This is only the begin.

STORIES OF A FUTURE TO BE TOLD

FENICE ALBATROS32

THIS IS ONLY THE BEGIN.

STORIES OF A FUTURE TO BE TOLD – PART 2

TABLE OF CONTENTS – PART 2

22. *IF THERE WAS NO MIHRIBAN*

On the way home, once they had taken the children, Sanem called Mihriban.

"Sanem? Daughter?" she immediately replied.

"Mihriban? Hello." replied Sanem.

"Who is that? Is it Grandma Mihriban?" asked Ates in the back seat.

"Yes, it's Grandma Mihriban." confirmed his mother.

"Hello Grandma!" she exclaimed loudly to be heard.

"Hello my chicks!" she greeted them softly upon hearing them.

"But where are you? I hear a big noise..." she said.

"We are in the car." replied Yildiz.

"Yes, we're on our way home." Sanem replied.

"Listen... I called to ask you.... it's been a long time since we had a girls' night... just you and me... would you be free tonight?" she asked.

"Here, if you already have plans with Aziz, don't worry, eh...let's make it another day." she said quickly.

"No, no, child. I'm there, indeed, you couldn't have asked me at a better time." she admitted.

"Aziz, he went to Istanbul on errands and stopped by Emre and Leyla to see Ilker. And I am currently in the camp spending some time, so I gladly accept." she replied.

"Perfect. See you at the loft then." said Sanem happily.

"Alright." she replied.

"See you soon grandma!" greeted the little ones.

"See you soon, my little ones!" she replied.

As soon as the driver parked, they were greeted by Can who came to meet them.

"Here they are, my beautiful family!" he said in high spirits, spreading his arms wide ready to embrace them all.

"Dad!" the children ran up to him.

"So?" he said taking them all in his arms and shoulders.

"How was school? Did you have fun at the grandparents'?" he asked.

"Yes! It was good!" said Yildiz.

"My friend went back to school." said Deniz all happy.

"Look, we drew you a picture at grandma's." said Ates.

"Ah, a drawing? Now I'm curious." he replied.

"But first... take your backpacks and help mummy carry things inside. We'll see the drawing inside. In fact, get them ready." he said.

"Come on. Run, run, run." he encouraged them.

Can picked up the work bag Sanem carried on his shoulder.

"Hello love, welcome." he greeted her with a kiss and a warm hug.

"I missed you so much." he said inhaling her perfume.

"You too. You don't know how much." Sanem said returning the hug.

Although always together even at work, that brief separation was pure physical pain.

Arriving at the end of the day tired and being greeted by his embrace for Sanem was like breathing again.

Can broke away from the embrace and looked at her, stroking her hair, making sure she was OK.

"I'm fine." she replied, knowing his gaze.

"The hand?" he asked.

Sanem showed him the stress ball. "It's always with me." she said pressing it.

"Good." he said taking the ball from her palm to observe the wound.

A long pink scar marked her hand. It was what remained of that strange accident.

Can brought it close to his lips with a sad look. "Don't make that little face..." she said, resting her forehead on his. Then with her good hand she brought his mouth close to her for a long kiss.

"Hmm... what a nice welcome..." he commented.

Sanem smiled slyly.

"Well, this is a small greeting, it must be enough for you until I return." she whispered to him.

"Why? Where are you going?" he asked snapping away, to get a better look at her.

"I'm not going anywhere. I'm not leaving the estate, that is." she clarified.

"I promised Mihriban a girls' night out." she said.

"No, Sanem..." complained Can remembering the past.

She made a contrite grimace and hurried to reply:

"Ah, no, no... it's not what you think. We won't drink, if that's what you're afraid of." she quickly reassured him.

"Ah... okay, then." he replied with a sigh of relief.

"No, it's just a way of saying we'll spend a few hours together after dinner. I realized it's been a long time since she and I have spent time alone." admitted Sanem.

"Is it a problem for you?" he asked her.

"No, it's not a problem at all. Of course, I'll miss you like air, but what can I do..." he said jokingly shrugging.

"I'll wait for you." he said.

"Hmm... really?" she asked kissing him.

"Hmm... really really." he replied.

"Dad, what happened to you? Are you coming to see the drawing?" said a small female voice that admitted no reply. It was Ates, standing in the front doorway, hands on her hips like a real little woman, in a determined pose, calling their attention.

"You are right, my daughter! You are right! I'm coming." he said.

"Eh, Daddy Can... you don't do that." said Sanem waving her index finger in the air.

"Yeah, Sanem junior lectured me." he said.

Sanem held back a laugh.

"Come, mum." said Can surrounding her with his arm. "Let's go and see what these little artists have been up to."

"Let's go." she said.

"Here I am! Here I am! I'm all yours!" Can exclaimed at the front door, spreading his arms wide in surrender.

Once they had had dinner and read a fairy tale to the children, Sanem joined Mihriban at the loft.

"Ah, here I am. I made it. Sorry for the delay. Tonight putting them to bed was more tiring than usual." said Sanem entering like a rocket to drop down on the comfortable sofa, where Mihriban was already sitting.

"Ah, daughter. Welcome. I was giving you up for lost. I thought you had forgotten." she admitted.

"Ah, Mihriban possible such a thing? I was the one who proposed it." she reminded her.

"Don't worry, I was joking daughter. I imagined you had been held back." she said.

"And... What did you want to talk to me about?" she asked her so point blank.

"Ah... and how did you know that I need to talk to you about something?" she asked blinking in surprise.

"Because I know you Sanem. From your tone, I knew right away that there was something. So tell me. What's going on? Nothing bad I hope." said Mihriban grabbing the still-full glass of red wine she had placed on the small table in front of her.

As soon as she nodded to take it, Sanem blocked her.

"Best to avoid it. After you hear this you'll definitely want to drink it all in one gulp." Sanem assured her.

"So you worry me... What's going on?" she asked seriously.

"Wait." she said getting up.

She closed the loft windows and returned to her.

"Mihriban I need your help." said Sanem speaking in a low voice.

"Why are you talking like this? Sanem you are scaring me. Really." she said alarmed.

"Can must not hear. No one must know. Neither Aziz nor anyone else knows. Except me, Muzo, Cey Cey, and Ayhan." she explained.

"I don't understand..." said Mihriban confused.

"Now you will understand." she replied.

"We have a problem. A serious problem in the agency." she began.

She told her everything. About Metin's phone calls she and Muzo had heard, about Deren's story, about her father, her grandmother, and everything she knew about it. And finally of their failed attempts.

"My God!" exclaimed Mihriban. "I can't believe it."

"Now do you understand why no one must know?" said Sanem to her.

"My hands are tied. I can't tell Can and I don't want to involve Aziz, for obvious reasons. Much less can I talk about it with Deren or Bulut or Burak... or even Deniz." she vented.

"We've been looking for answers for two months, but being able to rely only on the four of us in the neighborhood, it's really difficult," she admitted.

"That's it, daughter, I still can't believe it. How can Metin... I mean, I've been working with him for two years during your absence, I never imagined he would go so far as to do something like this..." thought Mihriban shocked.

"And Deren's father? Is that a father?!" she asked nervously.

"Ah, God, I'd better shut up otherwise..." she tried to contain herself.

"I'm sick of evil, calculating men like that... why do they exist, eh?" she asked rhetorically angry.

"Mihriban calm down. I know, you are perfectly right, but I need you lucid." reasoned Sanem.

"The cameras and recordings have led to nothing." she said.

"We need confirmation." added.

"Yes but why? I mean, what is it that Deren must not know, that's what I don't understand." admitted Mihriban.

"We don't understand it either." Sanem replied. "And if we stand still and wait we will never understand it!" she added.

"That's why I wanted to talk to you, you have shown yourself to be very skilled in the past in this kind of thing. So I ask you: do you have any ideas?"

Mihriban thought about it.

They both remained silent for a while. Then suddenly Mihriban snapped her fingers.

"Found it!" she exclaimed as a sly grin appeared on her face.

"What? What? What, what?" asked Sanem impatiently.

"I don't know if you'll like it though, that is..." she began.

"Never mind. You say it!" said Sanem ready and straight as an aerial.

"Alright. Remember when we were supposed to create that..." Mihriban clenched her teeth and fists at the mere memory. Then she took a deep breath, blowing out the air. "Arthur Capello, invented by Leyla?" she recalled trying to keep calm.

"Er... yes. Calm Mihriban." said Sanem seeing her like that.

"I am calm." she said smiling. "I'm very calm." she repeated trying to convince herself. When she did that it only took a second to hear the sound of breaking dishes.

"OK, and?" she asked.

"Do you remember what Leyla did for the presentation of Ayca?" she asked her.

"Um... a fake site." replied Sanem.

"Exactly. And who made that fake site?" asked Mihriban.

"The hacker who knew Emre. The one who worked for Aylin." recalled Sanem.

"Exactly." said Mihriban.

"So what? I don't understand." she admitted.

"Ah, Sanem! If you want to get confirmation from that phone, who is it that can give it to you if not a hacker?" blurted Mihriban.

Sanem remained silent for a moment. "A hacker, of course!" she exclaimed.

"He will surely have a way to hack into Metin's phone and see." she thought aloud.

"Yes, but that's illegal. And we'd have to do it against a lawman." reflected Sanem.

"Any other ideas?" she then asked.

"I don't have any Sanem. This is the best one I've had. I mean, the easiest thing would be, like you said, to be able to get my hands on his phone, but..." Mihriban thought.

"Wait..." Sanem brightened up.

"Ayhan once told me that in the dark part of the internet you can find anything." she recalled as a flashback of her best friend in contact with the hacker who saved Can from charges of stealing the project flashed through her mind.

"One minute... Ayhan!" she exclaimed brightening up. "Ayhan knows a hacker. What was his name? He had a code name." thought Sanem.

"Peacock? No, what was he like...? Black pigeon? No... Black falcon, of course!" she recalled.

"What does this have to do with, Sanem? We were talking about another hacker." Mihriban reminded her.

"Don't you understand? Metin knows that hacker. He has already been sent to jail once by Fikri Harika." she said.

"So what?" continued Mihriban, not understanding.

"So what if Metin, who I imagine is very careful about these things, realises and finds out who he is..." said Sanem.

"Ah, no... no, no. You're right." thought Mihriban getting to the point.

"I need to hear Ayhan. Maybe this Black Falcon could help us again." he thought.

"But we must not start with Metin. We have to start with Deren's father." said Sanem.

"Right... good girl! We only thought of Metin... But the real dilemma is him." agreed Mihriban.

"I'll call her right away." said Sanem pulling out her phone.

"Hello? Sister? Is everything alright? What's going on?" she asked.

"I have some news." said Sanem.

"Mh... tell me." said as she munched on some popcorn. Movie sound could be heard in the background.

"Am I disturbing you?" asked Sanem then.

"No, Cey Cey and I were watching a movie but he fell asleep, so it's more correct to say I'm only watching it, that's it." she clarified.

"Ah, OK. Listen, I'm here with Mihriban at the loft, and now she knows everything. We were reflecting and... something occurred to me." she said.

"What sister?" she asked.

"Black Falcon. Do you remember him?" asked Sanem.

Ayhan hearing that name almost choked on a popcorn.

"Ayhan?" asked Sanem worriedly hearing her cough.

"Yes, sister... I remember. Though I'd rather not." she replied in a choked voice.

"Ah, well. I think we should contact him and let him do some research." she explained.

"Why? I mean... why specifically Black Falcon? Why just a hacker that is." she asked in a shaky voice.

"Because you know him, Ayhan." retorted Sanem.

"Ugh, I always have to be the one doing these dangerous things. Are you forcing me into the dark side of the internet again after all this time? I don't believe it!" she ranted.

"Either him... or Aylin's hacker. What do you say? I bet Cey Cey at the mere mention of his name would be delighted." mused Sanem.

Sleepwalking Cey Cey that he was, asleep with his head on his wife's lap, his senses sharpened, when he heard the word hacker and Aylin on the other end of the phone, he sat up, drowsily.

"Did someone say Aylin? AHHHH!" he exclaimed.

"Ahhh!" shouted Ayhan suddenly, as she tried to keep the phone balanced, sending the bowl with all the popcorn flying everywhere.

Sanem jerked his away from her ear.

"No, only you said that!" replied Ayhan to her in a tone. "In your dreams!" she scolded him. Cey Cey lay down again and continued to sleep.

"God I was about to get dried up." she commented.

"Alright, sister. I'll see what I can do. I don't know if he still exists, but I'll try to contact him." she said.

"Alright Ayhan thanks." she replied.

"We'll talk about it, OK?" she said.

"Go, I got it. Bye." said Sanem hanging up.

"What does she say?" asked Mihriban.

"That she will try to contact him. It's been years, she doesn't know if he still exists." Sanem reported.

"She will let me know." He added.

"All right. That's something." said Mihriban.

"I was thinking... you didn't mention your sister in this story, though," she mused.

"After all, she was the one who told Emre to contact that hacker." Mihriban continued.

"So what?" asked Sanem.

"I mean, that she has made plans before. And she's part of the neighborhood... why isn't she part of this?" asked her curiously.

"Ah... for two reasons. One because my sister would tell me to mind my own business, not to meddle in other people's lives. She doesn't have a nose like me in these things. She would think I like to get into trouble, that there's a reason behind it, and blah blah blah." she said teasing her.

"And secondly... she would definitely spill the beans to Emre. She can't hide anything from him." said Sanem.

"And if she told him... most likely the word would get to Can.... And so on." she said.

"That's it... I understand, but don't you think that the more people in the agency know about it, the easier it would be to get information?" thought Mihriban.

"I don't want to upset the balance in the agency or at the Sanem. The agency is talking... I don't think it's appropriate." she said.

"I understand. You are right indeed. But count me in for anything." said Mihriban.

"If necessary I will find a hacker." she said, smiling.

"Ah, I am sure of it... you are capable of anything, my dear Mihriban." she said.

"Here, if I put my mind to it..." she replied nonchalantly.

"Ah, don't be modest." Sanem teased her.

"Consider yourself part of the group." she told her.

"Take care though... stay among us." she added.

"It will stay among us, don't worry." she said finally grabbing her glass.

"We can also drink now." replied Sanem to her gesture.

"Mh, but I think one glass is not enough after all you have told me." Mihriban replied.

"Didn't you have a barrel in the cellar, Mihriban? Let's put our mouths under that and see." joked Sanem.

Mihriban burst out laughing.

"I swear it's about the joke, not the wine." she replied seriously.

"Hmm, and I believe you, yes, Mihriban." Sanem teased her.

Mihriban laughed again.

"Ah, if you weren't here, Sanem..." she said.

With that topic closed, they spent the rest of the evening dealing with much lighter topics.

A few days passed and Ayhan discovered that Black Falcon no longer worked in the area. He had moved abroad.

This changed the plans.

Sanem and Mihriban saw each other again. This time she joined her at Sanem's office for coffee during a shopping break in the city.

Taking advantage of a quiet moment, the two caught up with each other.

It was Mihriban who proposed a new idea.

"If the hacker who had worked for Emre officially worked for the company or the agency, Metin couldn't say anything. In the company checks are necessary." Mihriban thought.

"Yes, but how do I explain it? How do I get him hired?" asked Sanem.

"Should I involve Emre and Leyla?" she added.

"Sanem I think you are making a mistake with them. If they knew, I think they would be on your side." said Mihriban.

"But I don't want that, you see? I don't want to force them to take one side or the other. I told you about the past between Can and his brother and I don't want to put them in the position of hiding something from him." she explained.

"Sanem, I don't see many solutions." Mihriban admitted regretfully.

"Oww... I know," Sanem said with her hands in her hair.

"Otherwise tell Can." she said directly.

"Are you crazy? Can wouldn't believe me. He would listen to me, yes, but then he would ask: "Do you have proof?" And what do I answer him? No?" blurted Sanem.

"I have to get confirmation first, then I will tell Can." she answered decisively.

"And I have to find it as soon as possible." she added.

"Alright, then we need to get a hacker to the agency or the Sanem. Where do you prefer?" asked Mihriban.

"No, I have a better idea." Sanem brightened up.

"Of course, why didn't I think of that before?" she asked herself.

She got up abruptly, picked up the phone left in her bag and dialled a number.

"Sanem, what are you doing? "Mihriban asked her.

"Ah, Muzo? Where are you?" asked Sanem on the phone.

"Ah, well. Come down to my office immediately, and bring Cey Cey too." she said and hung up.

"What are you doing, child, do you want to explain?" asked Mihriban.

"Now you will understand." she replied with a smirk.

Shortly afterwards there was a knock at the door from Muzo, followed by Cey Cey.

Sanem, who had uninstalled the cameras and locked the door from the inside, opened it and closed it once they were inside.

"What's going on?" asked Muzo.

"I need you to find me something on file. Cey Cey will help you. He knows what I'm talking about. Or rather who." she said.

"I don't understand." he replied.

"I need you to find me the documents attesting to the internship in the agency of a young man whose name or surname I don't remember, but dating back to about 10 years ago or maybe more." reflected Sanem.

"But if you don't know his name and surname, how can I look it up?" asked Muzo.

"Let me finish. For that you need Cey Cey. He will be able to tell you from the picture. Usually every person who is hired here is catalogued with CV information and photo. The person in question is Aylin's hacker." explained Sanem.

"Ahh! It wasn't a dream then!" shouted Cey Cey, turning to flee, slamming a headbutt into the closed door. He fell backwards and fainted instantly.

"Cengo!" shouted his friend. It was too late.

Muzo let out a sigh, rolled up his sleeves and then said: "I'll take care of it. I'll put it back and then I'll see to it." he said, dragging him out from under his armpits.

"If you open the door for me... I'll take the corpse away." he said holding back a laugh.

Sanem opened it and let him out. Cey Cey left wiping the floor like a mocho. On his way out backwards he knocked Cey Cey into the corner.

"Careful." warned Sanem.

"Ah, better that way, maybe Cengo will wake up." Muzo replied with his usual laugh.

"Hey, Cengo? Cenginz? You know you're not exactly a featherweight? Come on, wake up." he said as he dragged him away towards the lift.

"Let's try this one too." said Sanem once the door closed again.

"If it doesn't work?" asked Mihriban.

"If it doesn't work I'll be forced to ask my sister." she admitted.

MEANWHILE IN THE CORRIDOR...

Deniz came out of her office and saw Muzo and Cey Cey in that state.

"What's going on?" she asked running worriedly towards them.

"Nothing, just the usual Cey Cey fainting all over. She'll be fine now." Muzo reassured her.

"No, I really didn't mean that? What's going on, Muzo?" she asked pinning him by the arm as she continued to drag her friend away.

"What do you mean? I don't understand." he replied.

"Is it true that you are about to publish a book and Sanem is helping you out?" she asked.

"And how do you know?" he retorted.

"It doesn't matter how I know. Is it true or not, that you no longer work at Fikri Harika but here at the Sanem?" she continued to ask.

Muzo gave a sly smile.

"If you ask me for confirmation, it means you don't really trust what you think you know." he replied.

"Don't play such games with me." said Deniz seriously.

"Is it true or not?" she repeated.

"In English they say "Let's wait and see." so... if you please, I have a friend to drag away. Excuse me." he said, resuming his way.

"Hmm... that's angry!" blurted out Deniz taking the stairs to the floor above.

One floor away from Fikri Harika, passing through the archive she heard Metin on the phone. She recognized his voice immediately.

He stopped around the corner to wait for him to finish. She was going to surprise him, she told herself.

"No, no, sir I know that Deren is a woman of a certain class and elegance. I understand you." she heard him say.

"Yes, she is hardworking, workaholic, careful, precise, she is a leader in her field. There is nothing to say." he added.

Deniz's mood dropped headlong.

He gave up the surprise and called the lift upstairs without being seen.

As soon as the doors opened and she stepped inside, found Muzo and Cey Cey.

There she thought that Metin was in for another kind of surprise.

This time she looked at Muzo with a mischievous smirk.

The same evening Sanem received the photos of the documents she had requested with the words "Is that him?" from Muzo.

At that moment she couldn't take a look because Can was driving beside her.

She would check at another time.

The moment came when she decided to go to the garden to pick some vegetables for dinner, taking the opportunity to also check the flowers she had recently planted.

There with the water pistol in her rehabilitating hand, and the phone in the other, she was watering the plants with one and zooming in on the sent documents with the other.

She zoomed in on the photo. It was him. In that instant she remembered the moment when she knocked on his door. "Are you Hilmi?" asked.

"Hilmi! That's his name." she exclaimed before even checking the name in the document. When she found it, she had confirmation.

"Hilmi Duman." she readed.

There was a number in the CV. She tried to dial it.

"The number you have dialed is not in service." repeated a recorded voice on the other end.

"Ahhh!" blurted Sanem.

"Love? Are you alright?" asked Can as he approached.

"Um... yeah, I'm fine. I was just blowing off some stress. That's all." she lied.

Can hugged her from behind, kissing her on the neck.

"And here I was coming to see if you needed help." he said.

"Mh... actually... yes." she admitted.

"At your command Mrs Divit, please tell me, how can I help you?" he asked her.

"If you could collect some ripe fruits and vegetables for the children, I would be much obliged." Sanem played along.

"I, on the other hand, would like to take a nice bouquet of flowers to Mihriban." she added.

"Alright." he replied.

"This one's from me." said Can taking the water pistol from her hand. "I got it."

As Sanem headed a little further into the corner dedicated to flowers said: "Take care, gardener Can, choose the best ones, and don't ruin my garden, otherwise... it will be trouble for you."

"Ah... you put it that way Mrs Divit, so, eh! I understand. I'll try to satisfy you the best I can." said Can intentionally pointing the water jet at her innocently.

"Ahhh! Can!" exclaimed Sanem, taking cover behind the tomato plant.

"Are you crazy?" she asked taking cover.

"Ah, excuse me, aren't you satisfied with my service?" he replied.

"Ah, you are such a rascal!" she said, peeping out from the plant.

"I'm soaked!" she exclaimed observing herself.

"You are the worst gardener I have ever seen!" exclaimed Sanem. As Can walked around to spray her all over.

Then Sanem passed between the plants trying to get past Can but, he faster than her, caught clutching her before she reached the tap to turn off the water.

"You want war, huh? Can Divit? I'll show you then! I am Sanem Divit!" she said, slipping the water pump out of her hand.

"Ah, now what?" she said as she watered him all over, he however did not let go of her grip.

"I'm soaked by now, but you? Not enough!" she said as he insisted with the water.

At that moment, Deniz, Yildiz and Ates came running. The three champions of justice.

Without a second thought they took another garden hose and held it up in front of the three of them:

"Let Mama go or it will be war!" exclaimed Ates with her hands on her hips, like a little paladin, next to her brother holding the hose, and Yildiz on the other side in the same pose.

Can did not let her go.

"Ah, is that so, father? Then go Deniz, attack!" she said pointing with her index finger towards her parents.

In all this Mihriban and Aziz who had accompanied them home observed the scene laughing in the corner.

"They are really their parents' children, no doubt about it!" laughed Aziz.

"What a team, guys! The three of them would be able to move even walls!" said Mihriban.

"Oh, you can say that again. My extraordinary nephews." commented Aziz.

Meanwhile, the war began.

Deniz, positioned the direct jet, fire hydrant style. At that point, Can released his grip on Sanem and ran towards them to catch them.

The children started running away screaming in fear of being caught.

Deniz, was the only one who did not break away from the water pipe. He decided to fight his father.

While Yildiz and Ates were called back by Sanem who had hidden behind Can the scarecrow.

"Girls, come here!" said Mama.

"Ates, run!" said Sanem, as she hugged Yildiz who had just joined her.

Ates like a true warrior, as she ran, grabbed the watering hose, which her mother, running away, had left on the ground and with it protected herself from enemy attacks.

Eventually Can managed to convince Deniz to ally himself against the women of the house.

Thus two factions were formed: males against females.

Neither seemed to want to surrender so eventually the grandparents intervened to put an end to it.

"Sanem? I have something to ask you. Can you come?" asked Mihriban.

"Alright children, the war ends in a draw. You all won. Come on now." said Aziz, clapping his hands.

"But grandpa..." said Deniz.

Can looked at him. "Grandpa is right, the battle ends here, but... not before a nice dip in the pool! Whoever comes last no creap with chocolate!" said Can running off.

The children started running all wet. Extra creap for whoever takes the best dive!' added their dad.

Let's run!" said Deniz.

"I do a killer catapult dive!" he exclaimed.

"My bomb dive can't be beat!" exclaimed Ates.

"Mine will be a precise dive. " said Yildiz.

Can reached the pool and dived in, creating a tidal wave.

"Wow..." commented Yildiz.

"Dad, if you do that, there won't be any water left in the pool. Where will we dive?" asked Ates comical as ever.

Aziz followed them. "I'll be the judge." he said, lying down on the deckchair on the edge.

"Come on, come to me." said Can in the middle of the pool. "Show me what you can do,. he urged them.

"I'm coming!" exclaimed Ates as she jumped with a run-up, clutching her knees to her chest.

Once she had resurfaced, Grandpa Aziz gave his vote.

"Not bad, my granddaughter, not bad at all. Hmm... that's a good eight for me." he said.

Then it was Yildiz's turn and she did a very graceful and precise dive, just as she had predicted. Hers was a traditional dive but with an undeniable grace and poise.

"Nice... very nice Yildiz. neat." commented Aziz. "But I think in this case the competition is for the loudest dive." he said.

"I can't do it, Grandpa." said Yildiz.

"Ah, Yildiz, yours instead of a bomb dive is a feather dive. No one heard you!" commented Deniz.

"Nice, I like that name!" commented Ates swimming around his father.

"From now on the feather dive will be your dive, Yildiz." she told her.

Yildiz smiled. "I like it. I am satisfied with it. I don't mind winning." she said.

"Ah, well said, my granddaughter, it doesn't matter who wins. It matters having fun and feeling good." commented her grandfather.

"Come on, now for our last contestant!" introduced Aziz.

Deniz stepped back onto the lawn from the edge of the pool.

"Grandpa move over! 1.. 2...3...I'm coming!" he exclaimed as he ran and then jumped with his knees to his chest like his sister for a catapult dive.

The plunge generated such a splash of water that it looked like a meteorite had fallen, so high were the jets.

"Woah..." commented Ates, hiding behind his father's back.

Deniz resurfaced.

"Well?" he asked.

"Brother, are you crazy? You broke the pool!" exclaimed Ates in that brutally sympathetic manner of her.

Of course it wasn't true, the pool was dug into the ground.

A loud laugh escaped Can upon hearing those words.

Aziz was stunned.

"Nephew, thank you for warning me, otherwise I would have taken a shower! You were about to flood the house." he commented.

Ates looked at him and could do nothing but applaud. "He won, Grandpa. He won, I give up. I can't beat him!" she said, pointing at him.

Yildiz who had come out of the pool also watched the scene laughing next to her grandfather.

Everyone joined in Ates' applause.

Then Deniz, in the water, bowed his head in thanks to them. "Thank you, thank you."

"Um... the winner is Deniz!" decreed Aziz.

Then thinking about it he asked in his son's direction, "What was the prize?"

"Chocolate creap." replied Can.

"Ah, but then, if that's the prize, I think for commitment, likability, skill, and sportsmanship, they all deserve it." he said.

"Yes! Well said, Grandpa!" exclaimed Ates. "Creap for everyone!"

While this was going on, in the meantime in the garden, Sanem and Mihriban were picking flowers, and the vegetables that Can was to pick, they adjourned.

"Cey Cey and Muzo have found what I was looking for. Hilmi... that's his name. I didn't remember," Sanem said.

"I called the number on the CV, but it is no longer active. I should have guessed it after what happened." she admitted.

"What now?" asked Mihriban.

"I'll have to call my sister. And ask her." sighed Sanem.

"Will you tell her everything then?" she asked.

"I don't see any other choice, Mihriban. I am so tired..." she admitted.

"Then if you are determined, what are you waiting for? Call now that we are alone." invited Mihriban.

"You're right." said Sanem taking out her mobile phone.

She dialled the number. It was ringing.

"Hello? Sister?" answered Leyla from the other end.

"Leyla? Hi, what are you doing?" asked her sister.

"I just finished giving Ilker a bath." she replied.

"You?" she asked.

"Um... I'm picking flowers in the garden." said Sanem.

"Ah..." she replied.

Silence fell.

"Sister?" asked Leyla. "Are you OK? Why are you so quiet?" she asked.

"Um... I need to ask you something." she began.

"Mh...ask." she replied.

Sanem took a deep breath. She didn't know how to ask without getting an interrogation in return.

Mihriban gestured, urging her to speak.

"See, I wanted to ask you... do you have Hilmi's number?" she said hesitantly.

"Hilmi who?" asked Leyla confused.

"Hilmi the hacker, sister." replied Sanem closing her eyes waiting for her reaction.

"Um, I have it, but... why do you need a hacker, sister? What's going on? You're weird." she replied having caught her sister's wavering.

"What are you up to?" she immediately asked her as their mother would have done.

She could feel her inquisitive eyes on her.

At that moment she had a flash of genius.

"It's not for me, sister." she replied decisively.

"It's for Mihriban!" she exclaimed.

"What?!" exclaimed the person next to her. "Sanem what are you talking about?!" asked her in a whisper.

Sanem motioned her to be silent.

"For Mihriban? Why do she need a hacker?" she asked.

"Well, the other day in confidence, she asked me if I had her number, it seems someone hacked an account on her pc. I didn't quite understand." admitted Sanem signaling Mihriban to be silent.

"Ah... I'm sorry." said Leyla.

"But she asked me not to say anything to anyone. Especially to Aziz, she doesn't want him to worry about a trifle." she added.

"Ah, with the matter of Arthur Capello and Selim... I understand that Daddy Aziz is always on edge." Leyla included.

"Well, maybe even too much. That's why she asked me not to say anything. Please don't even mention it to your husband. Because I know you tell him everything, dear sister." she told her.

"Phew...alright. I'll send him to you." she replied.

"You know...lately I've realized that we need a hacker more and more. What do you say, sister, should we hire one in the company?" she asked nochalantly.

"I wouldn't be against it at all. On the contrary. We could keep an eye on the competition." she admitted enticed by the idea.

"Sister..." resumed Sanem. "That's not the point."

"Yes, I know, I know... it's for our own protection. You are right. All Emre does is tell me again and again." she replied with her eyes rolling.

"I think we should seriously think about it anyway." confirmed Leyla.

"Good sister, good thinking." she said.

"Anyway, I'll hang up and send it to you now. Come on, I have to go. Emre is waiting for me at the table." she said.

"Go, it's fine, don't keep him waiting. Thank you sister. See you tomorrow." she greeted her.

"See you tomorrow, bye." she hung up.

Three seconds later the message with the number came to her straight away.

"Ah, here it is. Sister, you're the best!" exclaimed Sanem at the phone screen.

Sanem? Why did you put me in the middle?" asked Mihriban.

"Well, that's the first thing that came to my mind!" she justified herself.

"But shouldn't you have told her the truth?" asked Mihriban.

"No, I thought it over, but it worked. My sister will now think seriously about hiring a hacker in the company. And maybe she will talk to Emre about it. I'm weaving the basis for a plan B, Mihriban." she explained.

"Ah, Sanem... I'll have to come up with something in case I'm asked questions. Because they will certainly ask me... thanks to you." she glowered at her.

"Sorry... but you still love me, don't you?" he asked her with a big smile to apologize.

"Yes I do... but when you do that... I would choke you." Mihriban jokingly replied.

Sanem laughed.

"Come on now, I'm calling." said Sanem.

"Go." urged Mihriban.

She dialled the number and initiated the call.

"Hello?" answered a male voice.

"Hilmi?" asked Sanem.

"Hilmi Duman?" repeated.

"Who is it?" he asked defensively.

"Don't you remember me?" replied Sanem with a firm, sly grin on her face.

Silence.

"We already know each other. I am Sanem Divit. Does my name mean anything to you?" she told him proudly.

"I don't know anyone with that name." he replied coldly.

"Ah... All right. Then let's hear if you remember it that way." she replied.

"Many years ago, I knocked on your door as Sanem Aydin and Emre threw you in prison. Do you remember now?" she asked.

"You pushed me by banging my head against the kitchen countertop. You were too busy running away. I still bear the marks, you know?" she said.

Silence.

"What do you want? It's been years. I paid dearly for that episode." he replied.

"I'm hanging up." he warned her.

"You want to hang up? Too bad, because I wanted to offer you a job." she said.

Mihriban looked at her fascinated. She had never seen Sanem like this.

"I mean, after all, you helped Emre... the one who sent you to prison... don't you want to help me?" she asked him sarcastically.

"It's a trap. You want revenge for what I did to you. Now that you are famous..." he let slip.

"Ah, so you know me... are you by any chance a secret fan of mine?" asked Sanem sarcastically.

Hilmi mumbled.

"Anyway..." said Sanem. "If you're not interested..."

"No, OK... let's hear it." he stopped her.

"I need a confirmation. You don't have to invent anyone this time." she told him.

"Would you be able to anonymously copy the contacts of a phone if I told you the number?" she asked.

"It's possible, sure." he said.

"But you must not be discovered, the person in question is very important." she warned him.

"What does that mean?" he asked.

"It means he is a lawyer. Do you understand? And he knows you." she said.

"How does he know me? Who is he?" he asked.

"Knock, knock? Who is it? It is the past knocking at your door, Hilmi! Who do you think I'm going to talk about?" she teased him.

"That lawyer?" he asked.

"That's the one." confirmed Sanem.

"Why are you investigating on him?" he asked curiously.

"That doesn't concern you. For your own good." she replied.

"Listen..." said Sanem, "He might be hiding something, that's why I need confirmation. That's all I can tell you. Then would you like to find out, whoever got your sentence might not be so honest?" charged Sanem.

At that moment she was afraid of herself for a moment. She felt as bad as Aylin. And that was her purpose. She knew that if she acted as determined and malicious as she did, he would play along.

And so he was.

"Alright. "he said. "I'll do it."

"OK, I'll send you the number. I'll tell you when to act. We have to make sure he doesn't have the phone in his hand at that moment, that he can't suspect anything." she warned him.

"OK." he replied briefly.

Sanem hung up.

"Sanem? Daughter? What was that attitude? My God, you looked like a different person. You were scary." said Mihriban blinking in surprise.

Sanem laughed.

"Ah, even? Good, that means it worked." she said returning to her usual playful tone.

"Why all this?" she asked."Because I knew from the start that he would be reluctant towards me, given the past." she said.

"So I thought that if I behaved more brazenly and maliciously like Aylin, instilling some terror in him, he would probably agree." she said.

"Ah, when you get down to it, you are just unbelievable!" exclaimed Mihriban.

"I could have used the pretext of having hit my head because of him to make him work for free, but that would have been a really unfair and cowardly move like Aylin, whereas I will not take advantage of it. I will pay him what I owe him." she replied, showing her goodness as always.

"Oh, that's the Sanem I know." Mihriban commented.

"I hope it leads us to something." admitted Sanem hopefully with a sop.

"Come on, let's gather everything and go, otherwise they'll get suspicious." said Mihriban.

The next day, in agreement with the group, they decided that the task of getting Metin off the phone would be given to Ayhan as it had happened a few months earlier. That evening during yet another yoga class he would pick up the phones. Ayhan, with Cey Cey and Muzo watching, would warn her to act.

And so it was. The plan went off without a hitch and Sanem, in contact with Hilmi, followed the operation as she monitored the progress of the lesson from the security cameras.

Once finished, Sanem asked Hilmi: "He won't understand what happened, will he?"

"No. He can't." he replied.

"OK, perfect. Send me all the material." she said.

Sanem took advantage of the fact that Can had gone for a run in the woods to analyse the contents. She opened the phone notes, where she had jotted down all the essential information of that mystery, including, the date of the exact day she heard Metin speak. In what Hilmi had obtained was everything: the first and last names of the contacts, the number, the time and the times he had called and received calls. It was thanks to that date that Sanem tightened the circle on some of the most present numbers. She then asked him to trace the first and last names of the numbers she had selected. They were all contacts of lawyers, Sanem guessed, because the names were all preceded by 'lwy'. Among the five selected by her, concerning that fateful day, were:

LWY. UFUK Y.

LWY. AHMET E.

LWY. MEHMET K.

LWY. SINAT O.

LWY. CEMRE D.

Sanem looked at them and thought: "Deren's father is hiding among them, I am sure of it."

She asked Hilmi for confirmation because she did not trust the names. Metin could just as well have registered him by a nickname, instead he was tracing the owner of the number.

While she waited for the results, she thought about her next move. When the children returned after an afternoon spent with their grandparents Aziz and Mihriban, Can had not yet returned. The first to greet her was Deniz, who was in an unusually good mood. Not that other days he didn't, but... it was different.

"Deniz? You look particularly happy, today. What's going on?" she asked.

"Mom, Deniz is on a high today." confirmed Ates. "Isn't he, Yildiz?"

"Yes... he is. He's happy." she nodded.

"Hmm, what is the reason for such contentment? Let's hear it." asked Sanem.

"Mama, Hatay is back to walking alone." he replied.

"Ah, your friend? Well, how nice!" commented his mother.

"Yes, well, he's still limping a bit, but he's fine." he said.

"Oh, I'm so glad he's recovering." she replied.

"Mom? When can we invite him here?" asked Deniz remembering her words.

"Ah, right! I promised you! That's right." she recalled.

"A promise is a promise!" echoed Ates.

"True, my loves, and mama always keeps her promises, so how about we invite him this weekend? Saturday or Sunday, eh?" she asked.

"But then if he can invite Hatay, then I want to invite Dilara." said Ates.

"Yes, that's right... let's invite Dilara." thought Yildiz excitedly.

"That's fine, that seems fair. If Deniz invites his little friend you can invite yours too." said Sanem.

"Alright, then we'll tell them tomorrow." said Deniz looking at the sisters.

"OK, if their parents or carers give permission, no problem for me, I would like to meet them." she repeated to them.

"And I'm sure Dad will want to meet them too." she added.

"Yuppie!" exclaimed Yildiz followed closely by Ates.

"Yuppie what? What's being celebrated?" Can asked as he returned from his run at that moment, all sweaty.

The children explained the reason, Sanem exclaimed: "Oh, he's here, Dad! Dad's here! Welcome!" she said, walking towards them.

"Now it's his turn!" she said. "He will celebrate with you." said Sanem aloud with a forced smile, then added in a whisper: "Please save me. They have irrepressible energy today. My head will explode if you don't relieve me. I need an urgent walk." she pleaded with him.

"Ooh... Is the situation that critical?" he asked.

"Looks like they've had sugar indigestion, too bad." said Sanem between her teeth with a forced smile, desperate.

"It's OK, I'll take care of them. Just give me time to take a shower." he said wiping the sweat on his forehead with a towel.

"Please hurry..." she begged him almost in a whisper.

"I'll run." he replied, winking at her.

Then summing up her usual enthusiasm, she said loudly: "Come on, kids, how about a couple of jumps on the trampoline, huh?" she proposed to them.

"Yessss!" all three exulted, loaded to the brim. They went out into the garden like rockets.

"And let's hope they get tired with this..." she said, following them into the garden. She settled herself on the deckchair to keep an eye on them.

Once they were done, Can came out with his hair still wet.

"There you go. Come on, kids, the last few jumps and then a nice bath awaits you. Up." he said, clapping his hands to call them to order.

Can joined his wife.

"Ah, thank you! Thank you, thank you! My hero!" she said, smooching his cheek.

"Mh..." he replied.

"Come on, go Mrs Divit, your shift is over for today." he said.

"I'll take a walk to the pier, if I can, enjoy the sunset for a moment and on the way back maybe wet the plants a bit. Then I'll be with you." she warned him.

"Take your time. We'll be here waiting for you." Can replied, kissing her on the cheek.

"Run, before they catch you again." he replied winking.

"I'll run. I love you." she greeted him.

"Me too!" he replied.

Then turning to the children: "So these jumps? Aren't you tired of this trampoline yet? You've been jumping on it since you were born!" exclaimed Can with open arms, reaching out to them.

"No! It's beautiful! We never get tired of it!" they replied in chorus.

"I can see that..." he commented to himself.

Meanwhile, Sanem did not take it easy at all, quite the contrary. She ran to the pier to be far enough away to make an important phone call. She scanned the number in the phone book and called. A deep voice answered immediately.

"Hello?"

"Is Mr. Volkan speaking? The investigator?" asked Sanem.

"Yes, who is it?" he asked.

"Hello, i'm Sanem. Sanem Divit. You know my husband, Can. Can Divit. Madam Remide had sent you to search him around the world. Do you remember?" she asked.

"Of course I remember Can Divit. Hello. Please, how can I help you, Mrs Divit?" asked Volkan kindly.

"Here, I need to find out everything about a person." she replied.

"OK, no problem... do you have a name or a picture?" he asked.

"Well, before I explain, I need to ask you a favour. It's a very delicate situation." she informed him.

"OK, I'm listening." he waited.

"Of everything I am going to ask you and this conversation, please do not say anything either to Mrs Remide, my husband, or his father, Mr Aziz Divit. I know you met him in Cuba." Sanem said.

"OK. Don't worry, there is professional secrecy." he reminded her.

"I know, but it felt right to let you know. That's it, related to the person I'm going to ask you about there might be someone very close to my husband. That's why I need proof before talking to him." she explained briefly.

"I understand perfectly. Mr Can, if you will allow me, having worked with him before, is a man who does not act without evidence in hand." he confirmed. Sanem discerned a smile in his tone of voice.

"Exactly." she replied.

"Don't worry, I won't say anything." he reassured her.

"Oh, thank you." said Sanem.

"And... Who do I have to take care of?" asked Volkan then turning serious.

"You must find out all about Deren Keskin's family. My work colleague and one of my best friends." she reported.

"OK." he replied.

"I want to know the life, death and miracles of her father in particular. Who is he? What does he do? Who does he work with? What does he want from the daughter he disowned?" she asked.

"Ah! And Keskin is not Deren's real surname, I know she changed it to distance herself from him. Keskin is her paternal grandmother's maiden name." added.

"OK, so you don't know the name of the person in question, did I misunderstand?" asked Volkan.

"No, that's right." replied Sanem.

" You see, I have reason to believe that the man has secrets he doesn't want his daughter to discover." she said.

"Perfect. Anything else?" asked Volkan.

"Yes, I need proof. I know he has her watched by someone who works for us in the agency. Metin, a lawyer and my husband's best friend. He has always had a crush on Deren, but she is now happily married to another lawyer, Bulut, and she is expecting." she summed up.

"Now do you understand? Any kind of evidence is welcome." she concluded.

"I understand. Without evidence you cannot tell your husband. Or Mr Can wouldn't believe you, is that it?" he asked.

"Exactly." confirmed Sanem.

"That's it, they've had disagreements about trust before, so... I want to be sure." she admitted.

"OK, I'll see what I can do." he replied.

"I'm sorry, I can't provide you a picture or name because unfortunately I don't know. I hope having told you the context though, will help." apologized Sanem.

"Mrs Divit, you have been more comprehensive than you imagine. Don't worry. I'll get right on it. I will contact you as soon as I have information." he replied.

"Alright. Thank you, I will be waiting to hear from you." Sanem said.

She hung up and sighed exhausted. She closed her eyes and breathed in the fresh, salty sea air, then sat on the edge of the jetty, her feet brushing the surface of the water. She really had to relax.

AFTER DINNER...

After a nice shower and dinner, while Can put the children to bed, Sanem settled into the hammock, letting the rocking motion rock her. When Can reached her, he found her completely asleep with her diary and pen resting on her chest. She was sound asleep. She was exhausted. So he took her in his arms, taking care not to wake her, and carried to bed.

THE NEXT MORNING...

While in the office, Sanem received information from Hilmi. He had sent her the names of the owners associated with the phone numbers. It seemed that the names matched the owners of the numbers perfectly, which meant that Metin had registered them in their real names. Having obtained the first news, Sanem was able to devote herself to her work. The morning passed quietly, and she was finally able to report and rejoice, with a slightly lighter heart, about a piece of good news that she had been hiding for a few days. The publisher had called. They had been so impressed by Muzo's draft essay that they were interested in publishing his book in several languages. When Sanem told him the news, he almost fainted.

"Are you kidding? I mean..." he let go of the chair in his office.

"Muzo? Muzo?!" exclaimed Sanem worriedly.

"Wait, drink, drink." she told him as she hurriedly poured him a glass of water with sugar.

"Pub... Pubb... Are they really going to publish my book? Did they like it?" he asked incredulously.

"Yes, I'm telling you they want to publish it in several languages. I'm not joking." he repeated.

Muzo burst into tears.

"Muzo..." said Sanem approaching him, stroking his back.

"My dear friend, don't be like this though... otherwise I'll cry too." she said.

"Besides, you can't cry like that, there's no brother of crocodile tears beside you." she added jokingly to cheer him up.

Muzo laughed.

"There..." said Sanem upon seeing him. "So I recognise you..."

But Sanem didn't realise that those hysterical tears were turning into one of his sonorous laughs. She only realised as she heard the tone of his voice change.

"Muzo?" asked Sanem worried about his outbursts.

"Are you OK?" she asked.

Muzo let out a laugh.

"There, it's gone." she commented.

"Yay! Great Muzo, you're great! You finally managed to climb the pyramid, you are approaching the top step. You started from the bottom, it's true... but your brains, your skills and your many abilities have taken you far. Bravo!" he said to himself, patting himself on the back.

"But are you talking to yourself out loud?" asked Sanem strangely.

"Yes why? There's nothing wrong with loving yourself." Muzo replied elatedly.

"In fact, why am I surprised... I've done worse." said Sanem to herself in an unintelligible tone of voice.

"Huh?" asked Muzo.

"Ah, nothing." she replied.

"Good." she added.

"Here, Muzo, I don't want to dismantle you like this, but the road is uphill, it's not over yet. You are only at the beginning. Don't let it go to your head." curbed Sanem's enthusiasm.

"An ascent you say? But I'm used to pyramids, girl! I eat climbs for breakfast now!" she exclaimed laughing.

"Muzo, look I'm serious. Now comes the tricky part. Now it really gets serious. There will be deadlines, and you have to show commitment and precision, otherwise all this will remain just a dream." she tried to bring him back down to earth.

"No, no, this will become reality. My dear Sanem, I will hold that book in my hands. Oh, yes!" he said confidently. "Well? What shall I do? Tell me, I'm ready." he said sitting at his desk, ready already with pen in hand.

"Um... I don't think you'll need that one, Muzo," he said looking at her.

He had taken out his heron-shaped pen.

"How?" he asked with his head elsewhere.

"Um, I think you deserve this now." she said, pulling out a gift pack from under her desk.

"What is it? Is that for me?" asked Muzo.

"Yes." replied Sanem.

"Ah, you remembered today is my birthday, thank you!" he exclaimed.

Sanem was stunned. Was it Muzo's birthday? She asked herself. Then she reflected. *"When is Muzo's birthday? I have never celebrated it. I never greeted his birthday, now that I think about it."*

"Ah, um, yes, did you see that? Of course I remember your birthday, possible?" she replied aloud with some hesitation.

"Ah, with this news and now a present too, it's the best birthday of my life!" exclaimed Muzo.

Sanem inwardly wiped the sweat imaginatively on her forehead, for having escaped the big one by making a good impression.

Then she softened.

"Come on, open it." she urged him.

"OK." he replied elatedly.

Muzo opened the box. "What?!" he exclaimed.

"This is yours, personal." said Sanem.

"My own pc? And one of the most expensive ones too?!" exclaimed Muzo open-mouthed, turning it over in his hands.

"Well, I think it's the right gift after such news." thought Sanem.

"What? It's perfect. Thank you, Sanem!" he said getting up to hug her.

"You're welcome, my friend." she replied happy for him.

"There, I'm an old-fashioned guy, you know that." he replied.

"I know, I mean, I've noticed you like to pen your poems... I meant your writings, but... now it's getting serious." she reminded him.

Muzo continued to unwrap the accessories, like a child at Christmas.

"And you will agree with me, that your pc was not in good shape, Muzo." added Sanem.

Muzo laughed. According to Cey Cey, it was a caterpillar tractor. Fan problems, it seems. I didn't quite understand his technical words." he said shrugging.

"Then let us make the official introductions. Muzo Kaya, meet Mr Pc. Mr Pc, meet Mr Kaya." said Sanem jokingly.

Muzo laughed. "Nice to meet you." he replied waving his hand in front of the screen.

"Happy birthday and congratulations, my friend!" reiterated Sanem happily.

"Thank you, my dear friend, Sanem Divit." he replied.

23. *MUZO B- DAY, NO BAD DAY!*

On that day, Cey Cey gathered everyone in the creative headquarters of Fikri Harika during the break, to celebrate Muzo with a beautiful cake. Both for his birthday and the publication of his book, which until then had remained secret from everyone.

Deniz took the opportunity to wish him a very warm welcome, as Metin was also present in the office.

In fact, she took advantage of the moment when he was passing in the corridor, on the phone, to greet him with a kiss on both cheeks.

Everyone was surprised by that gesture. Sanem was open-mouthed, followed closely by Ayhan.

Leyla and Deren laughed under their mustaches as they followed Deniz's gaze.

Out of the corner of her eye, she saw that Metin had seen, and his expression confirmed his jealousy.

Muzo, approached Cey Cey, who hugged him to wish him well, and so he took the opportunity to whisper in his ear:

"Cengo? I seem to have made an impression."

"Muzo, don't stretch yourself. For today I think you have received enough positive news,"he brought him back down to Earth.

Everyone asked about this mysterious book, but Muzo did not give his opinion. He did not tell the title to those who asked, nor the content of the book. He would only tell when it was published, or at least they would see it.

"Ah, Cengo is such a beautiful day, nothing could spoil it." he said.

"I also have my slogan for today, get this: Muzo B-Day, no bad day!"

"Ah, pun too... you're in the mood, I see.... Nice, nice." admitted Cey Cey.

"Eh, my friend, what can you do, talent is talent!" he replied, passing an arm around his full neck.

"Sure, right..." commented Cey Cey.

With the break over and everyone back to their work, as Muzo was delivering some documents from Sanem for Can in his office, the secretary arrived to inform the boss of an arrival.

"Mr Can?" asked the girl.

"Tell me, Zeynep." he replied.

"The actors have arrived for the clothing advertisement."she reported.

"Ah, show them in." he replied.

"Ah, Osman, Mr Can? Wasn't he the main character?" asked Muzo.

"Yes, Muzo. Him. And an actress to accompany him." said Can handing back the signed documents for him to take back to Sanem.

"Ah, no wife this time, then?" joked Muzo.

"Mh, not yet. Adile has not returned to work yet." he said.

"What do you mean? But isn't the baby already a year old?" asked Muzo.

"Yes." replied Can simply.

"And what is she waiting for? For her to be 18 years old to go back to work?" he replied.

"Muzo, I don't think that is any of our business. Adile will do what she sees fit with her motherhood, what do you say? Come on, get back to work." he silenced him.

"Under order, Mr Can." he said as he went out.

It was right at the door that, with a smile on his lips at the beautiful day he was having, he was confronted by the last person he wanted to see on the face of the earth... or rather see again.

She stopped abruptly. Cey Cey was ahead of her, trying not to let them meet, but she had not anticipated this.

"What are you doing here?" asked Muzo turning icy.

Deniz meanwhile, who had also gone up to join Bulut in his wife's office, stopped to observe the scene.

Can immediately came out of the office.

"Cey Cey, make the actors sit down. Where are they?" He asked as he looked up from the documents in his hand.

He saw the scene.

"Guliz?" he asked.

"Mr. Can... Welcome back." she replied with a smile, flanked by a man. Presumably her agent.

Can passed his gaze from her to Muzo.

"Um... Muzo, I forgot to give you these." he said, adding more documents in his hands. "Hand them over to Sanem." he said.

"Ah, Sanem is here in the agency? I would like to see her again." said Guliz.

Can smiled. "Sure. Um... have a seat, please." he said shocked as they entered the office.

"Muzo, go." he said. Then he added in Cey Cey's ear: "Go with him. And have Burak bring some coffee and tea."

"Alright, Mr Can." he replied.

"Muzo, come on." he said, leading him away bamboozled. His eyes fixed on a spot in front of him.

Seeing that scene Deniz approached.

"Ah, Deniz! Come here!" Cey Cey called her with a gesture. "I need help." he said.

Deniz at those words ran towards him.

"What's going on?" she asked.

"Muzo? Are you OK?" she asked, laying a hand on her arm.

"Muzo?" she repeated. "Who is that woman, Cey Cey?" she asked looking at him.

At those words, Muzo unlocked, walking long and fast away from the two of them.

"Muzo! Where are you going?" shouted Cey Cey after him.

"Cey Cey?" grabbed Deniz by the arm. "What's going on? Who is that woman?"

Cey Cey took a deep breath and then said: "It's Guliz. His ex-wife." Then he ran off behind him, leaving Deniz standing there, petrified.

"Burak? Burak?" called Cey Cey aloud.

"Tell me Cey Cey." he replied, springing up the stairs.

"Rejoin Mr Can, and serve the guests with what they wish." he said.

"Alright. But what's going on?" he asked, seeing Muzo go by like a rocket.

"Nothing, you go. I'm coming," he said, running after his friend who was about to take the lift.

Cey Cey couldn't get in with him so he ran down the stairs.

When Ayhan saw him coming breathlessly down the corridors of the Sanem, she called out to him.

"Love?"

"Huh? I can't now, Ayhan." he said running off towards Sanem's office.

"Where are you going?" she asked frowning.

"Did you see Muzo pass by?" he asked her then freezing.

"Yes...why?" she asked as her husband was about to run away. She grabbed him by the arm.

"Cey Cey what's going on? What's wrong with Muzo?" she asked.

"He was hurt, it's obvious." said Cey Cey.

"Hurt by what? Speak." urged Ayhan.

"Guliz... Guliz came to the agency." he said then slipping away from her.

"What! Guliz? And what is she doing here?" she asked, running after him in turn.

Meanwhile, Muzo had already entered Sanem's office like a fury.

"You knew, didn't you?" he said angrily.

"Why didn't you warn me, eh?" he shouted.

"Muzo? What... what are you talking about? Why are you so angry?" she asked innocently.

"That's why all this cuteness towards me, it's clear!!! The gift, the good news, the party... and maybe even the book, right?" he blurted out in anger.

"Muzo..." suddenly Cey Cey and Ayhan came in.

"Muzo I don't know what you're talking about." replied Sanem even more bewildered.

"Sure... sure...." he replied sarcastically.

"You want me to believe that you didn't know SHE was coming to the office today? Just today? Huh?" he asked.

"Who? Who are you talking about Muzo, huh?" asked Sanem then getting nervous.

"I'm talking about Guliz! She's upstairs in your office together with Can right now." he said in a rush.

"What! Guliz is here?" asked Sanem stunned.

She looked at Cey Cey.

"Yes, she is here. She arrived a few minutes ago for an appointment." confirmed Cey Cey lowering his head.

"She's going to shoot the commercial with Osman, and you want to tell me you didn't know?" continued Muzo.

"Eh, Sanem?" he shouted hearing her silence.

"Muzo, I swear I am finding out now. I didn't know. If I had known, I..." she tried to retort.

"I what? Huh?! What would you have done!? Would you have bought me a house, to keep me quiet? Would you have bought me a car? What?" shouted Muzo.

"Muzo, lower your voice!" exclaimed Ayhan raising his.

"Muzo, you are exaggerating." said Cey Cey seeing the tears in Sanem's eyes.

"I trusted... like a fool, I thought I could trust you. Sanem is careful, considerate of everyone, she won't do that." he blurted out.

"And yet you are no different from the others at all!" said Muzo shocked.

"Well done, I congratulate you!" he exclaimed clapping.

"Muzo, really I..." tried to reply Sanem.

"But why am I surprised after all... huh? It's certainly not the first time you have plotted behind people's backs, is it? On the contrary." he continued.

"Just see what you are mobilizing for Deren!" he exclaimed.

"Muzo!" resumed Cey Cey.

"You have fun don't you, making plans?" he sought confirmation.

Sanem cried silently, took a deep breath in order to reply, but suddenly a voice resounded in the office.

"Who is doing what, towards Deren?" asked Burak serious in face appearing in the doorway. His hands clenched into fists.

"Shhh!" exclaimed Ayhan. The office door was open.

"Burak!" exclaimed Sanem paling at seeing him standing there in the doorway.

"What do you mean? I heard everything. Who is plotting what, behind Deren's back. I want to know. Right now!" said Burak decisively.

"No, Burak, don't listen to him…" tried Sanem to reason with him.

"Ah, come, have a seat. They will explain it to you. In fact, let Mrs Divit explain it to you." said Muzo pointing at her with an arm around Burak's neck.

"I heard... I tell you." said Burak. "I'm not leaving until you explain to me what is happening to my sister-in-law." he said firmly.

"They're all yours." concluded Muzo as he walked out, greeting him with a pat on the back.

"Muzo? Muzo?" Cey Cey and Ayhan called him.

"Leave me alone!!! I want to be alone!" he exclaimed as the two ran after him.

He lost them again by taking the lift. At that point, Cey Cey ran to the Fikri Harika while Ayhan returned to Sanem. She went in, locked the door behind her so that Burak could not escape to his brother, and stood at the door keeping watch.

"Sanemsi? Are you OK?" she asked, seeing her trembling as she held on to the desk with one hand.

Sanem pulled up with her nose, took a deep breath, wiped away her tears and prepared to tell Burak everything.

Sanem motioned him to take a seat. Burak sat down in front of her. And she too sat down in her chair.

"Sanem?" asked Ayhan, drawing her attention. Sanem looked at her. Ayhan pointed to the cameras above them with her eyes. Then she told her: "I'll wait out here."

"Warn Can that I will be late. I have an urgent call." she told her.

"OK." she replied and went out.

Sanem turned off the cameras and locked the door.

Burak looked at her, frowning.

"It's for precaution, nothing else." she replied to his unexpressed question.

"What's going on, Mrs Divit, what are you up to behind Deren's back?" he asked directly, in a cold, detached tone.

"Listen Burak, I wouldn't have wanted you to know right now. But there's something you don't know." she began.

"What?" he asked.

"I'll tell you now." said Sanem.

He made him aware of her plan, and the answers she was waiting for, what she already knew, and who she thought was involved.

"I am waiting for the proof." she reiterated.

"That's why I didn't want to talk to anyone about it." she said quietly.

"I didn't want to wreak havoc on you, Bulut and especially Deren. My husband doesn't know either. Metin is his best friend." she said in a whisper.

"Do you understand?" she asked at that point.

"I understand, but you could have told me. I would have helped you. I mean, this is Deren we're talking about. I would have done my part, and I would have been less conspicuous, after all, I'm the last one here." he said.

"I didn't want to put you in trouble, Burak, you're a good guy, and you and your brother already have your own problems." Sanem reminded her.

"Besides... I was afraid you would tell your brother. And you know how he would have reacted, right?" said Sanem.

"It would have created chaos in the agency, more than there normally is. And with Deren in her state.... well, I didn't feel like it. That's why I wanted to act alone. But what I am doing is for her own good. To understand and protect her from what she told me." she explained.

"I have no bad intentions Burak. I swear." added Sanem sincerely.

"Then why Muzo..." began Burak asking, leaving the sentence hanging.

"Muzo said those things because he is angry with me. He thinks I hide Guliz's arrival from him." replied Sanem honestly.

"The woman I served upstairs? In Can's office?" he asked.

"That's right." she confirmed.

"And why?" asked Burak.

"Because she is the person who broke his heart so many years ago. She was his wife but then... it seems she cheated on him." she explained to him.

"Ah..." commented the boy taken aback.

"But I didn't know about her arrival at all." repeated Sanem.

"OK, but why did he say you like to make plans? Plotting behind the back?" asked Burak again. He wanted to understand. In this he was very much like his brother.

"In the past, in the early days of my career at Fikri Harika when I was just a novice pick-up and drop-off, I was very naive about work dynamics. I believed everyone. And I found myself trusting the wrong person and involved in evil plans. I was just a pawn, and I couldn't get out of it without hurting someone." Sanem recalled with regret.

"In fact I hurt the most important person in my life... and from there I did everything to make up for it. Every plan I made thereafter was to protect the people I love most. A bit like 'white lies', we can call them 'white plans'. And that's what I'm doing even now with Deren." she explained.

Burak thought about it.

"Do you really think he is behind this?" asked Burak, clenching his hand into a fist.

He knew Deren's story.

"I am waiting for confirmation." Sanem replied.

"I also want to be involved." he replied firmly.

"Whatever needs to be done in here, keeping an eye on someone, finding evidence... I'm ready." said Burak.

"I won't let anyone hurt Deren." he added.

Sanem smiled.

"Burak, this is not a game. I don't want to put you in danger. Your brother would take it out on me. And I don't want to." Sanem replied seriously.

"I am of age. No one can decide for me." Burak replied directly.

Sanem smiled. "You really are a golden boy, Burak. Deren was right." she said.

"You know, she often talks about you. She loves you so much. You are like a son to her. Her exact words." she confided in him.

24. *AN UPSIDE DOWN DAY*

Sanem entered the office.

"Ah, there she is." said Can when he saw her.

"Sanem?" called her Guliz in a cheerful tone.

"Guliz?" she replied in the same tone, hugging her.

"How are you? You look great." said Sanem.

On Guliz, despite her years, there was little to say. Aesthetically she had remained the same, only the clothes were perhaps 'more luxurious'. Other changes, if any, were yet to be seen.

"Oh, thank you. You too, you look great. How you've changed!" she added squaring her.

They hadn't seen each other in years, and it was certainly a shock to see her like this. She couldn't even imagine what she had been through since her departure. In front of her, she found a Sanem who was more mature and confident even in her bearing. A woman in her own right, tanned, with long, voluminous hair styled in light waves that framed her freshly made-up face. She wore a two-piece suit, consisting of a long black skirt with a high waist to below the knees and a white band around the edge. And a matching top that peeked out from under a formal, white jacket with gold buttons. On her feet matching white sock boots. Completing the look was her most important 'jewellery'. The ever-present Albatros brooch in her hair, her engagement ring, along with her wedding ring on her left hand, while on the ring finger of her right hand she wore a moonstone ring, matching the necklace and earrings Can had given her over the years. Added to this was a necklace dedicated to her family. It was a fine choker with a small red amber heart in the center, taken from the necklace Can had given her many years before, on either side of which were the symbols that represented them. To the left of the heart were a small stylised Albatross and a phoenix, entangled in flight, while to the right were the three small elements: a flame, a small star and a small wave of the sea to represent the most precious things in the world. Her children.

"Mr. Can was just confirming to me that you got married, and you have three children, right?" she asked once she had squared her head to toe.

"Twins." Sanem pointed out.

"Triplets? Really? Congratulations then." she said smiling and eager to gossip as always.

"Mh... thanks Guliz. I see you're always on the ball, huh... you don't waste time." Sanem replied, recognizing her old colleague.

"And so... Are you the actress for the clothing brand advertisement?" she asked in a formal tone.

"Mh mh." she replied nodding her head.

"How is that possible? I mean... why didn't I know about it?" asked Sanem casting a glance at her husband.

Can returned the glance in silence. He was speechless, bewildered too.

"Because I wanted it to be a surprise." she replied smiling.

Sanem feigned a gentle smile to hide her nervousness. "And you succeeded." she replied, smiling at her, then turned serious towards Can.

"It was a surprise for me too." he confirmed before she could say anything.

"How is that possible?" asked Sanem puzzled.

"Very simple, Sanem dear..." replied Guliz who was obviously listening to everything. "Because I know someone inside the casting agency. By now, they have been following me for years, so I asked for a favour and they did it for me. That's all." she replied with nonchalance and that mischievous smirk on her face.

"Ah, that's good. Good friendship." commented Sanem sarcastically.

"And... who's going to be the actor who's going to flank me?" asked Guliz.

"Ah, but how? Didn't they inform you? Someone as on the ball as you, how could you not know, my dear Guliz?" teased Sanem.

"It's Osman." replied Can briefly without any emotion.

"Osman? That Osman? Osman Isik we know?" asked Guliz spreading wide her eyelids in surprise.

"Yeah..." replied Can.

"Ahhh, I can't believe it!" she said literally jumping for joy. "Would you look at fate!" she commented.

"Yep... fate... it's really fate..." commented Sanem with a edge in her voice, casting a glance at the man behind her.

"And? The gentleman behind you, who is he? You haven't introduced us." said Sanem.

"Sorry, nice to meet you, Sanem Divit." she said, extending her hand to him, introducing herself.

"My wife, as well as a partner in the agency." specified Can.

"Sanem Divit... how nice that sounds..." Guliz commented, winking at her.

That attitude of a gossip, attentive to every detail from which to draw news, Sanem realised that she had not lacked at all, in fact, if possible, she had become even more intolerant of it all over time. Perhaps it was because of the distance from neighbourhood gossip, thanks to the healthy life immersed in nature that she and her husband had created for themselves, or perhaps because that was simply an aspect of the past that she did not remember with pleasure.

Sanem hinted a forced smirk.

"My agent, Mr Anil." Guliz replied.

"My pleasure, Mrs Divit." he replied, reciprocating the squeeze.

"Please take a seat." Sanem said, pointing to the chairs.

At that moment there was a knock at the door.

"Come in." replied Can as he took a seat at the desk.

"Can I disturb you?" asked a female voice.

"Ah, Leyla, come in." he said.

"Yes, Leyla, look who we have with us." said Sanem looking fixedly into her eyes with a forced smirk.

"Guliz?" she asked surprised.

"Leyla?" she replied approaching to greet her.

"Ah, what a surprise! What are you doing here?" she asked returning the kiss on her cheek she was giving her.

"Guliz, it's the actress from the commercial with Osman." explained Sanem with her static smirk that was gradually turning into a paralysis. Leyla noticed her eye twitching.

"Ah... and why didn't I know about this?" asked Leyla.

"Because Guliz wanted to surprise us, didn't she? Damn..." commented Sanem.

"Ah... " replied Leyla bewildered.

"Mr Anil and I have been in touch to arrange this meeting, but... he didn't say anything to me." she said then added: "Hello Mr Anil. Welcome." turning to him.

"Thank you Mrs Leyla. Um, as Mrs Guliz said, it was supposed to be a surprise." he replied.

Mr Anil was a mature person, with great experience in the field. He was so good and placid that it was easy to make him do anything and sometimes, forget about his presence. Leyla was not so surprised.

"And... Leyla? Why are you talking to managers now?" asked the usual curious one.

"You know, Guliz dear, so much has changed in here over the years, you'd be surprised." replied the Ice Queen herself with a wicked smirk.

Can cleared his throat.

"Shall we talk about work? Please Leyla." said Can, making her sit down.

"Ah, Leyla take a seat? You've been promoted then?" asked Guliz.

"I've been the customer representative for several years now...you've fallen behind, my dear Guliz." replied Leyla crossing her legs, with a mischievous smirk blinking naively.

"Anyway, let's talk business." she concluded seriously.

"Your word, Leyla." Said Can with a smirk giving way to her sister-in-law's sharp tongue.

"Thank you. Then the set will start in two days. The first costume fittings will be tomorrow." she said.

"Sorry Leyla, but didn't Mrs Deren take care of these things? What happened to her?" she quickly interrupted her.

"Mrs Deren is not in the agency at the moment. She had an engagement. I'm here. Shall we continue?" she answered briefly with a sigh. She was about to lose patience, it was clear.

"It's fine, please, we'll have a chance to talk later anyway." she replied.

Sanem opened her eyes wide as she exchanged a startled look with her husband.

"Mh, I had no doubt." she then replied through clenched teeth.

Can masked his smile by bringing a hand to his mouth.

"What did you say, Sanem dear? Oops, I meant Mrs Divit. "Guliz corrected herself by covering her mouth with one hand naively.

"Nothing, er... we don't have much time, so if we can speed up..." said Sanem looking at her watch.

"Sure, sister." replied Leyla.

Finally, Leyla was able to explain everything that was necessary. And in no time, Can declared the meeting concluded.

"Ah, so if we're done, why don't we all have a coffee together like old times?" proposed Guliz.

"I can't, unfortunately, Emre needs me." Can hurriedly replied to scurry off.

Leyla looked at him and held her hands. "Um... yes, yes indeed, he is waiting for you." she confirmed.

"Leyla?" asked a voice as he entered the office. He froze suddenly. It was Emre.

"Guliz?" he asked seeing her.

"Mr Emre, hello." she greeted him politely.

"That's right. We were just talking about you, love. You've come to claim your brother, haven't you?" she said, baring her eyes for him to play along.

"Ah, um... yes, I wanted to ask you something, but yes, of course, I was looking for my brother." admitted Emre with some hesitation.

"What a surprise." he added, approaching to greet the former employee.

"Isn't it?" commented Sanem. "It's just like that. Fate..."

"Welcome." he added.

"Thank you." she replied, returning the greeting.

"Are you visiting us?" he asked courteously.

"No, actually, Guliz will be the actress who will flank Osman." replied Leyla.

"Ah..." he exclaimed. "I didn't know that."

"And who did know..." commented Sanem.

"I don't think anyone in the agency knew." added Can.

"It's a surprise to everyone." he confirmed.

"And? How are you, Mr Emre?" asked Guliz to chat.

"Fine, Guliz, and you? You've become a full-fledged actress, then?" deduced Emre.

"Yes. The Orgatte commercial was my stepping stone," she commented with satisfaction.

"Do you remember?" she asked everyone.

"Mh, how could I forget." replied Leyla in an apathetic tone.

"Anyway, you two go." she said turning to the Divit brothers.

"Save yourselves while you still can." whispered Sanem in Can's ear as he kissed her goodbye on the cheek to follow his brother. "If you don't see me back in 15 minutes, come and save me." she warned him.

Can confirmed with a blink.

"It's been a pleasure Guliz." he greeted her before leaving.

"Thank you, have a nice day Mr. Can." returned the greeting Guliz.

"Alright, let's have a coffee." said Sanem. "Then sorry, but I have to run." she admitted as she looked at her phone.

"Perfect then." Guliz replied, then looked at Mr Anil. "Mr Anil, you can go." she said.

"Alright, have a nice day." he said saying goodbye to Sanem and Leyla.

Sanem had the feeling he wanted to run away. Poor man, he was right. Who wouldn't want to run away at that moment, she thought.

"Come on, let's take a seat at the counter at Cey Cey's." Leyla beckoned.

"Sanem?" closed Guliz.

"Guliz?" she replied in the same tone.

"But... if you are a partner, why don't we go to your office and have a coffee?" she proposed as if she were at home.

"You are already in my office, my dear Guliz." Sanem replied.

"Ah, you share the office with your husband? Ah, very romantic!" she exclaimed softly.

Then she turned to Leyla.

"Leyla, do you also share the office with your husband?" she asked.

"No, Guliz, mine is the usual office, you know it." she said pointing at it through the glass window.

"And Emre has his too, if you're wondering. We like it that way." she replied to remove all doubt.

"Come on, let's go to the counter." Leyla urged her.

On the way out Guliz obviously recognized faces in the creative team. She stopped to greet them, and they finally arrived at the counter.

"Cey Cey?" asked Guliz.

"And are you still at the counter like in the old days?" she asked him.

"Actually, my dear I'm a partner in the agency." he replied, expertly pouring a cup of coffee in front of them.

"Ah... you? A partner?" she asked surprised, blinking.

"Yeah." he replied all pleased.

"And you still pour coffee?" she asked laughing under her mustache.

"Why can't partners pour their own coffee?" he replied curtly.

Meanwhile, out of the meeting room behind the counter came Ayhan and Deniz.

"Ha ha!" exclaimed Guliz shocked. "Ayhan?"

"Guliz..." she said not exactly happy. She felt resentment for the pain she had caused to her friend Muzo.

"My God! How well you look! I almost didn't recognise you! Ayhan but what are you doing here? Or have you come back at last?" she asked, hugging her in surprise. She didn't know about Ayhan's obvious weight loss.

"Yeah... I'm back, aren't I, my hubby?" she said purposely hugging Cey Cey at the counter, showing off the ring.

"Ah! I can't believe it, you're married? Ahh!" she exclaimed going around the counter to hug them both.

"Congratulations! How nice!" she exclaimed squeezing them.

"You've seen Guliz... as you see there are many changes. She is no longer the Fikri Harika you know." replied Leyla.

"One minute... you work here Ayhan?" she asked.

"Um... yes and no." she replied.

"Both." Cey Cey replied proudly.

"My wife is a licensed life coaching. She teaches corporate yoga classes and more with Deniz." he said pointing at her.

Deniz at that point stood in the corner observing her and approached.

"Hello. Nice to meet you Deniz." she said cordially in a detached tone.

"Hello, nice to meet you, Guliz." she replied curiously with a smile, squaring her as she always did when faced with new acquaintances.

"Deniz, she is our company psychotherapist. Both from Fikri Harika and the Sanem." Cey explained quietly.

Sanem glowered at him.

"What?" he asked seeing her gaze.

"The Sanem?" asked Guliz. "What's that?"

"Sanem's company." confirmed Leyla.

"It's downstairs." replied Cey Cey calmly, making more coffee.

"Downstairs?" asked Guliz.

"Yes, instead of the publishing house. Remember?" continued Cey Cey. By now his tongue had taken command of his brain.

"Cey Cey!" growled Sanem.

"Wow... what a bombshell of news!" exclaimed Guliz.

"And what company is it?" she asked, growing curiouser and curiouser.

"What do you mean? It's world-renowned, don't you know it? Ah, I wonder!" exclaimed Cey Cey.

"It's my brand of organic creams and perfumes." replied Sanem surrendering with a sigh.

"Ah, really? You must give me a tour then!" replied Guliz elatedly.

"Um... that's not possible at the moment. Maybe another time." replied Sanem firmly.

Suddenly, as they sipped their coffee they heard an unmistakable voice.

"Ah, I can't take these shoes any more. My feet hurt!" said a firm voice.

"Uh... I smell coffee. Cey Cey is making coffee, do you smell it?" asked Deren popping around the corner, coming from the entrance flanked by Bulut.

"I smell it, I feel it. But you need to rest now." he told her thoughtfully, stroking her back.

The two were approaching the counter chatting amongst themselves. When they looked ahead and saw the group gathered at the counter, Bulut exclaimed first: "What's going on? Why are they all gathered there?" he asked.

They had all lined up, waiting for the scene. Sanem, Ayhan, Deniz, Leyla and Cey Cey.

"Ah, now I really want to enjoy the show." Cey Cey said, pulling out a bucket full of popcorn from under the counter, which he placed on top of the counter. Everyone took a handful.

Deren at that point raised his eyes, which she kept fixed on her phone, and saw.

"What's going on?" she asked.

Guliz got up from her stool with her mouth open, waiting for Deren to join her.

"I can't believe it!" exclaimed Guliz.

"Is that Guliz?" asked Deren surprised.

Guliz?" she called her.

"Yes... Mrs. Deren?" stammered Guliz for a moment.

"I can't believe it!" she repeated as she saw her advancing with Bulut hand in hand.

She greeted her with a double kiss on the cheeks.

"Guliz? What are you doing here? What a surprise..." she said dazedly, looking over her shoulder at the others for answers.

"Mrs Deren?" she asked.

"You look well, Guliz. How are you?" asked Deren of her.

Guliz aesthetically and internally had not changed at all. Now it was her turn to notice.

"I'm fine, thank you. You look good too, here... maybe... did she gain a few pounds? But if so, they look good on her." she said, committing a classic gaffe of hers by speaking out of turn.

Cey Cey spat out the popcorn.

"Help, she's going to spit fire now, I can feel it." he said as if faced with the scariest scene in a movie.

"Cey Cey... shhh, don't ruin the scene." resumed Sanem fishing out more popcorn.

Deren turned red as a pepper ready to explode.

Bulut knowing her, he knew the smoke would come out of her ears at any moment just like a pressure cooker. The topic of chili, as much as it was for a pregnancy, was very sensitive at the moment.

"Cey Cey?" asked Deren in an icy tone. "Did Guliz just call me fat or did she?" she asked looking her steadily in the eyes seeking confirmation to grind her to a pulp.

"Ah see? What did I tell you?" said Cey Cey to Sanem and his wife beside him.

He walked around the counter and joined her.

"No, no, Mrs Deren, she didn't mean that. She said that because she doesn't know..." said Cey Cey.

"Don't know what?" asked Guliz.

At that point Deren gripped her husband's hand tightly so as not to explode.

Bulut then, feeling his fingers tighten, took the floor.

"Um... hello. Nice to meet you, I am Bulut." he said cutely, shaking her hand.

"Nice to meet you, I'm Guliz. Actress." she replied automatically with a flirtatious manner as she squared him from head to toe. She was doing it from the first moment she had laid eyes on him. Deren had noticed.

"Ah, I am a lawyer. And I'm also the..." he replied.

"He's my husband, Guliz!" growled Deren, marking her territory like a bloodhound. She was observing how Guliz, as usual, was squaring him.

"Ah... you got married Mrs. Deren! Ah, she finally made it too, huh!" she said clapping, not realizing what she was saying.

"Guliz..." resumed Cey Cey. "You haven't changed at all." he commented, shaking his head.

"Why? What did I say?" she asked naively.

"Yeah, we've all changed here. Except you, I see. You, on the other hand, are still the same old flirtatious one." replied Deren straightforwardly.

Cey Cey turned around, exchanging a smug look with the others. Ayhan and Sanem opened their mouths wide with their popcorn hands in midair. Leyla crossed her arms smiling in satisfaction. Deniz did not understand, but felt a certain satisfaction in Deren's reply.

"Guliz but where have you been living for the last few years? Huh? In Burundi? Or in the Arctic Circle?" asked Cey Cey shocked.

"Has your brain hibernated by any chance? How can you not know anything? It made the news! It was the wedding of the year!" said Cey Cey bewildered that she had missed such gossip.

Sanem, Leyla and Ayhan were literally popping popcorn in front of here. They exchanged a complicit smirk. They were obviously team Deren.

Deren took a deep breath, looked at her husband and then said to herself: "I won't get angry. I will not get angry." she repeated with her eyes closed.

Once she had taken deep breaths, as if to overcome the pain of contractions, she opened her eyes and pointed them at her fiercely like a Velociraptor.

"Anyway... my dear Guliz, what you see, it's not extra kilos.... it is because I am expecting a baby. I'm pregnant!" she replied proudly.

"What! Ah... really? Oh my God, I didn't mean to...how embarrassing! Ah, congratulations!" she said, looking at her again. She was actually wearing the 'angel caller' necklace, she realised.

79

"Ah, married and with a baby on the way, who knew, huh?" said Guliz.

"Yeah... who would have thought it..." commented sarcastically Deren.

"Is there any other news that might shock me? More children on the way?" she then asked, looking at the others.

"Leyla has a child, did you know?" said Cey Cey.

"Ah, Leyla too? Ah, so many things I missed." she said.

"Right?" said Sanem with a grimace, plugging her mouth with a handful of popcorn to say no more.

"Ah, Cey Cey, where is Burak? I need his strawberry smoothie. Now!" blurted Deren in a fit of nervousness.

"Um, I'll go get him now, Mrs Deren, he'll be in the archive." said Cey Cey.

"Ah, here he comes." she then corrected herself as she saw him advancing.

Guliz also squinted. A tall handsome boy, with long black hair like Bulut. Resembling, even.

If thunderbolts had really come out of Deren's eyes at that moment, only ashes would have remained of Guliz.

"Brother? Deren? You're back." said Burak greeting them with a big smile.

"How are you Burak, are you all right?" asked Bulut.

"Yes, all good." he replied quietly shrugging.

Burak kissed Deren on the cheek.

"How are you?" he asked.

"Fine, my dear." she replied returning the smile, stroking his cheek.

"Burak, my brother-in-law. Before you ask." she said in Guliz's direction.

"Ah, pleasure. How young you are! Here... not that you're not Mr Bulut, but..." tried to explain Guliz in embarrassment.

"Don't worry. He's young in fact, he's barely of age." confirmed Bulut.

"A bit out of your league, Guliz, what do you say?" commented Deren.

"Burak is our intern at Fikri Harika, he's under my supervision." explained Cey Cey, giving himself a tone with his hands on his braces.

"Mh, I guess." Guliz replied with a grimace.

"So he works here... good." she added.

"Um, Burak, Bulut, meet Guliz, she was an OLD work colleague of ours many years ago." she said emphasizing the word old.

"But you said actress, or am I wrong?" asked Bulut.

"She's not wrong, I'm an actress now, I started with a commercial while I was still working here and then... I never stopped." she said with a laugh.

"Your name is actually not new to me. Where did I hear it?" thought Bulut.

"Maybe the Orgatte advertisement. That's where I got popular from." she said, shaking out a strand of hair in a star like manner.

"Or maybe because she is Muzo's ex-wife. You must have heard her from him." said Cey Cey. "Do you remember, at the estate?"

"Ah... of course! I remember now. Are you that Guliz?" asked Bulut pointing at her.

"Yeah, you recognised me now," she replied naively.

"Aren't you the one who betrayed Muzo with the captain of the ship in Papua New Guinea?" asked Bulut fearlessly.

Deren smiled.

"Bravo, my love! That is news to be remembered for. Isn't that right Guliz?" said Deren.

Behind them Ayhan, Sanem, Leyla, and with that sentence, even Deniz were literally devouring popcorn, holding back giggles.

Guliz uncomfortably replied, "Well... we all make mistakes, right? We are human. And anyway, the past stays in the past." she replied briefly to close that chapter.

"It had to..." commented Deniz. "But look at that, the past is showing up here again today." she said glaring at her, not realizing that she was speaking out loud.

Guliz looked at her, blinking in confusion.

Sanem and Ayhan almost choked on popcorn. Leyla, in the middle between them, helped them with two good, firm pats on the shoulders.

"Burak, could you please make me your strawberry smoothie?" asked Deren kindly.

"Sure, I'll go right away." he said not before shaking Guliz's hand.

"Nice to meet you anyway." he said.

"My pleasure." she replied reciprocating.

"Thank you dear." Deren replied. Burak gave her a tender smile.

"And? What about you, Guliz? Are you engaged? Married? Is there anyone in your life?" she asked her bluntly.

"No, no one as yet." she simply replied with a smirk.

"That's why she was squaring Bulut and Burak." whispered Sanem to Leyla.

"It's obvious." replied Deren through clenched teeth thinking the same thing as Sanem.

Meanwhile Metin made his entrance into the agency, they saw him pass in the distance and Sanem elbowed Burak, next to her at the counter making smoothie.

"Huh?" he asked distractedly. Sanem gave him a nod.

"Isn't that Mr Metin?" asked Guliz.

She noticed that he was walking briskly towards Can's office.

"Yes." replied Deniz decisively.

Guliz looked at her.

Cey Cey answered his doubts.

"Metin is back to being Fikri Harika's lawyer. And Deniz is his current girlfriend." he explained, pointing at her.

Deniz waved her off with a hand and a sly smirk.

"Ah, how nice... so you're all here?" she commented.

"Um, Sanem I'm going down to the company, I'd need to show you some documents as soon as I can." Bulut reminded himself.

Sanem seized the opportunity.

"Yes, I'll be right down." she said, gorging herself on the popcorn in her hand.

"Sorry I have to go." she said running off with her mouth full.

"But Sanem? What better occasion to show me your company?" asked Guliz.

Sanem put on the brakes. She gave a deep sigh and then turned back to her.

"God, give me patience, please. I can't save myself, can I?" she said in a whisper as she looked at Bulut, her back to Guliz.

Bulut tightened his lips while holding back a smile and shrugged.

"And Can hasn't shown up yet... ufff!" Sanem thought to herself.

"Alright, come, but it'll be a quick tour." she said hoping that was the end of it.

"Alright, let's go." agreed Sanem.

Cey Cey and Burak saw Metin coming out of Can's office. They kept an eye on him.

As they reached the stairs, Can joined them.

"Sanem?" he called to her as she, Bulut and Guliz came downstairs.

"Can!" she replied, turning around with a big smile. She was safe.

"I should talk to you. Could you come?" he asked her.

"Um... just a minute. I'll be right there. Just wait here." said Sanem to Guliz and Bulut as she walked up the few steps made to reach him.

"Sanem? What are you doing? I had come to save you, but..." her husband said between his teeth.

"No, Can, nothing, but... I can't get her off me! She wants to see the Sanem. She won't go away...she won't go away! I'll go crazy! I swear I'll go crazy!" she moaned in hysterics.

"Please come with me. I need moral support. I can't cope." she begged him.

"Why did you agree then?" asked her Can.

"Because, my dear hubby, I hope that after this, she will leave. If that is enough to make her go away then..." she let Sanem imply. "Anyway, I said it will be a short tour due to commitments." he added.

"Please... please." she begged him making eyes at him.

"And that's fine. All right. I'll come, but let him go, then eh! I won't tolerate all this gossip anymore!" blurted out Can in a low voice.

"You, eh? You... you don't tolerate it... my head explodes with how much I've heard her questioning and snickering! Look! Out of desperation I ate a bucket of popcorn and now look at me! Look how bloated I am! It's all still here, as my mother says!" said Sanem pointing at her belly.

"Ah, don't talk nonsense, you look great as always." he reassured her by kissing her on the forehead.

"Come on, we'll make each other strong." Can said taking her by the hand.

"After all, we have overcome worse. No?" thought Sanem.

"True." he replied.

"And... besides, you're a partner in the company so it's only right that you're there." she reminded him.

"Well, now that you have all the justification you need... can we go? Let it end as soon as possible!" said Can.

"You're telling me..." she commented.

They recomposed themselves, caught up and continued on to their destination.

As promised, the tour was very brief, as brief was Sanem's explanation of that space. While Can entertained Guliz she gave directions to the documents Bulut had told her about, after which they went up to the Fikri Harika for greetings.

"Well then..." said Sanem in dismissing her.

"Mama! Dad!" they heard their self calling.

Can and Sanem turned towards the entrance from which they saw Deniz, Yildiz and Ates running towards them.

They exchanged a glance. Sanem was surprised.

"Mama's little birds!" she exclaimed as she saw them spreading their arms wide.

"Here they are, my little pests!" exclaimed Can welcoming Yildiz and Deniz into his arms.

While Ates clung to his mother's legs for a hug.

Guliz opened his mouth wide in surprise as soon as she saw them. Then she brought her hands to cover it in emotion.

"Oh, how cute! Are these your children?" she asked.

"Yes." replied Sanem.

"Why couldn't you tell?" Can asked with two, of the three clasped in his arms.

"Ah, such sweethearts." commented Guliz looking at them. "They look so much like you, in fact." said Can writing them well.

"Right?" commented Sanem softening.

"But...where did you guys jump out from, I mean...who brought you here?" asked Sanem looking behind them.

Seeing no one he looked at Can.

"We brought them." said Mr Aziz arriving serene and happy hand in hand with his wife holding Ilker.

Once they reached him he recognized Guliz.

"Ah, Guliz? Daughter! What a pleasure... what a long time!" exclaimed Mr Aziz all happy.

Can and Sanem smiled. Guliz had not expected such enthusiasm from him. She did not know how Mr Aziz had changed after his illness and his long journey. She had not seen him since his departure.

Guliz stood in shock.

"My guess is that she's about to explode. With all the changes she has heard!" commented Sanem under her breath.

"She'll have gossip to tell for at least a year." commented Can.

"Yes... Mr Aziz?" replied Guliz stammering.

"You're back? What a pleasure to see you again!" exclaimed Guliz, unlocking herself from her torpor.

He held out her hand in greeting, looked at her and said: "Ah, come here girl, let me give you a hug."

Guliz was taken aback, once released from the embrace Aziz asked her: "And what good wind brings you here?"

"Here..." she said still in shock at such confidence.

"Guliz is the actress who will be supporting Osman in a clothing advertisement." Can explained.

"Ah... that's nice. Good girl. I am very happy that you have found your way." he told her sincerely.

Guliz looked at Sanem and Can shocked.

"Guliz, so what do you say about the new, more jaunty Mr Aziz. Huh? Do you like him?" asked Can to her.

"There, you too have totally changed Mr Aziz. I admit I'm a moment shocked. I remember you different, that is, no offense." she said.

Aziz laughed as he looked at his wife.

"I have the same effect on everyone." he commented.

"Ah, I didn't introduce you." he realised later.

Guliz-Mihriban. Mihriban-Guliz." he introduced her.

Guliz looked at her from head to toe, then looked at the child she was holding.

Mihriban, always gentle and kind, held out her hand and said: "How are you, my child, I am Aziz's wife. And you?" she asked.

To that question he replied.

"Guliz at one time, when I was head of the agency, she was my personal secretary until I left." explained Aziz.

"Ah... now I understand." commented Mihriban cordially, although her nose had already pegged her.

"Ah, the wife? The pleasure is all mine, madam." Guliz commented, increasingly surprised.

"Ah, what a beautiful child." she commented, thinking it was their.

"Ah, this is Ilker, Leyla and Emre's son." Aziz explained quickly.

"Ah, this is Ilker? What love. Hello." she said, touching his little hand.

Ilker was very shy, he clung to his grandmother's neck hiding his big blue eyes.

"Ah... he is ashamed." explained Mihriban with a smile.

Sanem asked her 'mother-in-law': You gave us a surprise, huh?"

"A surprise?" she replied frowning confused.

"What surprise, my daughter?" she asked.

"The children, I say, in bringing them here..." insisted Sanem.

Mihriban looked at Can confused.

"It's not a surprise. I asked to bring them. They were going out early today and since it's lunchtime, I thought it would be nice to have lunch together." explained Can.

"Ah, so you knew?" asked Sanem.

"Yes, he was the one who called." said Aziz.

Sanem looked at him realizing. "Ah..."

Can winked at her.

"You did well, my love. Very good idea. Isn't it, my little ones?" said Sanem stroking Ates' hair tightly by her side.

The children began to get restless so they tried to close that meeting. Mihriban, under the pretext of taking Ilker to his mother, invited the little ones to follow them to their parents' office, leaving the two alone with their guest. Aziz did likewise.

Leyla, however, was already coming towards them having seen her son.

"Ilker? Darling?" asked Leyla, taking him from Mihriban's arms.

As soon as he saw her, he clung to her neck.

"And you? My little nephews?" she said to the twins.

"Hi Auntie!" they exclaimed as they ran off towards their parents' office. On the way, Uncle Emre stopped them.

"Hop! And you little brats? Where did you come from?" he asked, blocking their way.

"Uncle Emre!" they exclaimed, hugging him.

"Ah, yes, give me a big bear hug. Come." he said, hugging all three of them.

MEANWHILE LEYLA...

"What a surprise! What are you doing here?" she asked her in-laws.

"Ah, my baby?" asked Emre coming up behind Leyla.

"Come to daddy. Come." he said taking him from her arms. He was not so light.

"Daddy? Mihriban? Welcome. How good of you to come." he greeted them.

"It's nice, of course, don't get me wrong, but... I didn't expect it. "Leyla admitted.

"Can wanted it that way." whispered Mihriban. "I'll explain now, let's go." he said, inviting them back to the office, joining the twins.

Meanwhile, Can and Sanem tried to close that meeting.

"Wow, here, I didn't expect all these changes. My head is spinning." admitted Guliz.

"Tell me about it..." commented Sanem.

"You really are a beautiful family!" she told them.

"I really thank you so much Guliz, but now, here, we should go." said Sanem.

"No, of course, I understand," she replied.

In the meantime she saw Ayhan running past them towards the entrance.

"Brother? Adile?" she said running to them.

"Ah, my favorite niece is here too!" she exclaimed. Greeting her in her mother's arms.

Can and Sanem took a deep breath and turned around.

"Osman?" called Guliz as soon as she saw him.

When he saw her, Can and Sanem, he walked over with his family.

"Welcome, Osman, Adile. Hello little one." said Can greeting them.

"Thank you guys, welcome," replied Osman.

"I thought you would arrive in the evening. Ayhan had said so." said Sanem looking at her.

"Because Ayhan knew so." replied Adile.

"Osman finished the shoot earlier today, so we anticipated. " she explained.

"Hi dear, by the way." Adile remembered to greet her. They exchanged a kiss on the cheek.

"Hello, dear. And you, little one?" said Sanem, making her smile with a tickle.

The little girl started laughing, with the dummy in her mouth.

"Ah, you give me the dummy?" said Sanem. "You give it to me?" the baby looked at her with her big blue eyes. She was dark-haired like her father and curly-haired, just like Osman, the rest was all mum.

"What if I take it from you?" asked Sanem taking it out of her mouth.

The little girl smiled at Sanem's funny faces, without crying.

"Ah, there's a big smile." she said.

Ayhan also joined in.

"Come to auntie. Come." said Ayhan taking her in her arms.

The little girl began to cry.

"Oh, no..." said Sanem.

"Come to Auntie Sanem, come." she said taking her in the arms.

"I don't think it's a good idea." said Can remembering the past.

"Watch and learn." said Sanem holding her to her chest.

The little girl immediately calmed down and started laughing.

"See?" said Sanem sticking her tongue out at him.

"This is a miracle!" exclaimed Ayhan.

"Could it be that she has now passed on to you the effect she had on the children?" asked Can looking at Ayhan dejectedly.

"It's just a matter of experience." Sanem corrected him.

"The children feel all the emotions you feel, if you're agitated, nervous or whatever, that's the result." she said.

"I am really impressed. Good my love, you are doing great." said Can kissing her forehead.

"Ah... she is more beautiful every day." commented Sanem.

Then to the little girl she said: "How big you've grown, huh?"

As Adile, Sanem and Ayhan talked about the baby, Osman exchanged a few words with Guliz.

"Guliz, long time no see. How are you?" he asked greeting her.

"All is well. I find you looking better and better." she replied squaring him.

Adile cast her a glance.

"Ah, thanks, it's fatherhood." he explained looking at his wife and then his daughter.

"True, it has that effect." confirmed Can laughing. He patted him on the shoulder.

"Um... I don't know if you know this." Can said. "But Guliz will be the one to join you in the commercial we have to shoot." he informed him.

Adile moved even closer to her husband.

"Ah, come on, so you're a full-fledged actress now too?" asked Osman of her.

"Yes. I made it." replied Guliz beaming.

"Good, I'm very happy for you. I remember you wanted it so much." he said.

"Yeah. I've come a long way." she confirmed.

"Did you?" asked Can then.

"What?" asked Osman.

"That she was going to flank you, I say." he explained.

"No, I didn't know that. But I'm happy to shoot with someone I know. It will be easier." he said.

"Yes, I think so too." she replied with heartfelt eyes.

Osman looked at Adile.

"Ah, this is my wife Adile." he said holding her close.

"Nice to meet you." she said shaking her hand not at all convinced of the woman.

"Nice to meet you, Guliz." she replied, returning the shake with a smile.

"I knew you were married." Guliz admitted.

"Ah..." intervened Sanem upon hearing those words. "So something you know? Unbelievable!" she commented.

"Of the world of actors nothing escapes me. It is of the outside world that I have lost track." she said, snubbing their world.

"We are the outside world so..." commented Ayhan getting nervous.

"Forget it, Auntie." replied Sanem mimicking the child's voice.

"Ah, look Uncle Cey cey is coming!" she added.

"We're really full up today." he said reaching them.

"Really. This meeting never ends, and today everything goes wrong. Nothing is going according to plan. It's just a bad day. I'm going crazy." vented Sanem, speaking in a low voice.

"Ah, go to Uncle Cey Cey." she then said giving her niece in his arms.

"Ah... Sanem, but so unannounced..." he blurted out.

"What notice?" asked Ayhan.

"In fact what do you want? For us to sound trumpets to warn you that we are about to pass your granddaughter in your arms?" asked Sanem.

"Is that how you will do it when you have children?" she added.

As soon as she laid the baby in his arms, she began to cry in despair.

Adile turned around.

"He doesn't like you." Sanem said with a laugh.

"He doesn't like uncles it seems. Only Auntie Sanem, isn't it?" she said, stroking her cheek. Beautiful dimples formed when she laughed.

"Take her. Take her, take her, take her." said Cey Cey fidgeting.

Sanem took her. "I really want to see how you two are going to do it... I really want to see." Sanem repeated as she slowly pulled away with the little one in her arms.

"She'll be hungry... for this." said Ayhan.

"I don't think so." replied Sanem.

"Sanem, I need to talk to you." said Cey Cey winking. She knew what he was referring to.

"What's going on here?" said Deren drawn by the child's desperate crying.

"Ah... who has arrived? The most beautiful little girl in the world?" she said in a voice that was both tender and shrill at the same time.

Disturbing.

Sanem, Ayhan and Cey Cey looked at each other shocked.

"My God, she won't talk to her child like that, I want to hope." said Ayhan.

"Poor child..." commented Cey Cey.

"What are you two confabulating?" said Deren looking at them.

"Ah, nothing." said Cey Cey shrugging.

"Osman and Adile have also arrived, I see." she said.

"Yeah." replied Sanem.

"And Guliz is still there." she added, extinguishing her enthusiasm.

"He won't budge. I'm exhausted. She really caught everything today. It's like a joke." thought Sanem.

"She's got her fill of news, now I hope we won't see her again for a while." said Ayhan.

"After she shoots, maybe..." said Deren.

"Keep her." Sanem said, handing the little one to her aunt Ayhan.

"What did you want to tell me, Cey Cey?" she asked approaching him.

"Let's go." he replied simply.

"Sorry." said Sanem walking away.

"Go sister. Go. You'll see she's not crying now." said Ayhan.

As soon as Sanem took two steps away, the little girl started crying her eyes out.

Adile was undecided whether to stay by her husband's side and listen to that Guliz or move closer, then she saw Deren intervene.

"Adile? May I?" she asked from afar.

"Sure." she replied. By now with the frequent collaborations they had, they had become part of the team and Adile trusted most of the members of the agency blindly. Deren was one of them.

"Sister-in-law, though, ufff." Ayhan complained.

Adile laughed.

Sanem stopped, cast a glance at Ayhan and smiled, then walked away for good with Cey Cey.

"Ah, come here. Don't worry little one, it's OK." Deren said, rocking her to her chest.

The little one liked her 'angel caller' necklace."

"Ah, you like it?" she told her. "Oh, what pretty eyes!" she commented.

"You're good at it, Mrs Deren." admitted Ayhan watching her with her arms crossed.

"Thanks, I'm rehearsing..." she commented with a smile.

Seeing the quiet little girl, Adile also calmed down, devoting her full attention to her husband's conversation.

Deren slowly took her around the agency, leading her to Cey Cey's counter, where Burak and Bulut were standing at the moment.

Both of them, seeing Deren with the baby in her arms, softened.

Bulut, seeing her like that, thought that he would soon be holding their child in her arms and smiled at the very thought.

Burak, happy to see her so serene, was even more convinced that he had made the right choice. He would protect that happiness at any cost.

While Can explained to the two actors how the job would unfold, Sanem and Cey Cey came down to the Sanem's office. She asked for Muzo, and he asked for Burak. Once they were up to date, they went upstairs and finally Guliz took her leave to prepare for his role, so they could finally enjoy lunch. Deren went out with her family, with Bulut and Burak by her side who had now become her bodyguards.

Osman, Adile and the little one went out to lunch with their uncles Ayhan and Cey Cey, while the Divit family gathered for an unplanned family lunch. Can, Sanem, the twins, Leyla, Emre and the baby, Aziz and Mihriban.

25. IN THE RIGHT PLACE,

AT THE RIGHT TIME

It was on their way back to the office that Can, having just left his wife downstairs, heard Cey Cey talking to Ayhan.

"I feel very sorry for my little sister," said Ayhan in a sad tone.

"Yeah..." confirmed Cey Cey sorrowfully. They were sitting in the small lounge set up behind the counter at the entrance to the meeting room. Being behind them, they both did not realise Can was there. He was on his way back to the office, but he really needed a coffee to get through the busy afternoon, but hearing those words, Can stopped.

"Muzo did not behave well." Ayhan said harshly.

"I didn't expect such a reaction at all. You know?" confided Cey Cey to her.

"That was really barbaric!" exclaimed Ayhan. "Yelling at him like that..."

"You are right. The reaction was exaggerated." said Cey Cey.

"My poor Sanemsi! You should have seen her after he left, the state she was in. She was crying and shaking like a leaf. I don't know how she pulled herself together and joined Guliz upstairs as if nothing had happened." said Ayhan.

"That's it, how he also managed to face Guliz right afterwards with a smile on her face, I really don't know." she added.

"That's her super power. Always smiling. Sanem is strong. And she is a leader. She can mask well even when she is sad. I know it well." said Cey Cey remembering the past.

"There, I understand that Muzo was hurt, but to think that Sanem deliberately avoided telling him about Guliz's arrival is madness. I mean, with all she did to help him.... She stood by him, supported him in writing that mysterious essay of his and even helped him get in touch with publishers. Would a person with such a big heart have ever not told him such a thing if he had known?" blurted Ayhan.

"I know, Sanem has been a really good friend. If it wasn't for her who knows what condition Muzo would be in now. Do you remember before he left?" said Cey Cey sipping his coffee.

"And who can forget it. He was beside himself. Only Sanem was able to talk to him." recalled her wife.

"No, no, Ayhan, it was anger that made him react like that. Seeing Guliz like that again, it set him off." said Cey Cey thinking back.

"I understand, Cey Cey, but that doesn't justify it. He was bad! He didn't even allow Sanem to explain, he immediately shouted the worst things at him, treating her very badly." said Ayhan.

"Do you know where he is now?" he asked her.

"No... I have no idea where he went." replied Cey Cey.

"Look, if you know and you don't tell me, we'll fight, I'll tell you!" she snapped angrily.

"I swear I don't know, Ayhan." he defended himself.

"You make me find out where he is and then you'll see. I have two little words to say to him!" said Ayhan angrily and protectively.

Can stood there in silence the whole time, realized his hands were sore, clenched into fists. Veins in evidence.

Instinctively he bent his neck to the right and then to the left, a gesture that foretold his rising nervousness.

He walked silently away without a word, black in face, back to his office. He took out his mobile phone and without a second thought called Muzo.

He did not answer.

"Coward." commented Can in the empty office, pacing back and forth out of nervousness.

Emre who saw him in that state from his office frowned, after taking a good look at him, got up to join him.

"Brother?" he asked as entered through the connecting door.

"What's going on? How come you are in this state?" he asked worriedly.

"I will find him. Oh, if I will find him! And when I find him..." he said, leaving the sentence hanging.

"You'll see." concluded Can with a smirk, walking past him.

"What? Who? What are you talking about?" his brother asked confused.

"I'm going out, Emre. I have a matter to settle." he said already outside the office door.

"But where are you going? Brother? Is there a problem?" he asked loudly behind his back.

"No." he replied directly aloud, moving further and further away.

"Emre? What's going on?" asked Leyla, seeing Can storming out of the office.

"I don't know. I wanted to figure it out, but he's gone." said Emre.

"Where? Why?" she asked worriedly. "Is there a problem?"

"I don't know. I saw him nervous, looking at his phone and pacing back and forth in the office, so I approached him, but I didn't understand."

"He didn't say anything at all?" she asked.

"He mumbled something like 'I'll find him, you'll see.' and things like that, but I have no idea who he was referring to." he admitted.

"My God..." commented Leyla. "What could have happened? I wonder if my sister is aware..."

"I wouldn't know. But maybe he's gone to her now." replied Emre.

"Come on, let's get back to work." he added. "You'll see it's nothing." he reassured her.

Burak who had heard that exchange, thought about going down to the Sanem, who, locked in her office was trying to contact Muzo without results.

"Where are you? Can we talk?" she texted him.

Meanwhile there was a knock at the door.

"Come in." she replied, setting the phone down in the corner of the desk.

"Excuse me. Mrs Sanem? May I?" asked Burak politely, peeping through the door.

"Of course, Burak. Come, have a seat." she said.

"Tell me. Do you need any pointers on the job? How can I help you?" asked Sanem seriously.

"Um, it's not work-related." Burak warned her.

"Ah..." she replied, thinking about the other matter.

"Is there any news?" he then asked.

"No, not on that front." she replied.

"OK, so what do you want to talk to me about?" she asked.

"Well, you told me to keep my eyes open and that's why I wanted to warn you." he said.

"Alright. Tell me. I'm listening." Sanem replied.

"Mr Can just left the agency in a hurry. He was very nervous. He seemed angry about something. Emre asked for an explanation, but even he didn't understand. Maybe he got a phone call, I don't know." said Burak.

Sanem straightened up in her chair.

"Well, I thought he was here, but he's not." he said looking around the office.

"No, he hasn't been seen here." Sanem confirmed.

"There, I know it's none of my business, but I thought it was only fair to warn you." he justified himself.

Sanem typed in Can's number replying: "No, no, you did great Burak. Thank you." he said.

Nothing, Can did not answer.

"Did you hear anything? I mean, did Can say anything?" he asked.

"According to Emre, he mumbled something like 'I'll find him, you'll see." he reported.

"My God, who will he find? What will he find?" wondered Sanem fidgeting. Then she snapped. "What if he's talking about Metin?" she whispered. "That would be the end!" she exclaimed, putting her hands in the hair.

"Or Muzo." thought Burak. "Could he not have heard what happened this morning?" he asked.

"I don't think so." replied Sanem confidently.

At that moment her phone rang. It was his mother.

"Ugh... mum! I just can't right now." she said declining the call.

Three seconds later her father called her.

Sanem looked at the screen.

"Dad?" she commented surprised at the screen. Usually it was her mother who called.

Had she convinced him to call for her? It could only mean one thing: it was urgent.

Without thinking too much about it, she answered.

"Hello? Dad?" she asked.

"Sanem, daughter?" said Nihat.

"Daddy, is Mommy calling you now too?" she asked.

"Sanem, you don't answer, and your mother wanted to tell you something important. So did I, actually. A strange thing, I would say." he admitted.

"What? What happened?" she asked anxiously.

"Can just called us." said Nihat.

"He called you? Why? What's going on?" she asked increasingly worried.

"I don't know, child. He asked for something unusual. That's why I called you." her father explained.

What did he say, Dad?" asked Sanem hastily.

"He wanted to know Muzo's address." her father replied.

Sanem froze. She remained silent.

"Hello? Hello? Daughter, did the line go dead? Are you still there? Ah, this technology..." commented her father on the other end.

Sanem unlocked. "What? Did he tell you why he wanted it?" she asked.

"I don't know, he just said he was looking for him." he said.

"Daughter, why is Can looking for Muzo? Did he do something at work?" asked her father worriedly.

"Why do you say that?" asked Sanem worriedly.

"Because he seemed nervous. Something was wrong. He didn't have his usual happy tone." reported Nihat.

"Ah... I don't know, father. I'm trying to contact him, in fact. If you see or hear from him again, tell him to call me. OK?" she asked.

"Come on, Daddy dear, a kiss." he added before hanging up.

"All right, daughter. A kiss to you too." replied Nihat seriously.

He hung up.

Once his wife had calmed down, Nihat decided to go out and reach Muzo's house to make sure everything was OK.

He saw Can's empty pick-up truck, then saw him ring the doorbell. Nihat stood around the corner of the street and watched.

He saw Can pick up the phone and put it to his ear.

Meanwhile in the agency, Sanem hung up the phone and gathered his things, telling Burak: "You were right. He is looking for Muzo."

"Then I think he knows what happened this morning." he replied.

"I think so do I. The question is, how much does he know?" she asked.

She picked up her bag, looked at him and said: "That's why I'm catching up with him. I'm off. For anything I'm on call."

"Alright. Good luck." Burak wished her.

"Thank you." she replied.

Once in the company car, her phone rang. She received the call she had been waiting for weeks.

"D.V." appeared on the screen. "D.V." was how she had added him to her contacts. The initials for "Detective Volkan."

Sanem answered on the fly.

"Hello?" she said. She looked at the driver from the mirror.

"Mrs Sanem, hello. I'm Volkan." he replied from the other end.

"Hello." she replied.

"I got the information you requested. I would need to speak to you in person." he reported.

"Um, I'm in the car right now, so that's not possible. Um, can we talk again at another time?" she asked in a formal tone.

"Um, sure, I understand, it's just... it's important." he added.

"OK, I will call you back as soon as possible." she replied.

"Ah, one thing, if you please. Just tell me one thing. Is it confirmed or not?" she asked.

Volkan knew very well what she was referring to.

She was asking whether Metin was really involved with Deren's father or not.

"It is confirmed." replied Volkan. "You were right, I have proof." he replied briefly.

"Alright, thank you, I'll contact you as soon as I can, thanks for understanding, see you soon." replied Sanem hurriedly.

He hung up. Then he turned to the driver. "Can you speed up? I'm in a bit of a hurry."

"I'll do what I can, Mrs Divit." replied the driver in the middle of the Istanbul traffic.

Arriving at Muzo's house, Sanem saw Can's pick-up.

"There, I'm late." he said, running to the door. She rang but nothing.

At that moment her father called her again.

"Dad?" she answered.

"Sanem, Can found Muzo." he replied in a low voice, hiding behind a tree.

"Where is he? He's not at his house. I just arrived." she said.

"No, Muzo is on a bench in the gardens on the coast near the neighborhood." he reported.

"I understand the place perfectly, I'm coming." she said without question. She didn't ask why her father had followed Can or why he spoke softly, at that moment she only cared about reaching her husband before he did something stupid.

As she approached him, Can was reminded of Sanem's words, when she told him that she had spoken to Muzo before he left, they had stood on the shore, and shortly before, after ringing his house, a sixth sense had told him that he would find him there. So he hurried.

He recognized his figure from behind, sitting on a bench in front of the sea.

"Muzo!" he called loud and clear a few metres away from him.

He looked up. He was still angry.

"Mr Can, this is really not the time. It's Sanem who sent you, isn't it?" he immediately went on the attack.

"No, Sanem doesn't even know I'm here." Can replied cold as ice.

"You... coward that you are... how dare you shout at my wife like that, huh? What kind of man are you!" he shouted at him.

"I have my reasons." replied Muzo.

"Oh, sure your reasons... and tell me, the reason would be that she did not warn you of Guliz's arrival, is that it? Is that your stupid reason?" he asked black with anger.

"He shouldn't have hidden it. She lied. She knew." insisted Muzo.

"You are crazy...really, I don't know what's wrong with you Muzo, but you are really delusional." said Can.

"Neither I nor Sanem, we knew Guliz was coming, we were waiting for an actress chosen by an external casting agency to flank Osman. No one had warned us that this person would be Guliz, and do you know why?" he asked.

Muzo remained silent.

"You don't know why... because you were too busy being offended and running away rather than listening to an explanation about it." Can scolded him.

"If you had stayed, if you had had the guts to stand in front of your ex-wife, maybe you would have seen with how many airs she boasted about surprising us all at Fikri Harika. How, with her connections, she had managed to convince someone from the casting agency to keep it a secret. That's the true reality!" Can said in one breath. The veins in his neck in evidence from the effort.

"I didn't know." said Muzo taken aback, not knowing what to say.

"You didn't know because you attacked MY WIFE like a dog and left." said Can brutally.

"Coward. You yelled at a woman! At my wife, who did everything for you. She stood by you in the hardest of times, and bent over backwards for you with your secret wise and all. She believed in you, how many others in your life can you say did the same thing? Huh?" He spit the truth in his face.

"I am not a coward." said Muzo.

"Ah, sorry, you are not, you are right, because you are not a coward, but a vile. I know a vile when I see one, because unfortunately I was one myself once. Running away does no good, Muzo. Things have to be faced, otherwise they become bigger and bigger bogs and heavier and heavier obstacles in our lives." he said seriously and firmly.

Muzo remained silent. "Face the past once and for all and put an end to this behavior of yours. You hurt yourself and especially the innocent people around you." he said sternly.

"Do you have any idea the state you left Sanem in, huh? Do you have any idea!?" he insisted.

"You have some.... You definitely saw her crying, but you and your past ghosts were more important, weren't you?" he said through gritted teeth.

"Don't you care about how you left her? About how she felt attacked? Well, I'll tell you. She was crying her eyes out and shaking like a leaf." Can yelled at him.

"Don't you ever dare again, do you understand? Never again do you dare to treat my wife like that, got it?!" he continued.

"Sanem, the last time she saw you here, she was understanding and light. I, on the other hand, will be brutally direct." he warned him.

"I don't want to see you in the company again until you have had the courage to finally solve your problems. Fikri Harika, but especially Sanem, are places born to express themselves. We have learnt from the past, and we have worked hard to ensure that they are both happy workplaces, where every member comes to work with a smile, and has to leave with a smile, not crying or shaking at someone's folly. Is that clear?" he said, staring straight into her eyes.

"Until then, you can forget about the book. Oh, and you are no longer a partner in Fikri Harika, I'm giving your one per cent to Cey Cey." he said.

"You can't decide for Sanem." said Muzo.

"Oh, I certainly do. If that is to protect her, I do. And I'll tell you more..." he said approaching him.

"If you dare to make direct deals with publishers or discredit Sanem again... I will ensure that the book never sees the light of day. Do I make myself clear?" he said.

At that moment, Sanem and his father came running in.

"There they are!" she exclaimed when she saw them so close. She feared that Can might beat him up.

"What's going on here?!" exclaimed Nihat in a stern tone.

Can and Muzo turned around.

"Can? What's going on?" asked Sanem running to him.

"Sanem?" he asked.

"How did you know I was here?" he asked.

"Ah..." he said looking at Nihat.

"Son, what's going on here? Muzo?" he asked. "What is this shouting, son? We heard you from over there." said Nhat pointing to where they had come out from.

"Muzo treated Sanem badly. He shouted in her face in the company. He made her cry and tremble." he said with clenched fists staring at him angrily.

Nihat, turned sharply towards Muzo.

"What! Is that true, Muzo?" he asked with a gloomy look.

"It's true." Can replied. "Ayhan said."

"Love? How do you know? I mean, did you talk to Ayhan?" she asked shocked.

"Something like that, I'll explain later." he said stroking her gently.

"And why would you do such a thing Muzo?" asked Nihat.

"Because Guliz, his ex-wife, came to the agency by surprise and he thought Sanem had hidden it from him. Both she and I knew nothing. But he as soon as he saw her, he ran to Sanem yelling at him without any chance of reply." said Can spitting out.

"Can..." said Sanem trying to restrain him.

"Love, don't look at me like that. It's only fair that your father knows too." he said.

"Is it true, child? Did he shout at you?" asked Nihat. The last word was to be his daughter's.

"Yes, but... it was in a moment of anger, that is..." she tried to lighten it up.

"Sanem..." resumed Can: "Don't belittle it." he told her.

"Muzo! Why are you yelling at my daughter, huh?!" ranted Nihat.

"Wow..." said Muzo getting up from the bench. "I have to tell you Sanem, you two were made for each other. You just can't stay away from plans, threats, trouble and poking your noses into each other's lives, can you?" he said looking at both of them.

"What are you talking about, Muzo..." said Can looking at him crookedly.

"I'm saying that... you two should talk to each other a lot more. You want to protect everyone, do good to everyone... and then what? You are the first ones who are not honest with each other." he said.

"What are you babbling, Muzo? Go, go. Come!" said Nihat dragging him away by the arm.

"What's wrong with you, huh? What's wrong with you, son? Why do you treat people like that?" he continued to scold him as they walked away.

"Good daddy Nihat, take him away, it's better." Can said wringing his hands.

As Nihat dragged him away, Muzo with a crazy smile added: "Can? Why don't you ask your wife what she's hiding from you..."

"What are you talking about Muzo? Walk!" said Nihat tugging at him.

Can glared at him, then furrowed his brow and looked at his wife.

"Can..." she began in a trembling voice.

"What did he mean?" he asked seriously.

"Are you hiding something from me, Sanem?" he asked.

Sanem took her husband by the hand. "Come now I'll explain everything to you." he said making him sit on the bench.

"What do you have to explain to me?" he asked defensively.

"Ah, love, let me explain, otherwise what was the point of saying the words you said to Muzo, eh? Did you think I didn't hear you?" said Sanem.

"Alright, I'm listening. You are right." he said with a sigh, then fell silent.

"I was waiting for confirmation before telling you this. It's a bit delicate, that's all." she said worriedly.

"Are you pregnant?" he asked her directly with a smile on his lips.

"Um... no, love I'm not pregnant. It's not that kind of confirmation." said Sanem stroking his cheek.

"The matter is a bit different and very serious." she pointed out.

"Ah... er, how serious? Should I be worried? Are you okay?" asked Can changing softening slightly.

"Yes, yes, love, I'm fine, it's not about me and my health. Don't worry. And it's not about you personally either, really." she specified.

"What do you mean? Sanem, I don't understand." he admitted.

Sanem took a deep breath and began to explain.

"Where do I start, let's see..." she said.

"Ah! Do you remember the story of Deren? His father and all?" she asked.

"Um, yes, I remember you asking me questions about his father. If I knew him and so on." repeated Can.

"That's right." she confirmed.

"One day Muzo, during the early days of working on the draft of his essay, confided something to me." said Sanem.

"What?" asked Can nervously at the mere thought.

"He told me that he had unwittingly overheard a phone call from Metin." admitted Sanem with some hesitation.

"Ah, so what? Metin is always on the phone." replied Can calmly.

"I know that, but the phone call was strange. Muzo heard him talking to someone from Deren. Verbatim words: "He is not suitable for Deren. And so on." he said.

"Maybe he was confiding in someone, I mean, we know he has no sympathy for Bulut. So I'm not surprised." Can replied serenely.

"In fact, I had a reaction like yours too, I didn't give it any weight, I didn't believe it... at first." pointed out Sanem.

"At first? What do you mean, Sanem?" asked Can.

"At that moment I thought it was Muzo's jealousy of Metin with Deniz, speaking." she continued her tale.

"But he added a detail that I didn't give weight to at the time. "He said: don't worry, sir, I'll keep an eye on her. Or something like that." said Sanem.

"The word sir struck me." she admitted. "But I let it go, I had other things to think about." she continued.

"What I didn't know is that Muzo didn't let it go, he started to observe it to understand it better." she said.

Can listened intently to her words.

"Just like the first time, he caught him several times in the same spot, in the archive, talking on the phone. Although he didn't find out anything new for several weeks. He only told me this afterwards." said Sanem.

"After what?" asked Can.

"A few months ago, I was the one who heard a phone call from him, Can." said Sanem. "At the usual spot Muzo said, I was waiting for the lift to go up to Fikri Harika. I had walked one floor, but my shoes were hurting." she said looking into his eyes.

"I was waiting for the lift to come when I heard him talking around the corner, so I instinctively hid and listened." she admitted.

"Deren must absolutely not find out, I understand." I heard.

"No, sir, they haven't seen each other since the wedding." Sanem recalled.

"Rest assured, I will keep an eye on her. I won't let her out of my sight." he repeated.

Can grimaced, confused.

"And who do you think he was talking to?" he asked her.

"I had no idea of course, but I was sure it was the same person from Muzo's phone call. Metin was reporting to a person he called sir.... On Deren." said Sanem.

"OK, but why would Metin keep an eye on Deren? And on whose behalf? That's absurd. I don't understand that." said Can.

"There, I didn't understand it either. What was the purpose? Above all, what was Deren not supposed to find out?" said Sanem.

"So I spoke to Muzo, telling him what I had heard and that I believed his words. He was right." she said.

"At that point, Muzo and Cey Cey went to work hoping to figure out who he was talking to, but they didn't get any more chances." she explained.

"I know you don't believe me, but I had a strange feeling after those words. That nothing good was hiding behind them. But I didn't understand what." said Sanem.

"Then... the nightmare night, do you remember?" she asked him.

"Of course I remember." he confirmed.

"Well, actually, I was thinking about that. And in a flash Deren's words about her father came back to me. Why does a lawyer of a certain level like Metin call a person 'sir'? Because he is older than him? But above all, why does he pass on information? What does he get out of it? He is a man of justice. Why do such a thing? With all these questions in my head, I came to two conclusions. Either he knew the person well, or it was a favour he couldn't say no to." Sanem tried to explain.

She waited for his reaction.

"Go ahead." said Can simply, wanting to hear the rest.

"During that dream, with Deren's words echoing in my head, Metin, London and everything else, it was like everything found its own connection. As if there was a common thread to everything. So I began to suspect that Deren's father was behind it, that being one of the most distinguished lawyers in London he knew Metin, one of the most distinguished young lawyers in Turkey, and that through him, he was keeping an eye on his daughter, lest he find out something." she connected.

"My God, Sanem..." huffed Can.

"Shh... I know what you are going to say. Sanem, what are you saying? You like to meddle in other people's business, blah blah blah. I know. And that's why I didn't tell you anything." she admitted.

"Before I told you I had to have proof or you wouldn't have believed me. After all, he's your best friend, you know? I didn't want to create friction between you." she said in a loving tone, trying to reason with him.

"And you have proof?" he asked.

"I have confirmation. Deren's father is behind all this, and... I'm sorry to have to tell you this but.... Metin passes information to him." she said, shaking his hand.

Can was silent for a moment. Then he looked at her and said: "How do you know that? How do you know for sure?" he asked her.

"Well, to get it I asked one person for help. In fact, two to be exact." she admitted.

"What did you do, Sanem?" asked her Can with an inquisitive look.

"I'll tell you, but don't get angry, OK?" she asked.

Can sighed. "It's not OK. Just say it." he said sternly.

"OK, it needed confirmation. I couldn't ask Deren, I didn't have any footholds to go into the argument, I would be conspicuous, so I couldn't. And I couldn't ask Deniz, because Metin is with her and doesn't know anything about this. I didn't want to involve you, because I knew you would be against it, so..." she said, lowering her gaze.

"Therefore, Mihriban gave me an idea." she said.

"Ah, Mihriban is also aware? Perfect. Maybe my father too." he replied, getting nervous.

"No, your father doesn't know anything." Sanem confirmed.

"Anyway, actually, I didn't even want to contact him, but I left it as plan B." she said.

"Sanem, who did you contact, for God's sake, will you tell me?" said Can getting more and more nervous.

"Black Falcon." she replied.

"Who? Black Falcon? And who is it?" asked Can confused.

"A hacker from our neighborhood. It's a long story, Ayhan and I knew him many years ago, and I asked her to track him down, but he is no longer active here, so... I was forced to go to plan B." she explained.

"Ah, Ayhan is also involved? Of course. How many other people are involved in this Sanem thing? Just so I know." he said staring into her eyes.

"Well... me, Muzo, Cey Cey, Ayhan, Burak and... now you too." she said almost ashamed.

"Even Burak?!" he asked in amazement.

"Yes, but he only found out this morning, just as the Muzo thing happened. There, he came in suddenly while he was angry and was accusing me of constantly making plans and..." she tried to justify.

At that point Sanem lowered her head, pulling up with her nose.

"Don't cry, continue the story. Come on." said Can unwilling to console her at that moment.

"Who did you contact Sanem?" he repeated.

"Hilmi." she replied with her head down.

"I asked him to get into Metin's phone, taking advantage of a yoga class with Ayhan. You know, don't you, that she picks up everyone's phones? There, I called him in, at that moment and he copied all the contacts in her address book and found me the rightful owners. I didn't trust the names under which they were registered, that's it." she spat out.

Can serious until that moment, he suddenly burst out laughing in disbelief.

"I can't believe it, really! Did I marry a cop or what? Eh, Sanem? All I needed was for you to investigate him and we were done!" he exclaimed.

His wife remained silent, turning red as a pepper.

"Well, I did that too. As a matter of fact." she admitted with a hint in her voice.

"Excuse me?" asked Can in amazement.

"I did, all right? I called Volkan and asked him to find out information about Deren's father, alright?" she boldly blurted out.

"What?! You called Volkan? But then I really live with Sherlock Holmes and didn't know!" said Can laughing out of nervousness.

"Sanem...you are incorrigible. Really." said Can.

"And? How did the story go?" he then asked.

"Hilmi found Deren's father's number on Metin's phone and his was the most called number." she explained.

"Volkan, on the other hand, called me now, while I was in the car, and confirmed the cooperation between the two but he has more to tell me. And it seems to be important. He wants to see me." concluded Sanem with a sigh.

"Sanem I mean, really...why did you do all this? Huh? Why did you set out to investigate Metin, Deren, his father and all that? After all, it doesn't concern us." he said getting up from the bench. He couldn't sit still.

"Can? Can... please come here." she said grabbing his hand pushing him towards her.

"I mean... based on what Volkan is going to say, whatever he says, how are you going to tell Deren, have you thought about that? I want idre, are you going to go to her and how are you going to justify that you found out these things? Huh?" he asked her.

"Oh, you know I hired a private investigator and researched your father, will you tell her? Or... You know, I wanted confirmation and so I asked a hacker for help.... huh?" blurted Can.

Sanem stood in stunned silence. And realized. "How do I tell Deren now?" she said looking at him with panic in her eyes.

"Ah, you mean to tell me that the 'Lady in Yellow' in you hasn't thought about it, is that it? I mean, after all this articulate planning, Detective Sanem Divit didn't think about it.... Bravo, what can I say?" he said clapping.

"I will find a way, don't worry, I have to talk to Volkan first though. One thing at a time." said Sanem bracing herself.

"I'm sure you'll find it, I mean, you really can do anything." her husband told her, shaking his head.

"Are you really angry with me?" she then asked him.

"I am, actually. I can't deny it, Sanem. I am worried and even a little nervous, yes." he admitted.

"One minute, one minute... Can Divit." thought Sanem suddenly.

"I mean, you are angry with me now, and not with Metin?" she asked.

"Thank you, thank you. He is the one playing dirty, and you are angry with me, is that it? Perfect, always Sanem loses out, of course." she said, turning on her heels to go home.

"Ah, Sanem..." he called after her.

"Where are you going?" he asked her.

"Away from here." she replied simply.

"Hello, Mr Volkan?" she then asked with the phone to her ear.

"Mrs Sanem?" he replied from the other end.

"Tell me when we can meet, I'm free." she said seriously.

"Even now, where do you prefer?" he asked.

"I'll send you the location. Join me there." she replied briefly.

"Alright, see you soon." he greeted her.

"See you soon." she replied, hanging up.

Meanwhile, Can caught up with her.

She increased her pace.

"Who were you talking to? Volkan?" he asked.

"What do you care?" she asked angrily.

"Come on, love, if you have to meet Volkan I'll come too." he said.

"Love? Ah, now I'm back 'Love', so. Until now I was just 'Sanem, Sanem... and that's it. You do this when you are angry!" she told him without stopping.

"Go run and work off your anger somewhere, Can Divit, I have things to do, see you at home." she said stretching her stride.

Can obviously did not leave her.

Sanem turned back then, and without giving him a glance, she passed him and continued towards her destination, strutting. She returned to sit on the bench from just before and posted her position.

Then she waited, looking at the sea.

Can sat down beside her in silence, holding back a smile at that move.

"Is this where you will meet Volkan?" he asked her.

"Can, please go! Weren't you angry? Go for a run, it's better. Now I'm the angry one." she said, turning away.

Can smiled. Sanem was using the offense tactic, he knew it well.

"No, I want to stay here, enjoying the view of the sea and my wife." he replied with a smile. Can's mask of anger faded.

"Hmm, sure... Can doesn't attack. Stop it." she quickly dismantled him.

"If you stay, be quiet. I want to rest my mind." she said.

Can had no time to reply that he saw Volkan coming.

He stood up. Sanem imitated him.

"Mr Volkan?" he greeted him.

"Mr Can? Mrs Sanem?" he greeted them.

Volkan looked at her. "He knows everything." she replied to justify his presence.

"Ah, OK." commented the investigator.

"What did you find out?" asked Sanem.

"Um, how about we move further away, under that tree over there is quieter." proposed Can.

"Do you remember, Mr Can?" asked Volkan with a smile.

"Yeah." he replied.

"Have you seen each other here before?" asked Sanem once they arrived.

"Yes, in the past. When I did research on Yigit." replied Can.

"That's it, when you do the research it's fine, when I do it instead... but still..." said Sanem in a low voice. "Back to us."

"Tell me, Mr Volkan," she said turning to him.

"So, Mrs Sanem, there are audios in here that I invite you to listen to." He said handing her an envelope with a CD. "Inside are also other material evidence you requested, when you see them, you will understand."

"Your colleague's father's name is Ahmet Erdogan, he was the second name on the list you provided me with." he explained.

"He was born and lived in Istanbul until he came of age, then, he moved to London to pursue his law studies. There he became a lawyer and through high society connections made his fortune by opening his own firm. He is currently one of the most famous lawyers in the world.

"At the age of 25, he married the Turkish actress Asil Nuvat, by whom he had a daughter, Deren." he said.

"Deren Erdogan, was born in Turkey, taking her citizenship, her father and mother lived here for the first years of her life, and then returned to London for her to attend the most prestigious schools.

After finishing her university studies, she decided to return to Istanbul to her paternal grandmother, and from there, there was a rift between her and her parents that led her to then change her surname to her current name: Deren Keskin."

"Paternal grandmother's maiden name." said Sanem. "I knew that." she confirmed seriously and attentively, with a nod of her head.

"Back in her homeland, Deren took care of her grandmother's health, which was beginning to present its first problems. And in the meantime, she looked for work, until she found it in your agency. It turns out that she has had no contact with them since then.

Meanwhile, in London, after a few years, his parents separated and then divorced, putting an end to their marriage for good.

Deren's mother has been in care for many years. Her husband's oppressive presence had caused her great depression for several several years. Now she has found serenity with a theater actor. A friend from the academy, it seems. A certain Amut Mustafa. Also Turkish. She now lives in America.

Deren's father, on the other hand, had another relationship, also now over, from which a child was born. I still have to look into that." he concluded.

"One minute. Does that mean Deren has a sister?!" exclaimed Sanem blinking impressed.

"Exactly." replied Volkan.

"How many years younger?" she asked.

"I don't know yet, Mrs Sanem, but I will find out. Don't worry." he replied confidently.

"Alright, what about the relationship with Mr Metin?" asked Can who had remained silent until that moment.

"Well, it seems the two know each other through the latter's parents. Mr Metin comes from a family of only lawyers, as I assume you already know, and the father during a stay in London many years ago, put in a good word about his son." he reported to them.

"Of course..." replied Sanem with a grimace.

"When Deren settled permanently in Istanbul, after changing her name, he kept an eye on her until he found out that his daughter had gone to work at Fikri Harika. There, thanks to his friendship with Metin's father, he found out that his son worked for the agency and approached him, asking him to check on Deren.

Ahmet Erdogan realized that Metin had a crush on his daughter, and used this to his advantage, giving the boy false hopes of a possible relationship with her." Volkan explained.

"That says..." commented Sanem incredulously with her eyes wide.

"So Metin has been keeping an eye on Deren all these years?" asked Can shocked. He was incredulous too.

"It seems so, unfortunately. At least until you drove him away." replied Volkan. "Excuse me Mr. Can, but in investigating lawyer Metin unfortunately I found out that for a while he no longer worked at the agency, am I wrong?" asked confirmation tactfully.

"No, you says well. We had disagreements in the past. It's no secret." confirmed Can.

"And what did you do during that time? He didn't keep an eye on her I guess." said Sanem.

"There, while he was working for Mrs Remide, it seems that Ahmet Erdogan, invited him to London several times during that period, probably to take stock of the situation." reported Volkan.

"There, but so Metin knows that Deren has a sister?" pondered Sanem aloud.

"Yes." replied the investigator.

"And he also knows who she is I suppose," he continued.

"I don't know for sure." Volkan replied briefly.

"The father was not at all happy to find out about his daughter's marriage to a lawyer other than the one he thought was right for her, that is." added Volkan.

"And so, you're saying he took advantage of Metin's renewed proximity in the agency to keep an eye on her again? But how can one be so obsessed, I wonder?" ranted Sanem.

"Excuse me." she said to Volkan, pulling herself together.

"Don't worry." he replied with a friendly smile.

"I think Mr Ahmet has done some research on Bulut Cehver and his family, that's why he is so displeased with such a union." he added.

"OK, he may be displeased, but what can he do about it now? He has to accept it." Can said.

"After all, he is the one who disowned his daughter." Sanem recalled. "What else does he want from her?" she asked.

"Excuse me, but now... are there other women in that man's life?" asked Sanem curiously.

"Just escorts to events, so it seems. A different one on each occasion. But no serious relationships." Volkan pointed out.

Can was shocked by such a rote story.

"But what does Metin gain from all this?" he pondered aloud.

It was Volkan who answered his question: "There are promises of important jobs in London, a job always open for him in his firm and a life and social position full of comforts, in exchange for this small favour."

"Small favour?!" asked Can in amazement.

"So Metin's fortune is due to him, or is it? Is that what you are saying?" asked Sanem in confirmation.

"Analysing, some of his lawyer friend's big clients come from Ahmet Erdogan's long list of wealthy clients. I leave the conclusions to you." Volkan said.

Can and Sanem looked at each other shocked. They were speechless.

"My God... who have I had beside me all these years..." said Can.

"I never really knew him then?" he wondered.

"I mean, Metin was always a super precise, meticulous person who was good at his job. It can't all be because of that man. I don't believe it... I don't want to believe it!" Can thought.

"No, I don't think it is, but maybe his friend, if you'll allow me, as good as he is, wouldn't be where he is now without certain social connections." replied Volkan reasonably.

"I fully agree." Sanem replied.

"Thank you, Mr Volkan for all this information, you have really given us a lot to think about." said Sanem pulling out an envelope folded in two. She placed it in the palm of his hand and without showing it, she handed it to Volkan clutching his own.

"This is a first part, as agreed. The other upon completion." whispered Sanem.

"You go ahead and check them." she added.

"I trust you Mrs Sanem, as I trust Mr Can." he said casting him a glance.

Can was absent.

"I thank you for your trust and your time." replied his wife seeing him in that state.

"I will continue the search, and will contact you as soon as I know more." he replied.

Can looked at him thoughtfully.

"Perfect. Goodbye." Volkan greeted them with a smile.

"Goodbye." the Divits greeted him.

ONCE THEY WERE ALONE...

"Can?" asked Sanem touching his arm. He had sat on the small wall surrounding the large tree they were standing under.

"Are you OK?" she asked worriedly as she sat down beside him.

"I'm fine, I just need to process... and reflect." he said with a low head.

"You were really hurt, weren't you?" she asked him.

"I just can't explain it." he said. "I'd like to pick up and go talk to him now." he said firmly, looking up at her.

"No Can!!! You're kidding, right? You can't do that." exclaimed Sanem tightening his grip on her arm.

"It would create utter chaos! More than I have already endured so far in keeping this secret. Please! At least wait until Volkan has told us everything, then you will talk to him. But not now. Don't do it, please. Do it for me. Or... if not for me, do it for Bulut and Deren." said Sanem beseeching him.

"Listen carefully, Can Divit, you must not tell anyone, do you understand?" he said shaking him out of that stupor.

"Alright, I understand," he replied without enthusiasm.

"Ah, good thing we're going into the weekend." Can commented to distract himself.

"Yeah, and thankfully, at the end of this busy day. Everything went wrong today. Muzo, Burak, Guliz... I'm exhausted. It's not easy to hold all the pieces together." said Sanem looking at the sea with a sigh. They were walking back to the car.

"But listen, you if you want, stay a while alone, run, go to the shed and chop some wood, or a boat ride, whatever you need. All right? Take your time and think well before making any rash moves. OK?" Sanem asked him, stroking his back.

Are you still angry with me?" she asked blinking her big doe eyes to make him smile.

"Come on, let's go home." replied Can, the corners of his mouth barely turned up.

Sanem hugged him tightly as they made their way to the car. Just like that time she joined him at the hotel, to convince him to forgive her and not leave on the Balkans.

"Alright... we have a really fun weekend ahead of us, you know?" She said in a good mood, trying to cheer him up. The twins' friends are coming to the estate!" she said laughing, exhausted at the mere thought of the chaos.

"Let the weekend begin!" she exulted charged.

Can silently pulled her close.

And so, concentrating on her good humor and gab, the only weapons Sanem knew to defuse the most difficult moments, she tried to silence the bad thoughts. Both hers and her husband's.

So to bridge that Can silence, she went from one nonsensical topic to another.

"Can? What if we buy a horse?" she asked. "That would be great, I'd love to learn to ride. We could reach the hut in the saddle, ride into the big flowery clearing in front." she said and then immediately changed the subject.

"Can, but in your opinion, does the chicken or the egg come first?" she asked in memory of old times.

 "We still haven't managed to answer that question in all these years, eh, what do you say?" she asked as her husband opened the car door for her, closing it once she was seated.

At that point making the turn, to reach the driver's side, Can rolled his eyes, sighed and let a smile escape.

26. *THE GRANDMOTHER*

The day which for Can and Sanem had ended prematurely, was not so for the rest of Fikri Harika. It was in mid-afternoon that Cey Cey, left alone as he was returning to his counter, received a phone call. The number was unknown to him, but he decided to answer anyway.

"Hello?" he said.

An unmistakable voice could be heard on the other end.

"Cey Cey, son, why aren't you doing anything? Work!" said an old woman. It was the grandmother.

"Grandma?" asked Cey Cey surprised. He looked at the phone screen double-checking the number.

"Eh, and who else could it be, silly!" replied the woman in her usual brusque and direct manner.

"Grandma, what number are you calling with?" he asked her.

"I changed the number. Did you think that by blocking me, your grandmother couldn't trace you? Well, you're wrong!" she told him with a laugh.

"Look grandma..." started Cey Cey stuttering.

"I'm dying," she told him.

"Again? What are you dying, come on grandma! Use another tactic. And that's it!" he blurted out.

"Fool that you are, I tell you I'm dying!" she insisted.

"But your voice sounds good to me for a dying woman." replied Cey Cey.

"I am dying, I tell you! Donkey!" she scolded him.

Cey Cey took a deep breath and sat down in the meeting room.

He closed the door behind him and took a seat at the head of the table.

As soon as he sat down, seeing the overview of all the empty chairs around him made him imagine for a moment a meeting with him at the head.

"Yes, gentlemen, we are gathered here to figure out "is grandma dying or not?" let's face the evidence we have together." he said in a formal almost news-like tone.

"You fool! What are you doing? I can see you!" she shouted.

Cey Cey nearly fell out of his chair. He was forced to pull the phone away from his ear. His dream vanished in an instant.

"What are you kidding? I die!" she insisted.

"Ah, and what would you be dying of? Let's hear it." said Cey.

"Not of what, you fool! But 'why'!" his grandmother corrected him.

"Hmm, why?" he then asked.

"Because you won't let me see my grandchildren." she said.

"But what grandchildren, grandmother! You are delirious!" he said.

"That's what you're dying for, huh? You are going mad. Say it now." sneered Cey Cey at her.

"Shut up! Fool that you are! I'm telling you the grandchildren are coming and I won't see them. And it's all your fault!" said the grandmother.

"I'm dying for it!" she ranted.

"Again with these grandchildren..." he commented. "And then why is it my fault?" he asked.

"Because you block me, you don't call me, I can't call you. Me, if you don't let me see them, I die. Understand?" insisted the grandmother, complaining.

"But what do I have to show you, grandmother? There is no grandchild!" lost patience Cey Cey.

"You are lying! You don't want to tell me, but I know. I can feel it." she said with a clairvoyant manner.

"Ah... What do you feel grandmother?" asked Cey Cey worried about her abilities.

"Your wife is pregnant, stupid!" shouted he.

"Ahhh!" he shouted back at the mere thought.

"Don't yell at your grandmother!" she exclaimed.

"No, Ayhan is not pregnant grandma, what are you talking about, she is just fine." retorted Cey Cey in denial. She was having a panic attack.

"You are blind! Fool that you are!" said her grandmother.

"I hear and see everything!" she repeated.

"Grandma, maybe then you see too much. You also see what is not here." replied Cey Cey. "Is that a secular power by any chance?" he then asked curiously.

"You will see, I will die. And I will not see them." she repeated.

"Ah, but you are only 109 years old! You are still a child." he said, complimenting her.

"I am dying." she repeated.

"Now I'm dying." said Cey Cey waving a file found there on the floor. He felt faint.

"No! You cannot die! I must see my grandchildren. Until then, you cannot. I won't let you!" ranted the grandmother.

"Ah, so now you also decide when I can die, is that it? Thank you, grandma." blurted Cey Cey, anchoring himself on the table to keep himself upright.

"I have to go now. You go to your children, go. Bye!" she said decisively, hanging up instantly.

"Bye grandma, bye," he replied with a huff, hanging up in turn, without strength.

"She's going crazy... I swear she's going crazy." he said as he staggered out of the meeting room to get some air. He stopped at the counter to pour himself a strong coffee.

With his back turned, he did not notice the arrival of someone.

"Cey Cey?" asked a familiar voice.

Cey Cey turned around slowly, scared like in a horror movie. Perhaps he really was going mad.

When he saw her, he asked: "Zu zu?"

He lit up, turning around to reach her. She had a huge box in her hands. Cey Cey felt like deja vu.

"Zu zu? What are you doing here?" he asked upon seeing the box.

"From the Grandmother." she said, handing it to him.

"She had a dream, and so the whole village filled this box for you." she explained.

Zu zu was still the same, it seemed like no years had passed since the last time. She had grown, but only Cey Cey realized this, knowing her so well from his various visits to the village. This time too, her long hair were styled in huge braids.

"Zu zu? Thank you." he said, taking the box. He kissed her on the forehead and then with a sad look, she left.

At that moment Ayhan came running up like crazy. They were alone now, the agency had emptied. On Fridays, the working day ended early and no one had noticed Zu Zu. This time the box was safe. Cey Cey in the meantime had placed the heavy box on the bar counter and, with his back turned, was peering inside it, when Ayhan sneaked up behind him, making him flinch.

"Cey Cey?" she called out to him sharply, on purpose.

Cey Cey jerked.

Ayhan laughed.

"Ah, that's funny..." he commented with a grimace.

"Cey Cey? Love?" she called him softly all agitated, elated. She couldn't keep still.

"Ayhan, are you alright?" he asked looking at her.

"You look like a coffee addict. Did Mrs Deren stop and you started now?" he asked her.

"No, I didn't start it! Nor can I." she said.

"Ah, well, that's good." he replied quietly, going back to rummaging inside the box.

Ayhan didn't ask and didn't mind. It wasn't the first time he had seen Cey Cey counting bags of coffee beans inside boxes, or tea bags, so she didn't ask.

"Darling?" she called him again.

"Tell me Ayhan? I'm almost done, now let's go home." he warned her.

"Phew... Mr Cenginz, look at me!" she then said in a tone.

"Tell me, Ayhan dear." he finally replied, crossing her eyes.

"I don't resist anymore. I have been holding back for three days. I have to tell you!" she said.

In the space of three seconds, Ayhan brought her hands to her belly and suddenly exclaimed: "I'm pregnant!"

Cey Cey did not realize immediately, so instinctively replied: "Ah, okay..." continuing to adjust the counter.

"Cey Cey?" she called angrily to him.

At that point he realized.

"Ahhhhhhhhh!" he exclaimed with his hands inside the box. He looked at it for a moment, then slipped them out from inside and started running like a madman all over the agency, relentlessly. He took the stairs, the lift, did all the floors with soft arms and gelatinous legs. He got as far as the Sanem, where he ran aimlessly through all the corridors, then back up again. He opened the windows and, as he had done before, straddled the windowsill, leaning out for air. Ayhan ran after him, trying to hold him back, as Muzo had done so many times before.

"Cey Cey! Cey Cey! Are you crazy, what are you doing?!" she said, pulling him down.

He then, not having run out of energy yet, continued his run, returning to the starting point at the counter. He looked at the box, stuck his head inside it, closing the flaps, and screamed in the dark:

"She's pregnant!!!!!!"

"Cey Cey, calm down, what are you doing?!" yelled Ayhan.

Once he ran out of air in his lungs in there, he came out with a rattle in his mouth, spitting it out. He took a deep breath, then his eyes crossed and a second later he collapsed to the ground. Unconscious.

Ayhan approached him. "Ah, Cey Cey? Cey Cey?" she called to him, slapping him across the face. Nothing. He was gone.

Meanwhile, Cey Cey found himself inside a dream, his grandmother's words echoing in his head.

"I die..."

"You can't die yourself..."

142

"She's pregnant..."

"If you don't let me see my grandchildren I will die." said the voice.

Ayhan then took a bucket from the bathroom nearby and filled it with water. Then he poured it all over him.

"Desperate times call for desperate measures... " she said.

Cey Cey, soaked, did not move, he spoke in his sleep.

"Ah, Cey Cey, does that sound like the way to react? Ouch, though!" she said, hurling the bucket to the ground that almost hit the unfortunate man's head.

"Ah, that was close." said Ayhan with a hand to her mouth seeing the bucket so close to his head.

"Now I'll take a pan and give it to his forehead, so he has reason to sleep then." she said decisively.

But knowing it would do no good, she picked up the rattle from the ground, realising it was for children. Then instinctively she approached the box and looked inside. She saw that it was full of baby stuff. Bibs, onesies, toys, stuffed animals and much more. There was a world inside.

"So he knows?" she wondered. "Ah, my silly little pastry..." commented. Then slowly began to take things out of the box one by one and sat down in the little lounge behind the counter to wait for his awakening.

Suddenly, however, Cey Cey's phone rang. It was on the counter.

Ayhan got up and picked it up.

"Hello?" answered.

"Ayhan? Congratulations daughter!" exclaimed the grandmother.

"Grandma?" she asked.

"Yes, put the phone to my grandson's silly ear!" she said.

"Alright. Just a minute." she said leaning over him.

"One minute... you sent the box, didn't you? That's why Cey Cey knows." she thought before dropping the phone to her husband's ear.

"Zu zu just came to bring it. Of course I told him. I see everything, child." the grandmother replied.

"Now put the phone to his ear on speakerphone." she told her.

"Ah, OK." replied Ayhan.

"I got it." she said once done. She had placed the phone on the floor on speakerphone to her husband's left ear.

"Cey Cey! Cey Cey, you fool get up or I die!" she threatened him.

"Eh, what?" he exclaimed waking up in a daze. "Grandma..." he said snapping.

"Ah, good morning, princess. Did you wake up? What are you doing, huh? I told you not to die! I must see my grandchildren!" she exclaimed.

Cey Cey shook his head.

"But why am I all drenched?" he said looking at himself.

"Because you are a fool! Get up and congratulate your wife! Now!" shouted Grandma.

"Ah, grandma again? Ayhan is not pregnant." he said. "She just asked for a pint! But what pregnant!" he said translating the sentence in his own way thinking it was a dream.

Then he remembered.

"Ah!!! Ayhan is pregnant!" he exclaimed bringing his hand to his mouth.

"Yeah, good morning, Mr Cengiz, you're going to be a daddy!" Ayhan said teasing him.

Cey Cey without saying a word ran to hug her, holding her close.

"Ah, thank you, finally a human gesture!" exclaimed Ayhan returning the hug.

"Son? See that you don't faint again. And take care of your wife and the creature. Is that clear? If not, I will kill you and then die. Alright?" said Grandma.

"All right, grandma. Hang up." said Cey Cey.

Cey Cey looked at his wife with a quivering moustache and big doe eyes.

Ayhan said to him: "Are you happy?"

Cey Cey began to moan, and in answering, his voice became small and shrill.

"I am. My God, I'm going to be a father." he said.

"But what happened to your voice now? Did you swallow helium?" asked Ayhan laughing.

Cey Cey squeezed her in a hug.

"Ah, Cey Cey, easy." she resumed.

"Ah, sorry." he replied, still in that little voice.

"How long will this tone last?" asked Ayhan seriously.

"I don't know." he replied in that voice.

"Ah, you are so weird. God help me. If he was a mini Cey Cey who knows what other weirdness I'll have to see! God, please give me strength and patience." she repeated with her gaze turned to the sky.

"Come on." she then said. "Let's go home. Pick up everything." she said pointing to the box.

"Did you see that?" asked Cey Cey.

"I saw." she replied.

"Ah, we have nine very long months ahead." said Ayhan. "Eh, Daddy Cey Cey?" she said imitating Muzo passing an arm around his neck.

"Daddy Cey Cey..." he commented squeaking in that mousy voice. He was holding back tears. As he walked away with the box in one hand, he blew his nose sonorously with the other.

Yet another trauma was added to his long list.

27. WEEKEND WITH FRIENDS

That evening, to lift the spirits in Divit's house, there were the children and the news about Ayhan. It was shaping up to be a very promising weekend.

The next day, the twins' friends would come with Emre and Ilker. While Leyla and Can would join them after the set with Osman and Guliz.

The following day, however, they had decided to celebrate the happy event with Ayhan, Cey Cey, Osman, Adile and the baby. It was a way of saying goodbye to the family of actors who would be returning home that evening.

Saturday afternoon arrived and Sanem welcomed the children and their companions.

Dilara, invited by the girls, arrived with her mother. While Hatay, arrived accompanied by an old lady.

Sanem welcomed them with all the enthusiasm she had. She was as excited as her children's first day at school.

When the little ones noticed her enthusiasm, Ates immediately commented: "Mummy didn't make them the owl sandwich too, did she?"

Yildiz stretched his neck to check the table set up. "Hmm... no, it seems not." she replied.

"Ates, for you now owl sandwich = excited mum, is that it?" her brother asked her.

"Ah, don't start with the maths, eh! Ugh, all those numbers... at home too?" she huffed.

Her brother laughed. "What numbers? All that for using an equal, Ates?" he asked her. "Where's the maths here?" he asked.

"Of course this is maths! I saw it in a book. Where there are all these symbols, it's mathematics. And it irritates me, so stop!" she told him, scratching her arms itching.

"Then scratch." her brother replied, sticking his tongue out at her.

Ates stopped scratching the mosquito bite on her arm and glared at him seriously.

"Ha ha, but how nice you are!" she commented.

"Ah, look they're here!" exclaimed Yildiz.

"Mama?" called Ates to her. Sanem was in the kitchen tidying up.

"Mama, they're here!" repeated Deniz.

"Ah, I'm coming!" exclaimed Sanem hurriedly stowing her apron. She had prepared the table on the porch with snacks and drinks. In fact, the children wasted no time and ran to meet their little friends, heading straight to play on the trampoline.

It was the first time Sanem had the opportunity to get to know other parents from the school up close.

They introduced themselves and got to know each other.

Dilara's mother, Mrs Alis, was a well-groomed woman with an easy manner. Outwardly she might have given the impression of a serious and unsociable lady, but in reality she discovered through talking to her, that she was just a mixture of defensiveness and shyness. She also discovered that she was not from a 'wealthy' background, she had also been a 'child of the neighbourhood' and was well acquainted with people's prejudices. She recounted that she had met her husband in the last year of high school. He was the newcomer. His family, well-to-do, had just moved to Turkey.

Finding such an exquisite person was for Sanem a breath of fresh air that eased the initial pressure her family (especially her mother and sister) had put on her.

In fact she was delighted when shortly afterwards she saw Leyla arrive with Ilker.

The old lady, however, did not say a word the whole time, looking uncomfortable.

So, Sanem tried to engage her more.

"How is Hatay? My son Deniz told me about the accident." she added.

"Hatay is better now, well, he's not fully recovered, he's doing some rehabilitation. The doctor suggested keeping him on the move so that the current limp disappears completely." replied the lady.

"For the cast?" asked Dilara's mother. A sign that she knew too.

"Yes." replied the woman.

"Ah, then the trampoline is perfect for that." replied Sanem laughing. "Here he can do all the gymnastics he wants, run, play... whenever he wants, really." she offered.

"My son seems to be very attached to his grandson." she said with a smile.

The woman was about to reply when Alis commented: "The estate is really beautiful, congratulations." she said looking around.

"Ah, thank you!" replied Sanem, "It's our piece of paradise." she admitted proudly.

"I'll give you a tour, if you like." Promptly proposed Sanem.

"Mama!" exclaimed Dilara, joining her.

"Tell me, my child." she said. Then realized. "Ah, come here, how shameful, you haven't even introduced yourself to Mrs Divit." said Alis.

"Don't worry, they are children. They want to play, and it's only fair. That's what they are here for after all, right?" said Sanem winking at Dilara.

With that gesture Sanem won over the little girl, who approached shyly, repeating what she had been taught: "How are you, ma'am? My name is Dilara." she said, holding out her hand.

"Oh, nice to meet you Dilara." Sanem replied, reciprocating that squeeze. "I am Sanem. You can call me that." she confided in her in a whisper.

The little girl then went up to her ear and covering her mouth so as not to be seen said: "Mama wants you to call everyone sir or madam."

"Ah, but with me you can make an exception. I don't like the name "ma'am", you know?" she told her in a whisper.

"Neither do I." admitted Dilara.

They both burst out laughing.

"What do you confab with Mrs Divit, Dilara?" asked Alis.

"Ah, don't worry, my sister knows how to win children over." said Leyla taking part in the conversation. "She will understand shortly."

"Ah, sorry. I did not introduce you. As Leyla just pointed out, she's my sister. Leyla, this is Mrs Dilara and Mrs Behice," she said pointing at her.

"How are you?" replied Alis immediately with a friendly smile.

"Nice to meet you." Mrs Birce replied more formally.

"No mum." replied Dilara to mum's question.

"Hmm..." she commented. "What did you want to ask me?" she reminded her.

"Ah!" she remembered.

"Mrs Sanem? Um... I meant to say, Sanem? Ates said you have chickens, is that true? Can we see them?" she asked.

"Dilara!" her mother shot her back.

"No, don't scold her. I only asked to be called Sanem. 'Madam' never appealed to me." she admitted, wrinkling her nose.

"And of course you can see them. Let's go!" she said.

Alis stood up together with Sanem.

"Sister? Mrs Birce?" she asked.

"Um, sister, I'll stay here with Ilker." she said.

"Is it very far?" asked the lady.

"Um, no, it's around the corner here. Would you like me to give you a hand?" offered Sanem seeing her struggling.

"No. Daughter, thank you, no need." she replied briefly.

Sanem looked at the woman. She couldn't understand her.

"Mama look! How many are there!" exclaimed Dilara.

"Did you see?" her mother told her.

Sanem looked at her watch and then proposed: "Children, why don't you show your friends how to feed them, huh?"

"Yes!" exclaimed Ates.

"Wait." she said, opening the gate. "Follow me, come inside" said.

"Are you afraid?" asked Dilara and Hatay.

"No, but they don't peck, do they?" asked Dilara seeing them so close.

"Give us your hand Dilara." said Yildz and Ates. "You'll see they won't do anything to you."

Deniz, entered, Hatay on the other hand had stood in the doorway hesitantly.

"Come on. They won't do anything." Deniz encouraged him.

"No, I'd rather go out." he said, returning behind the net.

"Come on, Hatay!" insisted Deniz.

Sanem looked at him.

"Deniz, don't insist, if Hatay doesn't want to, let him do what he feels like." resumed Sanem. She observed that the grandmother had remained silent in the background. And the child kept his distance from her. It seemed strange to her.

Slowly, from inside the cage, after filling the children's little hands with feed, she walked around the enclosure until she reached Hatay's height. He was watching the hens at his feet. So Sanem lowered herself in front of them, and talking to them, as she was wont to do, gave them food. Seeing that the child was watching her, she addressed him.

"You don't like chickens much, do you?" asked Sanem.

"Not much." he admitted shyly.

"And what is your favourite animal?" she then asked with a smile.

"Dogs." he said "Because with them it's easy to interact, with chickens on the other hand, apart from pecking..." dropped the sentence Hatay.

"Ah... I get it. In fact... " admitted Sanem.

"I really like dogs too, you know?" she told him.

Then she whistled.

"Haydut!!!!" she called him.

Suddenly they heard barking. And from around the corner came Haydut with one of Can's slippers in his mouth.

Perfect, she told herself. Can would be happy. *He had stolen yet another pair from his.*

Sanem came out of the cage with the children, attracted by the dog, closing it behind her.

"Haydut, again?!" scolded Sanem with her hands on his hips upon seeing the slipper.

"No! Daddy's slipper!" exclaimed Deniz.

"Oh, oh, Haydut is in trouble. When Dad finds out…" thought Ates with a grimace.

Meanwhile, from the exact moment the dog popped up, Hatay lit up.

"Come here scoundrel." called Sanem to him.

Haydut looked at her with the slipper in his mouth.

"If you don't come here, no bone for you. Understand?" she said pointing her finger at him.

Asil smiled.

Hatay was attracted to the dog. Undeterred, he immediately approached, stroking his muzzle. "Hello, boy!" he said smiling.

Faced with that celebration, he looked at him, and began to wag his tail, letting go of the slipper. He threw himself on the floor with his belly out, ready for a cuddle.

"How is that possible?" asked Sanem as he looked at Deniz.

Deniz returned the look of surprise and bewilderment at how easily he had managed to make the dog yield.

"Wow, that's a gift! He can train dogs." said Ates.

"Well done, Hatay. You have a way with dogs, I see. I can tell you like them. And they like you." commented Sanem.

"Come on back to the shade, children. Aren't you hungry?" said Sanem under the sun.

"Haydut you too, come." said seeing the dog's expression.

"You have found a new friend Haydut today." Deniz told him.

Once on the porch, Sanem asked Hatay: "Would you like to feed him?"

"Sure!" he exclaimed happily.

"Then come, let's prepare the bowl." Sanem told him, motioning to follow him into the kitchen.

Once they were ready, they went back outside and placed them next to his kennel.

Haydut bore down as usual, while Hatay sat on the floor beside him watching him fascinated.

At that point he called out to him. "Haydut? Look!" he said, pulling out a brand new bone from behind his back.

The dog pointed at it, sitting upright in front of him.

"Do you want it?" asked Hatay.

The dog barked once.

"Ah, he answers, look mama!" exclaimed Ates.

"I saw, I saw." replied Sanem.

"Hatay, next time he steals a pair of slippers I'll call you, to take them back." joked Sanem.

"No problem." he replied.

"And... go!" he said, throwing the bone into the middle of the garden in front of the pool. Haydut ran, caught it, and squatted quietly in the green grass, munching it greedily.

Hatay followed him, sat down again at his side, and unexpectedly the dog rested its muzzle on his crossed legs, letting him pet it.

They remained like that for a while.

The other children took two snacks and went back to the trampoline, Hatay preferred to stay with Haydut.

Grandma smiled.

"Good with dogs, eh?" asked Sanem.

Mrs Birce replied: "Actually, it's the first time I've seen him so smiling and comfortable." she admitted.

"He's been through a lot." she added.

"He's a good boy, though." Sanem commented. "She'll be proud of her grandson I guess." added again.

"There... actually, Hatay is not my grandson." the lady finally clarified. "I mean... I am not the grandmother."

"My God, I'm sorry, what a bad impression I made." said Sanem covering her mouth.

"Are you his aunt?" she then asked.

"No, not even." replied the woman.

"What do you mean? My son told me you are his grandmother because of that. Forgive me for calling you that several times, but I swear I didn't know." she apologized again.

"Don't worry, not many people know." Birce admitted. Then after looking around, confirming the children's distance, she said:

"I am Mrs Birce Unal." said and then added: "Hatay is in my care. I am his social worker."

"Ah... his social worker?" asked Sanem surprised.

"Yes, Hatay was born under not at all simple circumstances." explained the lady.

"ah, poor baby." commented Alis.

"Now I understand." replied Sanem who remained silent.

Mrs Birce looked at her.

"What are you referring to?" she asked.

"Deniz always told me that Hatay had no parents." Sanem recalled.

"But he had a grandmother, didn't she, then?" she asked.

"No, unfortunately." admitted Mrs Birce regretfully.

"If I am not too prying... what happened to his parents?" asked Sanem feeling sorry for the poor child.

Leyla and Mrs Asil remained silent in listening.

"Are they..." tried to ask Sanem hesitantly.

"Dead? Ah, no." replied Mrs Birce.

"They are alive and well, as far as we know. Hatay was born under difficult circumstances, in a place where babies should not be born. And icing on the cake, once he was born, his mother did not recognise him. He was an obstacle for her." she recounted.

"His mother abandoned him as soon as he was born?" asked Leyla shocked.

"Yeah. In fact, his mother did everything not to carry the pregnancy to term." said Birce.

"My God..." commented Alis bringing a hand to her mouth.

"But Hatay clung to life with all his might." he concluded.

"And he did it." she added with a smile.

"My God...that's really terrible." commented Sanem.

"And the father?" she asked. "I mean, a grandmother, a relative...didn't he have anyone who could take care of him?"

"Not that I know of." Birce replied. "I don't think he has any relatives, or if he does, no one has ever come forward." she explained.

"Excuse me, but I didn't understand, does he live with you? Are you taking care of him?" asked Leyla.

"No, I can't do that, it goes against my job. I'm just making sure he soon has a family that will give him all the attention he deserves." replied the lady.

"So you are looking for a family to adopt him, did I get that right?" asked Sanem.

"Exactly." replied Mrs. Birce.

"And... are there any volunteers?" asked Leyla.

"Well, Hatay is not a simple child at all. He has his own traumas, and it is difficult for him to feel at home. He has always lived in the family home since he was born. And he's still like that." said Birce looking at him as he stroked Haydut.

"He doesn't know what it means to have a home, a loving family, a father, a mother, brothers..." he said with a sad look.

"He's always been alone." she concluded.

"That's why he's so on his own..." commented Sanem nodding, casting a glance at the poor child who was so peaceful.

"Mrs Sanem, if you please, I would like to say a few words. I was very glad of your invitation today, Hatay needs to be in company, to have friends, to laugh and have carefree fun." opened Mrs Birce.

"Oh, the pleasure is all mine. My son seems to really care about him, and that only pleases me." she admitted.

"There, and here we come to the point." said Birce, "If your son talks to you about him, I'd love to know what you think. Having a point of view of one of his little friends, it might help." she said.

"Maybe he confides things to him that he doesn't tell me given my position. He's a very intelligent child." she added.

"Mh, of course, of course. If I can be of more than willing help. And I will tell you more, Hatay can come to us whenever he wishes. Be it for the animals, for my son's company or for something else. The door of our house is always open." offered Sanem with a heart of gold.

"Thank you." replied Mrs Birce, a serious-looking and perhaps gruff, but good-hearted lady. She reminded her a little of Mrs Remide.

"Ah! Deren has arrived." said Leyla seeing her getting out of the car.

Sanem stood up. "Deren?" she asked in amazement.

"Yep, that's her all right. Look, and there's Bulut and Burak too." she said seeing them close the doors.

"Deren?" called her Sanem flinching to be seen.

"Ah, Sanem!" she greeted her. All three of them set off down the path to join her. Sanem noticed their clothing. All three were casual, including Deren. She was almost in camp clothes. Sanem ran towards them with open arms, looking at Deren questioningly.

"Deren? What are you doing here? Weren't you supposed to be on set with Can?" she asked.

"I'm done, Can dismissed me earlier and since Bulut had to come and sort some things out in the garden we said to visit you. Did I make a mistake?" asked Deren uncertainly.

"No, no! Deren, what are you talking about! Of course you can come whenever you want, you don't need my invitation. I'm just surprised. I didn't expect this. And in camp clothes too..." she said, looking at her.

Bulut and Burak laughed.

"With two of us, it was easier to convince her." Bulut said, looking at his brother.

Also dressed in t-shirts, shorts and boots.

"The doctor said the sea air, sun and fresh air would be good for me, so I said to myself, what better place than Sanem's estate?" she asked rhetorically.

"You did well. There is no better place." she replied confidently.

Burak looked around in curiosity.

"Nice here." he said.

"Ah, and Burak will give me a hand in the vegetable garden." Bulut quickly explained.

"Ah, Burak, forgive me. Meanwhile, welcome to the estate. So we have a new labourer, eh?" she teased him, exchanging a wink with Bulut.

He laughed.

"We'll put him to work, see what he can do." said his brother.

"I'm ready." replied Burak.

"Bulut, give him a tour of the estate. I'll join you as soon as I can." said Sanem, casting a glance at the porch.

"Ah! Who are those?" asked Deren, seeing two women together with Leyla.

There are two little friends of the twins playing with them.

"Ah, then I won't bother you, I'll go for a walk with them." said Deren.

"See you later." she added.

"No need really. You can join us if you want." Sanem told her.

"Don't worry, I'll take a walk and then join you. You go back to your guests." she told her.

"OK, as you wish. I'll be waiting for you, eh!" reminded her Sanem.

"Alright. Alright." said Deren as he set off.

Sanem went back to entertaining the guests until Can and Emre arrived.

"Ah, Dad's here, Ilker, look!" said Leyla.

"One minute." realized Sanem. "But wasn't Emre supposed to be there instead of you today? And weren't you supposed to be on set? What's going on?" she asked confused.

"Ah, now you realise? Good morning, sister!" exclaimed Leyla laughing.

"There was a change of plans. Can wanted it that way." he replied shrugging.

"When? How? Why don't I know anything about it?" asked Sanem bewildered.

Meanwhile, Alis and Mrs Birce were entertaining the children while they were having a snack.

Leyla got up to meet Emre. "Look, there's Daddy! Do you want to go to Daddy?" she asked.

Ilker flinched. Then Emre, with a beaming smile, spread his arms and stretched his stride to join his family and take his son.

"Daddy!!!!" exclaimed the twins as they ran towards him.

"Ah, there are my little sailors!" he exclaimed as he lowered himself with his arms outstretched ready to greet them.

Dilara and Hatay stood aside.

"Come daddy, let us introduce you to our friend." said the two princesses of the house pulling him by the hands.

"This is Dilara." said Yildiz.

"Yeah, and this is CapCan." replied Ates.

"Hi Dilara. What a beautiful name. How are you?" said Can.

"Nice to meet you Mr. CapCan." she replied, holding out her hand, Can kissed it like a true gentleman. Then he caressed her, smiling at her.

"And what have you been up to?" he asked.

"We jumped on the trampoline!" exclaimed Ates jumping on the spot.

"I had no doubt." replied her father.

In all this, Hatay watched the scene afar, from the sidelines. Sanem saw a certain sadness in his eyes, and noticed that Deniz saw as much, in fact he approached him.

"Dad!" he called him aloud. "Come here, meet my best friend Hatay," he said.

Sanem smiled.

Can approached him. "Oh, nice to meet you Hatay. I am Can. Can Divit." he said hoping he would tap the five he was proposing in the air.

Hatay stood still. Then he held out his hand, saying: "How are you, my name is Hatay. Hatay Yuksel." he said in a formal tone.

"Yuksel?!" asked Deren behind Can's back. She had just arrived with Bulut and Burak at her side.

Deren was shocked. Bulut and Burak looked at her.

"Deren are you alright?" her husband asked her.

"Huh? Ah, yes, everything is fine." she lied. Then he approached the child and playfully said to her: "What a beautiful surname you have!"

Can also remained silent and confirmed. "Really nice surname." he said. Then seeing the child's frown, he added: "Don't mind her, she is like that." he said, pointing at Deren.

Mrs Birce seeing that exchange came closer.

"Um, Hatay, why don't you go back and play with Deniz?" she proposed politely.

The child looked at them seriously and then obeyed, approaching Deniz.

"Something wrong with the surname Yuksel?" asked Mrs. Birce.

"Ah, um... no. Sorry, it reminded me of someone for a moment. Then I realized I was mistaken." explained Deren.

"Um... Is he your grandson?" she then asked. "He's such a sweet child." added Deren to cover her figure.

Sanem remained silent waiting for Mrs. Birce to give the explanation she wanted.

"Um, he's not. I'm his social worker, actually. You, on the other hand? Who do I have the pleasure of talking to?" Mrs Birce asked.

"Social worker?" asked Deren. Can also looked at his wife puzzled. Sanem nodded.

"Um, let's come in, let's not stand." said Sanem inviting everyone to sit on the porch.

At that point he made the official introductions.

"Mrs Birce, this is my husband, Can." she said.

"How are you, ma'am. Can Divit." he said, extending his hand to her.

"My pleasure, son. I am Mrs Birce Unal." he replied.

"She, on the other hand, is Deren, a friend, and work colleague, accompanied by her husband and brother-in-law." she said introducing Bulut and Burak as well.

"This is Emre, Can's brother and my sister's husband," she said, pointing at him.

"Nice to meet you ma'am." said Emre, holding Ilker in his arms, shaking her hand.

"My pleasure." replied the lady.

"Ah, such beautiful youth." she commented.

Once they had also introduced themselves to Dilara's mother, Emre and Leyla decided to go home, Ilker had collapsed from sleep in his father's arms.

Dilara's mother too, after a brief conversation, decided it was time to go home, so they too left. That left Deren, Bulut and Burak, Can, Sanem and Birce among the adults. Deren as Sanem greeted her guests, observed the child.

"Bulut? We are going to the garden!" Yildiz and Ates exclaimed specially.

They liked to make him angry.

"Ah, no, eh! I'll catch you, eh! Clever little girls!" exclaimed Bulut.

"They really are your daughters, eh, Sanem?" he then said before snapping to protect his work.

The girls had already left.

"Wait, I'd better come too. I'm scared for my flowers!" Sanem admitted.

"Will you excuse me for a moment? With your permission." said Sanem addressing Mrs Birce directly.

"Please, don't worry." she replied.

"Can you handle this?" she asked to her husband.

"Of course." he replied.

"Come here, you two, let's make a wreath!" she called back, trying to distract them.

"I'll come too!" said Burak.

"Come, come, so I can take the opportunity to show you something you haven't seen yet." said Sanem.

"Ah, if you're talking about Can the scarecrow, I already know everything! Bulut just told me." he said, hiding a smile.

"It's comical, isn't it?" asked Sanem laughing in turn.

"There, creative, I'd say." replied Burak.

Meanwhile, left alone, Deren took the opportunity to ask Mrs Birce a few questions.

"Excuse me, but I was struck by what you said earlier. How come that child is in the care of social services? I mean, what happened to his parents?" asked Deren.

Can was also curious, but did not ask the question, having realized that his wife knew about it. He would have asked her.

Mrs Birce looked at her. She noticed around Deren's neck the necklace calling angels.

"Sorry, maybe I was too impulsive, but you know... lately topics like: custody, children and family, they touch me a lot." she said bringing a hand to her belly.

"Ah, I understand. Congratulations by the way." Mrs. Birce told her.

Deren thanked her.

"Well, she wasn't intrusive or anything. I know well that, when I accompany Hatay and say that I am a social worker, the question arises." the old lady replied.

"Here, my husband and I, we are also dealing with a custody case that concerns us closely, that is... in our case, however, the person at the center of this, is an adult and we, in order to protect him, would like to obtain custody of him legally. My husband, who is a lawyer, is taking care of that." Deren explained, seeing the woman a bit uncertain about her curiosity. She thought that sincerity might open her up as much as possible.

"Ah, I see. Well, in your case, speaking as a social worker, I can tell you that in cases of majority, there is a need for the approval of the person in question, but it is also true that if the boy or girl is not financially independent, then he or she must be entrusted to those who can guarantee stability until he or she is independent. The family that decides to offer custody, for the sake of the subject, must be assessed from every point of view, especially if it is at the centre of a legal debate. Usually such an evaluation is carried out by a figure like mine." she explained.

"Ah... there, I admit that some of the points you explained I did not know." Deren replied, casting a glance at Can, beside her.

"Here, excuse me, but... the social worker, in these cases, what exactly does check when visits the family?" asked Deren then.

"That's it, of course it changes from situation to situation, but in principle I can tell you that once it is ascertained that the boy's family is not suitable to take care of him, the social worker visits the family that wants to take him in, making sure that it is the best place for the person in question. Our job is to ensure the best for the people we protect." she said.

"Hmm, I see..." Deren replied thoughtfully.

"Well, if you're wondering exactly what we look at, in principle I would tell you that the important aspects are: a close, loving family, a welcoming house, with the space necessary for the child to feel welcome and at home. But a large part depends on the talks we have with the foster parents. That is why, even when the foster children come of age, they are still followed up by us over time, with visits and talks, to make sure that everything is running smoothly. Sometimes they are also followed up step by step by a psychologist if they have suffered abuse or trauma." Birce explained.

Deren listened attentively. Without knowing it, she had hit some very important points for her.

"I don't know if I was helpful... I don't know you case, of course." Mrs Birce added, hearing Deren's silence.

"No, no, you are been really helpful. More than you can imagine. I thank you." said Deren. "I just hope the little one's situation is not that bad." Deren added.

"Well, his situation is very complex, unfortunately." repeated Birce with a sigh.

"Did Hatay have a trauma?" asked Deren.

Birce nodded. "As I explained to Mrs Sanem, Hatay was born under circumstances that were not at all simple. And his parents did not want to know anything about him."

"What exactly do you mean by not simple conditions, excuse me?" asked Can.

"Well, I mean that the place where he was born is not suitable for children." replied Birce.

"What do you mean? Where did the mother give birth?" asked Deren increasingly curious.

Birce made sure the children were at a distance before answering.

"In prison." she replied.

Deren became paralyzed. "In jail?" she asked again.

"Yeah..." replied Birce.

"Is that why he was entrusted to you?" asked Can. "Because his mother couldn't take care of him?" he asked.

"Not really." replied Birce.

Then she added: "It wasn't just the place of birth that was the problem... i mean, his mother didn't recognize him."

"She didn't recognize him?!" exclaimed Deren stunned.

"She didn't want him from the beginning, and although she carried the pregnancy, during all the months, she tried everything to interrupt it. But at the last we managed to convince her to at least give birth." said Birce.

"The mother had a lot of sessions with the psychologist to be convinced, and finally she seemed to change her mind. She gave birth, but she didn't want it. It was an obstacle for her.... A mistake," Birce explained.

"Hatay..." thought Can.

Birce looked at him nodding.

Deren realized at that moment. "Hatay means mistake..."

"Excuse me but Yuksel is a surname given by whom? If his mother didn't recognize him..." asked Deren.

"No, once she was convinced to give birth, the mother, despite her decision, decided to give him one last 'gift' if you can call it that."

"What kind of mother is she!" exclaimed Deren without restraint. "Giving one's child a name like that is like branding him for life." she blurted out.

Mrs Birce nodded silently.

"Deren..." resumed Can for her tone of voice.

Deren apologized. Then she remained in thoughtful silence.

"What about the father?" asked Can.

"What father?" was Birce's reply.

Can realized he was not there.

"Is he dead?" asked Deren.

"No, we don't know for sure, but we don't think so, the mother never revealed. Surely the biological father doesn't even know he has a son." replied Mrs. Birce bluntly.

"Just a minute!" she exclaimed at one point.

"So the surname also belongs to the mother, or is that wrong?" she recalled.

"Well, from the documents, we understand that it does, but who can tell..." replied Birce somewhat confused by the case at hand.

Deren looked at Can with wide eyes.

"Excuse me, but how old is Hatay? He looks older than my children..." asked Can.

"Hatay goes to the same school as your sons. They are not the same age, of course. They are not in the same class, he is 10." she explained.

"Excuse me, but I have to ask at this point. What is the mother's name?" asked Deren increasingly convinced of an idea that was running through her mind.

"She remained anonymous." replied Birce. "So she wanted." added.

"What do you mean? She just said her mother gave her name... so Yuksel might not be her mother's surname, I'm confused." admitted Deren touching her forehead.

"True, her mother gave her name, but as she chose the name, she might as well have chosen the surname as well." she admitted.

"Ah... for a moment I thought..." commented Deren with a sigh of relief. Then she returned thoughtfully.

"Excuse me and where does Hatay live now?" asked Can.

"Hatay has been living in a group home since birth." replied Mrs. Birce. "I've been dealing with his case since the beginning and I'm looking for a family who can take care of him." she explained.

"He hasn't found the right family yet?" asked Deren.

"Deren..." resumed Can.

"What? What did I say?" she asked.

Then she reflected and realizing the misunderstanding, she quickly corrected herself.

"No, I'm not accusing her... I mean, I'm not saying she's not good at her job, on the contrary... I'm just surprised that since her birth the right family hasn't been found yet." explained Deren.

"Well, it is not an easy case, and I have to be very careful and selective with candidates. My aim is to protect the child and guarantee him the best possible future." said Birce confidently.

"I cannot compromise." she added.

Can nodded. "Absolutely right, I completely agree with her."

"I'm sure he will find the best family for him." Deren added with a friendly smile.

Can watched his son enjoying their self with his little friend and felt like adding:

"Probably if he has spoken to my wife I am sure she has already told this, and just in case I will repeat myself, but... if Hatay likes to come and play with my children... I mean, if we can get him distracted in any way, you can call us without any problem." said Can handing her a business card from Fikri Harika, his and his wife's contact details were written on it.

When Mrs Birce, after thanking him, took the business card in her hand and read the name of the company, she froze. For a moment her bespectacled eyes remained fixed on the piece of paper in her hands, then she slowly lifted her gaze, still fixed, and placed it on Can.

For a split second Can read the shock in her eyes.

Then she turned that expression into a friendly smile, thanking him again.

"Well, now I think it's time to go." she said as she stood up.

"Hatay?" she called to him.

Deniz and Hatay approached.

"Hatay, it's getting late. We have to go back." she said.

Can immediately read the change in the child's mood. The smile on his slightly sly lips faded.

"But I was having fun." he replied.

"I know, baby, but we'll be back, I promise, OK?" said Mrs. Birce.

"Ah! Are you leaving?" asked Sanem as she returned to them with Bulut and Burak.

"Yes, Mrs Sanem, it's time to go back." she said.

Sanem noticed the displeased look on her son's face and went up to him, stroking his hair. He leaned back on her legs.

"Ah, but we are waiting for you again, aren't we Deniz?" his mother asked looking at him.

"Yes! Come back again! We'll have a good time!" exclaimed Deniz regaining some enthusiasm.

"Sure, come back anytime! Our doors are open..." confirmed Can.

"Hear that, Hatay?" asked Mrs. Birce, holding him close.

Hatay nodded.

"We are waiting for you whenever you want. And Haydut too. Look, he came to greet you." said Sanem, seeing him approaching.

Hatay looked at the dog, who came up to sniff him.

The boy stroked his muzzle and greeted him. "Hello Haydut. Hello boy." he said cheering him on.

"Thank you all for the invitation, and the availability." replied Mrs. Birce cordially.

"Thank you for coming." Sanem replied.

She then leaned over to Hatay and asked him: "Did you have a good time?"

Hatay replied, nodding, then added: "Very much." with a smile.

"And did you have fun?" she asked her son.

"A lot mum." replied Deniz.

"Oh..." commented Deren witnessing the scene, hormones raging. She pouted, about to cry.

"Well, come on then, I'll see you soon. And in the meantime you'll see each other at school!" recalled Sanem.

"Right." confirmed Can.

"Come on, say hello to everyone Hatay." said Birce.

"Bye..." he said shyly.

"And how do you say?" added Birce.

"Thank you... for everything." he said looking at Sanem. She knew he was referring to Haydut.

"Ah, Can, you know Hatay is a master with Haydut? He saved your slipper!" said Sanem.

"Ah, my slipper again... then I must thank you!" said Can approaching to exchange a five with him.

Hatay reciprocated with a smirk. The more he observed him, the more familiar that smirk seemed to him.

"It'll mean you'll teach me how to deal with that rascal next time." Can added with a gentle smile.

"Come on, Hatay, let's go." said Birce.

They said goodbye to everyone and then left.

"Bye Hatay! See you soon! See you at school!" barreled Ates along with her sister, energetic as ever as she waved at him from afar.

"What a dear child..." commented Bulut.

"Yeah..." replied Deren, casting a glance at Can.

"Huh? Come on, let's all have dinner together, shall we?" proposed Sanem pleased as a child.

"No, but we don't want to disturb, that's it..." replied Deren immediately.

"But what disturbance, Deren!" exclaimed Sanem "Don't say that even in jest, right Can?" asked Sanem confirmation.

"No, indeed, my wife is perfectly right." he replied.

"And afterwards let's take a nice walk to the pier to look at the stars." said Sanem.

"We will introduce the Phoenix and Albatros to Burak, won't we children?" asked Sanem.

"Yes!!!" they exclaimed.

"It's our boat, you know? We are the sailors and dad is the captain!" exclaimed Ates.

"Oh, really?" asked Burak surprised.

"Sure, and Deniz is studying to be captain, isn't that right daddy?" added the bratty little one of the house.

"That's right, my daughter." replied Can.

"Then it will mean that you will show what you have learnt to Burak." said Sanem.

"We will teach you a lesson." replied Ates speaking directly to him.

"Ohhh..." commented Bulut.

"I'm really curious to hear this lesson." replied Deren.

"Come on, pupil Burak... to the table." commented patting his brother on the shoulder.

Everyone laughed.

28. SUSPECTS

After a quiet Sunday spent in the company of Osman, Adile, the baby, Cey Cey and Ayhan, a new busy week began. Can was still a little angry with Sanem over the Deren affair.

Monday arrived and he hoped to distract himself a little by concentrating on the much work going on, but when he reached the office that morning, after saying goodbye to his wife, heading downstairs, he found Deren there.

She was sitting comfortably on his sofa. Through the glass windows he noticed that his brother Emre had not yet arrived.

Both had arrived earlier than usual.

Deren was anxiously waiting for him.

When Can entered, he did not notice her immediately. Only when he reached his desk chair did he realize who was in front of him.

"Good morning." Deren greeted him.

"Good morning... Deren? What are you doing here? What's going on? Is there a problem?" asked Can in bursts.

It was not like her to wait in his office.

Deren got up and closed the door.

"We need to talk." she said.

"From the look on your face, it doesn't look good." Can commented, observing her serious expression.

"Listen, if there are any problems with any projects, give me time to turn on the PC to check two things and then let's have a meeting right away, alright?" said Can quickly putting his hands up.

"No, Can, don't worry it's not about work. I need to talk to you about something else." Deren replied seriously.

"Now you worry me... What's going on?" he asked frowning.

"Come." she said motioning for him to sit next to her.

Can silently obeyed.

He looked at her and then asked puzzled: "Is Bulut alright?"

"Bulut? Of course he is fine! Why would he be sick?" she asked rhetorically.

"OK, then talk, don't keep me on tenterhooks." Can urged her.

"Well, I don't know where to start..." admitted Deren.

"From the beginning... I think it will be easier." he replied sarcastically.

"Here... Can Saturday I noticed your expression... it wasn't that different from mine." she began.

"My expression? What was wrong with my expression? What are you referring to Deren?" asked Can increasingly confused.

"I think you also thought the same thing I think..... About Hatay." she said shyly.

"Hatay? Deren, seriously you closed the door of my office to talk about Hatay?" asked Can.

"Can... don't you understand?!" blurted Deren.

"What don't I understand?" he asked in turn.

"Ugh...you men.... Can but are you serious? Don't tell me the surname Yuksel doesn't mean anything to you at all..." said Deren.

"Ah... that... you say."

"Huh, what else?" she replied rhetorically.

"See, for a moment I admit I thought about it, but you heard, didn't you? It can't be her. It's a coincidence. Let's not stare at each other's heads." he immediately replied.

"A strange coincidence though... don't you think so?" asked Deren of her.

"I mean, as soon as I heard that last name pronounced, the blood froze in my veins. I thought the past was knocking on our door again." said Deren touching her chest.

"And the story?" he then added.

"A woman in prison giving birth, and deeming her son such a mistake that she gave him that name." she continued.

"But she might have made it up... and then there's not just her with that surname in the world." Can continued, knowing who she was referring to.

"In the world surely not, but what are the chances in a prison?" mused Deren.

Can at this remained silent.

"One minute!" exclaimed Deren then.

"How old did you say Hatay is?" she asked.

"10..." replied Can as he began to mentally count along with her.

"And when was Aylin arrested?" she asked.

Can began to count.

"9 years?" asked Deren confirmation.

"9 years or so yes..." confirmed Can.

"Did you see that? Come back!" she exclaimed more and more convinced.

"Deren... don't panic. It's true, by now we're used to always being suspicious of everything that happens to us... but I think we're going too far now. You're spending too much time with my wife, playing the lady in yellow. Enough of these mysteries." he blurted out.

"Because Sanem has an eye!" she exclaimed "She has instincts and is never wrong about these things." Deren replied.

"One minute..." she then thought. "Is Sanem investigating something, by any chance? What's going on? What mysteries? She already guessed it, didn't she?" asked Deren.

"Then I'll go and talk to her. I will have more satisfaction." she said getting up.

"Deren... Deren... don't be silly, wait." stopped her Can.

"Calm down. Come here, sit down, where are you going?" he asked her.

"If you came to me it means you wanted to talk to me about it, right?" reminded him Can.

"Yes, but if you don't believe me, what's the point of continuing the conversation?" she replied with a hand already ready on the door.

"Let me ask you a question." she then said assuming a professional pose, hands on her hips. Like a true creative director.

"Maybe he isn't, but if he was...if Hatay was his son...with that name and age...who do you think the father might be?" she tried to make him think.

"Think about it! I haven't slept all night for that, and a name in mind I have unfortunately." replied Deren.

"No, you're wrong..." he denied strongly, realizing.

"Get your brain working a bit, Can! Who had a long history with Aylin, before her arrest?" she insisted.

"I think the answer is simple." replied Deren as she left the office.

Can wanted to stop her, and ask not to talk to Sanem, already intrigued in another mystery... but Deren's words reverberated in his mind and for a moment, just a moment he thought:

"If it were true, Emre could be Hatay's father..." Realizing what this entailed, without a second thought, he dialled a number on his phone.

A strong, deep voice answered on the other end. "Hello? Mr Can?"

MEANWHILE DOWNSTAIRS...

"Good morning!" she smilingly greeted her co-workers Sanem as she reached her office. As soon as she entered she found Ayhan and Deniz inside.

"Ah, good morning girls! What a coincidence! I was going to call you any minute." she said, putting down her bag and immediately turning on her PC.

"So we have to send some samples to the lab, and today we'll get some important approvals for the next summer line of creams. We will also have a meeting up at Fikri Harika to approve the latest drafts of the packaging. So I need you to keep me informed of every step. Whatever news there is today, pass it on to me immediately, OK? I have to run upstairs from Can for some work. Also, where is Muzo? Has he not arrived yet?" she asked looking around.

"Have you seen him?" she asked.

"Um... Sanem, I don't think he will come.... For a while." Deniz replied shyly.

"Why? What else happened?" she asked.

"Well, we know about the argument he had with Can." replied Ayhan.

"Papa Nihat, after giving him an earful, took him home. And..." she said.

"And... there at the door was me waiting. I had to talk to him." replied Deniz.

"I had realized that something was wrong. And seeing him run away like that... I decided to join him." continued.

Together with Nihat we entered the house, and once he calmed down, he left him in my hands. At the end I forced him to start a therapeutic course with me." explained Deniz.

"Ah..." commented Sanem.

"Yeah, and that's why I asked Ayhan for help. She will help me keep him good. Cey Cey will also do his part." she added.

"OK, but what does that have to do with work? I mean, there's a book being published... he can't give up work for that." replied Sanem.

"How? Didn't Can tell you?" asked Ayhan.

"I thought you knew and agreed..." she admitted, blinking in surprise.

"Can pushed Muzo away until he solves his problems once and for all. No agency, no Sanem and no book." she reported.

"What are you saying?" asked Sanem surprised. "What? What...when did this happen? Why do I find out now? "she wondered.

"I don't know, but that's not all, he even passed his 1% shares to Cey Cey." added Ayhan.

"How can he decide for me? How can he not have told me, huh? He can't stop Muzo from publishing the book!" exclaimed Sanem angrily.

"I'm going to talk to him now!" she said as she started towards the door.

"Sanem... " Ayhan called to her, preventing from leaving.

"Can is right. And your father agrees with him too..." she reported.

"And to be honest, we agree too." she admitted.

"Muzo cannot work under these conditions, or sooner or later he will jeopardise everyone's work, and especially your image." Ayhan reasoned her.

"Do you understand why your husband did this?" asked Deniz.

"I know Can is protective, but I don't understand why he didn't tell me, acting behind my back." Sanem said furiously.

"To protect you, Sanem! Because in order to help you, you are willing to put yourself at risk. And that is both a good and a condemnation. Can, and your father are being tough because they know you." Deniz explained to her.

"Muzo needs calm and quiet, and as his therapist, for the success of the treatment, I ask you to stay away from him. Don't call him, don't look for him... let the therapy take its course and you will see that he will look for you." said Deniz decisively.

"Alright..." Sanem replied simply.

"Alright? Really? You won't make a fuss?" asked Deniz.

"I said alright." she replied testily looking her straight in the eyes.

"OK, then we need to ask you one more thing." said Ayhan.

"Ask." she replied with a sigh.

"Here, for the therapy we need to leave work early, until he is cured, so at a time to be determined, we will not be in the office."

"What, you're leaving me alone?" She asked. "And how will I do ?"

"You have Burak and Cey Cey who will never leave you. You can rest assured. They will take care of everything." Deniz reassured her.

"And what will you do with him?" asked Sanem.

"I will try to make him deal with his relationship with Guliz." replied Deniz.

"And I the relationship with his mother. I think being abandoned was a trauma for him." added Ayhan.

"All right, look, I want to be informed of his every progress." Sanem replied.

"Alright, sister." replied Ayhan.

"Sorry but I really have to go now." she added as she ran off.

"Where?" asked Ayhan.

"To the meeting." she replied.

Arriving at the top of the stairs she found Cey Cey.

"Ah, Sanem I was just looking for you." he said transfixed.

"I know, Cey Cey, the meeting... I know, I'm on my way." she said rolling her eyes.

"No, here...I mean, yes, but...we have an emergency. You have to replace Mr Can in the meeting." he said.

"Replace?" asked Sanem.

"Replace, yes." he confirmed.

"Why? Where is Can?" asked Sanem.

"I don't know, he left in a hurry, he didn't tell me. He just informed that he would be late, and to be replaced by you and Deren." explained Cey Cey briefly.

"Ufff... right now?!" blurted out Sanem.

"Why? Love problems?" asked Cey Cey raising and lowering his eyebrows with a mischievous look.

"Cey Cey..." began Sanem glaring at him. Then squinting her eyes into two slits she approached him.

"I know very well that you are in cahoots with Ayhan and Deniz about Muzo..." she said.

"But Sanem, I..." tried to retort Cey Cey.

"Open your ears wide, Cey Cey. Tell to the dear Can Divit that when he comes back, I want to talk to him UR-GEN-TLY!" she said pointing her finger at him.

"And don't you dare tell him on what subject... don't you dare! Or I'll make a bad quarter of an hour for you and him!" she exclaimed angrily, overtaking him to reach the office.

"Ah! All this negative charge is not good for you, Sanem... ah, I can feel it in my whole body right now." said Cey Cey trembling.

When Sanem entered the meeting room, the participating Fikri Harika members were already present. Sanem sat at the head of the table in Can's place, looking angry and hurried.

Her sister, Emre, Metin and Deren looked at her.

187

"Sanem?" asked Deren as soon as she saw her enter.

"Where is Can?" she asked looking over the door.

"He will not participate. I'm filling in for him." she replied finally looking up from the files she alliened by slamming them vigorously on the table.

"Sister all right?" Leyla asked tactfully.

Sanem glowered at her. He immediately noticed the thunderbolts leaking from her eyes, and only replied: "Alright." returning in silence.

A few minutes later the clients arrived and the meeting began. Sanem was professional and competent as usual. At the end, Deren approached her to congratulations. Sanem thanked her, and once they were alone, she tried to talk to her about the Hatay matter, but she was too nervous to listen, so she quickly dismissed her by telling she had an urgent engagement. She went back downstairs to take care of the rest, locked himself in her office without going out for hours.

Suddenly there was a soft knock at the door.

Sanem looked up. It was Burak.

"Come Burak." Sanem replied coldly.

"Sanem, Can has just returned to your office..... You asked me to report it to you." he said shyly.

"Perfect, I thank you." she said getting up. "Take these to the archive while you're at it. And don't anyone dare come into our office now. Pass the word! Am I clear?" she asked seriously.

"Crystal clear, I'll report right away." he replied, returning to his work.

Sanem walked briskly out of the office. As she reached the lift she found Ayhan.

"Sanemsi..." she tried to stop her.

"Not now Ayhan." she replied decisively, overtaking her like a train.

She took the lift and went up, once in the agency at a brisk and determined pace, with thunderbolts in her eyes, she reached the office. Can was sitting at his desk.

She entered without knocking, closing it noisily behind her.

As soon as Can saw her, he lit up with a smile. "My love... I just heard." he said.

"Sorry I didn't attend the meeting." he added, getting up to walk towards her.

Stopping there in front of him with breathlessness, not from running, but from suppressed anger, she immediately exclaimed: "How dare you, huh!" "How can you think of doing such a thing! Huh?!!!"

Can froze.

He closed his eyes and sighed.

"Love... it was Deren, wasn't it?" he asked. "Deren told you everything, didn't she?"

"Ah, Deren knows too then? Great!" exclaimed Sanem like a fury.

"I bet the whole office knows but me, doesn't it?" she blurted out.

"Because who am I after all, eh? Nobody, right?" she continued.

"Love what are you talking about, you're my whole life!" replied Can.

"Sure...right. Your life..." replied Sanem with a sarcastic half smile.

"Look, I would have told you about it, alright?" he started to say.

"You would have told me about it? Ah! But thank you, what an honor, Mr Can Divit! Because I don't count for anything after all, right?"

"What are you saying, Sanem?" he replied frowning confused.

"What am I saying?!" she shouted.

"How dare you make decisions for me, huh? On MY writing job how dare you interfere, huh?" ranted Sanem with eyes of fire.

Can remained petrified. His brow furrowed.

"Who are you to decide to interrupt a collaboration of mine, huh? Tell me, Can!" she shouted.

"Have I ever done that with you? Have I ever dared to tell you who you could or could not work with? Have I ever dared to interrupt a collaboration that had already started without your knowledge? In your name? No! I never have! And I never will!" exclaimed Sanem.

Can understood that he was referring to Muzo.

"Listen, Sanem... calm down." he said trying to get closer to her.

Sanem kicked away his hands that were trying to calm.

Can was hurt by her refusal, but tried to calm her down anyway.

"Love, listen... Muzo needs serious help! And you are too good to him!" he said.

"It's true! I am good, OK? And maybe naive too. I am like that!" said Sanem with a shrug. "I always have been. For me, you can never be too good!" she added.

"Are you jealous by any chance?" she then asked, attacking him.

"Jealous? Me? Of Muzo? How many times have I told you it's not like that!" repeated Can irritably.

"I swear it doesn't sound like that at all." retorted Sanem crossing her arms.

"Sanem, I'm not." repeated Can with a sigh.

"Then WHY? Huh? WHY did you speak to Muzo on my behalf and tell him that he would not publish his book? Huh? And why did you give his percentage to Cey Cey, huh?" she attacked him.

"Was there any need for all this? Are you happy now that you took over everything?" she insisted.

"I didn't take control of anything." Can replied.

"Oh, no! I found myself with a fait accompli for the umpteenth time and you say you didn't take control, is that it?" ranted Sanem.

"Sanem, sometimes you are too good! And when I see people taking advantage of your goodness, it is my job to protect you. I am your husband!" she reminded him.

"I don't need to be protected, OK? I can take care of myself!" Sanem replied.

"Can, don't hide behind the excuse of protecting because it no longer attacks. When you do that, you go back to being the old possessive Can! You clearly haven't learnt anything from the past!" she exclaimed like a fury.

"If you want I'll tell you again, since you show that you don't know me. Nice to meet you, I am Sanem Aydin and I don't like accomplished facts! I don't like people who make decisions for me! Neither by a stranger nor by my husband!" she shouted angrily.

"Sanem, Muzo made you suffer." he recalled.

"Can you be talking about an incident you didn't even witness! You only acted on hearsay!" she exclaimed furiously.

"But it was true!" he exclaimed, getting nervous.

"It's true, I was hurt. I don't deny it, but Muzo, who already needs help, didn't deserve all this." Sanem took his side.

"Sanem why do you insist on helping him, huh? Do you like being treated like this?" he asked nervously.

"You don't understand... And maybe never will understand, it seems. It's a pity... it's really a pity." she replied with a disappointed look.

"A pity for what?" asked Can.

"A pity that you, despite saying otherwise, you have remained exactly the same! If anyone needs help here, it's you!" she exclaimed.

Sanem headed for the door. Ready to open it.

"Sanem, don't be like that... he had made you suffer and I don't allow anyone to make you suffer." he continued.

Sanem looked at him: "You say you don't allow anyone to hurt me? Huh? Then you should talk to yourself, because the only person who is making me suffer more than you can imagine, is only you, right now!" she said.

Then smiling, said: "You will never have control over me! And no one but me will ever have it! You are not my master. Now watch and learn how much control you have over me!!" she said as she left, slamming the glass door violently.

The whole agency jolted, everyone's eyes on Sanem who was leaving at a brisk pace.

Deren, Bulut, Burak, Emre and Leyla immediately came out of their offices.

"Sister!" called Leyla. Sanem did not turn around.

"My God... I haven't seen a fight like this in years." Ayhan commented open-mouthed as she saw Sanem come out.

She was unapproachable.

"I've seen them fight... but I don't think I've ever seen them fight like this in their entire history." commented Cey Cey beside her at the counter. "I feel some bad energies around." he admitted, pulling out Allah's eye to sanitize the air a little.

Then Ayhan commented: "Ah, sister.... ah. I told you not to do that..."

"What's going on?" asked Deren worriedly.

"I don't know." replied Emre, both of them standing outside their office doors.

"I'm going to my brother." he said.

Emre went back into his office, and from there through the inner door, he reached his brother.

He was sitting on the sofa, his face covered by his hands. His knees were wobbling with nervousness.

"Brother? What happened?" asked Emre.

"We had a fight, alright?!" He grumbled again nervously. "You all surely heard it anyway. What's the need to ask?" he said.

"Alright, alright, brother..." replied Emre, raising his hands in surrender.

"Calm down." he added.

"What did you fight about? Let's hear it. Let it out. I am here. I'm listening." he said as he sat down beside him.

"Why did Sanem leave like that?" he asked.

"Nothing, that's it... she heard what I reported to Muzo, when I took him back for making her suffer." Can replied curtly.

"Ah, for making her cry, you say?" asked Emre.

"Exactly." he confirmed.

"I was not present in the office, and when I heard Ayhan talking to Cey Cey about it, I was at a loss and called Papa Nihat to tell me where he lived. I caught up with him, but found him at the little park nearby." he recounted briefly.

"And what exactly did you tell him? I mean, what exactly were the words that infuriated Sanem so much, brother? I've never seen her furious like that. Not even in the past." he admitted.

"Muzo, it made her cry, and when I told him to stop with that cheeky attitude of his, and with that sly smirk on his face, I told him that until he solved his problems, he shouldn't show his face at the agency, at the Sanem, and that his book might as well forget about it." said Can.

"Brother..." commented Emre dumbfounded.

"What?" he asked.

"Are you serious?" he asked.

Can glowered at him.

"Brother, don't look at me like that." said Emre. "You did the one thing Sanem hates... confronting her with a fait accompli!" said Emre.

"Now I understand why she was so angry. Look even I get it." he added.

"Don't start Emre." his brother cheered him.

"Oh, of course I'll start! What has gotten into you, huh? How can you tell Muzo that he will not continue the book with Sanem? It's not your job." he pointed out to him.

"Emre, Muzo is not well, and Sanem is too good! He is taking advantage of it! Sanem wouldn't say no even to a fly, you know that. That's why I did it! Sometimes you need someone to bang the fist on the table." he said.

"Brother, I understand your gesture, you didn't do it out of malice, you did it to protect her, OK, but... so from right, you go to wrong, and look! What did you get out of it? A big fight." Emre said, pointing to the door.

"Your wife stormed out." he concluded.

"She'll get over it. She'll understand that I was right." replied Can seriously.

"She'll get over it?" he repeated. "You're not going to do anything about it then?" he asked.

"Emre, she needs to cool off, and so do I, please." Can begged him.

"What do you mean, brother! You're not going after her?" Emre blurted out.

"No, I won't go after her. It means that when Sanem bangs her head on it, she'll understand." replied Can as he stood up.

"Ah, is that so?" he asked.

"It is so." Can stubbornly replied.

"Then why didn't you let her bang our heads from the start, without interfering, huh?" he asked her.

Can stared at him in silence.

"Brother, really, when you act like that, I don't understand you." he admitted.

"Why are you being possessive, huh? Don't you trust Sanem? Wasn't what you experienced in the past enough for you? How many more times do you have to bang your head to understand that, huh?" blurted Emre.

"My sister-in-law is very smart, she knows very well when to approach or push a person away. Don't you remember with Yigit?" he said.

"I remember how long it took for her to realize what kind of man he was!" Can recalled.

"Because he was one way with you and another way with her, that's why it took her so long. But when she realised, what did she do?" he tried to reason with him.

Can remained silent.

"Didn't she push him away for good?" insisted Emre.

"Yes." replied Can simply.

"So what? Isn't that what's important?" he added.

"Yes, but why wait for him to suffer when you can put a stop to it right away, eh? I mean, why doesn't she trust me?" he asked.

"Ah, brother.... Again with this trust, trust, trust." snorted Emre rolling his eyes.

"What about respect instead?" he asked. "Brother dear, in a marriage, there is that too, not just trust. And you my dear, this time, you disrespected her, invading her space, even interfering in her work as a writer. Tell me, you even became a writer and I don't know?" he ended the sentence jokingly.

"Emre, don't joke. I'm not in the mood." Can replied.

"I mean, ok give your judgement for the agency and the Sanem, after all you are partners in both, but of her writing work, are you, by any chance, her manager? I don't think so." he said.

Then he looked at him.

"And may it not cross your mind!" Emre scolded him, pointing her finger at him.

"You have your pictures and she has her writing. I mean, has she ever interfered on your behalf with the photographer's agency, for example? No. Not that I know of at least." he corrected himself.

"It's not the same thing." Can replied.

"How 'isn't it the same thing', brother? Don't be stubborn! You're being a wayward child right now!" he resumed.

"You don't want to admit you're wrong, but you'll figure it out." Emre replied, nodding.

"Anger is clouding your brain right now." he added.

"When something upsets you, you rage, and attack without thinking."

Can turned sharply to look at him.

"Behind all this, there's something else bothering you too, isn't there?" asked Emre.

"How do you know?" asked Can worriedly.

"Because when you get to these levels, it's usually because you're hatching something inside. Something you can't or won't externalize, and that wears you down inside, until you explode unjustly." he examined him.

"Wow, I didn't know I was a lab subject..." commented Can, hinting at a smile.

"Years and years of study." joked Emre. "Am I wrong?" he asked.

"No." replied Can as he returned to sit on the sofa.

"That's right, have a seat, you better get it out of your system or someone will pay the price."

"Tell me Mr. Can Divit, what is it that upsets you so much?" said Emre with a psychologist's manner.

"Emre..." pronounced Can with a conflicted sigh.

"Ouch, the matter is more serious than I imagined." he commented seeing his brother's gloomy expression.

"I have to tell you something, but I don't know how to tell you." Can admitted in distress.

"Brother, you're scaring me though. Speak." he urged him.

Can began to tell him Hatay's story until he reached the crucial point.

"I mean, I don't know if this is the right time to tell you, maybe I should wait until I have evidence in hand, but... I also think you should be ready, just in case..." he said dropping the sentence.

"What are you saying brother? What does this have to do with me?" asked Emre.

"Here, it's just Deren's theory, OK? So take it with a grain of salt." he warned him.

"Here, according to Deren, Hatay could be Aylin's son." said Can.

"Hatay is Aylin's son?" asked Emre with wide eyes.

"That's it, we don't have proof, but... if you think about his history, his mother in prison, who didn't want him, who gave him that name as a trademark for life, who rejected him because an obstacle, and who turns out to be registered at the registry office with the surname Yuksel (although we don't know if the surname was really put by her.) admitted Can.

"There, actually if you put all these things together, it's easy to think so." he added.

"OK... OK, but what do I have to do with this?" stammered Emre in shock.

"Brother, get your head working a bit." Can urged him.

Emre thought in silence.

"Hatay is ten years old." Can began. "And you were with her until just before her arrest." he said.

"She gave birth in prison... well, actually, she did everything she could to lose him, but in the end the baby was born healthy and strong." said Can.

Emre realized.

"Hatay could be my son, is that what you are saying?" asked Emre.

"There, I don't know for sure of course, but it was Deren who put the flea in my ear. I admit I didn't really think about it." said Can.

"That's why I wasn't in the meeting this morning. I contacted someone who will give us confirmation or not." he explained.

"No... no, I mean..... It can't be. It's not like Aylin not to tell me anything. You know that too, don't you? She would definitely do anything to make my paternity known if that was the case, she wouldn't let an opportunity like that pass her by. Especially in prison." thought Emre on the verge of a breakdown.

"Well, I too thought the same thing at the time, but we know what that woman is capable of. I mean, we can expect anything from her." Can replied.

"Unless she's up to something bigger." he then added.

"What are you thinking about?" asked Emre.

"Well, in this whole story, if it were true, there's one part that doesn't add up for me." Can admitted.

"Which is? Brother spit it out." asked Emre agitatedly.

"Because Aylin who wanted to lose the baby at all costs, decided to keep it, even naming it. Doesn't that sound strange?" he reflected.

"Well, actually..." admitted Emre.

"Unless she kept it for a very specific purpose." Can mused.

"And what?" asked Emre.

"I don't know, but we'll soon find out." said Can patting his brother comfortingly.

"Sorry, if I've ruined your day, but I think you should know, I mean... you'll have to think about the consequences if this turns out to be true. You know what I'm referring to, right? With Leyla and all...' Can said.

Emre realized at that moment.

He widened his eyes in terror.

"My God... what if it's true... how do I tell Leyla?" he asked, putting his hands in his hair.

"That's why I was unsure whether to tell you now or with the confirmation in hand, brother, I didn't want to agitate you ahead of time, but... now." he said.

"No, no, brother, you did right, in fact, I thank you. It's just that my head is now bursting. I don't know what to do. I have to think." he said touching his head.

"My head's exploding too, brother." Can said.

"What do you say if me, you, and Dad go for a boat ride for a few days, huh?" he asked.

"Dad!" exclaimed Emre, putting his hands in his hair again.

"How am I going to tell Dad if it's true? He'll kill me!"

"If Leyla doesn't do it first." commented Can.

"Ah, thanks brother, you're helpful." Emre replied.

"If you don't want Dad, you and I can go." Can replied.

"I can't leave Leyla alone with Ilker." he thought.

"I'm sure Sanem will call her sister. They will all stay together." replied Can.

"Two days will be enough, you'll see. Volkan will be quick to find what we need, so we'll come back with an answer." thought Can.

"I don't know brother. Let me think about it, OK?" asked Emre.

"Come on, let's go to the gym then. We need to blow off some steam." he said getting up from the couch.

"What about work?" asked Emre.

"Leyla and Deren will take care of that. Come on." he said. Urging him to get up.

"Alright." he replied confused and shaken.

29. THOUGHTS, CLARIFICATION

AND TWISTS

After unloading in the gymnasium, Can and his brother returned to work.

All afternoon Can thought about Sanem. He was restless. With a clear mind, he was beginning to realize his mistake.

Once home that evening, he was greeted by his father, Mihriban and the little ones.

"Um, Sanem is not back yet?" he immediately asked.

"No, son, she warned that she would be late for work." replied his father.

"Ah, I see." replied Can lowering his head.

"Son, are you all right?" he asked seeing her expression. "Something wrong?" he asked.

"No, no, Dad, just tiredness." he lied.

"Ah, then get some rest, if you want we'll stay with the children, it's no problem, in fact, if you want to take the night off, we won't say no, won't we love?" he asked looking at his wife Mihriban.

"No, no... I thank you, you have already done so much. I will spend the evening with my little ones. I have missed them." he said, hinting at a smile, but it did not light up his eyes.

Aziz realized this, but said nothing.

"Yay!" exclaimed Ates running to his father.

"Night with Daddy!!!" exclaimed Deniz.

"Yay!" exclaimed Yildiz.

"Well, I'd say your kids are more than happy, so, grandparents take off then. Bye little ones!" exclaimed Mihriban.

"Bye grandma!" they exclaimed in chorus.

"Bye little rascals!" greeted them jokingly.

"Hello grandpa!" greeted them at the door.

"Dad? What are we up to?" asked Ates.

"Mh... you tell me, I'm at your disposal. But first... I need a nice, tight Albatross hug." he said, lowering himself to their height by spreading his arms wide.

The children wasted no time and catapulted themselves onto him. Can hugged all three of them, letting himself fall backwards. They all found themselves lying on the floor of the house.

He inhaled their scent and smiled serenely for the first time all day.

MEANWHILE...

Sanem left the agency and headed into the neighborhood. He arrived at Muzo's front door and rang.

He answered the intercom in a sleepy voice. "Who is it?" he asked.

"Um, Muzo, hello. I'm Sanem. Can I bother you for a second?" she asked politely.

Muzo surprised by this unexpected visit, did not refuse her and let her in.

Once she reached the flat, Muzo motioned her to take a seat in the living room.

The first thing Sanem noticed as soon as he saw him at the door was his livid eyes, the sign of someone who was not well. That wasn't just tiredness, she told herself.

Pretending nothing was wrong, she flashed a gentle smile and took a seat on the sofa he indicated.

He was still wearing his pajamas.

"I'm sorry, did I wake you up, by any chance?" he asked.

"No..." he replied, but the look said otherwise.

"I'm surprised to see you, what is the famous Sanem Aydin doing at a poor devil like me?" he asked.

"Don't say that Muzo." resumed Sanem.

"Listen, I came here, to tell you that I didn't know anything about it, OK? Not about Guliz and not about what Can told you, OK? I didn't tell him to come." she quickly specified.

"I know... I figured it out." he admitted seriously.

"Really?" she replied surprised and relieved.

"Mh mh." he replied.

"Good, I'm glad." replied Sanem hinting a smile.

"So listen, maybe for the time being I can't let you have the agency and Sanem's percentage back, but on the book I'm the only one to decide. And if you still want it, we can continue whenever you want." she said.

"Right now I'm not in a position to continue." he admitted.

"You know that, don't you? Deniz or Ayhan will have told you." he said.

"Yes, I know." admitted Sanem.

Muzo lowered his head.

"I seem to have been diagnosed with abandonment syndrome." he said almost ashamed.

Sanem raised his head sharply.

"I didn't know that." he admitted.

"Yeah..." he said with a deep sigh.

"But how are you? I mean, how are you feeling?" she asked worriedly.

"Like this." he said shrugging with the look of someone who lives knowing that something is broken inside.

Sanem felt pity and compassion. She could understand Muzo's feeling very well.

For a moment she wondered if she too had this effect in the eyes of others. Then she shook her head at the memory and, hinting at a smile, said: "Listen, you probably don't feel like doing anything right now, even breathing seems difficult. But... from experience, I

can tell you that this bad period will pass. So will many others."
she said.

"I don't know, honestly... it seems to me that this bad period never
ends, you watch! Leaving didn't help, I mean, I was sick before
and I'm sick now." he said.

"Muzo...don't say that. My friend, do you know why you are sick?
Because you didn't solve your problem before and even now. You
left, it is true, but you just avoided it. And as soon as you came
back, you relapsed." Sanem explained to him.

"You ran away, but I think you can't solve this on your own. And
now you've realized it too, haven't you?" asked Sanem in
confirmation.

Muzo nodded.

"I'm sorry, for treating you like that. I was really an animal. I
wasn't myself. Can was right." he said regretfully.

"I have already forgiven you long ago." Sanem replied with a
smile.

"Listen, I know that the words I'm about to say will sound
repetitive and matter-of-fact, but it doesn't." she said.

"You are not alone. You have all of us, even if we fight, if we
attack, if we carry the MuZo. (pun, in italian "muso" means to
keep muzzle, with the same pronunciation of his name)" said
Sanem winking at him.

Muzo, looked at her hinting a slight smile. "That was bad." he
commented.

"Oww!" blurted Sanem, adding: "At least the corners of your
mouth turned upwards."

"Anyway, what I mean to say is that it doesn't all end with a squabble. Our friendship, our projects together, don't end because of that. There will always be ups and downs." she said.

And as she said these words, she thought of Can.

"Well, yes, but I was really bad there, to yell at you like that. I don't know what came over me, here.... It was like my mind went blank for an instant. I was seeing everything red... red with anger." he admitted.

"Can was right to give me a scolding." he added.

Hearing Can mentioned several times, Sanem blurted out. "Can didn't do right at all! He should have stayed in his place, he shouldn't have allowed himself to say such things to you!" she replied decisively, getting nervous again.

Muzo looked at her impressed by her outburst.

"Did you quarrel, by any chance?" he asked.

"Forget it." Sanem replied.

"Listen, I don't want you to fight over me." he added.

"It's not like that. Old Can is back to visit me. Every tot comes back to test me." she said with a sigh.

"Anyway, let's not talk about me." said, changing the subject.

"Look, I'm not saying this because of the work in progress, but because I know how much you care about that book." Sanem replied.

"Here, if you don't want to, you don't have to feel obliged to continue. I can cancel it without any problem. But if instead, you feel like continuing this work, I will support you. I will visit you here whenever you want and we will continue from where we left off as nothing happened." he proposed.

"Right now I think my creative vein has gone out." Muzo said.

"Don't say that. It's only because you've let yourself go, but I'm convinced that deep in your heart there's still a flame burning, ready to bring that dream to life." she encouraged him.

"There, writing is what saves us, is that what you are saying?" asked Muzo.

"Exactly, my friend. It is our motto now. From the most difficult moments one can draw great energy." added Sanem with conviction.

"What I feel like saying to you is. give yourself all the time you need. Be well, let Deniz and Ayhan guide you and you will see that everything will work out." she said.

"Now you feel empty, you think you've made scorched earth around you, you feel alone in the midst of a sea of thoughts that you don't know how to unravel, so write. Get a notebook and write down whatever's on your mind, or dedicate yourself to the book you've already started, but write." she advised him.

"I'm already doing that actually." he admitted embarrassedly.

"Great. That's already a good step forward." replied Sanem.

"Remember Muzo, it is from the ashes that the Phoenix is born." she added, touching her hand in comfort. "You just have to believe." she said.

MEANWHILE AT THE ESTATE...

Can had just put the children to bed and sat in the hammock outside watching the stars. He had been waiting on the sofa for his wife to arrive, and not seeing her began to worry.

He picked up the phone and stared at her contact, the first one in the phone book. He changed his mind and thought of a message. As the bar blinked waiting for him to type the words, he realized that he did not know what to write.

Sanem was furious with him. He knew it well, and he also knew well that she had to blow off steam. He decided not to send her anything.

Put the phone down beside him and let himself be cradled in the hammock. His thoughts then shifted to his brother. So he picked up the phone again and sent a message. "What's up? Everything OK?" he asked.

Waiting for a reply, he placed the phone on his chest and, bringing an arm under the nape of his neck as a pillow, he thought back to Hatay's story.

The times when that child had been at the estate came back to him.

He dwelt on his physical appearance.

Hatay was a very tall child for his age, he thought. He had black hair, a short cut, very similar to Aylin, in fact.

His eyes were dark, quite the opposite of his brother's, he thought. But Aylin also had dark eyes.

This child might well have taken after his mother, he thought.

He lingered over the cut of the eyes. It was narrow, nothing like Aylin's.... and Emre's? He asked himself. He moved on. The mouth could well be associated with both, but in the smile, there was something familiar that Can could not decipher offhand.

As he pondered this, his brother's reply came.

"Well, everything's fine. I'm a bit tired, I'm going to bed now. Goodnight brother." he replied simply.

Can returned the message and once he placed the phone on his chest he closed his eyes, trying to relax.

IN THE NEIGHBOURHOOD...

Sanem left Muzo's house very late. Tightly wrapped in his jacket, he walked slowly towards the pier. She reached the rocks that had once been the refuge of her tears, and sat down to look at the sea.

sHe lost herself in thought, smiling at times from the nostalgia of the moment. She stayed there for a while until her sister sent her a message.

"Sister, how are you? Everything OK? If you want to talk I'm here." Leyla wrote.

Sanem was in no mood to talk, so she simply replied: "I'm fine, don't worry. We'll talk tomorrow." she replied.

She sighed. He got up and decided to walk slowly towards her parents' house.

It had been a long time since she had spent time alone with them, she told herself.

She had no intention of returning to the estate that evening.

As she walked along one of the lighted promenades along the Bosphorus full of people, taking her time, illuminated by the light of a street lamp, sitting on a bench at a distance, she noticed two familiar faces.

Sanem was petrified.

Without a second thought, she moved off the meandering lit path, hiding on one of the dark flowerbeds. She quickly gathered her hair in a low ponytail and pulled out a scarf from her bag to wrap it around her neck, so that her look would not be totally recognisable. As she closed the bag she realised that she had Deniz's sporty brim cap with her. It was dark blue with an anchor embroidered on it.

He put it on, hoping it was not too small.

The circumference was tight, but not excessively so. She made it fit.

So, in the dark, decided to move closer, slowly, hiding behind the tree closest to them, hoping to hear something.

She watched them in silence.

"What do you want Metin?" she heard her say.

He answered her to speak more softly, so from that moment on, Sanem heard nothing more, but thought it was time to capture that moment. But how? She asked herself. She absolutely had to use the flash, but that would attract attention. She had to involve someone. Get someone else to take the picture. But who?

She looked around, noticing a Simit salesman with his own cart. She thought about approaching him and asking him for a selfie posing as a tourist, but before this could happen, her eye fell on a dark tree behind her. She noticed the familiar profile of a person, who, recognising her, showed himself for a few seconds in the moonlight. It was Volkan. He too was witnessing the scene. Before she knew it, a message came to her from him.

"Mrs Sanem, you'd better leave the place before they notice you. I'll let you know as soon as possible." he wrote.

"OK." replied Sanem simply, walking away in the dark, past the flower beds, to the pavement of the main street and from there into one of the streets that led back to her parents' house.

Before entering the street home she took off her bonnet, untied her hair and removed her scarf, placing everything in her bag.

She passed by his father's shop, he was in the till and was closing it.

Nihat was sitting with his head down, counting the daily takings.

Sanem cleared his throat and knocking on the open door said in a thick voice: "Mr Nihat, you don't have any fresh ricotta cheese left by any chance?"

His father, accustomed to all the customers, replied with a low head. "We are closing, ma'am." he said.

"Ah, but is that possible? A shopkeeper never closes while he still has customers in the shop." Sanem replied.

"Come back in the morning, you will find even fresher ricotta cheese." he replied, tapping the numbers on the calculator, without looking at her.

"But I need it now. You know, my wife is making a ricotta cake that is mouth-watering! She's left in the middle of the recipe and needs it right away." said Sanem.

"Ah, the ricotta cheesecake..." commented Nihat, passing his tongue over his lips with mouth watering as his stomach grumbled at the end of the day.

"Ah, maybe accompanied with some nice nuts, and some good honey." he thought daydreaming.

"Ah, let's see if I have anything left!" he said as he looked up at the customer. "Heaven forbid the recipe gets ruined by Nihat Aydin." he said.

Sanem was leaning against the doorframe with her arms crossed.

She smiled as soon as he looked up, waving at him.

Nihat stared at her dreamily.

"Little joke!" exclaimed Sanem as soon as he recognised her.

"Sanem! Daughter!" he exclaimed.

"Hi daddy!" she exclaimed.

Nihat immediately ran to hug her.

Sanem opened her arms to greet him.

"What is my little bird doing here at this hour?" he asked looking into her eyes.

"I just left work now and went to see Muzo, Dad." she explained.

"Ah... and how is he? I heard..." her father said referring to the diagnosis.

"Yeah, I went to see how he was and made myself available for anything." she admitted.

"Sanem...despite the way he treated you?" his father asked seriously.

"Dad, don't put yourself there too. My husband is enough." she replied exhausted.

"My little bird, Can is right. He acted like a man. He protected his woman, what did you expect him to do?" asked Nihat.

"Let's not talk about that, OK dad?" she tried to close the topic.

"Alright. Listen to me, it's not like you two had a fight over this, right, you and Can?" asked Nihat seeing her change the subject.

"No, Dad, don't worry." replied his daughter so as not to worry him.

"Coming out of Muzo I told myself to visit my daddy." she said smiling.

"You did well, daughter! You did well!" he exclaimed all happy.

"And? What are the little ones doing?" he asked as if he never saw them enough.

"The little rascals are at home with Mihriban, Aziz, and Can." she replied.

"Ah, greet them so much when you return." replied his father."And tell Mr. Aziz, that I expect him soon for a good game of Bakgammon." he added.

"I will tell him, I will tell him..... Tomorrow." replied Sanem.

"How tomorrow?" asked his father.

"See, they gave me the night off, Dad. That's why I'm here at this time, otherwise I'd be long gone at the estate." replied Sanem.

"Ah..." exclaimed Nihat.

"I want to stop by and say hello to Mama." ahe said.

"Ah, then stay for dinner with us. In fact, stay over, in your little room like in the old days, how about that?" her father proposed, winking at her, elbowing her.

"Just what I was hoping for." Sanem replied.

"Then let's go for dinner. Up." hurried Nihat to say, closing the shop's shutters.

"Come, I'll take care of it, dad. "Sanem said closing the door and throwing down the shutter.

"Ah, daughter you don't have to bother." said her father.

"Ah, but what bother, I'm a shopkeeper myself!" she recalled proudly.

"Ah... so let's see." said her father testing her.

Sanem closed everything cleverly as in the past.

"That's it." she said contentedly when finished.

"Let's go." said her father hugging her.

As they walked the few meters that separated the shop from the house, Sanem noticed the space in his mother's old shop empty.

"Ah, Brother Tekil, has it closed down?" asked Sanem to his father.

"Yes, he moved." Nihat replied.

"He opened his tailoring shop in the street where he lives, a lease had opened up apparently." he replied.

"Ah..." commented Sanem. "There, good for him." she commented. "So he will be closer to his family." said.

"Yeah." commented his father. Arriving in front of the house without being stopped by anyone, Sanem became worried and asked: "Dad, where is Melihat? Why is everything closed? What's going on in this neighborhood, huh?" she asked strangely, furrowing her brow.

Her father slipped the key into the door and before turning it, turned to her. "She's gone on holiday!" he exclaimed all delighted.

"Ah, really?" asked Sanem surprised.

"Yay!" Her father exclaimed, pretending to wipe away a tear.

"Dad... don't be like that otherwise I'll cry too." said Sanem, then added "Of joy!" she exclaimed.

They laughed like two children.

"You know I was thinking of throwing a party! Did you hear that silence? Unreal! I don't think I've ever heard such silence in all my life." said Nihat moved.

"How long will it last?" asked Sanem then.

"As long as possible, I hope!" was his father's prompt reply.

"Look, I can even dance in the middle of the road without her noticing." he said, dragging his daughter with him to the middle of the roadway, spinning her around in an impromptu dance.

"Daddy!" exclaimed Sanem, feeling suddenly jolted.

They both laughed, then Sanem, caught up in the moment, grabbed her father's hands and together they tangoed their way along the entire length of the street in front of the house: from shop to house and back, in absolute silence, until they heard Mevkibe whispering to them from the upstairs window.

"Nihat? Sanem! Have you gone mad? What are you doing in the middle of the street at night at this hour?" she asked.

The two stopped below the house, and still with intertwined hands looked up at her.

"Come into the house now, come on!" she scolded them in a whisper so as not to attract attention.

"Two children... two children..." she commented as she closed the window and then reached the front door.

Sanem and his father entered the house laughing.

Mevkibe stopped at the foot of the stairs.

"Sanem daughter, what are you doing here?" she asked surprised to see her.

"Ah, Mevkibe! Is this the way to welcome your daughter?" asked Nihat looking at her crookedly.

"You could show a little more joy." he said.

"I came to see you, Mama." Sanem replied, seeing that her mother was still staring at her. She was analyzing her, she knew.

"Shall I leave?" she then asked, honing her abandonment technique. She placed her hand on the door handle and without being seen winked at her father.

Her mother immediately replied: "No, child, I just didn't expect to see you. Here, not at this hour." she replied.

"You're all right, aren't you? You didn't have a fight with Can, did you, child?" she asked quickly.

"No mum. I missed your treats." she replied.

"Sanem is staying with us tonight, she just left work." said her father.

"She will sleep in her room." he added all happy.

"What do you mean?" asked Mevkibe.

"Something bad happened, then." she deduced.

"Ah!!! Mevkibe, why does something bad have to have happened? Huh? My God!" exclaimed Nihat exasperatedly as he started towards the kitchen, having put on his slippers.

"Indeed... come mum, I'll explain now." said Sanem hugging her. "But let's sit down at the table, because dad is starving." she said taking her arm, after kissing her on the cheeks.

They reached the kitchen.

Mevkibe immediately hurried to add an extra place at the table, while his father was already ready sitting at the head of the table with his napkin stuck in the lapel of his shirt, and cutlery in hand, like a wolf ready to devour its prey.

Sanem smiled and, as before, prepared to cheer for his father. She immediately prepared the glass full of water for him.

Her mother as usual was never caught unprepared, she always prepared large quantities of food, not only to share with the neighborhood but also knowing she had a good fork at the table.

Sanem started cheering as soon as she saw a tray full of dolma laid on the table. 'Go daddy! Go dad!" she exclaimed.

Not even time to put the tray down that Nihat went on the attack.

Mevkibe let her husband satiate himself by stuffing himself with the contents of that tray.

In the meantime, she took out a smaller one reserved for herself and whoever else was at the table.

It was always like this, she always had to prepare double portions of dishes.

While he gobbled, accompanied by his daughter's cheers, Mevkibe pulled a steaming spinach borek out of the oven.

As soon as Nihat caught a whiff of it, he immediately left the dolma to pounce on it. Anticipating this move too, Mevkibe let Nihat gobble down the larger borek starting from the center, his favourite part, and then pulled out a smaller one.

At that point, Mevkibe and her daughter were also allowed to dine.

As they ate, Sanem explained how she had come to them at that hour, where she had been and all that.

"Ah, that poor son is really sick." she commented when the subject fell to Muzo. "Not that he's ever been really well, eh!" she said pointing to her head. "But you did well to visit him. Well done daughter!" added Mevkibe.

After dinner and catching up on neighborhood gossip, munching seeds on the sofa under the window as in the old days, her mother came out with: "Ah, if only Can had been here too! I need his advice for the neighborhood association." she said with a sigh.

"I have to think of something new." she admitted.

Sanem listened to her in silence.

"Tell him on the way back that I'll call him soon." she concluded.

"Alright, Mama, I'll tell him." was Sanem's brief reply.

After that she took advantage of a yawn from her mother and invited her to go and rest. Her father was already asleep, lying on the sofa next to them.

Sanem wanted to be alone. She needed to think quietly.

So after persuading her father to get up, and saying goodbye to both of them, she retired to what had once been her bedroom.

It is said that when we are upset we always go home.

Opening that door was a plunge into the past.

His father had not let his wife touch anything. Everything had stood still, as if time had frozen at the last time she had closed that door to begin a new chapter of her life.

She looked at all the items that were most important to her.

The Albatros poster, the post-it note with the password 'Albatros' affixed to the dressing table mirror, the white flower crown created during the Arzu Tas photo shoot and many other items.

On seeing them, she was overwhelmed with nostalgia.

She took off her slippers and sat on the bed, looking up at the ceiling. That room had been for her a refuge and guardian of secrets, laughter and tears. So many tears.

Once safely inside her bubble, she let out a silent cry. She did not exactly know the reason for those tears either.

It was as if the past, the present and the future suddenly exploded from her eyes. A mixture of conflicting emotions that she only found vented in that way.

Some highlights of her history with Can came back to her mind, from the saddest to the happiest. Looking at her small wardrobe she thought of the last morning she had spent in that room, when hanging there was her wedding dress ready to leave with her to the estate for the ceremony.

She remembered the excitement and the grin from ear to ear that showed no sign of easing from her face when at first light she was already awake with excitement as she contemplated the poster of the Albatross in front of her. She smiled in turn, thinking about how far she had come since that day, and how things had changed. Thinking about the last few days and the fight that morning, her smile faded, giving way to a mixture of anger and old grudges.

She instinctively found the bed uncomfortable, so she got up to reach her beloved desk chair. Puffing, she looked at the sky beyond the window in front of her. Her gaze lingered on a row of trees on the horizon, beyond the neighborhood houses, and there his mind connected with other thoughts.

She thought back to the scene she had seen in the park.

She frowned thoughtfully.

She still could not believe what she had seen.

"Does that mean that Metin knows Ezgi"

"Why does Metin know Ezgi?" she asked herself.

Thinking back to the way she had answered Metin, Sanem deduced that they had known each other for a while.

With her words, "What more do you want, Metin?" she had rolled her eyes, as if this was not the first time he had bothered her.

She reflected.

"Just a minute... Could Metin bother Ezgi?" she wondered.

"Are they friends?" wondered Sanem.

"What a strange coincidence…" she thought. "Both of them in different ways are close to Deren."

"Or... is she also part of the plan with Deren's father? No, no, I don't even want to think about it. That would be absurd. No, I refuse." she said to herself, shaking her head.

"Though grandma's dress and all..." thought a little voice inside her. "No, no, Sanem don't be silly. It's not possible." she said to herself.

"Hmm... although... Metin could have lured her to the wedding having realized the closeness with Deren. That wouldn't be so strange." she continued.

"I mean, why else would a lawyer like him talk to a wedding dressmaker like Ezgi. What reason would he have?" she thought.

Suddenly, Sanem's eyes went wide, closing her mouth.

"Or.... One minute. Hold it! What if Metin... My God! Isn't it that Metin is making contact with Ezgi about Deniz? Oh Lord, they're getting married!" she exclaimed, plugging her mouth as she pulled her wheelchair back into the middle of the room.

She stood up.

"What does it mean? Deniz is getting married... I mean, my trusted therapist psychologist is getting married, and she doesn't tell me anything?!" she thought angrily.

"Ah, if that were the case other than 'Little Lamb' as she always calls me.... she'll have to call me 'Bull' because of how furious I get." She thought.

Then she sat back down. Her gaze grew serious.

"But if she marries Metin... what will happen to Muzo?" she wondered sadly.

"Maybe that's why no one knows?" She thought then. "Are they marrying in great secrecy so as not to upset Muzo further?" she wondered.

Only Deniz would do such a thing. Certainly not Metin.

At that point, Sanem without realizing it, let her head go backwards on the back of the chair looking at the ceiling as she gave herself the push with one foot to turn around.

"What a mess..." she thought aloud.

It was at that moment that the flow of her thoughts was interrupted by the sound of a message.

Sanem straightened up from his chair and picked up the phone placed on the desk.

It was Volkan.

"Mrs Sanem,

if it is all right with you, I would ask you to meet me tomorrow morning at dawn, in the same place as our last meeting.

I await your confirmation.

V."

To those lines she immediately replied.

"OK."

After this exchange Sanem picked up the phone and went back to bed, her eyes turned to the ceiling, she couldn't help thinking about this increasingly intricate matter.

"If Volkan wants to talk to me, maybe then it's true that something shady is going on between Metin and Ezgi?" she asked herself.

Her brain could think of nothing else.

Suddenly all this thinking gave her a headache.

And so slowly, exhausted, she curled in on herself and closed her eyes.

30. TIMING GAME

At 5 am Sanem's brain decided to get going again, despite the few hours of sleep, which forced her to get up early.

She reached the kitchen where she prepared a nice steaming tea for herself and her father, who, as was the custom, would shortly wake up to open the shop.

When Nihat saw her awake at that hour, sitting at the table in the garden, he joined her still sleepy rubbing his eyes.

"Good morning daddy." she greeted him with a smile.

"Good morning..." he replied, yawning.

"Daughter? Why are you up so early?" asked her father.

"Here, I was waiting for you to wake up so we can have tea together and let you know I'm coming home. I have to change and run to the lab. They called me in for some developments on a new fragrance I've been working on for some time." she lied partly.

"Ah..." her father replied, waking up.

"Sorry, I won't be able to have breakfast with you." said Sanem.

"Don't worry, my daughter, it was already good that you stayed here to sleep." he said. "Breakfast together will be for another time."

"We will make it up. I promise." she replied as she got up to serve tea to her father.

"Enjoy it. I'm off." said once she placed the cup in front of him and greeted him with a kiss on the cheek.

"Bye child! Take care on the way." he repeated to her as always.

"Don't worry daddy, I'm not driving. The driver is waiting for me at the entrance of the neighborhood." she reminded him.

"Ah, I know, but still, you can never be too careful." her father replied.

"Say hello to mummy for me, will you?" she asked her.

"Of course, my child." her father replied, sipping his tea. Come back more often!" shouted after him as she had already reached the front door.

As soon as she was out, she turned to the right at a brisk pace. She felt watched, as she did every time she was in the neighborhood. Surely some neighbor was watching her, or if not them, surely her father or mother from some windows.

Once she reached the exit of the neighborhood, she looked around and turned left, slowing her pace to reach the park nearby.

At that hour there was no one around. Just a few rare people running. As she approached the spot indicated to her, under a large tree with thick foliage she noticed the figure of a man wearing a hat.

His back was turned. It was definitely Volkan.

She crossed the road and caught up with the man behind her.

When he heard footsteps approaching, the man turned around. Volkan took off his sunglasses and greeted him with a smile.

For a fraction of a second, just a fraction of a second, she had thought to looking at another person.

Fortunately that was not the case. She breathed a sigh of relief and greeted him.

"There is news, I presume." Sanem deduced.

"There is." he confirmed. "I think I have discovered the secret, Mrs Divit." he declared.

Sanem squinted her eyes. "Really?"

Volkan nodded.

"You found out last night?" she asked remembering the scene.

"Not really... I'll explain now." he said.

AT THE DIVIT'S HOUSE...

Meanwhile, at the estate, Can awakened in his hammock by the first light of dawn, and returning to his room, not seeing his wife at all he hung up on the phone taken aback by worry. The nervousness of the previous day had given way to fear that something had happened to her. On the phone he saw no message or missed call, a sign that she had not contacted him.

He tried to call her. The phone was switched off.

"Where are you Sanem... where are you..." he repeated to himself.

While preparing breakfast for the children he sent a message to his brother.

"Good morning brother, is Sanem at your place by any chance?" he sent.

229

Meanwhile, the little ones hurriedly joined him in the kitchen.

"Good morning." he greeted them.

All three rubbed their sleepy eyes, while Yildiz and Deniz yawned as they took a seat at the table, Ates, frowned and asked: "Dad? Where's Mum?"

There, the very question Can feared most that morning.

"Um... I'll take care of you this morning, I'll take you to school. Mum... had to leave early for work." he said hastily.

"And when did she come back? She wasn't even there last night...' she reminded.

At that point, Yildiz and Deniz also raised their antennae.

"Um... you're right, child, and do you know why? Because mum stayed over at uncles Leyla and Emre's."

"And how do you know she left early for work then?" asked Deniz.

"Because I just spoke to her." he answered offhand, serving the eggs on their plates, already full of vegetables and cheese.

"She sends her love, and she's sorry not to be with you this morning." he then added, to sound more believable.

At that point Can, seeing the children's faces, clapped his hands, and said: "Come on, to the table!"

As they ate, he walked away from the kitchen counter to the children's room.

He heard a notification on his mobile phone.

He went back and picked up the phone from the living room sideboard on which it was resting.

"Is that Mum?" asked Ates immediately with her mouth full.

Can checked.

"No, it's uncle." he replied seriously after reading the message.

"No, Sanem is not with us. Why? Did something else happen, brother?" replied Emre.

"No." replied Can simply.

He tried to call her back but got no answer. It was still switched off. As he stared at the phone, thinking where she might be, he realised. Maybe he knew where to find her.

"Come on, children, quickly, we have to leave the house before this morning." he told them.

"Why?" asked Yildiz.

"Because otherwise we will find too much traffic." he replied.

"What about the other days then dad?" commented Deniz.

"Just because of that, you've seen that there's construction going on along the road we take, right?" insisted Can.

"Oww but then we'd have to gorge ourselves, Dad!" blurted Ates with her mouth full.

Yildiz and Deniz laughed.

"Alright, Ates, my daughter, eat normally, but hurry up and get dressed afterwards, alright?" said her father.

Unable to answer for the too-big bite, she raised her thumbstick, nodding.

"Ates... you're always the same." his brother commented.

Ates narrowed her double-slit eyes, staring at him as she chewed with great vigor. She looked like one of those squirrels with cheeks full of acorns.

Too sweet.

MEANWHILE...

Sanem shocked by Volkan's revelations stopped on a bench by the sea to think.

"What will I do now?" she asked herself.

She waited for the documents he had promised to send.

The story was so clear now and so absurd at the same time, that for a moment Sanem thought about not showing up at the office at all and working remotely at home.

But then she realized that she would have to come to the company anyway, she lacked the material.

She looked at her watch. She realized that she had been sitting longer than she thought, so she hurried to call the driver who joined her shortly afterwards.

"To the estate." she said as she got in.

On the way, however, a question arose, so she composed a short message for Volkan.

Once she arrived, she asked the driver to wait for her and entered the house. It was empty. She freshened up, changed, took the necessary things and went out again.

MEANWHILE...

After dropping the children off at school Can headed into the neighbourhood. He parked in front of Muzo's house, got out and before he could ring the bell, he found Ayhan hurriedly leaving.

"Can?" she asked almost jerking in fear of suddenly finding him in front of her.

"Ayhan?" he replied. "Good morning."

"Um... Good morning." she said. "I'm late, I know, but it was my turn to stop by Muzo. I had to check that everything was OK." she tried to explain before he could say anything.

"Don't worry, it's good I found you." Can replied.

"Why? What's going on?" she immediately asked frowning.

"Have you seen Sanem? I mean, has she seen herself here?" he asked pointing to the house behind him.

"Um, she came by for a visit yesterday, according to what Muzo said, then she left." Ayhan replied.

"Are you sure about that? You're not lying to me, are you?" he asked staring into her eyes.

"Lying to you? Why would I lie to you, Can? I didn't understand. What happened to my sister?" asked Ayhan worrying.

"Nothing, nothing... never mind," replied Can sighing.

"Ah... now I understand." exclaimed Ayhan. "Cey Cey told me last night about your fight at the office. She didn't sleep at home, is that so?" asked Ayhan.

Can nodded.

"I tried to call her a lot of times, but her phone is off." he admitted.

"Until last night, I thought I should give her her space to cool off, but when I woke up this morning and saw that she still hadn't returned, I started to worry." Can admitted.

"Maybe she went to Leyla's. thought Ayhan.

"No, she's not at her place either. I asked my brother." replied Can dejectedly.

"Mhh..." said Ayhan reflectively.

"If you want I can drop by Mevkibe and Nihat's, I'll try to see if she had been by them." she proposed.

"No, thanks, I think I'll go by there now. Since I'm here..." he said.

"If you hear from her though, let me know right away, alright?" asked Can.

"Alright, sure." she replied.

Can opened the car door.

"Can?" called Ayhan.

"Don't take it to heart. And don't worry too much. Sanem is definitely fine, she just needs some time alone. When she's like this she does everything she can not to be found. She's been like that since they were little." she tried to console him with a smile.

"I know." he replied.

"You will see that she will reappear on her own.... when she is ready." added Ayhan.

Can nodded unconvinced.

"See you in the company." he greeted her.

"See you later." replied Ayhan as she set off on foot.

Once had moved the car in front of Aydin's house, Can got out and rang the bell.

A few seconds later it was Mevkibe who greeted him.

"Can? Son? Welcome!" she exclaimed enthusiastically as soon as she saw him.

"Mama Mevkibe? Good morning." replied Can with a big serene smile as he did every time he saw his beloved mother-in-law.

"Come, come, come, come, come on in." she said inviting him inside.

"Um... OK." he replied even though he was in a bit of a hurry. Entering and putting on the pair of slippers with his name embroidered on them that Mevkibe had made especially for him since he had become his son-in-law, she continued, towards the kitchen, saying: "Ah, this time Sanem has really been true to her word."

"Why?" asked Can.

"Like why son? But to get help from my personal adviser on new activities to propose for the association. Isn't that why you are here?" she asked.

"Um... of course." commented Can with a slight initial uncertainty.

"You know, I was just telling Sanem after dinner last night, son!" she said as she entered the kitchen.

"Tea, son?" asked, heading for the cooker.

"Of course, I never turn down a good tea." Can replied.

"Have a seat at the table, my son. It will be ready in a few minutes." she said placing the ready-made kettle on the stove.

"Have you had breakfast? I made a hot borek this morning, you must taste it!" she said preparing.

Mevkibe was like that, talking non-stop. I wonder by who got Sanem from?

"Eh, meanwhile think, son... what could I do in association? That's it, we constantly need to raise funds for work in the neighborhood. I don't know what to come up with anymore." she admitted desperately.

"One minute." he then added. "But shouldn't you be at work at this hour?" she asked looking him straight in the eye after glancing at the clock hanging on the column in the middle of the kitchen.

"Well... actually I should, but, lo and behold, I was in the neighborhood, so I said to myself: "I'll run and help my beloved mother-in-law." replied Can.

"Ah, my son! You are too dear!" she said, running to hug him.

Can reciprocated.

Mevkibe placed a steaming cup of tea and borek in front of him.

"Enjoy your tea, son." she said.

Can sipped the tea, and then tasted the borek, starting in the middle, just as Nihat did. Then he gave her a sidelong glance.

"Don't worry son, eat, eat, eat." she encouraged him.

"How is it?" she asked, as Can chewed with gusto.

Once he swallowed, he replied, "Really, really good! Bless your hands, mother Mevkibe!" he said, taking her hands in his.

"Oh, I'm glad, eat, eat, eat, son. These muscles must be fed properly. Help yourself." she said, pleased to see him eating with taste.

Once he had his encore, as Mevkibe was explaining to him in depth about the association, the light bulb went on in Can.

"Mama Mevkibe? I had an idea." he said suddenly.

"Tell me, son, right away, tell me, tell me, tell me." she said grabbing her glasses, paper and pen, ready to write like a pupil waiting for the teacher's words.

MEANWHILE...

Arriving at Fikri Harika, Sanem silently reached her office downstairs. Unlike other mornings, she was in no mood to stop at the counter with the others at Cey Cey's. sHe didn't want to meet anyone. Not after what she had heard.

Stepping out of the lift, in front of the entrance to his company, Sanem stood in front of Metin.

"Sanem? Good morning." he greeted her with a polite smile.

"Good morning Metin." she replied without too much enthusiasm. She was in no mood to pretend or hold back.

She got past him.

"Are you all right?" he asked seeing her like that.

"I'm fine, thank you. You?" he asked more out of politeness than genuine interest.

"Great, couldn't be better." she replied beaming.

"I notice a certain good mood today, or am I wrong?" she asked then focusing her attention on him.

"Not wrong." he admitted nervously.

"What's going on? If I may ask." said Sanem.

"There will be good news soon." he said, "But I can't say anything yet." he added.

"Who are you telling..." commented Sanem thoughtlessly.

"You too?" asked Metin wrinkling his forehead in confusion.

"Huh?" asked Sanem.

"You too have some news you can't share yet?" he asked.

"Exactly... you know, when you write a story you want everyone to know, but you can't do spoilers due to bureaucratic issues?" replied Sanem mischievously with a mixture of truth and fiction.

"Ah, I get it... you've written a new book but you can't let anyone know about it yet? Did I understand correctly?" he asked.

"Very well…" she replied lying.

"If only you knew what story I'm referring to." thought Sanem to herself.

"Don't worry… " said Metin in a low voice, "Your secret is safe with me." he whispered.

"And sure, you're the master of secrets lately." she would have liked to answer him Sanem, but only a whispered: "Thank you", came out of her mouth.

"Sorry I have to go now." she hastened to leave him.

"Sure, see you." replied Metin.

"Bye." she replied.

Sanem walked transfixed into her office and closed the door.

She slumped in her chair, thinking: was he sincere or was he probing the ground to make sure I knew? She was now suspicious of everything.

A few hours later his sister like a tornado entered in her office, knocking three times, then locking the door behind her.

"Please come in, sister, I would say, but… you're already in." Sanem replied sarcastically, looking at her unwillingly.

"What are you doing?" she asked when she saw she was locking up.

Her sister pointed her finger at her and said decisively: "Now you explain to me what's going on. Where were you last night, huh? Why is your phone perpetually off?" she asked nervously in anger.

"No, it's not off." she replied confused, rummaging through her bag looking for it. Once she pulled it out however, she realized that her sister was right.

"It must have run out without me realizing." she commented.

"Where did you sleep last night? Why didn't you come home? What's going on between you and Can, huh?" she asked.

As Sanem was asked that series of questions one after the other, she felt as if she were going back in time, when her sister demanded that she, as a minor, had to account to her for every step she took.

Angered by that attitude she stood up and said staring at her seriously: "Sister! What happens between me and Can only concerns me and him, OK?! I don't have to explain myself to you or anyone else if I don't want to. Please respect my will." she answered her in a low voice.

Leyla hearing that tone lowered 'the crest', replying: "It's alright, sister, sorry, I put too much emphasis, it's just that I'm worried about you. When Can called Emre this morning and said you hadn't returned, that's it... I panicked, sorry." she said, dropping exhausted into the desk chair in front of her.

"What, what?" asked Sanem. "Can called you?" she asked.

"Well, actually, he didn't call, but he sent a message to Emre this morning asking if you were at our place." she pointed out.

Sanem remained silent.

"Where have you been Sanem?" her sister asked in a quieter tone.

"I stayed at mum and dad's." she replied. "I needed to be alone. But, I didn't tell them anything. They only know that I was late for work. The children were with Mihraban and Aziz."

"And Can..." replied Leyla. It was not a question.

Sanem looked at her.

"Sanem what happened?" she asked with a sigh. "Why did you fight like that yesterday?" she asked displeased.

"What is the reason for all that anger?" she added.

"The exasperation sister. Exasperation!" repeated Sanem nervously.

"This last period has been so strange, intense, chaotic, frustrating and challenging that my head is cracking." she admitted, touching her temples.

"I don't know what I can say and what I can't say, I don't know what's right anymore... and in all of this, the old possessive Can comes peeping back, too." she said.

"One minute, one minute, one minute..." her sister stopped her.

"What do you mean I don't know what I can say or is right to do anymore?" she asked.

"What are you hiding Sanem?" asked her sister.

"Sister, listen, it would be too long to tell now, okay? I promise that when I am ready I will tell you, but not here." replied Sanem.

"And especially not now." she said getting up to gather her things.

Leyla looked at her.

"Where are you going?" she asked.

"Out. I made a mistake coming to the office today." she said without adding anything else as she hurried off.

Her sister did not even have the chance to ask her anything. Confused, she watched her leave.

Once outside Fikri Harika, Sanem breathed heavily, she felt as if she had been in apnoea for a long time.

Her driver, who was waiting outside, got out to open the car door and let her in.

As soon as she saw him position himself behind the wheel, Sanem said: "At home."

"All right, Mrs Divit." replied the driver.

Meanwhile, Can arrived at Fikri Harika that it was almost lunchtime.

The meeting with his mother-in-law had taken longer than expected but had borne good fruit.

Soon a very important community service would open in the neighborhood.

Before going through his own office, he decided to join his wife downstairs. From Mevkibe he had obtained all the information he needed without asking for anything, and he knew that Sanem had stopped by the workshop early, as she often did, before reaching the company, so she had to be there.

He couldn't wait to share her mother's good news.

He hurried down the stairs whistling, and so to her office, when he knocked and entered and saw it was empty, he frowned in confusion.

The desk was all tidy, as always. Sanem never left anything out of place.

"Has she not come yet?" "Or has she not come at all?" he wondered.

"Maybe she's up at the agency." he said to himself.

So he left the office, closing it behind him.

As he reached the stairs again he passed Deniz.

"Deniz? Have you seen Sanem?" he asked.

"Ah, Can, hello. Um, no, I haven't seen her today." she replied.

"How... she didn't come to the company?" asked Can.

"I don't know, I just arrived recently, I had therapy with Muzo." she said sorry she couldn't help.

"But maybe she's upstairs." she added seeing Deniz's confused expression.

"Alright, thank you." replied Can running off.

"You're welcome." replied Deniz to the wind.

Can flew up the stairs back to the agency, as he reached Cey Cey's counter, he looked for her among the many faces around.

"Cey Cey, have you seen Sanem?" he asked distractedly with a glance towards the offices.

"Ah, good morning, Mr Can. You're late today." Cey Cey greeted him first.

"Eh, yes I had an engagement." he replied distractedly.

"Anyway no, Sanem didn't show up here," Deren replied for him as he arrived at the counter.

"Can? What's going on, are you OK?" she asked seeing him distracted.

"Huh?" he replied turning to look at her.

"Everything's fine, everything's fine." he replied.

"Well, everything may be fine, but it didn't seem like it yesterday." Deren said.

"I said all is well." repeated Can in a tone that did not admit of repartee.

"Mrs Deren, usually you are the one to take me back in these circumstances, but this time I am forced to do so with you. Don't you understand that Mr Can does not want to talk about it?" rebuked Cey Cey.

"Mr Can, I would suggest you ask Leyla. She is her sister and probably knows where she is." proposed Cey Cey.

"Thank you." replied Can as he reached Leyla's office.

He knocked and entered.

"Can, good morning." she greeted him.

"Good morning, Leyla, have you seen Sanem? Or do you know where she is?" he asked.

"Um... yes I have seen her. She was in her office until just now, then she went out." she replied.

"Left...and where did she go?" he asked.

"I don't know, she didn't tell me. When I asked her, she simply said: "Out." and ran off before I could ask anything else." She admitted.

"Ah... what mood was she in, do you think?" asked Can.

"Confused I dare say... she wasn't in a chatty mood, that is." precise.

"Can, is everything alright between you two?" she then asked.

"I swear everyone is asking me the same thing. To be honest, at this point, I don't even know anymore, Leyla." admitted Can.

"I know she spent last night at our parents'." she added.

"Yes, I heard that too. Your mother told me this morning when I stopped by." he replied.

"Ah, you stopped by?" asked Leyla.

"Yes, and before that I spoke to Ayhan whom I met there in the neighborhood, and she didn't know anything either." he added.

"But there was one sentence she said that really struck me. "If Sanem wants to disappear, she knows how to do it... or something like that, she said. Is that true?" he asked focusing her.

"Can, I saw her very tired. Maybe she just needs a rest." replied Leyla briefly.

"Yes, tired... of me." he replied.

"Don't say that..." said Leyla.

"Whatever happened between you, try to make peace with her, OK? Try to understand each other and come to terms. I'm sorry to see you like this." she admitted sincerely.

Can nodded and quietly went back to his office.

AT DIVIT'S HOUSE...

Meanwhile, once at the estate, Sanem put on more comfortable clothes and took a long walk to the jetty, carrying her diary and pen. She let herself be lulled by the silence of the sea waves, transcribing everything she felt. Once she was free, she snapped the diary shut and breathed deeply with her closed eyes turned towards the sea on the horizon. She stayed there for a while, enjoying that peace. Then once she had gathered her thoughts, relaxed and with one less weight in her chest, she headed resolutely back to the estate. Before returning home, she had to talk to someone.

Now she knew what to do.

31. *STUBBORN*

Sitting in that large living room, Sanem waited to speak to the only person capable of understanding her at that moment.

Her very loyal sister Mihriban. Her second mother.

"Here are our teas." she said, emerging from the kitchen with a tray.

They were alone, Aziz had gone out. Taking advantage of the beautiful day, he had decided to drop by Nihat's. There was still the promise of a rematch from his last defeat at backgammon, and it was also a way for in-laws to be together. From there the two would then pick up the children from school and Aziz would take them to the estate.

"So daughter, tell me about it. I am surprised to see you home at this hour. Something is wrong, isn't it?" she asked.

"I swear, Sister Mihriban if I don't tell someone... my brain will burst." said Sanem.

"My God...what is tormenting you so much? Don't scare me. Come on, tell." she urged her.

Sanem took a sip of tea, and began with the following sentence:

"I have discovered everything." she said.

"What did you find out?" asked Mihriban naively.

"Deren..." she merely pronounced.

"Ah!!!" she exclaimed. "And?"

"I would rather not have known. Because now I'm in such a situation that I don't know what to do, I don't know how to behave.... " she admitted, snorting in exasperation.

"What do you mean? Come on, tell me! Don't make me die of curiosity." Mihriban begged her.

Sanem began to recount everything that had happened from the last time she had spoken to her until the discovery that morning.

"My God, child, I can't believe it.... is even worse than I imagined." she commented at the end of the tale.

"Yeah, you see now? I didn't even want to go to the office this morning, I did everything I could to avoid crossing paths with others. There are so many people involved that, how am I going to look them in the face now knowing the truth, huh?" she wondered snappily.

"If I spoke, it would create a ruckus in the agency and the company, and I don't want that..." she admitted.

"But you know not, that sooner or later the truth will come out..." replied Mihriban.

"I know, but do I really want to take responsibility for telling the truth, compromising the relationship between me and the people involved?" she asked desperately.

"This is the punishment for meddling in affairs that do not concern me. Can was right. I should have played dumb from the start and worried about the problems in my life." she replied.

"But you did it for the good you want for the people around you, not with bad intentions." Mihriban justified her.

"And then sorry, what do you mean my problems, Sanem? What problems are there in your life, child?" she asked, dwelling on those words.

Sanem hinted a slight smile and with sad eyes confided: "In all this mess, I also missed fighting with my husband." she said.

"Did you fight with Can?" asked Mihriban surprised and sorry.

Sanem nodded. "And why?" she asked back.

Sanem told him about the fight the day before at the office and the rest of the evening.

"Ah, child... what need was there to come to this, eh?" commented Mihriban.

"I can't stand it! I can't stand it when Can is possessive, making decisions for me. I never liked it, even in the past! And he knows it very well, he was one of the reasons I moved away when I was working at the publishing house with Yigit for the publication of my first novel, and you know very well what it led to too." vented Sanem.

"Well, child, you're right about that, I mean, Can shouldn't have spoken for you without your consent, I'll give you that, but... he didn't do it with bad intentions." she tried to justify it.

"I know! But have I ever allowed myself to make decisions for him about his career as a photographer, for example? No, never! Not even for the companies we are partners in, have I done that... so what right does he have to do that to me? Just because I cried? I'm sorry, because I've never cried for him? It doesn't make sense! He's jealous!" Sanem vented.

Mihriban remained silent.

"We always told ourselves that we had learnt and would continue to learn from our mistakes, and instead, here we are!" she concluded.

"Sanem, child, you are right, but I think you need to focus more on your marriage to Can than anything else at this point. Look at you! You have three wonderful children that so many would dream of having…" she tried to reason with her.

Sanem listened, shaking out her hair, which in the heat of speaking had partly covered her eyes.

"I think you need to eliminate everything around you, and devote all your attention to Can and your children. Maybe with a nice boat trip alone, what do you say? Maybe in the middle of the sea you will find your way and your balance again." Mihriban proposed.

Sanem remained silent, then replied: "I don't know."

"And don't think about that again. After all, nothing happened, right? I mean, Metin didn't hurt or threaten anyone, so remember, if it's meant to be, it will happen." She said, trying to cheer her up.

"OK, but how will I ever look Deren in the face again? And Deniz? And Burak? I put him in the middle as well." she recalled.

"Sanem, it's very simple. Let go. You can't make everyone else happy if you're unhappy yourself first, you know? Look around, I mean, Deren is happy and peaceful with her family.

Ezgi is her close friend, Metin has done nothing wrong and continues his affair with Deniz. In the eyes of the others in the agency at the moment, those who have problems are only you and Can." Mihriban pointed out to her.

Sanem nodded, "That's true. You are right."

"So to Ayhan, Cey Cey, Muzo, and Burak you can simply say that there is nothing new. You will see that slowly even their attention will be focused more on work than anything else." she replied with conviction.

"And remember that if we notice anything suspicious, knowing the history, if any of our loved ones were threatened, we could intervene. I am and always will be with you, my daughter." Mihriban concluded, laying a hand on hers.

"Thank you, Sister Mihriban. I am so happy to have you in my life!" she said hugging her.

"Ah, my daughter, the same goes for you. Do you by any chance want to make me cry?" she asked wiping the outer corner of her right eye.

Sanem broke away from the embrace and with her new-found humor looked at her resolutely: "Fine, but Can has to apologize to me!" she said stubbornly.

"Oh, Mrs Sanem I am convinced he will." she replied seeing her determination.

As they laughed, the triplets arrived.

"Mummy!" they exclaimed as they entered when they saw her.

"Ah, mama's little birds!" she exclaimed spreading her arms wide as the little ones swooped into her arms sinking into the sofa all at once. She began to snog them all inhaling deeply of their scent.

"My God how I missed you!" she exclaimed.

In the meantime, Aziz, who had stayed behind, also entered.

"And you missed me, huh?" she asked.

"A lot." replied Deniz.

"How much?" asked Sanem again.

"So much." replied Yildiz.

"So, so, so much!" exclaimed Ates, spreading her arms like a little Albatross.

"Wow, that's a lot!" she exclaimed, clutching all three of them to her chest again.

Sanem looked at Aziz. "Daddy Aziz? So who won this time?" she asked.

Aziz, first made a sullen face and then smiling, spreading her arms nonchalantly, replied: "Of course me!" he said with a big smile.

"Ouch, I wonder how poor Nihat will be now..." commented Mihriban.

"Ah, Dad... why does he insist on fighting you again? We all know you're the best at backgammon." replied Sanem.

"He definitely does it to practice, he hopes to get to your level." said Mihriban winking at him.

"Mom, we drew you a picture!" exclaimed Yildiz.

"Mum? " pronounced Ates frowning seriously, placing her hands on her hips.

"Why did you abandon us last night?" she asked.

Sanem looked around, her eyes wide with fright. She met Mihriban's gaze for a split second, then looked at her watch, and getting up abruptly, said: "Come on kids, let's go home so we can all play together!"

Aziz looked at Mihriban confused.

In no time Sanem said goodbye to everyone and took the children away, and before Aziz could ask anything, it was Mihriban who put all doubts to rest.

"Why did she say that?" asked Aziz.

"No, nothing... basically last night Sanem came back very late from work, there's a fragrance she's been studying that's been giving her some headaches for a while now, so when she arrived at the estate the children were already in bed, and this morning she had to run off again at dawn because she received the results of some tests. So the little ones didn't even see her when they woke up. That's why Ates said that." she concluded her lie naturally.

"Ah... I get it." replied Aziz relaxing as he took a seat next to her on the sofa.

Meanwhile, when they arrived home, the children showed the drawings they had made.

It was Yildiz who explained it to her. The drawing was made up of several sheets put together, three to be exact, one for each. "This is you, this is us, and in the middle is a big heart." she explained, as his brothers joined the pieces together.

"Wow, you actually made this?" asked Sanem in amazement.

"Mh mh." they replied in chorus.

"Wow, that's beautiful, my little birds! And who came up with this idea?" she asked.

"All three of us." answered Ates promptly.

"No, actually, Ates had it," admitted Yildiz.

"As always." confirmed Deniz.

"Ouch though, you guys play along too!" snorted Ates who had turned red with embarrassment.

"You were all good!" exclaimed Sanem. "You move me like this." she admitted, touching the outer corners of her eyes.

"Come here!" she said, clutching them to her chest again. This time it was the twins who kissed their mother on the cheek.

"Oh..." commented Sanem pouting to hide the lump in her throat.

"We missed you so much mummy!" exclaimed Deniz.

"Oh, my loves, you too!" replied Sanem.

Once they had detached, it was Ates who brought a smile back to everyone's face, exclaiming seriously, her little finger pointing at her mother:

"Don't ever do that again! OK?" she said in a tone that admitted no reply, as if she were the mother.

Sanem smiled as she saw herself in that expression somewhere between serious and amused and replied: "Alright, Mum." giving a military salute with her hand brushing her forehead.

"You're grounded!" all three exclaimed in chorus.

"So what are you going to do with me now?" she asked putting her hands up in surrender.

"Now? Let's play!" exclaimed Ates jumping up.

"What shall we play?" asked their mother.

"Hmm..." thought all three of them.

They joined in a circle with each other confabulating. Every now and then they peeked in their mother's direction and beyond.

They looked outside.

"Have you deliberated?" asked Sanem.

"Huh? Delibe... what?" asked Deniz.

"What does that mean?" asked Yildiz.

"It's a term they use in.... forget about it, it's not important. It's a way of asking if you've done, that is." she explained simply.

"Oh, yes! We did!" all three said, crossing their arms. They looked at her slyly.

"Hmm, this doesn't look good." Sanem thought to herself.

"You will be our prisoner!" exclaimed Ates.

"In what sense?" asked Sanem fearfully.

"Since you were not with us yesterday, to prevent you from running away again, you will be our captive Indian." she explained.

"We already have the tent outside in the garden." pointed to Deniz.

"Me and Ates Indian like you, we will have to rescue you from the clutches of the bad soldier Deniz who imprisoned you." Yildiz explained.

"We will also bind you." Ates added. "So you cannot escape again."

"But first... we have to dress for the occasion. And you will help us mum." said Ates.

"Alright, since I'm your prisoner, I can't say no." she replied, playing along.

Lately they had been in a fixation with Indians. They loved to hear stories about them.

"So let's do this, let's get cards, crayons and everything we need and we'll make our own accessories." said Sanem.

"Yesssss!" exclaimed Yildiz, immediately running inside to get the necessities.

"Let's position ourselves on the table outside." she said pointing to the porch outside. Better to detonate a bomb outside than in the house, Sanem thought.

"All right, Mama." all three said in search of the materials.

Sanem moved outside. After a while she saw a box with legs coming, from behind it came Yildiz.

Behind her was Ates, holding some toys, and Deniz, behind in turn, with other things.

Deniz had changed, putting on a plaid shirt and a pair of denim shorts.

Ates too, had put on a little brown dress that was too long, in fact Sanem usually fastened it around her waist with a belt to make it more practical.

Yildiz, on the other hand, had not changed.

When Sanem saw them like that, she tightened her lips to keep from laughing.

"The style and love of 'special' combinations you definitely got from your father." she thought. "My God, now I wonder if that one time he dressed you up didn't leave its mark on you." she admitted.

"Don't say that. Dad has great style!" Deniz immediately protected him.

"When it comes to disguises, definitely..." commented Sanem.

At that moment they looked at each other as brothers. They had not seen before, as they came from different rooms, each collecting the necessary toys left around.

Ates looked at Deniz and blurted out: "Deniz, what trousers are you wearing?" she said, pointing at them.

"Why?" he asked, looking at himself, blinking in puzzlement. Nothing was wrong, he thought.

"Have you ever seen in books or cartoons, a soldier wearing shorts? Oh, Come on!" she blurted out.

Sanem burst out laughing at the expression and frankness with which she said it.

Yildiz meanwhile took out a book, which, Sanem thought, the twins were inspired by.

Yildiz hurriedly opened it, flipping through it quickly to the page in question.

Then she walked over to it and pointed to a soldier on horseback.

Had it not been for the maturity she had assumed with the years, she would surely have commented on the same thing, without a second thought.

Ates, seeing the picture, took the book from her sister's hands, and placing it next to her brother, said: "Do you think you're the same?" she asked, pointing to the figure he was supposed to be drawing from.

"Phew... but with long jeans it's hot!" exclaimed Deniz.

"Ah... are you or are you not a soldier? Then you can take some heat." she said.

"But I didn't even want to be a soldier." commented Deniz.

"Ah... and what did you want to be? The damsel in distress?" asked Ates.

"If you want, we'll tie you up like a salami, instead of Mama!" she thought.

"Yeah, why didn't I think of that first! That way, while you're tied on the spit, me, Yildiz and Mama will do the Indian dance around you!" she said.

"Ates..." her mother said, taking her back, but not avoiding a smile.

"No, no, I'm being a soldier." replied Deniz immediately.

"Oh, yeah, huh!" echoed Ates.

Deniz, observed her for a moment, then laughed under his mustache.

"What are you laughing about?" she asked looking at him seriously.

"Why you? How are you dressed, eh, sister?" asked Deniz laughing.

In that foot-length brown dress, I really want to see how you dance around her or how you run... you look like... what's her name?" he asked in search of the name looking at his mother.

"Who Deniz?" she asked.

"That all-hair character... mh... wait." he said reflectively.

"All hair?" asked Yildiz.

Deniz snapped her fingers, mimicking the ditty she was referring to.

"Ah... the Addams family!" exclaimed her mother.

"That's right! What's the name of the one that's all furry, Mom?" he then asked.

"Cousin Itt!" she replied.

"That's him!" he confirmed.

"Ah, this is war then! You'll see how the Indians will beat the little soldier... you'll see!" said Ates staring at him with a mischievous smile.

"Alright, alright, come on, let's go back to the room and choose something suitable... since you want to look like the book..." said Sanem silencing everyone.

"And you Yildiz why didn't you get dressed?" asked Ates.

"Because I wanted to bring the box. And then I couldn't find anything suitable." she admitted.

"Now we'll think about it together. Let's go." said Sanem leading the way.

Once in the room, positioned in front of the open cupboard, Sanem started looking for something.

Ten minutes later she found everything she needed. Long denim trousers for Deniz, a belt for Ates' dress, and a simple beige dress for Yildiz.

She changed too, wearing a brown suede dress, perfect for her role.

Once the little ones were settled, she brought them their garden boots; they weren't in theme, but given the game ahead they were ideal.

Then she disappeared into the walk-in wardrobe of her room and took a cowboy hat that Can kept in his wardrobe as a souvenir of one of his trips. He put it on Deniz's head, then went back outside to create some accessories with the colored cards for the girls' dresses whose hair he had already styled with braids.

He created headbands with the circumference of their heads to which she applied a fake feather. Then she created a necklace of fringes for both of them to attach to the neck of their dresses.

"There." she said contentedly once completed. "Now you look perfect!"

"Well... one has never seen Indians in garden boots, but..." tried to say softly Ates.

"My child, if I put on the suede boots you have in your wardrobe, do you know what they will look like in a few hours? Green and full of mud. So you will make do with the chantilly ones." Sanem said.

"Chantilly? The Cream?" asked Ates already licking her mustache.

"No, love, the chantilly are these boots here." she said pointing to the ones on their little feet.

"Ahhh... but that's what the cream is called too, isn't it?" she asked.

"Well, it's pronounced similarly, but they are different." Sanem tried to explain.

"Ah..." she commented.

"Then are we ready?" she asked.

Deniz brought the box with the toys. For herself she took the belt with the fake gun.

Ates took an axe, while Yildiz took a bow.

"Now we are ready!" they exclaimed posing.

"Ah, but then if you do that, we need a good photo!" exclaimed Sanem as she picked up her phone. She took a couple of them, after which they started to play.

Sanem ran around the garden until the soldier picked her up and took her to the Indian tent in the garden, making her kneel in front of it. Then with string, he tied her hands behind her back.

At that point, Sanem started to call for help from the two girls who, according to the story they were staging, were the only survivors in the village. The girls seeing their mother like that started attacking the soldier, each with her "Weapon." They coordinated and started to attack him. Yildiz threw the sucker darts from her bow, to push the soldier away, and Ates, had to try to go around him to save Mama, cutting the rope around her hands with her axe.

Deniz and Ates glared at each other. As foretold, one wanted to prevail over the other, until Yildiz out of desperation, seeing that the game seemed to end no more, silently took the water pump, and pointing it at her brother began to splash him.

"Great Yildiz!" exclaimed Ates, reaching out to Sanem to untie her and save her.

Deniz turned away from the jet: "That's cheating, though!" he exclaimed.

"Indians didn't have water pumps like this." he added.

"But we are modern Indians!" exclaimed Ates. "And we have this and more. Look, we even have chantilly. Repeated Ates proudly, mispronouncing the boots, mistaking them for cream.

Sanem laughed.

Deniz at that point replied to her sister: "Ah, you're always right, Ates!"

Meanwhile her two sisters started running around Sanem with one hand in front of their mouths, doing the Indian dance.

"Well, now that you've freed me, how about we take some things off and go to the jetty to enjoy the sunset?" asked Sanem.

"Yessss!" they exclaimed jumping.

"Then run. Run and put your previous clothes back on and let's go." she said.

"In the meantime, I'll gather some things here." she added, then shouted: "Don't put your shoes on, though. You will put your boots back on!" she reminded them.

"Alright!" she heard answer from the room.

After a while, the children returned to their shoes and joined her as she put everything back in the house.

"Ready?" she asked.

"Ready!" they exclaimed.

"Mummy, I'm hungry!" exclaimed Deniz.

"Ah, don't worry, your mum has already taken care of it. I have prepared a small snack for you to eat on the pier." she said, showing a small bag, which she had in her hand.

"Yay!" exclaimed Yildiz.

"Let's go then. Everyone hold hands." she said taking Deniz's hand, which created a chain with the sisters.

Meanwhile, Can had arrived home. He hurried out of the car to see his entire family again.

He entered the house and exclaimed: "I'm back!" as he was wont to do.

Usually at those words, the children ran to him, but not that night. Hearing that silence, he asked aloud: "Hello? Children? Are you playing a joke on me? Are you hiding? Watch me catch you!" he said.

Nothing, no sound was heard, so Can slowly checked the whole house, but not a shadow of them.

He went out into the garden, there was no one there, so he reached the loft, there was no one there either.

He checked on the roof terrace, but nothing.

Coming down he thought to look in the garden, and seeing Sanem's flowers moving, he thought she was there, so approaching he asked: "Sanem?"

He noticed a figure crouching behind the plants, but once in front, he asked the question and realised it was not her.

Bulut stood up.

"No, I am not Sanem." he replied.

"Bulut? When did you arrive?" asked Can.

"Now." he replied.

"Ah, I didn't see the car, that's why." Can replied.

"Did you happen to see Sanem, or the children?" he asked.

"Um, no... they haven't been seen here for now." replied Bulut.

"Ugh... where will they be?" huffed Can.

"Everyday lately I feel like I'm playing a treasure hunt. They are never where I think they are." said Can.

"They'll be at Mihriban's," Bulut threw in.

"I can take a look if you want." he proposed.

"All right, I'll try to see at the wharf in the meantime. Who knows..." said Can.

"I'll let you know if I find them." said Bulut.

"Alright, thank you." Can said, walking away in large strides.

As he reached the entrance to the estate, he was confronted by Haydut.

"Haydut! Come here!" he said, calling him to himself.

Can was the one member of the family whom Haydut obeyed the most, so he quickly joined him.

"Where is my family, do you know?" he asked him.

Haydut barked.

"If you take me to them, I will give you a nice bone. I swear!" he exclaimed.

The dog stuck out his tongue, savouring that moment, and after barking twice, snapped forward, sniffing the floor.

"In fact, if you'd rather, I'll give you a pair of slippers identical to the ones you're already mauled me in, since you like them so much!" he added to the stakes.

The dog seemed to understand, and concentrated even more on the search, sniffing the path leading to the jetty.

Getting closer and closer Can said: "If you show me the jetty, know that I know the way too, dear Haydut." he said.

Then thinking to himself he realized: "Can, what are you doing? Are you really relying on the dog to find your family? Have you come this far?" he asked.

"Come to your senses." he said to himself.

He lengthened his stride and overtook the dog, who was used to roaming free around the grounds of the estate.

Haydut seeing himself overtaken, barked at him and ran after him, overtaking him in turn. There was good loot at stake and he had no intention of letting it slip away.

When, emerging from behind the hedge, he saw his family sitting on top of the jetty, singing and joking, he breathed a sigh of relief.

There it was, happiness. His whole world.

Haydut barked and joined the children on the jetty.

They all turned to look at him.

"Haydut, all right, all right, I get it, you win!" exclaimed Can, behind him, catching up with him. The dog for joy wagged his tail, cheered everyone, and then after a spin, jumped into the water.

"Haydut!" Sanem picked him up as he stood up with the children, to avoid being splashed by the plunge.

The children, seeing their father, ran towards him. Sanem, on the other hand, stayed in place, scolding Haydut to return to dry land from the meadow next door.

When he saw him return to shore and shake off the water, she relaxed.

Meanwhile, the children, climbing on Can were watching Haydut laughing, while their mother scolded him.

Can approached, and Sanem stiffened, taking on a serious expression.

She mentally prepared to have a word with him, but when she saw Bulut emerge from behind the hedge coming towards them, she called out.

"Bulut?"

"Ah, you are here then." he said, looking at Can.

"I called you twice, but you didn't answer me, that's why I reached you. "he said.

"Ah, I guess it was silent from the office. Sorry." said Can with the children in his arms.

"Hello children." he greeted them.

"Hello, brother Bulut!" they reciprocated.

"Ah, Bulut, I was just looking for you!" said Sanem passing Can and the children.

"Tell me Sanem." he replied, following her at a distance.

Can observed her.

"I had a spectacular idea." she said passing an arm around his neck in a friendly manner to whisper what she had to say.

"You know the secret perfume I've been working on for so long?" she reminded him.

"Yes..." he replied vaguely.

"Here, I've decided to let it go for a while. I'm not getting the results I was hoping for, and I need more time to study the formula." she explained.

"OK, but won't that create damage for the release of the new Sanem collection?" he asked.

"No... and do you know why? Because this is where I got the idea." replied Sanem.

Can didn't hear much of their conversation because the children were trying to draw the focus all on them.

"And that would be?" asked Bulut.

"If all goes well, we will have three new fragrances. But first I have to get to work." said Sanem.

"Here, I have made a list of flowers I need, since you are here, could you pick them from the garden and bring them here to the workshop?" she asked.

"Sure, I was already cutting some flowers when I met Can. No problem. Let me see." he said, taking the list in his hand to check.

"I'll take care of it." he concluded confidently after a brief glance.

"Thank you very much, Bulut, and sorry to bother you." Sanem replied kindly.

"Don't mention it." retorted Bulut.

"And? What's your business around here? Sanem asked. "Deren and Burak all right?" she asked.

"Ah, yes, yes, all fine." he replied serenely.

"And the baby?" asked Sanem.

"The baby is growing... judging by the belly. But Deren is very nervous about tomorrow." said Bulut.

"Tomorrow?" asked Sanem. "Why?"

"Because we will have our check-up tomorrow, and we hope this time we can see him/her." said Bulut.

"Ah, so you will know the sex?" asked Sanem excitedly.

"Hopefully this is the time. Play hide and seek." explained Bulut.

"Ouch, I haven't had a chance to talk to Deren these days..." admitted Sanem.

"Ah, you will have a chance in the morning, don't worry, the visit is in the afternoon. "Bulut said.

"Ah, then I'll expect her in the morning for a chat. Tell her." she said.

"Thank you Sanem, if you can calm her down, I will be eternally grateful. "Bulut replied.

Sanem laughed. "Watch out because I will ask you for several crates of tomatoes in return!" she replied jokingly.

"As many as you want!" proposed Bulut immediately.

"In fact, I will plant two rows of tomatoes in your honor. There is a vacant space in the garden, I will call them Sanem's tomatoes." he said.

"It's a deal then." she concluded, laughing.

Then she turned to Can and said seriously: "Can, I have to work. You're with the kids, right?"

"Um... OK, but..." he tried to answer uncertainly.

"Perfect." closed the topic Sanem, striding away.

"Children, see you at home. It's time for you to wear out Dad's batteries a bit now." then she turned and strided away.

"Daddy, come, let's all watch the sunset together." said Yildiz taking him by the hand. She was the only one on the ground.

Can's gaze, however, was once again on his wife's shoulders.

It grew dark, Sanem was concentrating on stepping on the flowers Bulut had brought in her mortar.

Meanwhile at home Can had the children eating dinner, and taking advantage of Mihriban's visit, who had come to bring a freshly baked chocolate cake, he asked to check on them as he realized that Bulut had left some of the flowers there for Sanem. Thinking she might need them, he decided to bring them to her.

Arriving at the top of the workshop stairs, he was attracted by the smell of flowers and fragrance. He saw her busy mixing and sniffing ampoules, so slowly down the first few steps he said:

"Sanem? May I?" he asked.

Sanem continued to do her work, answering firmly and professionally: "Come." as if she were in the office.

"I brought you these, I think Bulut forgot them." Can said, placing the flowers beside her.

Sanem looked at them.

"No, they are not Bulut's. They are the flowers I picked. And they are not needed here." she replied, concentrating on a cruet from which she counted ten droplets to insert into the beaker in front of her in which she was creating the perfume.

"Ah..." he replied not knowing what to say.

Sanem had not yet looked him in the face.

"What are you doing?" he then asked to get her attention.

"A perfume, it seems obvious." replied Sanem.

"A new one?" he asked.

"Yes." she replied, stirring the concoction.

"Can I smell it?" he asked.

"Smell what? It's not ready yet." she replied.

"OK, but can you tell me about it? You can tell me what flowers you used." he proposed.

"Like it makes much difference to you whether I put one flower or another." Sanem said, setting the mixture down in front of him.

She sighed, turned and looked at him.

"Can, what do you really want to talk about?" asked Sanem directly, looking him in the eye for the first time.

"About you." replied Can.

"About me... mh." replied Sanem. "Let's hear then what you have to say about me? I'm listening." she said.

"Because I have nothing to say about me." she specified.

"OK... er, where did you spend the night last night?" he asked, trying to keep his tone of voice calm and collected.

Sanem smiled mockingly.

"You definitely know where I stayed. Someone must have told you for sure otherwise you wouldn't be asking me in this tone. Am I wrong?" she asked. She started bottling two ampoules to be left to rest.

Can for a second was taken aback by the answer, then admitted: "It's true, I know."

"Then why do you ask?" asked Sanem.

"Because I want to know from you, alright? I want to know where my wife slept last night." he answered decisively.

"I want..." repeated Sanem.

"I want, yes, I'm your husband, right? I have the right to know where my wife has been, no?" he asked, he was starting to get nervous.

"Like you have a right to go and investigate to know where i was, right? Is that what it means to be a husband? And then you come here, already knowing everything and say you want to know from me? Are you kidding me?" blurted Sanem.

"If it was so important to hear it from me, you would have talked to me from the start, not acting behind my back and then popping up and pretending nothing happened." she added.

"Again with this acting behind your back?" asked Can rolling his eyes.

"Why not?" asked Sanem. "You keep doing it and you don't even realise it." she added.

"Alright." said Sanem then. "You want to know where I've been? Well I'll tell you. I went to Muzo's, and then to my parents. I had dinner and spent the night in my old room, but you already knew that, didn't you? Are you happy now? Are you relaxed? Good!" Sanem concluded, arranging all the products in front of her. She had lost the mood to experience anything else, so she was getting ready to leave.

"No, I'm not relaxed, OK?" replied Can.

Can stopped his wife's arms forcing her to look at him.

"Leave me." she said seriously.

"No. I'm not leaving you." he replied.

"Why?" asked Can. "Why did you do that?"

Sanem smiled out of nervousness. "Why did I do that? Are you really asking me why I did that, Can? After what happened yesterday?" ranted Sanem.

"Why do you think I did that, huh? Because I needed to be alone! I needed to think about how to fix the mess you put me in without my knowledge. Because I was angry and disappointed... and I still am!" spat Sanem.

"And you just picked up and left without saying anything.... didn't you think about the children?" asked Can.

273

"All they did was ask about you. Where is mummy? Why is mummy not here? When is she coming back? And so on."

"One minute, one minute!" Sanem immediately blocked him.

"Now you are also accusing me of not being a good mother? Is that what you are doing Can? How dare you, huh?" she replied.

"Do you really think I would leave my children out of the blue without saying a word?" she added.

"Well, since you're accusing me, I'll tell you that too, my dear Mr Can. Because you obviously didn't investigate thoroughly enough." she said decisively, slamming her notes on the table.

"Leaving work late, I called Mihriban, because it was her and your father's day to pick them up from school. We talked and I asked her if she could look after them longer, and if necessary spend the night with them, in case you were busy. When I spoke to her on the phone I put them through, to hear their voices and what they had done at school and all that. So don't you dare tell me I'm a bad mother! Don't you dare!" replied Sanem angrily.

Can remained silent, speechless.

"Do you know why I acted that way? I'll explain that too since you don't get it. For their happiness. I preferred to walk away because I didn't want the children to see that something was wrong. OK? I couldn't bear to see their sad faces, or their questions, which would surely come!" she admitted.

"If that means being an irresponsible mother, then yes, Can, I am a bad mother!" Sanem concluded.

"I didn't say that." Can retorted.

"Not in those words, but you thought it." said Sanem.

"If there's anyone I didn't say anything to, it's you." he added.

"And since I am such a thoughtless person, next time, if you want to investigate properly, contact Volkan. Maybe you'll have more success with him." Sanem concluded, shaking off Can's arm to climb the stairs of the laboratory and leave.

Can immediately sprinted after her.

"Sanem!" he called.

"Sanem!" he repeated.

He reached her blocking her way.

"Can, let me pass." she said resolutely.

"No." he replied just as decisively. "Why are you doing this, huh?" asked Can.

"Why do you think, huh? Get your brain working a bit, isn't that how you tell our employees?" she reminded him.

"What do you want me to do? Do you want me to apologize? If you want me to apologize, I apologize. Excuse me." he said simply.

"Ah, save your breath, Can!" she replied.

"True, it's an apology I want. But a real apology! Sincere, coming from the heart! Not fake ones just to make me happy, I don't know what to do with those." she ranted.

"But you can't even understand your own mistake, how can you apologize?" she continued.

"You always do this. You act like this, and then you come here, and say sorry, thinking everything will work out. I'm sorry but it won't, not this time, Can." said Sanem.

"And what are you going to do? Will you run away in my presence like you have been doing these days?" he asked nervously.

"No, we will act like nothing in front of the children for their sake, but don't think I have forgiven you!" said Sanem.

"Now, if you allow, I would like to be alone." she added.

Can turned his back and walked away, then before disappearing behind the small house beside the jetty he had just reached, he turned to look at her.

He saw Sanem reach the end of the jetty and clutching her knees to her chest, rested her head on them. She let go the lump in her throat and the tears that were ready to escape found a way out.

Can watched her with shining eyes. He noticed how her shoulders lifted continuously.

Sanem was sobbing. Clasping her arms around her knees, she slowly began to rock back and forth.

Seeing her like this, silent tears ran down Can's cheeks uncontrollably. He let himself fall to the ground, leaning his head against the wall of the small house, in the same spot where he had once found Sanem at the crack of dawn after a sleepless night.

He stood there pondering for a while, not realizing that Sanem had walked past him on his way home without noticing his presence.

Once inside, Sanem, her eyes swollen with tears, felt inhumanly tired.

She did not bother to let Mihriban and Aziz see her like this. At that moment she felt empty. She didn't care, she was tired of holding the strings of everything.

As soon as Mihriban saw her return, sitting on the sofa next to Aziz, she immediately sprinted to join her.

"Sanem, daughter, what happened? What is that face?" asked Mihriban.

Sanem with a hoarse voice broken by too many tears, simply replied with bleary eyes: "Please don't ask questions." she said noticing Aziz's shocked expression.

"I thank you for looking after the children, but now if you will excuse me, I need to rest." he said.

"Alright, if you want, you rest, we'll stay here, no problem." Mihriban immediately offered.

"Can, where is he?" asked Aziz.

Mihriban glared at him.

"Good night." said Sanem simply, disappearing into the corridor.

"What happened now?" asked Aziz worriedly.

"Aziz,... you too though! Can't you see the condition she's in huh?" his wife pointed out to him.

"Come on, get up. Let's go." urged Mihriban.

"You know what's going on between them, don't you?" Aziz squared her suspiciously.

"No, I don't know..." replied Mihriban vaguely. "Come on let's go." she said pushing him out.

"Mh, let's go yes, so you can tell me everything you know at home." he said.

"Mh, alright dear, let's go." she said rolling her eyes.

Sanem reached her room, took a good shower, put on her pajamas, and like a zombie looked at the bed, throwing down the corner of the blanket on her side, then on second thought reached the children's room, slowly opened the door, quietly, and looked inside. She saw that the cots were empty, and for a moment she panicked, but when she turned to the wall of the door next to her, where the big bed was, and saw all three of them there, she breathed a sigh of relief. Without making a sound she walked over to them, caressed and kissed them, then stopped to observe them.

On a pillow, clinging to Deniz at the edge of the bed, was Ates. Those two, despite being cat and dog, loved each other very much. On the other pillow, however, slept Yildiz peacefully, content to have her own living space.

Seeing them like this, Sanem broke into a slight smile, and without being heard, climbed into the middle of the bed. She passed an arm around Yildiz, who still sleeping, rested his head on top of her. On the other side, when Ates and Deniz opened their eyes, feeling the bed move, and caught a glimpse of their mother, half-asleep, they snuggled into her, under her other arm.

Sanem stroked them for a while until tiredness got the better of her.

AT THE SAME MOMENT AT THE JETTY...

Can, on the other hand, remained thinking for a while behind the walls of that little house and slowly returned home.

When he arrived in front of the kitchen door, through which he used to enter, he found his father sitting on the sofa outside.

"Can? Son? Where have you been?" his father asked as soon as he saw him, jumping out of his chair.

"At the wharf dad, why?" he asked downcast.

"What are you doing here at this hour instead?" he asked.

"I was worried about you, I saw Sanem coming back, and... I realized something is wrong. What's going on son, huh?" asked Aziz.

"Dad, I don't really feel like talking right now." he said without strength.

"Ah, son, no buts. I know you. If you don't talk and shut yourself up, that thing, whatever it is, will wear you down from the inside." he said.

"So come here, have a seat." he said, pointing to the empty seat next to him.

Can sighed. "Alright, but not here." he said peering inside.

"Don't worry, Sanem has gone to bed. If that's what you're worried about." his father replied.

"And how do you know?" he asked.

"She said it herself. She was in such a condition, that when I saw her I admit I got scared." he admitted.

Can sat down beside him and nodded, head down.

Aziz patted him on the shoulder in encouragement.

"Did you fight?" he asked.

"Yes." he replied.

"Why?" asked his father.

"Because of another previous quarrel." replied Can.

"How? When?" asked Aziz. "Come on son, speak up, don't force words out of your mouth, come on." he urged him.

"We had a fight in the agency yesterday, if you talk to any of the employees they can confirm that." Can replied.

"OK, but why?" he repeated.

"Over an issue with Muzo..." said Can. "Alright, I'll tell you from the beginning." he concluded then with a big sigh surrendering to his father.

"And... well, Can actually, how can you blame her... sorry son..." replied his father after listening to the tale.

"You too?" asked Can. "Emre said the same thing."

"Like you too? Son, don't you see your mistake?" asked his father.

"Maybe i do now." replied Can.

"Ah... and? Go on." urged Aziz.

"Because of that fight last night, Sanem did not come home. She went to Muzo's, and then stayed with her parents." he explained.

"Ouch... that means that's why she asked me and Mihriban to look after the children until late then." he thought. "Was she very angry?" he asked.

"A rage." replied Can.

"OK, and? Why did you fight tonight?" he then asked.

"I hadn't seen her since yesterday, that is, I dropped by Mevkibe's this morning, and that was the only way I found out she had stayed with them. Her phone was always switched off." he continued.

"Then when I arrived at work, I did not find her, I found out that she had already left, and so when I arrived tonight and found her at home I wanted to talk to her. But when she saw me, in Bulut's presence, she said she had to work and went to the workshop asking to bring him flowers. I stayed with the children." he said.

"Then, when Mihriban came to bring dessert to the little ones, I saw flowers here on the table, and I thought they might be needed so, I joined her. And there..." he dropped the sentence, leaving the rest to the imagination.

"You had a fight." his father concluded.

"There, as she looked at me with eyes full of anger and disappointment, I actually wanted to tell her that I had missed her like air. Her look, her face, her voice... but all it took was one spark and we started arguing." he confessed.

"I asked where she had been, because I needed to hear her voice, even though I already knew the answer, and it all erupted from there." he explained.

"It was a moment, I don't know how we got there either, but out of concern, and everything else, without realizing it I asked if in leaving the children like that, she had been thinking of them and..." she dropped the freshee again thinking back to the scene.

"Can!" his father took him back.

"I don't know, that is... I didn't mean to accuse her like that, but she thought I had called her an irresponsible mother, a bad mother... and I didn't know what to say." he admitted confused.

"Like you didn't know what to say, son? You should have apologized!" his father looked at him, blinking naively.

"That's what she said too." Can replied.

"And sure..." confirmed Aziz.

"I told her: if you want me to apologize, then i apologize." he quoted his words.

"Son, are you serious? But how did it occur to you to ask her what she wanted? Of course she wanted an apology." replied Aziz, "A heartfelt apology, though." he stressed.

"Can, I don't understand, but are you regretting what you said or not? Because I can't understand, honestly." his father replied confused.

"I am, but when I heard the children ask 'where is mummy? Why is mummy not here? When is she coming back? And all the rest... I don't know, I didn't know what to say, I was in so much trouble that... when we started arguing, it just came out like that." he tried to justify himself.

"Can, you just because, you were attacking each other, saying such a thing, you hurt her. Son, don't you remember how insecure your wife was when she was a new mother? How many times she said she didn't feel up to it when she couldn't get them to calm down, or give them everything they needed?" he reminded him.

"And then sorry... you didn't know what to say? You should have protected your wife, and not shown it to the children." his father scolded him.

Can smiled. "That's what she said too. She said she didn't come home so the children wouldn't suffer."

"There... she has a point. I mean, sure, not coming home to your family isn't nice, but breaking a balance to the children, it can have severe consequences on your relationship with them, son. I learned that in the hard way." Aziz reminded him.

"Ah... all the fault of that thing with Muzo!" commented Can. "If he hadn't made her cry, I wouldn't have done any of this and we wouldn't be where we are now."

"Son, you do well to protect your wife, but you can't eliminate from her life everyone who makes her cry or suffer... otherwise she would have no one left around her... including you." he replied directly.

"What do you mean?" asked Can looking at him sharply.

"What I mean is that you also made her suffer in the past, if it was because of that then she should have eliminated you from her life long ago, you know?" she tried to reason with him.

Can looked at him carefully.

"Why didn't she do that? Because she loves you. And she accepts both to be happy and to suffer sometimes. And that goes for everyone she loves." Aziz got to the point.

"You're right." Can finally realized.

"What a fool I've been!" he exclaimed realizing.

"Yeah... you have to make it up to my dear, and properly." said his father.

"Sanem doesn't deserve this." he added.

"Come on, since my work is done, I'm going to bed. And you rest." his father said seriously.

"We'll think of something tomorrow, a Divit meeting is urgent." said Aziz.

"Thank you dad, good night." he greeted him.

"Goodnight son." returned Aziz more serene.

Can re-entered the house, but before reaching the room, he passed by the children. Opening the door, he too was frightened for a moment when he did not see them in their beds, but once he looked towards the big bed, he was enchanted. His whole family was sleeping wrapped in a big hug with their mother. Sanem in the middle had a distraught face, her cheeks streaked with tears. Can, swallowing the lump in her throat, and smiled.

"How could he have been so despicable to her?" he asked himself.

Pausing to look at them, he thought:

"There could not be a kinder mother than you, my love." he whispered.

Slowly, she walked out of the room.

Once outside, Can wiped the inside corners of his eyes and after pulling up his nose, he looked at the closed door and thought while clenching his fists: "I will make it up to you, my love."

"I will make it up to you," he repeated.

32. *LET DESTINY TAKE ITS COURSE*

Can spent the whole night lying on the bed with his hands behind his head, thinking. He saw the sun rise, at first light, and so, not being sleepy, he decided to get up and go for a run. Perhaps, among the various ideas buzzing around in the head, he would make up his mind.

Once home, he found his family just up having breakfast in the kitchen.

Sanem's back was turned, while the children said good morning to their father.

As she had announced, she acted as if nothing was wrong for the sake of the little ones, but Can noticed, as soon as her gaze was out of their reach, how it darkened.

Despite the fact that the children demanded his constant attention, he never let her out of his sight. As he took his seat, and Sanem placed his breakfast in front of him with a smile, he immediately noticed her face swollen with tears, despite the fact that she had tried to disguise it with make-up.

And he noticed how once she turned her back to him, facing the kitchen, her expression changed in a second. It was like a switch, turning on and off. And it was costing her dearly, he could see that.

Once breakfast was over, Sanem urged the children, as usual, to go and get dressed.

She, on the other hand, already ready, took off her apron, and thinking she was alone, leaning against the kitchen counter, poured herself a glass of water in which she poured a soluble sachet.

A medicine.

As she turned the teaspoon inside with one hand, she massaged her temple with the other.

She did not realize that Can had meanwhile, after showering and changing, joined her in the kitchen, ready to take the children to school together as usual.

"Are you OK?" he tried to ask her behind her back.

"I'm fine." she replied seriously, without turning around, after downing the medicine in one gulp.

Then she headed for the corridor, calling loudly: "Children, are you ready?"

Sanem reached the small room and closed the door behind her.

Once they reappeared, ready with their backpacks on their shoulders, they reached the car and set off.

Once accompanied, the short drive to the agency was silent. Sanem turned on the radio, resting her head on the seat, waiting for the medicine to take full effect.

Can cast glances at her whenever possible. Every time the road allowed.

Once they reached the front of the agency, Sanem spoke.

"I'll get off here, thank you." she said seriously as soon as Can slammed on the brakes because of the queue, she had to get to the underground car park.

In a moment, Sanem was already outside, he followed her with his eyes to the entrance, until someone behind him honked. The queue had disappeared, and he had unknowingly stood still.

So, back to his senses, he raised his hand in apology and looked in the rear-view mirror and gave the gas.

Meanwhile, Sanem immediately headed downstairs to her office as soon as she entered.

As she walked down the Sanem's corridor, saying good morning to her colleagues and friends, she paused when she saw that the door to her office was half-open.

She frowned in confusion, looking around to ask someone, but they were all gone.

She approached and with her hand on the handle, she jerked the door open, looking inside.

Sitting on her sofa adjacent to the entrance were her sister and Mihriban.

"Sister? Sister Mihriban?" she asked confusedly as she entered.

"Ah! Finally!" they both exclaimed as soon as they saw her.

"What are you doing here?" asked Sanem.

"Daughter, what happened? I'm worried about you. After last night..." dropped the sentence Mihriban.

"Gosh, sister Mihriban!" she exclaimed seeing her sister nodding. She too had already been brought up to speed.

"Faster than light! Damn, I was complaining about the neighborhood where gossip was born even before the facts happened, and look at this!" she exclaimed as she placed her bag on the coat rack next to her desk.

"Daughter, we are worried about you. Don't you understand?" she replied.

"Fine, I'll just explain it once." Sanem replied.

"Sister, what happened to you? You have a face..." said Leyla.

"I know, I've had a big headache since I got up." she admitted.

"Well... with all those tears..." commented Mihriban.

Sanem glowered at her. She settled back in her chair and began to narrate as she brewed tea in her dedicated little corner.

"What, she told you this?" blurted Mihriban.

Sanem nodded.

"Sister? You don't say anything?" asked Sanem. Leyla had been silent the whole time.

"Well, of course I'm sorry. But more than blaming one or the other, I'm trying to understand Can." she admitted.

"In what way? Sorry, child, you don't think what he told her was right, do you?" replied Mihriban nervous about the situation.

"No, that is..." tried to explain Leyla.

"If Emre said something like that to you, how would you react?" asked Mihriban.

"I wouldn't react well, of course. But Emre would never tell me such a thing anyway." she added confidently of her husband.

"Never say never, sister..." commented Sanem as she rolled her eyes.

"Alright. Do you want me to honestly say what I think, sister? I'll indulge you right now." replied Leyla decisively.

"I think Can misses his wife terribly. And not after what happened, but even before." said Leyla.

"Even though I have been silent all this time, I have been watching you. And I noticed his expression." she admitted.

"But what are you saying, sister! But if we are always together at home and at work!" retorted Sanem decisively.

"Is that really so, sister? Think a little." she tried to make her think.

Mihriban remained listening.

"Is it just me, or has Can been alone in the company for a while now? Where are you?" she asked her.

Sanem felt impressed. She stared at her in silence.

"And I don't think it's that different at home either, or am I wrong? Commitments, work, being late, or not coming home at all..." she reminded her.

"You have changed, sister. You've been weird for a while now. And when you do that, you're definitely up to something. I know you." Leyla said.

Mihriban cast a glance at Sanem. She in turn looked at her, and noticed a blink on Mihriban's part, she was telling her, "tell her." she knew.

"Um, I'll leave you two alone. I'll wait out here." Mihriban said as she reached the door, which she closed behind her, keeping watch.

"There is something then!" exclaimed Leyla. "And Mihriban knows about it, doesn't she?" deduced.

"All right, detective, all right." replied Sanem impatiently. "I'll tell you, but... you must absolutely promise not to say anything to anyone." she warned her.

"Alright. Sister, but you're scaring me like this." she replied.

Sanem, as always disconnected the cameras, a now habitual gesture when she had to deal with certain topics.

He then sat down next to her, and whispered the whole story in her ear as her sister, reacted: "What?!!!"

"My God..."

"You're kidding, right?!!"

"I wish I was joking." replied Sanem.

"Now I understand why Hilmi..." she reflected.

"I can't believe it." she said bringing a hand to her mouth.

"Yeah..." commented Sanem.

"You mean..." began Leyla.

"Shhh! Sister!" resumed her immediately, Sanem.

"Do you understand now?" asked Sanem.

"I understand, and Can knows?" asked Leyla.

"Some of it, but she doesn't know what I found out, because as I told you we had a discussion." she said in a low voice.

"And what are you going to do now?" her sister asked.

"Nothing. Absolutely nothing." replied Sanem.

"Like nothing?" replied Leyla, baring her eyes.

"I'll leave that to fate." Sanem replied.

"And take a good look at me! You will do the same, understood? Don't make me regret telling you, eh! That you won't get away with telling anyone, not even your beloved Emre. Alright?" she said.

"Alright, alright, I promise. Look I'll write it here." said Leyla visually marking an x on the armrest of the sofa.

"Now I understand why you are so..." said Leyla.

"Hmm, that's nice... Thank you sister." she replied sarcastically.

They both took a sip of tea, then Sanem relaxed at having gotten this off her chest again, she admitted:"Anyway, I really thank you, sister."

"Why?" asked Leyla.

"For opening my eyes." she replied.

"You're right, caught up in all this mess, it was Can who lost out." she admitted. "I can see that now."

"I detached myself from him, without even realizing it, out of some sort of protection for him, you know?" she thought.

"I think subconsciously I want to keep him away from all this mess as much as possible." she admitted.

"That's it... I understand Sanem, but that way it's your marriage that loses out." he whispered. Then she added: "For something that, moreover, doesn't even concern you!"

"I know, and for that I'm sorry, but he also put his own spin on it, I mean, the whole Muzo thing, and what he said to me yesterday, had nothing to do with it." he insisted.

In the meantime Mihriban peeped through the door.

"Come, come, Mihriban." Sanem told her.

"Ah, may I?" she asked.

"Of course, I know everything now." Leyla replied.

"But... as I was saying, sister, no matter how bad the words he used, don't hold it against me... but I can't be angry with him, because I'm sorry." she admitted.

"Before the fight, I told myself that I would only focus on our marriage from then on, and look at the situation we are in instead." said Sanem.

"Ah, child, don't say that, everything will work out, I'm sure of it." Mihriban consoled her.

"That's right, and listen carefully, this is your birthday week. Don't put yourself down." she reminded her.

"Yeah, maybe, Can, she'll make it up to you on your birthday with a nice surprise, who knows?" said Mihriban.

"My birthday? I didn't even remember it, to be honest." Sanem replied.

"What? Why do you say that sister..." said Leyla shocked.

"I've been having such unlucky birthdays for several years now that my brain must have removed the day of my birth too, it seems." was Sanem's reply.

"Why?" asked Mihriban.

"Since the beginning of our history with Can, my birthday has always brought bad luck. Shall we remember Fabbri's cheating party? Shall we remember the following year, when I spent it in a psychiatric clinic? Or shall we talk about the two years traveling the world, when due to stormy seas and a boat breakdown, we were unable to celebrate? Or shall we add the year of our return, that due to severe nausea I was more dead than alive?" she said all at once.

"All right, sister, all right, we get it." said Leyla.

"Breathe, child!" said Mihriban.

"But the next years then were good, weren't they?" asked Leyla.

"Mh, beautiful... just beautiful... sister, but don't you remember anything? If you want I'll continue with the list." said Sanem.

"There was the year I was out promoting the children's trilogy, the year the little ones all three got sick with chicken pox, the year we rushed to the hospital because of Dad's diabetes, the year we discovered Dad Aziz's peanut allergy." said Sanem watching Mihriban nod.

"What a scare, don't remind me." she said touching her chest.

"But that's not the end of it, of course." Sanem continued. "The year Can was asked to give a speech for a photo agency event." she recalled. "And we spent the day together with all the most influential photographers in the world without being able to celebrate."

"Let's see, have I forgotten something? Ah, yes, and the last year when we had to urgently take Haydut to the vet for boils." concluded Sanem.

"You're exaggerating, sister..." thought Leyla.

"Am I exaggerating? Leyla do you really think I made all this up? I wish!" was her prompt reply.

"I'm afraid of my birthday now, do you understand?" said Sanem.

"I have a calendar full of all the things that happened just on my birthday." she confided to them.

"In my history with Can, the date of my birthday is cursed. I have the evil eye!" she said, instinctively taking Allah's eye from the desk to raise it in the air in front of her suspicious that some negative energy is already swirling around. Once she had shaken it a little, she put it down.

"But what do I do?!" she asked herself as she put it down. "I'm having a bad birthday this year anyway, given the situation. That's all the luck I need..." she commented.

"In fact, I'm almost curious to see what bad things will happen to me this year." she said, hinting at a smile.

"Well, I don't know what to say, child... I didn't think you had such a bad luck history with birthdays. Because that is bad luck indeed!" confirmed Mihriban in distress.

"We should pour lead, what do you say?" she asked her.

Sanem shook her head and replied with a shrug.

"I expect nothing." she said simply. "And I won't organize anything. It's just a waste. It will simply be just another day for me." she concluded.

Then thinking about it she added: "Who knows, maybe this year I'll be the one who gets sick."

"Don't even joke about that sister. Ufff!" said Leyla touching her ear lobe and then tapping her knuckles three times on the coffee table in front of her.

"Come on, let's go upstairs. I want to talk to Deren, she has visitation today and I promised Bulut I would try to calm her down." she said getting up.

"Ah, she has the visit? But do they know what they are waiting for?" asked Mihriban.

"No, they hope to find out today, that's why Deren is nervous." replied Sanem leading the way for the others.

"Ah, how exciting!" exclaimed Mihriban quivering.

33. CONVERSATIONS

Once they reached the counter and greeted everyone present, Sanem asked Burak to call Deren for a break all together.

"Good morning, Deren!" greeted her when she saw her coming.

Sanem hadn't seen her for a few days, but noticing her, thought her belly had grown visibly.

"Good morning Sanem! How are you?" she asked hugging her.

"Good, how about you?" she asked placing a hand on her increasingly prominent belly.

"Good come on, even though I'm nervous. Look, my hands are shaking!" she said showing them to her.

"Ah, Bulut told me you have a visitor today." she informed her.

"Yeah, this little person in here already has a temper! He or she doesn't want to be seen." she said, stroking her belly.

"Ah, don't worry, I'm sure he or she'll show up today." Sanem replied confidently. Remember, he senses everything and if he senses that you are nervous or agitated he might do the opposite of what you want." she said.

"Yes, Sanem is right, you just have to be calm. Be serene. Think of something that makes you feel at peace with yourself. "Leyla suggested.

"Think about coffee, Mrs Deren!" exclaimed Cey Cey at the counter as he prepared them some tea.

"Shall I make you a cup?" he asked, winking at them.

"Cey Cey... don't be cheeky!" exclaimed Deren.

"Ah, Deren, think about meditation, your yoga classes." suggested Burak to her.

"Hmm... right, why didn't I think of that before?" replied Deren.

"Think about what you focus on, when you go into meditation. What is it that helps you relax?" she asked as she finished drying Cey Cey's freshly washed cups.

"Grandma." replied Deren instinctively.

"There you go. Think of her, and you'll see that it will show." said Burak as he placed a glass of his favorite smoothie in front of her.

"Thank you dear! If you weren't here..." said Deren.

Burak smiled, winked at her and then walked away with the tray full of more full cups to be delivered to the creative department.

"Oh, Burak really is a love..." commented Mihriban with heart-eyes.

"Yeah... he'll be a really good big brother." commented Deren.

"Deren... can I ask you a question?" asked Leyla.

"Sure, Leyla dear, ask away." she replied.

"I was wondering, no... as a child did you ever like having a brother or sister?" she asked.

Sanem nearly choked on her tea on hearing that question. She looked at her sister with wide eyes.

She began to cough.

"Oh, Sanem..." worried Mihriban and Deren immediately.

After a few coughs, she recovered.

"Leyla, do these sound like questions to you?" asked Sanem. "I mean, why do you have to remind Deren of the past?" she asked.

Deren replied quietly.

"No Sanem, don't worry. Leyla didn't say anything wrong." she replied.

"See?" asked Leyla mockingly.

"Actually, it's something I've started thinking about a lot since I found out I was pregnant." she admitted.

Mihriban, Sanem, and Leyla listened to her carefully.

"As a child, I never really thought about it." she admitted. "Maybe because I was too focused on myself. And my family situation was not the best..." she reflected aloud.

"But growing up, in my teenage years, I sometimes thought in certain situations what it would be like to have a protective big brother... ready to protect me, that is, someone on my side." said Deren.

"And now that you're pregnant, do you think the same thing, or..." tried to ask Leyla, dropping the subject.

"Well, now, under these circumstances I think I would have liked a sister much better.... Maybe because she could understand me better in my circumstances? I don't know." she admitted.

"Someone to share emotions with..." commented Leyla, smiling at her sister.

Sanem reciprocated.

"And in that case, since we are playing this out, would you expect an older or younger sister?" asked Mihriban.

"In the past I would have definitely said no to the younger sister, because I would have had responsibilities and she would have stolen my clothes... and so on." she replied, smiling.

Leyla on hearing this pointed at Sanem.

"Hey!!!" she pouted, crossing her arms.

The others laughed.

"But honestly now... it wouldn't matter. I mean, when I think of Burak being like a son or younger brother to me.... That's it, what I mean is... I don't see the age difference as a wall anymore, in fact!" said Deren. "Or maybe I'm just getting older." she admitted.

"Ha ha... who's getting old?" asked Mihriban frowning. "Let's not start with that kind of talk girls, or it ends badly here, I tell you." she said. "Nobody here is old, least of all yours truly." she said winking at them.

The girls laughed.

"Ah, you are right sister Mihriban. We are all young here." Deren said.

"You are my young sisters." she concluded.

IN CAN'S OFFICE...

Meanwhile, Can had received the same surprise as Sanem.

His father and brother were waiting for him impatiently on the sofa.

"Come on..." he commented when he walked in and saw them.

"Good morning brother," Emre greeted him.

"Son, we need to talk. Come, come, come, you will not escape us." his father said, signaling for him to take a seat with them.

"Good morning. I bet Dad has already brought you up to speed, am I wrong?" asked Can looking at his brother.

"You're not wrong." replied Emre.

"Son, we will help you find a solution, come." insisted Aziz.

Can took a seat on the small armchair next to the sofa.

"Actually..." he said as he sat down. "I think I've already found the solution." he admitted.

AT THE BAR COUNTER...

In the meantime, Leyla and Mihriban, while Sanem was busy continuing her conversation with Deren, with a glance of understanding headed for the bathroom.

"Daughter..." said Mihriban in front of the mirrors as they washed their hands.

"We must get Can to make it up to her!" she exclaimed.

"Sister Mihriban, do you think Can will listen to us? He will do what he wants. He just does his own thing you know, right?" she said.

"I know, I know, but those two have to make peace!" whispered Mihriban.

"And how are you going to do that?" asked Leyla.

"The birthday! Can has to make it up by giving Sanem the birthday She never had." said Mihriban.

"Right... great idea indeed, sister Mihriban." she approved.

"Then listen to me. Right now Aziz is in Can's office talking to him." She said.

"Emre is also with him." added Leyla.

"Perfect, then... let's go!" said Mihriban, crushing a five with Leyla.

They washed their hands and walked out as if nothing had happened.

Passing by the counter they saw Sanem get up.

"Sisters..." She said mimicking the inverted commas.

Cey Cey there, feeling left out asked: "What about the brothers?"

"Sisters and brothers..." said Sanem in a blatant tone, spreading her arms wide. "Is it OK now?" she asked casting a glance at them.

"Now it is." replied Cey Cey strutting.

"I'm going back downstairs. See you." she greeted them.

"And... Deren, let me know." she added.

"Alright, I will." she replied.

"Alright, bye sister." replied Leyla.

"Go daughter, go. Bye!" greeted Mihriban with her hand.

The two of them looked at each other and within three seconds sprinted off towards Can's office.

"Ah! What's going on now?" asked Deren seeing them leave like that.

"What's up with people in the agency all of a sudden I'm starting to wonder too...." commented Cey Cey.

"Since Burak's been around, the people drinking at the counter are behaving even weirder..." she thought as she looked at a fixed point in front of her, after which focusing on Burak who was picking up the empty cups from the creative department, she called out to him. "Burak!!!"

"Cey Cey, listen carefully!" said Deren taking him by the apron he was wearing.

"Don't you dare! Don't you dare blame Burak with your nonsense, or I swear, as true as my name is Deren Cehver I will make you pay dearly! Am I clear?!" she said seriously, with Cey Cey's mustache inches from her face.

Cey Cey saw the flames in her eyes, and clamped his mouth shut before a scream escaped him.

"The devil... the devil..." he whispered. "With the long tail and the pitchfork..." he continued in a panic.

"Ah... evil... " he whispered, moving away fearfully from the counter.

He hid behind the pillar of the creative department, from which his moustache sprouted.

When Burak reached her, his expression changed in a second.

Smiling, amiable, and kind, she reminded Burak of the doctor's appointment for 4 p.m. He would also attend with his brother.

When Burak's back was turned to her to set the cups on the piano, Deren turned sharply towards Cey Cey staring at him, acquiring that murderous expression again.

" Ah.... My God, she's possessed. She's possessed! We need an exorcist. Ah!" he said, hiding behind the column. Slowly he reached out a hand until he picked up the eye of Allah, hanging a little higher up on the column. He brought it in front of his face, and slowly, he stepped out, and approaching the counter pointed it at him, making unintelligible sounds as if to cast out the demon.

"Ah..."

"Auh..."

"Ihh..." he exclaimed.

After which he removed Allah's eye from his face and looked at her.

Deren had come closer, and Cey Cey found her murderous expression practically in front of him.

She stifled a cry in her hands, and in three seconds she was gone like a rocket, downstairs.

Burak who was drying cups, witnessing the scene burst out laughing.

"There, settled." Deren replied quietly. "Now I can also calmly go back to the office." she replied all happy.

Meanwhile, at Can's office door, after three knocks, Leyla and Mihriban came in like a tornado.

"Good morning." they both said, composing themselves in a hurry.

"Er, good morning." greeted the men.

"We need to talk." they said.

"Come on... right now?" Can asked.

"Right now." they replied.

"What's going on?" asked Aziz.

"Can, you have to make it up to her!" exclaimed Mihriban.

"I know." he replied.

"Ah, well, that's already a step forward." replied Leyla.

"We were just talking about that, come on." said Emre making room next to him and his father on the sofa.

Seeing them both transfixed, Aziz poured two glasses of water for them.

"Come on, drink up." he said. They both thanked and after draining the glass, Mihriban took the floor.

"We talked to Sanem." he exclaimed.

Can became highly concentrated.

"And? What did she tell you?" he asked impatiently.

"He told us what happened, and we were talking about his birthday...so.... One minute!" suddenly froze Mihriban.

"Can you remember that Saturday is Sanem's birthday, right?" asked Mihriban.

"Of course I remember Mihriban! How could I forget?" replied Can seriously.

"Ah, there, I think you need to make it up to me with an unforgettable birthday, Can!" spat Mihriban excitedly.

"Ah, but you look! Can had the same idea! He just told us about it." replied Aziz.

"Ah! Really?" asked Mihriban. In no time, she got up and went to hug his godson. "Well done son, well done! Way to go!" she said.

Can responded to the hug a little confused.

"Just a minute!" he reflected.

"What exactly did you talk about with Sanem on his birthday, explain," said Can.

"Well, Can, she told us that basically... thinks her birthday is bad luck." said Leyla after a moment's hesitation.

"What?!" exclaimed Aziz.

"Why would my sister-in-law think that?" asked Emre confused.

"Well... she told us how punctually for a few years now on her birthday something always happens." summed up Mihriban.

"How?" asked Aziz looking at Can.

"What kind of things?" asked Emre.

"Here, she mentioned Fabbri's birthday party, her birthday at the clinic.... " said Leyla in distress pausing to look at Can.

"The nausea from the pregnancy, the run to the hospital for dad's diabetes..." added Leyla.

"Then she said the kids' chicken pox, if I'm not mistaken. The hospitalization for your peanut allergy, love..." continued Mihriban.

"Then what else?" Mihriban asked helpfully.

"Mh... the storm and the broken boat when you were on the road." she said

"Ah, Haydut with the forasacs, I think... and Nihat's diabetes." said Mihriban.

"And... the tour for the presentation of the children's trilogy..."

And a certain invitation to your photo agency for a talk, I think she said." concluded Leyla with difficulty.

"My God... did all these things really happen on her birthday?" asked Aziz shocked.

"There, it seems so. She says she even pinned them on the calendar every year." replied Mihriban.

Can jumped up and reached the window. He felt terribly guilty.

"It sounds like a joke." commented Emre.

"Yeah, I didn't realize my problem happened on his birthday." Aziz admitted.

"Neither did the rest of us." admitted Mihriban and Leyla together.

"My God, how many birthdays has my poor daughter-in-law missed without saying a word then?" wondered Aziz absorbed.

Can remained silent gave the answer, "10..."

"10 years?" replied Aziz in amazement.

"Yeah... this year it's 11 years we've known each other." Can replied.

"No! No, no, no, no! Son, we definitely have to do something!" exclaimed Aziz.

"What else did dhe say?" asked Can to Mihriban and Leyla.

"There... I think she's kind of lost the will to celebrate." Mihriban tried to say mildly.

"That's it, she's curious about what else will happen this year, already considering your situation is not the best." said Leyla.

"Eh, sure! Poor girl, how can you blame her!" exclaimed Aziz sorrowfully.

"How unfortunate... Indeed." commented Emre.

"Son, you have to show her otherwise! You must prove her that her birthday is not unlucky, but the luckiest event that we are all happy to celebrate!" said Aziz.

"She said that she does not expect anything. And that: "maybe this year I'll be the one feeling bad." quoted Mihriban verbatim.

"Eh, no! No, we will not allow that! Can, son, we have to find a solution." his father immediately blurted out.

"Yeah, we will do everything so that nothing and no one disturbs his birthday this year." said Mihriban.

"Exactly." confirmed Emre.

MEANWHILE...

As Sanem was on her way to her office downstairs, typing a message on the phone for Volkan while walking with her head down, she bumped into someone. The phone flew to the floor. When she looked up, noticed it was Metin. Before she could even duck to pick up her phone still on the conversation, he stepped in front of her.

"Oops, sorry. You're not hurt, are you?" he asked her.

"Um, no, sorry, it's my fault, I was focused on the phone. I didn't see you." she admitted.

When she saw Metin's hand reach down to pick it up, her heart started beating wildly. He was just about to grab it when he saw the screen of her phone go blank. It had fortunately gone into stand-by.

Metin picked it up, and instinctively checked that the screen turned on.

When he saw the time appear with the background lock image, Sanem breathed a sigh of relief.

"It didn't break." he said handing it over to her.

"Yeah... thanks." she said taking it from her hands.

Going to standby, the phone had returned to the home screen, and having the lock pin, Metin wouldn't be able to see anything. She was grateful for that.

"Phew! Thank goodness." replied Sanem. "It's still working. Otherwise the lab who can hear it!" she said, trying to be as believable and normal as possible.

Metin smiled. "Then maybe it was better if it broke down." he thought.

"Then you would have some peace." he said staring into her eyes.

"I don't think so, they would definitely find another way to contact me." she admitted.

"I see." she replied.

"Well, thanks again." repeated Sanem quickly, having to continue on his way.

"Nothing. Be careful next time." he advised her.

"Sure." she replied before returning to her office where she recovered from her fright.

Checking her phone, once unlocked, she saw that the message screen was still there. She looked at the name under which she had registered the contact: "Detective V."

Shaking her head to herself, she changed it in a flash, renaming it just "V." Completed the text of the half-finished message and sent it. Then she let herself relax in her chair, trying to relax.

A few minutes later he received a reply.

She poured herself a cup of tea and after a sip concentrated on her work.

Around 5pm, immersed in the files on her desk, she heard a knock at the door.

"Come in." she answered without looking up.

"Sanem?" asked Deren, peeping in.

As soon as she recognized the voice, she looked at her.

She had a bright smile, excited to the core. Deren approached, her eyes shining in front of her.

"Deren? Come, come." Sanem said, motioning towards the parlor.

Deren took a seat as Sanem quickly made her way around the desk to join her. She, too, was looking forward to it.

"And...? Don't keep me on tenterhooks!" pleaded Sanem beside her.

"Ah! My hands are shaking." she said, looking at them. She closed them into a fist hoping to stop them.

Sanem then without a second thought took them between her own to give her courage.

"If you are in this state, that means you know, doesn't it?" asked Sanem.

Deren nodded, smiling.

"It's... it's a girl!" she exclaimed beaming.

"Ah! Congratulations! My God, a little Deren!" exclaimed Sanem bringing her hands to her mouth in happiness.

She embraced her tightly.

"Ah, I'm so happy for you!" she exclaimed, wiping away a tear that had escaped her control.

Sanem gently laid a hand on Deren's belly. "Hello little one!" she greeted her.

"And Bulut? Burak, how did they react?" asked Sanem.

"Ah, Sanem you should see her, she is so cute! We saw her profile. Wait..." she said pulling out the ultrasound scans from her bag. "Look." she said handing it to her.

"Ah..." commented Sanem on seeing her.

"My God, how sweet!" she exclaimed. In the last ultrasound, you could really see the well-defined profile.

"Anyway, Bulut and Burak were happy. Bulut is in love." she said.

"He was nervous, I had never seen him like that." admitted.

"Ah, I guess." Sanem replied.

"Look at you, you have such a bright smile too..." commented Sanem.

"Ah, my dear Deren, it means you have learnt to laugh." she joked, remembering Cey Cey's words of yore.

"What do you mean?" she asked almost resentfully.

"I mean, that I've never seen you so radiant and smiling since I've known you." Sanem explained.

"Pregnancy is making you glow, my dear." she said.

"Ah!" Sanem in a moment snapped to her feet, picked up her notebook and started jotting something down.

"Sanem? What are you doing?" asked Deren puzzled. "What's gotten into you?" she asked.

"I had an idea!" she said "If I don't write it down I might forget about it, and I definitely don't want to, because it's a very... but very good idea." she said.

Deren watched her as she wrote quickly and smiled serenely.

"Done!" she concluded a few moments later satisfied, closing the notebook hastily.

"Sorry, but you know how it is..." said Sanem.

Deren looked at her nodding.

"Why are you looking at me like that?" she asked when she noticed her expression.

"You know, when you do that, it makes me very proud to have been your superior for a while?" she said.

Sanem understood.

Even Deren when she had a creative outburst absolutely had to write it down before inspiration faded. Wherever she was, if she had an idea it absolutely had to be written down, even if it meant using what she had around, including the shoulders of some colleague as a desk.

"Ah, Deren, are you trying to move me by any chance?" she replied.

"And... what's your idea? Can you tell or is it a secret?" asked Deren.

"Mh... I think it will be a secret... at least for a while." admitted Sanem.

"Alright." replied Deren.

"I can only tell you that you just gave me the idea." she confided in her.

"Me?" asked Deren.

"Mh mh." nodded Sanem. "But back to us." she said.

"So tell me about it! It's been a while since we've talked to each other. How is it going? I mean, what plans do you have with Bulut in view of the birth?" she asked.

Then she added: "Do you already have any names in mind?"

"Mh... names in my head I have a few. With Bulut we've talked about it a few times, but we can't agree yet." she admitted. "I want it to be perfect for her."

"I guess. But there is still time. Don't worry." said Sanem.

"Ah! And then... now that we know the sex, I think I'll have a baby shower later on. I already have some decorations in mind." she said all elated.

"Ah, I get it, it will be a kind of wedding 2.0." replied Sanem jokingly.

Deren glared at her.

"I'll shut up." said Sanem passing an imaginary zip over her mouth.

"Besides... there's something that's been on my mind for the past few weeks." she admitted. "Now that my mind is no longer so clouded by nausea." she said with a shudder at the mere memory.

"Yeah... Bulut told me that." confirmed Sanem.

"Anyway..." replied Deren, shrugging her shoulders to banish the memory.

"I was thinking of moving house." she admitted.

"Ah..." commented Sanem surprised.

"Yeah, because lo and behold, my flat is starting to get cramped. There are already three of us, and soon there will be four of us." replied Deren. "I don't know, but the more the pregnancy goes on, the more I convince myself that it would be the best decision." she admitted.

"OK, what about Bulut? Burak? By the way, how is Burak's case going?" Sanem asked.

"Well, Bulut has presented several pieces of evidence against his brother, and pending the verdict in court, temporary removal from his parents has been arranged. They will do checks on this. They will examine the whole home environment, not only the father, but also the mother, and at that point they will decide. The timeframe is long unfortunately. The lawsuit is in a few months." she said.

"I just hope I'm not so huge that I have to miss it." she admitted regretfully.

"I mean, what could be done to speed up the time?" asked Sanem.

"Not much." she admitted. "The only one would be a smoking gun from the mother, but... she's not going to talk." concluded.

"I understand. Deren, if we can help you in any way, just tell us." offered Sanem as always.

"Thank you, I know." she replied.

"OK, enough sad talk now, on such a beautiful day!" changed the subject Sanem.

"And... we were saying? You'd like to move house." she said.

"Yeah..." she said.

"And tell me, what do Bulut and Burak think?" she asked.

"They don't know yet." she admitted.

"Ah..." replied Sanem surprised. Only to ask the fateful question: "Do you have any places in mind?"

Deren looked up and smilingly admitted: "Yes."

"Ah... and that would be?" asked Sanem.

"My grandmother's house." replied Deren immediately.

"Ah! But that's great!" exclaimed Sanem happily.

"There, we would really have a lot more room for everyone there." admitted Deren.

"And would you like to move there before the birth or are you in no hurry?" asked Sanem.

"That's it, I don't even know if Bulut and Burak would agree.... Also because the house needs to be fixed up after all these empty years." said Deren.

"Well... if you want my advice, I would, if I were you, take advantage of this joyous day to propose it to them. What do I know, maybe you could take both of them there and show them your idea. Maybe they will understand." Sanem said.

"Hmm... good idea. Indeed." thought Deren as she stood up.

"Then I'll run." she said hurriedly. "Carpe diem." she exclaimed.

"Good girl, seize the day." she repeated. "Alright, see you." greeted her Sanem.

"Bye!" she said as she closed the office door behind her still all excited.

Once out, Sanem completed her work for the day and then left to join Muzo and pick up the children from her mother's.

To her surprise Muzo had worked on the essay! And a lot too, handing over a ready-made draft for her to correct. She was surprised and delighted. Once she had taken the twins and returned to the estate, she entrusted them to Can and ran to the workshop to finish the work she had interrupted the night before.

Perhaps because of Deren's good news, or because of the idea she had in the office, her work finished smoothly and without a hitch. And before long, the fragrances were ready to be tested on the skin.

She waited ten minutes, noted down all the characteristics she felt and, satisfied with the results, prepared the samples to be tested in the laboratory the following morning.

Afterwards she went home, put the children to bed and with her creative streak still active, decided to move to the loft where she started working on her new idea.

She had no time to waste if she wanted that to be the perfect gift for Deren's pregnancy.

She stayed awake until 2 a.m. without realizing the passage of time. She was so focused and inspired as she had not been in a long time that she surprised herself.

She didn't even realise when around midnight, Can approached the loft to have a look around.

He too had spent the rest of the evening on the garden porch, writing things down, but his inspiration was not as satisfying as Sanem's. In fact, the floor outside was overgrown with paper balls. He got up in search of inspiration. It was so difficult to write such things...He remained looking at her around the corner of the loft, covered by the curtains.

She was so beautiful, so immersed in her own world, he told himself. Completely focused.

"I wonder what she must be doing?" He wondered.

Suddenly he saw her raise the paper in the air in front of her and smile at the result.

And there it was, his inspiration.

Instinctively he smiled too. And before that feeling disappeared, he returned to his seat, picked up his pen and began to write.

34. THE BIRTHDAY CURSE

The weekend arrived and on Friday night, at the stroke of midnight Can placed a letter he had written in his own hand on his sleeping wife's bedside table and went out.

Sanem only realized the letter in the morning, when after yet another night spent sleeping with her children, she went to her room to change.

Entering the still dark room quietly, it took her a few minutes to realise that the bed was empty. Made up. As if no one had slept there.

"He must have gone out for a run." she thought.

She went to the windows and drew the curtains, letting the light in. She looked around.

Yes, the room was indeed empty.

Suddenly, however, she was attracted by something.

She walked over to her bedside table and noticed a sealed envelope with her name written on it.

She immediately recognized Can's handwriting and opened it.

She sat down on the edge of the bed and began to read.

"My beloved Sanem,

I don't know if, and when, you will read this letter.

Perhaps recognizing my writing you will avoid it, as you have avoided me these days, but a little voice inside me hopes you will open it.

The last few weeks have been turbulent. And I am mainly to blame for that. I realize that now. I have thought a lot these last few days of silence, I have tried several times to approach you, and explain to you in words, but on your part, I have found a high and solid wall, which has made me back up several times. I know that you are offended and angry with me, and I understand and respect your desire to keep your distance. That is why I am writing these lines to you.

You know that unlike you, writing is very difficult for me. I have spent sleepless nights searching for the right words, and I don't even know if the following are the right ones, I can only tell you that I wrote from my heart because I want you to know this:

I love you Sanem.

I love you to death.

I have always loved you and I will always love you.

You are everything to me.

You are my breath, my life, my soul, my world and my universe.

At this point Sanem was forced to stop. Because the tears and the heavy lump in her throat prevented her from going on. She covered her mouth with her free hand. She breathed slowly, and forced herself to continue.

It may be too late now and you will never forgive me, but you are right. I deserve your coldness.

Because once again I was mean, intrusive, possessive, and I hurt you. I hurt you in the ugliest possible way.

I curse myself for what I said and thought about our children.

I wanted to retort at that very moment, but I couldn't. The words got stuck on the tip of my tongue.

You are not a bad mother at all, nor are you irresponsible.

You are a present, funny, loving and caring mother, and as I have said before, our children could not have a better one. In my eyes there is not, and never will be, a better mother than you.

For this, forgive me if you can.

Please forgive me Sanem, because these days without you, have been eternal. Without your face, your smile and a look from you I feel lost.

Happy birthday, my great love.

Despite everything, I wish you to spend it peacefully with the people who can make you smile the most, because you deserve the best.

Always.

Can.

Arriving at the end, even more devastated than before, she immediately ran out of the room holding back the desperate crying she felt growing inside. She needed air. With one hand covering her mouth to hold back her tears, she reached the kitchen, threw open the door and went out into the garden.

At that moment Mihriban came out from around the corner, holding a cake with candles on it.

"Ah! Good morning to my birthday girl!" she exclaimed happily.

Sanem turned and stared at her.

When Mihriban saw the state she was in, he immediately placed the cake on the table outside and asked: "Sanem? Daughter? What happened? Why are you in this state?" asked Mihriban agitated.

Sanem pointed to the letter and before Mihriban could ask him anything else. She composed herself and said: "Ehm... You stay with the children, they are sleeping. I have to go." Sanem said snapping away.

"Go where? Eh, Sanem?" she asked as she walked away. Got no reply.

"Hey Sanem!!!" she shouted, but she did not turn around as she walked straight out of the property.

Without a second thought, she reached the place where she had shed all her tears in the past.

The jetty.

Today, too, she would fill that sea with hers. She ran at breakneck speed still in her slip tight in her satin dressing gown. On her feet she still had her slippers. She had cried the whole way, and reaching the hedges leading to the jetty she slowed her pace, catching her breath. The words of that letter echoed in her head.

"Where are you, Can?" she thought.

"He stepped aside to respect my wishes."

"What did he mean? Where did he go? Where?!" she tormented herself.

"Why? Again! Just today!" she thought.

She stepped onto the jetty and with those words still in her head, she walked with her head down until she spotted a figure sitting on top. It was Can, who, like so many times before, had come to think.

"Can?" she thought as saw him.

She ran towards him calling: "Can!"

He turned around and seeing her come running, he stood up worriedly.

"Sanem?" he replied seeing her crying. In an instinctive gesture, he spread his arms wide.

Sanem dived into them in no time. Can held her in his protective wings. With her head sunk into his chest, she began to sob loudly. Can worried and grateful at the same time for that contact was silent for a moment, bewildered.

Confused, he asked worriedly: "Sanem? What happened?" he asked hesitantly as he hugged her tighter.

He lowered his head, trying to look at her, but she sank her head further into his chest. Looking at her Can noticed that in one hand she was clutching a handwritten paper. Then he closed his eyes and understood. He asked in a shy whisper: "Did you read it?"

Sanem nodded his head yes as the tears showed no sign of stopping. Can gave a grateful, closed-eyed sigh. And with one hand he held her close, while with the other he tried to calm her down by stroking her hair. Slowly her breathing began to become slower. So Can hugged her, with his head resting on her shoulder, and inhaled deeply, asking the fateful question.

"Do you forgive me?" he whispered in her ear.

"I forgive you." she said. "But don't ever leave me again, please." said Sanem.

"Neither do you." replied Can.

At that point they looked into each other's eyes.

Can took his wife's face in his hands, wiping her tears with his thumbs.

"Forgive me too, Can." said Sanem.

"Forgive you? And for what?" he asked, stroking her.

"For leaving you alone." she replied. "I misbehaved with you too. I shouted at you like that..." she said regretfully.

"Shh! It's in the past." replied Can, seeing her fidget again.

"You don't need to be forgiven, but if it makes you feel better, I'll tell you, you're forgiven." he replied, hinting at a smile.

"Did you really write those words?" asked Sanem confirmation.

"Yes..." he replied shyly, hiding his face red with embarrassment over her shoulder in an embrace.

They stared at each other for a time that seemed like an eternity. It was as if they were rediscovering each other for the first time, both looking for change, for signs, for something different, as their hands caressed each other's faces for the lack of each other's faces.

At that point it was Sanem who broke that silence: "Can? You are my constellation," she said in reply.

"I love you madly, Sanem Divit." was her prompt reply.

"Me too, Can Divit." she replied and then overwhelmed him with a kiss, in the true sense of the word. So much so that they both fell into the water.

Returning to the surface, Sanem shouted, "Ahhh! It's cold!"

Once again the sea, literally this time, had brought them together, showing them that the way forward had always been and always would be together. Can at that point laughed heartily. Sanem, with her shaggy hair, was so sweet that Can could not resist. He approached her and drawing her to him with élan, he whispered: "I'll warm you up."

Sanem smiled gloatingly, and Can thoroughly enjoyed that smile. A rainbow of pure joy after a dark storm, so he would have called it.

"Ah, how I had missed this." he said serenely.

"What?" asked Sanem.

"Your smile. Now I can finally breathe." he said, going apnea with her in his arms and then surfacing.

"Ah! Can? But at least warn! I was about to drown." she said coughing like crazy.

"Ah! Happy birthday my life!" he exclaimed happily and blissfully.

Suddenly, beside them, they saw his pom-pom slippers, as she had nicknamed them, floating on the surface of the water. It was then that Can recognized them and paid attention to her clothes.

"Love?" he asked.

"Yes?" she asked, like a poor soggy cat.

"But did you leave the house in your nightgown?" he asked.

Sanem looked at herself for the first time.

"Ah! My favourite slippers!" she exclaimed as she saw one pass by her.

Breaking away from Can to join her, he realized that the soaked dressing gown was getting in the way of her frog-like style. So she took it off, remaining only in the petticoat, which clearly showed her form in the water. When Can noticed this, suddenly the temperature of the sea heated up terribly and like a predator with his prey, he silently swam after her until reached her and caught her in a lethal grip.

There was no need for words, their burning gazes and their grip on each other did the rest. In an instant their lips found each other and before passion took over, they were back on shore and from there on the "PHENIX & ALBATROSS."

35. CELEBRATIONS

Once they were inseparably reunited, as happy and in love as on the first day, as they walked home hand in hand, Sanem laughed.

"What are you laughing about?" asked Can serenely.

"Mh, I was thinking that right now it's like time has stopped, I feel like I'm back to 11 years ago, when we were just at the beginning of our relationship. So happy and carefree…" he said.

"Ah, but we are and will be again, don't worry. Many surprises await you, you'll see!" exclaimed Can, kissing their entwined hands.

"Hmm..." she replied hesitantly.

"Aren't you happy?" he asked seeing her hesitancy.

"Well... you know, I mean, you know I love surprises." she replied cutely.

"Then how come you're not jumping for joy?" he asked her.

"Because surely something will happen that will prevent us from celebrating." replied Sanem confidently.

"But it's OK, that's it... I mean, I already got my present now after all." she replied mischievously.

"Ah, but if you do that... I'll eat you up with kisses." He replied, reciprocating that look.

"Anyway, I'm not giving up. There will be some nice surprises. I promise. Nothing and no one will be able to ruin this day!" he pointed out.

"Mh... we'll see." Sanem replied, not very convinced.

Back home, she received her first surprise. She celebrated with her whole family. Her parents had joined them together with Leyla, Emre, Ilker, as well as Aziz and Mihriban. As they arrived hand in hand, they exchanged a look of understanding. They had made peace and everything was proceeding as it should. The table outside was adorned with festoons and the table was laden with every delicacy, most of them her mother's. It was easy to recognize her hand.

"Best wishes daughter!" her father greeted her when he saw her.

At that moment Sanem thanked Can and the boat for changing her clothes. She was wearing a tracksuit. Same for her husband, they seemed to match. She only noticed at that moment.

She looked at Can suspecting that it was all planned. But she did not ask. She preferred to enjoy the moment.

"Best wishes my daughter! It's good that I gave birth to you. Look! We'll have a nice breakfast together," said her mother cheerfully.

"What is it called?" asked Mevkibe to Aziz.

"Brunch." she replied.

"Ah, yes, a 'brach'." Repeated Mevkibe never been good with names in her life.

"Eh, whatever..." commented Sanem hopelessly upon hearing her pronunciation.

"Ah, mama but look how many delicacies are here!" she exclaimed after greeting her.

"See?" she asked.

"Wow, I'm really surprised. You've outdone yourself. Did you make everything or is there also something from Mihriban?" she asked.

"Some of it is hers." she confessed, hugging the mother-in-law who had approached her.

"Wow, really good, it looks like a shop! I swear!" exclaimed Sanem.

"Eh... indeed it does." her mother replied.

"Eh?! What do you mean?" asked Sanem. "What did I miss?" she asked looking around.

"Well, credit to your husband. I told you no? That I needed an idea for the association, didn't I?" she reminded her.

"Yes, I remember." she replied. But then suddenly Sanem remembered that she hadn't told Can about that at all, clouded by anger. She opened her eyes wide, realizing.

"Well, I admit that this time you really were of your word, child. The next morning Can came over and chatted a bit and had a brilliant idea." she said.

"What idea?" she asked as Can came over to hug her wife.

"Melihat, Mihriban and I decided to open a takeaway shop." replied her mother all excited.

"Ah... but that's a wonderful idea!" she exclaimed enthusiastically as she looked at her husband.

"Here, I thought that since the neighborhood is in constant need of money for maintenance and work, why not use the wonderful talent in the hands of your mother and all the women in the neighborhood and beyond, providing a service to the people?" replied Can.

"One minute, one minute, one minute... so you will put up for sale the dishes you usually exchange in the neighborhood, is that right?" asked Sanem.

"Exactly." replied her mother.

"Wonderful. Really, why didn't I think of that before?" she wondered.

"Well, we all know the neighborhood is good food." said Mevkibe pointing to her husband as an example. Nihat strutted proudly.

"So we will create every speciality we know how to make. For example, Melihat will make borek," his mother continued.

"I will make dolmas and other recipes, sister Irmat will take care of the sweets, and anyone who wants to join in, is welcome. For example, Mihriban has offered to cook some vegetarian dishes, the ones your father likes so much!" she exclaimed, winking at her daughter.

Sanem cast a glance at her father who glared at everyone. Also, by the way, he offered to do the barbecue." she said. "I wonder how come?" added her mother as she rolled her eyes.

"Ah..." commented Sanem looking at his father mischievously. "Clever boy..." she told him.

"So you're going back to basics like with the catering, dad, huh?" she added.

"Here..." said Aziz flanking him. "If the opportunity comes, we will promote that service as well." he replied.

"Ah, but you've really thought of everything, I see." replied Sanem surprised that Daddy Aziz was also involved.

"Your sister for example, said that when she can she will prepare her fried intestines." added her mother.

"Ah!!! Then I will prepare my very famous and delicious raw meatballs, what do you say, Can?" she said jokingly looking at her husband.

"That's it, you can do anything, you know, and I'll always support you, but I think customers should get used to simpler flavors before trying that... sophisticated dish." he praised her sarcastically. He actually wanted to end the sentence with 'MORTAL', but desisted for the sake of his newly found peace.

Sanem answered him with a foul tongue.

"Daughter, you don't want to scare away our customers before they get here, eh?" her mother said, knowing her.

"Alright, alright, I'll keep the recipe just for Can. He loves it, doesn't he?" she insisted looking at him.

"Mh mh. I love it! I can't live without it. I'm too jealous, I think I'm not ready to share that recipe with the whole world." he admitted.

His wife laughed.

"And... where will it take place and when especially?" asked Sanem to her mother.

"In a few hours we have the inauguration. And of course you are all invited." she replied without a second thought.

"Ah! Today? And where?" asked Sanem.

"At my old shop. 'Mummy's' has now changed to 'Neighborhood Delights'.' She informed her.

"Ah, that's right! That place was empty. I knew it wouldn't stay vacant that long." she admitted as she looked at her father.

"Wow..." thought Sanem then open-mouthed. "I'm shocked." she admitted.

"You will come and support me, won't you daughter?" asked her mother.

"I'll drop by, of course I'll come! We can't miss it, can we?" she replied seeking her husband approval.

"Whatever you want my dear, today is your day." he said kissing her on the forehead.

"Ah..." commented Mihriban melting with her heart-shaped eyes. "How sweet..."

After hugging the rest of the guests, they sat down at the table, and there between bites the children gave their gift to their mother.

An orange blossom wreath they had made from flowers from the garden just as she had taught them.

It was Deniz who carried it on a cushion, while Yildiz placed it on her head. She was followed by Ates holding a respectable bouquet of wild flowers, just as she liked.

"Here mum. These are for you." she said handing them over. They were bigger than she was. They were practically flowers with legs, Sanem noticed as he approached.

Then all three little ones lined up in front of her and said in chorus: "You are our queen."

"Our Queen of flowers." pointed out Can as he joined the line of children.

"Ouch... but now you make me cry, though." said Sanem wiping her eyes.

Then it was the turn of her sister's presents, Mihriban and Aziz and her parents.

Once the 'brach', as Mevkibe would say, was over, the whole family reached the neighborhood to help out in the shop.

What Sanem didn't know was that Fikri Harika was in charge of advertising, so the entire neighborhood was plastered with flyers and invitations to 'Mahalle Lezettli (neighborhood delicacies)'. The street was festively decorated and not only that, when they arrived Sanem was surprised to find all her friends and work colleagues there.

Deren, Bulut, Burak, Ezgi, Osman, Adile and the baby, Ayhan and Cey Cey, Muzo and Deniz, and all the employees of both companies. It was a great celebration. For a moment, amidst the singing and dancing, she felt as if she were reliving the spring festival, her favourite holiday. But there was still time for that.

In the middle of the street, a long buffet table had been set up with all the specialities the shop had to offer.

What could one say? Sanem had not expected this at all. She was surprised to learn that they were all there mainly to celebrate her as well as her mother.

The birthday girl enjoyed persuading customers to come to her mother's shop. Everyone played their part.

The twins, for example, enjoyed convincing the other children in the neighborhood, especially their close friends with whom they played whenever they were at their grandparents. Suddenly, Can approached her and taking her by the hand pulled her away from the crowd, exchanging a nod with her father and Mihriban.

"Um, Can? Where are you taking me?" he asked as they were moving further and further away. In the meantime it had become late afternoon.

"I'm kidnapping you. If you have no objection..." he replied, stopping suddenly in the middle of one of the deserted streets in the neighborhood.

"What? Now? And..." she was about to say, but her husband finished the sentence for her.

"If you're going to say 'what about the children'? Know that they are in good hands." he replied, resuming walking towards the car.

"And where are we going?" she insisted.

"Surprise." he replied simply.

"What kind of surprise?" continued Sanem curiously.

"Mh, you won't be able to extort anything from me, my dear wife, just know that! I can only tell you that we will go to a place where it will be just you, me and nature. Is that enough of an explanation?" he asked.

"Ah!" Sanem brightened up. "Really?" she asked covered her mouth with her hand. "Are we really going where I think we're going?" she asked brightening up like a child.

"Now we'll see if what you think is what I think." he replied, winking at her.

Once they reached their destination, as they got out of the car, Sanem exclaimed with a sigh: "Ah, how I've missed this place!"

"You expected it then?" asked Can.

"Well, when you said, "You, me and nature" instinctively imagined this, but I wasn't so sure. For a moment I thought you wanted to take me to the mountain hut. Do you remember?" asked Sanem.

"How couldn't I remember? You ran away with the motorboat, and you got lost. And I had to run after you." he recalled vividly.

Sanem stuck her tongue out at him. "I wasn't lost, it's just that the mountain was all the same, snow, snow... snow everywhere I turned!" she exclaimed.

"Ah, I get it... it's nature's fault then." said Can.

"Of course, otherwise my unerring sense of smell wouldn't have a problem." Sanem replied confidently.

"The mountain is my way of life!" she reminded him.

"Well, now you're going to show me if you're still doing well in the wilderness." said Can closing the boot of the car from which he had taken blankets.

"Pss, of course I'll show you. I remember everything!" she said tapping her temples with her strutting fingers. They headed for the shed.

Can preceded her to open it.

"Ah, this smell of wood... how I have missed it!" continued Sanem, remembering the smell that distinguished that place.

"So many memories..." commented Can raising an eyebrow mischievously.

"And... Are we staying here tonight?" asked Sanem.

Before Can could answer, Sanem opened her eyes wide like a greedy child in front of her favorite dessert.

"Just a minute... don't tell me you're going to cook the meat or I might do a triple cartwheel somersault here on the spot. Now!" she exclaimed.

"Oh, I'll do it! Of course I'll do it!" he commented as he checked the amount of wood.

"Just to see you do that jump, I'd do it." he added, winking at her.

"Mh... let's see if I still remember the rules of living at the cabin." said Sanem.

"Rule 1: change into more comfortable clothes." she said opening the chest of drawers where they used to fish for something.

She opened the top drawer and pulled out a change of clothes for herself and her husband.

"Mh, great." said Can. They changed, and once the shed was open again, Can asked intrigued: "Rule 2?"

"Mh, check the amount of wood and pick vegetables from the garden." she recalled.

"Mh, wood is OK. The food is not. So while I reach the shops nearby, you think about the vegetable garden?" Can asked.

"I'll take care of it!" replied Sanem confidently.

"Alright, I'll be right back then." he said kissing her on the forehead and then disappearing away.

As soon as he reached the car, however, Can's phone rang. It was Volkan.

"Mr Can? I have the information you requested." he said.

"Can we meet?" asked.

Can was taken aback. He did not expect to receive an answer that very day, so he replied: "Today is impossible, I am out of Istanbul right now and will not be back until tomorrow."

"I think you should know as soon as possible." Volkan replied.

"OK, I understand, I'll see if I can reach you tomorrow then." he replied.

"OK, I'll be waiting to hear from you." Volkan retorted.

"Perfect, thank you." replied Can before hanging up.

"Just today..." he commented to himself before getting into the car.

Once back, the evening passed as quietly as it had been in a long time. Everything went as he had hoped. They cooked meat with a nice salad just like in the old days, called the children to see what they were doing, and said goodbye with the promise that they would meet again the next day.

When, squeezed on the small sofa in front of the crackling fire they hung up, Sanem sighed: "How nice it would be if they were here with us, eh?"

"After all, they've never seen this place." she thought. "They only know the shed back home."

"Well, that would be nice, sure, but how do you think we'd all fit in here?" asked Can looking at those four "walls."

"Right." commented Sanem sadly. "That's why the other hut exists."

Seeing his pout Can then replied: "One day we'll take them on a trip here. OK?"

Sanem brightened up. "Good idea."

Can noticed the sparkle in her wife's eyes.

They looked up at the stars and relaxed as they hadn't in a long time.

"It was a nice birthday." she blissfully admitted snuggling against his chest as sleep was slowly taking over her. She was relaxing to listen to the beating of his heart.

"Hmm... but it's not over yet." whispered Can to her ear.

"What do you mean it's not?" she asked, waking up sharply.

"No... the celebrations are not over yet my dear." replied her husband with a smile.

"How not, Can? It's past midnight. It's not my birthday anymore." she said.

"Ah, don't say that. It's still your birthday! And it will be for the next 10 days." he informed her.

"What do you mean?" she asked confused.

"I kidnapped you, didn't I? You're mine." he replied, kissing her cheek.

"For 10 days?" she said surprised, bringing her hand to her mouth.

"And the job?" she asked.

"At Fikri Harika Emre and Leyla will take care of it, at the Sanem Bulut will be your representative. I asked Deniz to let your producers know that you would not be available. So it's OK." he said. "Don't worry."

"You're not angry, are you?" he then asked.

"No... I'm just shocked." she admitted.

"And... Are we going to stay here ten days then?" she asked increasingly curious.

"Hmm... I can't tell you. It's a surprise." he replied.

"I... I didn't understand." admitted Sanem scratching her head.

"Great. That's fine. You'll understand soon." he replied stroking her hair.

"It's fine..." she replied before her eyes closed.

"I love you so much..." she said before sleep took over.

"Me too..." he whispered hugging her tightly to him. Closing his eyes in turn to better savour her scent.

He relaxed as well. Then he observed her, she had collapsed.

Taking advantage of the moment, Can with his free arm sent a message to his father. He had an idea in his head.

The next morning, close to each other, they were woken by knocks on the door.

They heard each other again, and Can pretending to still be half-asleep sent Sanem to open the door.

He had been awake for a while and stood beside her, got up and opened the door.

"Who is it?" she asked peeping out of the hut.

Meanwhile, Can was already standing behind her.

"It's us!" exclaimed the children peeping through the door.

"Ah! What are you doing here?" asked Sanem as he found them standing in front of him.

At that point, Aziz appeared.

"I brought them." he replied.

"Ah, Daddy Aziz? But how did you know we were here?" she asked and then turned around. At that point realized that Can standing there was smiling smugly with his arms folded, a sign that his plan had succeeded.

"You... You did this!" she exclaimed. "Scoundrel!"

"What is this place?" asked Yildiz.

"Is this the hut you were saying, dad?" asked Deniz.

"Exactly son." he replied.

"Well, I'm off." said Aziz.

"Alright, thank you dad." Can greeted him.

"And best wishes again, daughter." he added.

"Thank you very much, Daddy Aziz." she replied still shocked.

"So did you enjoy the surprise?" Ates asked.

"Did I like it? I loved it!" she exclaimed, taking her in her arms.

"Come on, let's show you around a bit." Can said.

"This is the first hut. The one Dad was inspired by to recreate the one at home, you know?" asked Sanem.

"It's actually similar... but is this all here?" asked Deniz peering inside.

Can and Sanem laughed.

"Well, it's actually a bit small, but... it's a perfect hiding place." admitted his father.

"Hiding place from whom?" asked Ates curiously.

"From the world." replied her father.

"Yeah... it's dad's secret photography studio this, you know Yildiz?" said Sanem seeing her daughter observing the environment carefully.

"What? Really?" asked the child brightening up.

"Come. Come to daddy. Said Can taking her in his arms. "Now I'll show you everything." he said.

"You should know that Mummy and I always used to come here before you were born." said Can.

In the meantime, Ates, having come down from her mother's arms, joined the 'tour' of the hut with her brothers.

When Can's attention shifted to the outside, a sign that the inside tour was complete, with a frown and furrowed brow looking at her parents, she asked: "Excuse me, but where is the bathroom?"

"That's right, where is the bathroom?" repeated Deniz also looking around.

Can and Sanem looked at each other holding back laughter.

"Ah, a little patience my child." Can replied. "The tour is not over yet." he said.

They took them to the vegetable garden hidden behind some bushes.

"Ah, there's a vegetable garden here too, like at home." said Yildiz.

"Yes..." replied his father.

"It's a bit small though." commented Ates.

"Eh, the out world shed is like that." commented Sanem as if in the clouds.

"Why out of this world, mama?" asked Ates.

"That question will be answered by your father," replied Sanem.

"Because before it was Can & Sanem's cabin, this was my lonely refuge, before I met your mother." recounted their dad.

"When I used to come here, unplugged the phone and enjoyed nature." he explained.

"Ah... now I understand." replied Deniz.

"I like it here. It's so quiet. And fairytale-like." said Yildiz breathing in the air at the top of her lungs, just as her mother had done a moment before.

"I want to see the bathroom." said Ates feeling observed. She still hadn't said anything about the place. "Until I see it I can't decide," she replied confidently.

"Come on then, let's go." said Can taking her by the hand.

He accompanied them to the end of the vegetable garden. Beyond the vegetation was a sort of wooden cabin. A sort of small house, matching the cabin but very rough.

"Here." he pointed at Can.

"This is the bathroom." he said once in front. "On the door was a carved wooden sign that said WC.

"But... the bathroom is a mini shed?" she said surprised and confused at the same time.

"And why is it separate from the shed, daddy?" she asked.

"Because the bathroom was born after the shed." he replied.

"What do you mean?" she blurted out.

"See, I built the bathroom." said Can.

"Really?" asked Deniz surprised.

"Yes." confirmed his father.

"And why right here, Dad?" asked Yildiz this time.

"Because it has the best view." he replied, pointing to a small porthole that overlooked the hills that stretched beyond the vegetation.

"Can I see it?" she asked.

"Wait." he said, checking first that everything was OK.

"It's OK. You can look." he said.

"But there's nothing else here!" exclaimed baffled Ates.

"No shower... no sink..." she said. "And how did you do, Dad?" she asked.

"My daughter, you are very lucky because you have all the comforts of the world, but you see, in some places in the world they don't have as much luck." Can tried to explain.

"What your father is trying to tell you is that he, when traveled the world with his camera saw all this, and he knows how important it is to have... what do I know... water from the tap or even just a toilet. The way of life here is very simple. And that's the beauty of this place. After all, you come here to be in touch with nature, not for the comforts." Sanem said, looking at her husband. Can nodded.

"Like going camping then." said Deniz.

"Exactly, son. In camping you have to get everything: Wood, a place to make the night more comfortable with your tent or sleeping bag, cooking food with what you have, and so on."

"But then... we are rich!" exclaimed Ates.

"I wouldn't say rich... rich we are here." said her mother touching her heart. "Because we understand the value of things we usually take for granted. We are rich inside."

"That's why I tell you we are lucky. Having a warm bed, a roof, food, and water to wash are luxuries we should never take for granted." said Can.

"Coming here reminds me of countries that are not so lucky. Do you understand?" he asked after they finished talking.

"Nice, I like it." said Ates.

"But the bathroom doesn't." she added a moment later, confident.

Everyone laughed.

"Well now that the tour is over, let's have breakfast and then go." said Can.

It was their first family breakfast in that cabin. They were making memories with their children even in their refuge away from the world.

Sanem prepared the tea while the girls set the table, Can and Deniz instead went to the bakery for freshly baked simits.

Once they had finished their breakfast, they all set off towards their new destination.

"Where are we going?" asked Ates curiously.

"I wonder too, my little bird." replied Sanem surrendering with a sigh.

"We are now returning to the estate. I want you to get ready to lower the sails because we're leaving!" Can informed her.

"What?!" exclaimed Sanem.

"What about school?" she asked.

"No school!" exclaimed happily the children.

"I have already talked to their teachers. Don't worry." replied Can having thought of everything.

"With the boat, dad?" asked Deniz snapping in the back seat despite the belt.

"With THE PHENIX & ALBATROSS." he confirmed.

"Yuppy!!!" exclaimed Ates. "A boat trip!"

"It's not going to be a trip, it's really going to be a holiday! So once you get there, I want you to pack your bags, Divit family!" exclaimed Can.

"Whatttt!?" exclaimed Sanem.

"First real boat trip?" exclaimed Deniz on a roll.

"And where will we go?" he asked.

"Oh, we'll have some stops to make." replied his father looking at him from the rear-view mirror.

"Ah, like pirates?" asked Ates.

"Yeah, love, like pirates." replied Can smiling.

"So you guys get your backpacks ready, while I go and refuel the boat. I'll meet you directly there in two hours. Alright?" he said.

"Yeeeee!" exclaimed the children.

"Well, what can I say... you really thought of everything!"commented his wife still in shock.

"But honey, your suitcase?" he then asked.

"Me? Mine's been packed for a while now. Don't worry." he said once he had parked at home. He winked at her.

"You... You are really... unbelievable." Sanem replied with her eyes narrowed to two slits.

The children came running down to the house, while Sanem was taken for one last kiss before they left.

After that, her husband took the road to Istanbul. He was to meet Volkan.

The appointment was at the usual place, in the small park, under the canopy of a large tree.

Her euphoric mood was put to the test and she began to crack after hearing the news about Volkan.

He had found strange information, as if someone was trying to cover up the truth. But everything they currently had, was easily traceable to Emre, unfortunately.

Can, however, knew that dealing with Aylin meant being confronted with evidence concealed or falsified to her liking, so keeping her spirits high and her hopes up, he decided not to believe it. At least not until they had tangible proof in their hands.

Having said goodbye to Volkan, he hurried to call his brother to inform him of what he had just discovered.

He joined him shortly afterwards under that same tree.

"It's not possible, it's not possible!" exclaimed Emre nervously and agitated.

"Brother... calm down." Can replied.

"How will i calm down? Everything leads to me, brother! How can I calm down, huh?!" he exclaimed in a panic.

"Listen. Look at me." he said, blocking his arms, forcing him to look into his eyes.

"There is only one way to know the truth." he said.

"And what is that?" asked Emre desperately.

"You have to do the DNA test." replied Can.

"Sure and I according to you, how do I get the comparison with Hatay's, huh?" he asked sarcastically.

"Simple. Through his social worker." replied Can.

Emre remained silent.

"And how?" he asked more calmly and seriously.

"I bet you didn't notice how that woman snapped immediately upon hearing our last name that day at my house." Can recalled.

"No... I didn't notice anything strange about her attitude, brother." he admitted.

"Neither did I at first. Deren pointed it out to me." continued Can.

"What do you mean?" asked his brother.

"Well, the woman is trying to learn more about that poor child's family dynamics, she confided it to me and I'm convinced she knows something... or at least she's done research. And maybe she found out that the mother worked for our company. She must have seen the news and everything... and when she found us in front of her, she jumped." explained Can.

"It's just a guess, eh, but I think that woman knows something, and you thinks.... Who better than her can confirm if the mother is really Aylin?" he asked.

"Yes, but we already know it's her. Volkan has confirmed it." Emre reminded him.

"We will have one more confirmation then." replied Can. "Come on, let's go." he said.

Once in the car, Can called Mrs Birce and asked her to join Fikri Harika.

They were in the Sanem meeting room, away from prying eyes. The meeting was also attended by Deren who was aware of the facts.

She confirmed both about Aylin and that she was aware of her bad relationship with the Divit family. She admitted that she was surprised that day that had come into contact by chance with someone who had known Hatay's mother so closely.

Can's assumptions were right. The woman knew very little about Aylin. At that point, it was Emre who brought her up to speed on what she never wanted her to know. Their relationship.

And hence the demand to know whether Hatay was really his son who had been kept hidden all this time. Faced with so much evidence, the woman began to put the pieces together and also understood the reason behind the choice of such an inappropriate name for an innocent child. So without a second thought, she took advantage of the opportunity she had in front of her after years of emptiness, and agreed.

Can told the woman to speak directly with her brother from then on. They would still stay in touch.

At that point, Can could leave knowing that he had done everything possible.

Back at the estate, he and his family set off on their first route. A very close destination that he couldn't wait to show his children. The island of Orak.

The time had come to take his children to the top of that seaward promontory for an update on his life. And so they did.

The children all in their little sailor hats had a great time. Sanem held onto Ates, the most dangerous of them all. It was a spectacular day. The sun, the sea, the breeze… The seagulls flying freely over them fully represented the whole family's sense of freedom at that very moment. Only at that exact moment did they realize how much they needed it. It was as if they had always lived in apnoea for the last few months and only now, as they rose to the surface, did they begin to really breathe. They were truly a family of travelers. That evening, once they were back on board and showered, the children collapsed from sleep.

At that point Can joined Sanem at their favorite spot on the boat.

Under the stars they lay under the boat's mast.

"You'll catch cold." Can told her, coming up behind her with a blanket. He wrapped it around her shoulders.

"I missed it so much..." said Sanem.

"What?" asked Can.

"All this." she admitted. "I would never have guessed." she added, laughing at herself.

"The stars are beautiful." she added.

"But you are the most beautiful." retorted Can wrapping his wife in his arms. Sanem also wrapped him under the blanket.

"Yildiz would have loved these stars." thought Sanem.

"Ah, she'll get to see more of them. Don't worry." Can reassured her.

"You really surprised me, Can Divit." his wife then admitted.

"Happy birthday, my love." he repeated again.

"Thank you." she replied kissing him on the cheek. She caressed him looking straight into his eyes, then with sly eyes in a knowing expression said: "I know what you're doing."

"What?" he asked naively.

"You're trying to undo the curse of my birthday." said Sanem.

"Hmm... and I'm succeeding, it seems." He replied confidently.

"Don't sing victory too soon, Can Divit." retorted Sanem a little sad.

"If my reasoning doesn't mislead me, you chose to take a ten-day trip to make up for ten years of birthdays gone awry, am I wrong?" she asked.

"Mh, clever as ever, my dear Detective Divit." he replied, smiling jokingly.

"That's a nice thought, but... there was no need for that. Really." continued Sanem.

"Oh, yes there was. We all needed it. You, me, the kids... don't you see how just getting away from all the problems did us good?" he said.

"It did." she admitted.

"And... what is our next destination CapCan?" Macho asked at that point.

"Mh, we have two days of sailing to get to our next destination, I can tell you that for now." measured Can words.

"Ah! We will be leaving Turkey then?" asked Sanem squinting.

"Exactly." he replied. "Today's was just a test to see how the children were doing, and... I'd say they're ready." he said.

"Cooked to perfection." exclaimed Sanem winking at him.

"It will be an unforgettable trip, I promise." said Can.

Sanem let go against his chest. Then suddenly she straightened up.

She looked him straight in the eyes and said: "We're not going to the Galapagos, are we?" she asked worriedly.

"No, my love, I said the sailing would take two days... how could we get to the Galapagos in that time, eh?" he reminded her.

"Ah, that's it, because we can't go with the kids, Can." Sanem replied seriously.

"I know, don't worry. We'll go somewhere safe." he said, stroking her hair.

During the two days on the open sea, the Divit family filled their days with various games and activities. Sanem showed the children how to cook by rocking the boat, they caught fresh fish together, which Can cooked. They saw dolphins swimming happily alongside the boat, Yildiz took photos with his camera and they watched the most beautiful sunsets and stars they had seen since they were born. On the day they approached land, Sanem with binoculars in hand, looked at the horizon and immediately recognized the approaching coastline.

"I can't believe it, Can!!!" she jumped like a little girl.

"Have you figured out where we are?" he asked happily.

"Are we arrived?" asked Yildiz.

"Yesssss... my God I'm so excited!" she exclaimed going to hug her husband tightly at the helm.

"Ah, Gino! Gino is waiting for us kids!" she exclaimed.

"I'm so hungry!" said Deniz.

"Ah, then we couldn't have arrived at a better time!" exclaimed Can.

"Who is Gino?" asked Ates.

"Gino is the best pizza maker in the world!" exclaimed Sanem.

"Pizza?" snapped all three children as soon as they heard that magic word. Three days at sea had put their appetites to test.

"We're all going for pizza!" exclaimed Can.

"I promised you, didn't I?" he reminded his wife.

"Ah, I can't believe it! This really is the best gift in the world!" she exclaimed as happy as a child.

"Then all ready in position for maneuvers." said CapCan, who had meanwhile entered the port of Naples.

The family followed the captain's directives and before long, they were on dry land.

After the first stop at Gino's, and having satiated the whole family's appetite, they took a tour of the city, showing the sights to their children through stories of their first trip to the land.

The following days they decided to visit the Amalfi coast, stopping in Positano, Amalfi, and Capri, where they stayed several days. On the last day in Capri, Can received a phone call from his brother.

Leyla had caught a request for a paternity test in Hatay's name on his mobile phone. Chaos had erupted.

"What?!" he exclaimed into the phone. It was now evening and Can was standing in the bow, while the rest of the family was inside. Sanem was helping the little ones take a shower.

He hadn't noticed, however, that Sanem had approached him.

"Alright. I understand, brother, don't worry. We'll leave tomorrow anyway, see you soon and talk about it." he said, ending the call.

He touched his forehead in shock.

"That's all we need..." he commented in a whisper.

"Can?" asked Sanem at that point who remained silent behind him.

"What's going on?" she asked worriedly. "What happened to Emre?" she asked.

Can realized it was time to bring his wife up to speed on the events.

"I'll tell you, but promise you won't be angry with me, please." he said already upset for his brother.

"So you scare me though, what's going on?" she asked again.

"After dinner." he said pointing at the children.

"Alright." she replied reaching for them again.

Once dinner was eaten and the little ones were asleep, Sanem joined her husband at their usual place, and there she told him everything she knew about Hatay.

"Please don't be angry with me for not telling you." he said to her.

"I'm not mad at you at all, love. I'm just upset!" she said in shock.

"My sister..." thought.

"I know..." he commented.

"It's a good thing we're coming back." she admitted with a sigh.

"Yeah, but i'm sorry it ended like that, though." Can admitted.

"Love, you don't have to take it to heart, your surprise turned out just as you wanted. I'm happy, and quiet, and we were going to leave tomorrow anyway, so don't make an issue of it." said Sanem.

"Well, even if the ending isn't quite what I expected, I want to at least give you this." he said, pulling out from behind his back a black box with a big red bow on it.

"For you." he said handing it to her.

"A present?" she asked curiously. "What is it?"

"Open it and see." he replied.

Sanem opened it. The first thing that jumped out at her was the title: "The Divit Family's First Boat Trip."

"Did you make this?" asked Sanem stunned, pulling out a finely bound album with a sturdy cover.

"Mh mh." confirmed Can.

Sanem leafed through it all in silence watching that journey of theirs through Can and Yildiz's eyes.

"These are Yildiz's." he said pointing to the pictures on the last pages.

"She put in so much effort and wanted to give her own touch. It was only right that she had her own space." he explained proudly.

"These... this is us." Can said simply.

"We need to remember this whenever we are under stress or angry with each other." said Sanem. She understood her husband's purpose.

It was not just an album, but a note for life.

"I will make one for every trip we take." Can promised.

"It's really beautiful, my love. I have no words." replied Sanem throwing her arms around his neck.

"I love you madly, Can Divit. More than myself. Both in sunshine and in stormy seas. Never forget that." she whispered to him.

"More than myself, my love. Now and forever. You are my sun." he said, seeing her smile.

"Ah, you romantic rascal!" she exclaimed before planting a passionate kiss on him.

And so illuminated by the only light of the starry sky, with a city in full motion behind them, they gazed at the horizon of the sea before them, knowing that nothing and no one could really separate them.

36. THE CALM BEFORE THE STORM

Dear diary,

I need to write. Yes, because something is changing.

These five months have been wonderful and have passed so quickly that it's as if I suddenly blinked my eyes and.... hop! Here we are.

But let's start from the beginning.

The relationship between Emre and Leyla after that discovery has soured. They've been going through really difficult months. Especially my sister.

It's not easy to accept that perhaps, there is a remote possibility that, such a powerful ghost from the past, could come back to haunt them.

Emre is devastated, and as much as I love my sister, I'm sorry to see him like this.

Can is helping him in any way he can. Volkan seems to be working only for us these days!

Emre is doing everything to make sure that this is not true. There have been delays and problems with the results these months, he had to retest, but still nothing. Strange. If it were his he would be ready to take responsibility, as he should be, but will my sister be ready for this? So far it seems not.

As far as I know, they sleep in separate rooms and Leyla fills her days with work and Ilker to take her mind off things.

Can and I have done everything we can to bring peace and quiet back between them, but I admit it's difficult with these conditions. I only hope that everything will work out for the best, for the sake of my little nephew.

Ayhan and Cey Cey, on the other hand, are going full steam ahead with preparations for the arrival of the twins. Yes, Ayhan is expecting a boy and a girl. We are all curious to see two mini Ayhan-Cey Cey come into the world.

But before them, of course we await the birth of Deren's baby girl. It is a matter of days now, she could give birth at any time.

Deren is exhausted, forced to take maternity leave. However, she continues to work remotely, the only thing that seems to keep her brain busy and not think about her huge belly.

Muzo meanwhile finished the proofreading of the book, in recent months we have been working on the cover design and the advertising campaign with Can at Fikri Harika. Can publicly apologized to Muzo, and he accepted. Soon everyone will know about this mysterious book. Especially Deniz.

Therapy with her seems to have brought back that initial closeness between the two. Now in the agency they laugh and joke without hurting each other like two very good 'friends'... though perhaps that is not quite the right word for it.

This 'closeness', if you want to call it that, has obviously created a bit of suspicion in Metin, who, if possible, is even more attentive and present than before. From the look on Deniz's face, however, it seems that this attitude of his is not welcome. When he arrives and intrudes into the conversation of the two masked with that gentle smile of his, I notice Deniz roll her eyes several times. Talking to her, it seems that apart from that, things between them are fine for the time being. Well, as in... always in the same habitual way.

I don't think Deniz is ready to talk about it yet, and I haven't delved into the subject. But that hasn't stopped me from keeping a constant eye on Metin. And if I'm honest... dear diary, not as of now. In fact, despite what I said, have always silently continued to keep an eye on Metin. I know, I know! I said I wouldn't meddle, and I'm keeping my promise, but what can I do? It's stronger than me. I have a sixth sense about this whole thing that I can't suppress. After all, I'm not doing anything wrong... I'm just making sure nothing bad happens to Deniz and Deren. That's all. I just do it for them.

My mother, on the other hand, after opening the 'Mahalle lezzetli' (neighborhood delicacies) shop, based on Can's idea, is going strong. The idea of harnessing the skilled hands of many women in the neighborhood who already shared their food with their neighbors is just perfect. All the ladies in the neighborhood participate and from morning to night they fill the shop with every food possible. They are paid for this and part of the proceeds, after deducting expenses, is used to finance the work in the neighborhood that the association takes care of.

Everyone can contribute their own specialities. For example, Mihriban brings her healthy, vegan food whenever she can.

And recently, talking to my father, Can and I suggested putting up a sign to promote the catering service more, since he and Aziz love to barbecue, it might be a good idea to support my mother.

Miriban and Aziz are spreading the word as much as possible to support their in-laws, and the whole of Fikri Harika participated by spreading flyers everywhere. We have been anxiously awaiting the day of the spring festival, (me especially!) where the neighborhood has always been dressed up for the festival, amidst fragrances and traditions.

For several years I missed it, but this year it was great to be able to participate. Especially for the children.

It makes me extremely proud and happy to introduce the twins to and experience the traditions that have always been part of my family.

Being at an age where curiosity is sky high and eyes always alert and ready to learn new things, it was truly unforgettable. It was wonderful to see them tasting food created especially for the occasion, having fun with songs, dances, and games. Also present this year were Ayhan, Cey Cey, Osman, Adile and the baby, who took the opportunity to visit their old trainee in the butcher's shop who had worked for them for years. He became the new owner by taking over their old family business.

As for me, on the other hand, the Sanem is proceeding apace. The release of the 'Pink Lady' line internationally could not have made me happier. Especially considering its history.

All it started as a personalized gift for Deren's baby shower with the name 'Pembe gul' (Pink Rose), in honor of her grandmother and more. In fact, the whole line, consisting of oil, cream, scrub, cleanser and perfume is all based on different roses. I worked on it for months. Every time she told me how she had pain in her legs, or stretch marks and all that, I asked myself: "Sanem? How come it never occurred to you to create a line for pregnant women? You still have your grandmother's recipe book, why not use it?" After all, I know very well what it means to see your body change to make room for a new life. In my case, three! Whenever she asked me for advice, I responded with the methods recommended by my grandmother, and so the idea of creating a personalized gift inspired by hers was born.

Her expression when she realized what they were was priceless. When she received it she was shocked, but happy. She was my first customer, and seeing the results, she proposed to put it on the market.

And so it was. But with a different name proposed by Deren herself, sure that it would have been a great success abroad. Pink Lady, to be precise.

Another novelty was the children's fragrances, inspired by my beloved little birds. Three fragrances: a fresh and sparkling one reminiscent of a sea breeze, a warm and enveloping one reminiscent of burning wood with a pungent note, and another, eternal, intense, natural, impervious and unattainable like an edelweiss, with a note of sweetness.

In the agency we have concluded some very good contracts, and for a few weeks now, after several years, we have been working with Makinnon and his secretary, Mrs Minè, again. (ex Fabbri secretary)

They too are pleasing the market. It is certainly a gamble, considering that children's perfumes usually only have super sweet and sometimes nauseating fragrances reminiscent of candies, and in some cases, even cough syrups. Could it just be my nose that repulses them because I am used to more natural fragrances? Probably.

The best thing about all this, however, has been the children's appreciation. Now every morning they are super happy to be able to spray their own fragrances, so another dream of mine has come true.

Although they have to learn to dose themselves. Sometimes they overdo it in the shower! The air becomes unbreathable! My God... when I think about it, I get nauseous.

But that's normal, isn't it? Every perfume, even the most delicious in excessive quantities, becomes nauseating...

What can I say? As for the rest... well, something else is cooking at the moment. But it's still too early to talk about it.

37. TIME BOMB

METIN

It was a morning like any other in the agency, all a general rush from one side to the other, printouts, meetings and coffee flavoured brainstorms, but I took no notice. I only had one goal at that moment. I had to do something, and I had to do it now.

I was about to contact her, but as luck would have it, just as I was walking towards Can's office, she was walking towards me.

"Good morning Metin." she greeted me as usual.

"Good morning Deren." I greeted her.

"Metin? Are you OK? You seem nervous today." she replied.

"Deren, I need to talk to you about something important. It's urgent." he said seriously.

"About what? What happened?" asked Deren worriedly.

"I'll tell you what. Let's meet at the café down the street, over coffee I'll tell you about it." I said.

"But you're scaring me like that." she replied surprised.

"You don't have to scare yourself. You just have to listen to me. You'll understand when you hear." I insisted.

"Alright..." replied Deren confused.

"See you in five minutes." I concluded, continuing straight on my way.

A LITTLE LATER...

Deren reached the bar and sat down slowly given her nine-month-old baby bump.

A little later she saw Ezgi arrive.

"Ah! Ezgi?" she called her as soon as she saw her pass by.

"Deren?" she replied surprised. "Hello! What a coincidence!" she exclaimed happily.

Deren tried to get up.

"No, stop, stop." Ezgi stopped her, lowering herself to greet her with a hug.

"What are you doing here?" asked Deren.

"I'm meeting someone. He has given me a date here." she said.

"Ah, a hot date?" asked Deren mischievously.

"No." she replied seriously. "Not at all." she added, looking around. "But I don't see him, maybe I'm early." she said.

"And what about you?" she asked in turn.

"I..." she started to say, then seeing her standing there, she added: "Have a seat here. Come. Let's wait together." she said.

"I too am waiting for someone. A colleague from work." Deren replied.

Meanwhile Metin came out of Fikri Harika and went to the bar.

When he arrived he saw them both sitting next to each other at the same table, he smiled to himself, thinking how lucky he was that day.

He approached.

"Girls?" he greeted them with a smile.

"Ah, Metin, there you are." Deren replied.

"Ezgi?" he greeted her.

Deren looked at Ezgi and then at Metin.

"You two know each other?" she asked.

Ezgi was at a loss. She wished she had not shown up for that meeting at all, and now more than ever.

"Yes, we know each other." Metin answered for her. "And for a long time, too." he replied.

"Ah! Really? I didn't know that." commented Deren dispiritedly.

"Better that way, then. Ezgi is waiting for someone, and I have asked her to sit with me while we wait." Deren explained.

"Oh, you did very well." replied Metin with a mocking smile.

"Isn't that right, Ezgi?"

Deren furrowed her brow. "Why do you say that?" she asked.

"Because he is the person I was supposed to meet with." Ezgi replied icily.

"Ah!" commented Deren. "What do you mean?" she asked even more confused.

"Yes... I admit it. I wanted to meet both of you in the same place." said Metin.

"Why?" asked Deren.

"Yeah, why are you being mysterious?" asked Ezgi in a resentful tone.

Deren looked at her. Ezgi seemed to resent his friend and didn't understand.

"Sorry, but now I'm so curious..." interrupted Deren. "How do you two know each other?" she asked.

"Now you have to tell me." she said carelessly taking a sip of her smoothie.

"Oh, I'll tell you. That's what I'm here for." he replied.

"What do you mean?" asked Ezgi doubtfully.

"I mean that you have a mutual acquaintance." he replied without mincing words.

"Have you ever thought that your stories are very similar? Almost complementary I would say." he corrected himself.

"Metin what are you babbling about?" asked Ezgi impatiently.

Metin looked at Deren.

"There, I actually admit that I have thought about it. I mean, it's true, we both had a difficult past, maybe that's why we get along so well." replied Deren.

"Good girl, Deren. The past. You hit the right spot." replied Metin.

"And what exactly is it that you have in common about the past, shall we hear?" he asked.

"Well, for example I never had a good relationship with my father and.... I understand that Ezgi is also in the same situation, or am I wrong?" asked Deren.

"That's true." he admitted.

"But I didn't understand... what is the point of all this Metin? What are you getting at, huh?" asked Ezgi.

"Wait. You said you're in contact with a person we have in common... who is this person?" asked Deren instinctively bringing a hand to her tummy.

Metin took a deep breath and spat out: "Your father!"

"Our fathers?" asked Ezgi.

"You... why are you in contact with my father? How? When?" asked Deren confused and taken aback.

"Alright, let's see if you get there." said Metin.

"What does your father do?" asked Deren.

"He's a lawyer, but if you say you know him, you know that much, I mean... you're one of them too." she replied.

He looked at Ezgi.

"And your Ezgi?" he asked.

"Mine is also a lawyer." she replied.

"Really?" asked Deren turning sharply to look at her.

"I don't understand, Metin. What are you trying to say?" asked Ezgi in a panic.

"Ah... I get it!" Deren exclaimed. "You mean our fathers are colleagues? That they know each other?" she asked.

"No." replied Metin.

"Deren how old are you?" he then asked.

"Metin! But does that sound like a question to ask a woman? And married, too?" she asked in amazement.

"One minute..." Ezgi exclaimed brightening up.

"You said: I know your father... why did you use the singular?" asked Ezgi.

"Bingo!" he exclaimed.

"Bingo? Bingo what? I'm not getting it." admitted Deren taking another sip of smoothie.

"Why did you say that?" asked Ezgi raising her tone of voice.

"Because he is your father." he said.

Deren nearly choked on her straw as she drank her smoothie.

She coughed.

"Who?!" shouted Ezgi.

"The famous lawyer Ahmet Erdogan." replied Metin.

"WHAT?!" Deren exclaimed petrified.

"WHAT?! ARE YOU JOKING?" blurted Ezgi.

"I knew you wouldn't believe me and that's why I prepared these two envelopes for you." he said, holding them out in front of them.

"WHAT KIND OF JOKE IS THIS METIN? Huh?" ranted Deren then, getting up ready to leave.

"I'm saying that he is the father of both of you. You two are sisters. Deren the elder and Ezgi the younger." he replied quietly.

"I'm not joking. It's all written inside." he said pointing to the envelopes.

At that point Ezgi also stood up black with anger.

Everyone in the club turned to look at them but they didn't care at all at that moment.

"THIS IS YOUR SELLING, ISN'T IT?" shouted Ezgi.

"Because I don't reciprocate what you feel, do I? You are doing this on purpose... you know very well that my father is a very painful point in my life. That's why you're doing this, isn't it? What kind of man are you, huh?" she said.

As the furious quarrel between Ezgi and Metin played in the background of Deren's thoughts, like a distant echo, she with tears in her eyes and shortness of breath, commented in a hushed voice "sisters?"

Of those screams, of that conversation she heard only sweeps, and at that moment she honestly did not care at all. She only heard Metin say: "It was only right that you should know..."

"Yes, but why now? Why now?! You have no proof. These are definitely fake! How else can a person bring two girls together and say such a thing like this, in a bar, eh?" continued Ezgi with their argument.

While the two were busy arguing, Deren found the courage to open the envelope.

The first thing her eye fell on were two photos. One with her father and mother. And one with her father, another woman and a newborn child. Turning it over she noticed the name written on the back: "Ezgi."

At that moment the background noises became more and more muffled as the thoughts became more and more overwhelming. Her ears were ringing. Conspicuously, as the other two continued to argue, she stepped out. And as if in a trance, without knowing what she was really doing, she motioned to her driver waiting outside to give her a hand.

The man immediately jumped at her nod, caught up with her and helped her into the car. Once inside, he got behind the wheel and asked: "Madam, shall I take you to the hospital?" he asked worriedly.

"Are you all right?" he asked.

"I'm fine, I'm fine. Take me to Grandma's." replied Deren in a trembling voice. She felt like she was in a bubble....

"Madam are you sure? Do you want me to call your husband?" her trusted driver insisted.

"Just do what I told you." Deren replied coldly between tears.

Meanwhile, Can and Sanem arrived at the agency.

As soon as they crossed the entrance, Sanem's phone rang. It was the editor for Muzo's book.

He motioned Can to continue while she apologetically went back outside to answer it. There was too much buzz inside.

As she was waving goodbye to her American publisher, she saw Ezgi passing in front of her, at a brisk pace across the street. Her face was distraught and from what she could see she was crying. She noticed her dabbing at her face with a handkerchief.

She followed with her gaze and meanwhile ended the conversation and hung up.

"Ezgi?" she called to her hurriedly. But she probably didn't hear because she got into a taxi a little further on and then disappeared.

Sanem frowned displeased and puzzled.

"Why was Ezgi in that condition?" She asked herself.

She returned and reached her company.

"Good morning Sanemsi." greeted Ayhan as she walked out of the break room with a sweet in her hand.

"Good morning." she replied distractedly, her mind still on what she had just seen.

"How are you?" she asked focusing on her.

"Fine. But what an effort!" she said touching her baby bump.

"I know right." replied Sanem as she reached her office.

Ayhan followed her and took a seat on the sofa.

"What about you? Why do you look like that?" she asked.

"Me? Ah, I saw something strange, but... never mind." she replied.

"Rather…" she began the speech as she turned on her pc.

"Where is Deniz? Can you send her to me?" she asked.

"Um... that's why I'm here." replied Ayhan. "Deniz is not here. She didn't come and I really don't think she will come today." she said.

"Why? She didn't say anything to me. Is she ok?" she asked.

"No, sister. Not at all." Ayhan replied.

"What happened?" she asked as she took a seat at her desk.

"They broke up." said Ayhan with a sigh.

"Who did they break up?" asked Sanem.

"Her and Metin. Last night." she replied.

"What?! What do you mean? What happened? Talk!" began Sanem worriedly.

"Alright, but calm down." replied Ayhan feeling under pressure.

"You're right, sorry." she tried to contain herself.

"It seems Metin proposed to her last night." she said.

"What!?" exclaimed Sanem.

"Yeah... and she refused." Ayhan continued.

"How did she refuse? I mean, I don't understand. What made her refuse? She doesn't love him anymore, does she?" she said. "I knew it, even if she didn't want to admit it." Sanem continued.

"That's it... that's partly it, but that's not just why she refused." said Ayhan.

"Ah! What's that?" asked Sanem even more curious.

"Alright, sister I'll tell you the whole story properly, otherwise you won't understand." said Ayhan with a sigh.

"Tell it." she insisted.

"Well, you know that she and Muzo are back to being friends like before or maybe even more, right?" began Ayhan.

"Of course I know." Sanem replied.

"Here, at this time, Muzo given the closeness, tried to open her eyes to Metin. It seems Deniz has been venting several times about some attitudes she didn't tolerate about him lately. Always jealous, overly present in front of Muzo, etc... and things between them have been getting worse and worse. I mean, at least on Deniz's part." Ayhan took a breath.

"Two days ago they had a fight, and while I was at Muzo's, Deniz came in crying. She vented to us, at which point he, seeing her like that, did something, Sanem." said Ayhan.

"What did he do?" she asked.

"He told her the story of Deren." she admitted.

"What did he do!?" asked Sanem incredulously.

"Yes, he did, sister." confirmed Ayhan.

Sanem stood petrified for a moment, then reflecting, replied:

"OK, but she doesn't know the whole story. In fact, you don't know the whole story." she corrected herself.

"What do you mean, sister? Why do you?" asked Ayhan, raising his antennae.

Sanem took a deep breath and then admitted. "Yes, I know other things. Don't hold it against me, but I didn't tell you anything so as not to get in your way. But in all this time I never stopped keeping an eye on him." Sanem emptied the bag.

"One minute, one minute..." said Ayhan "What exactly do you know?" she asked frowning.

Sanem replied in a whisper." Metin and Ezgi know each other, and he seems to have had a crush on her for a long time." she said.

"Ah!" exclaimed Ayhan. "What are you saying!?"

"One night I caught them together on a bench at the gardens near our neighborhood." she recounted at that point.

"And I heard that she was very annoyed. Later Volkan confirmed that Metin is smitten with her, but not her with him." Sanem pointed out.

"Woha!" exclaimed Ayhan with an open mouth.

"I'll tell you... I'm more surprised that it was Deniz who left him, than vice versa. Because I was really convinced that Metin would have dumped her any day now, if the other had agreed." she added. "That's why I was keeping an eye on him. I didn't want him to hurt her or Deren." explained Sanem.

"Sanem! Wow, Muzo found out the same things! That's why he warned Deniz at that point." commented Ayhan bewildered.

"One minute! Muzo knows all this! What do you mean?" asked Sanem open-mouthed at the twist.

"Well, it's true, Muzo hasn't been well, but the illness thing and all, it wasn't that bad. It was our plan." she admitted.

"What? A plan of yours?" asked Sanem even more stunned. "Did you make fun of me?" she asked.

"No, we didn't, sis. Listen." said Ayhan.

"Mihriban informed us why you didn't give us any more info, I mean, you had your own problems with Can and we also didn't want to get in your way, so Muzo wanted it that way." she explained.

"What do you mean?" asked Sanem. "Like Muzo?"

"Yes, it was all his idea. After your quarrel, he never gave up on Metin. He kept investigating on his own and asked us for help." confessed Ayhan.

"We who?" asked Sanem.

"Me, Cey Cey and... Burak." she replied.

"Now I understand why none of you have ever come to ask me anything about it," reflected Sanem.

"Here, sister don't be angry with us, please." said Ayhan sorry.

"No, I am not angry. I'm just surprised." she admitted. "It means Muzo never stopped keeping an eye on Metin so.... wow, I'm impressed." she admitted.

"One minute... but how did he therefore manage to get the information I know?" she asked.

"Simple... because he was also present that night at the gardens you described. It really seems like you both saw the same thing." acknowledged Ayhan.

"No way..." commented Sanem bashfully.

"OK, but what about the rest?" she asked. "How do you know?"

"Here, I don't know. Who knows! Maybe he followed Volkan! Can you imagine that? Muzo following a detective..." she said laughing.

"Ah... it's not so hard to imagine after all." admitted Sanem.

"And... Deniz how is she?" he asked.

"Well, not well, that's why she didn't come. Muzo stayed to keep her company." she said.

"Oh... Muzo, my friend with a gold heart!" exclaimed Sanem softening.

Ayhan confirmed.

Meanwhile upstairs, at Fikri Harika, Bulut entered the agency with a beaming smile. He was in a great mood, he had just got what they had fought for all those months and could not wait to tell his wife and brother the good news.

At the counter he found Cey Cey.

"Good morning Cey Cey. Is Deren in her office?" asked Bulut.

"Ah, good morning Bulut. What's going on? Huh? You seem to be in a great mood today." he observed.

"I am Cey Cey. I am! I couldn't be happier. So where is she?" he asked agitated again.

"Um... Derosh is not in her office. Wait." he said seeing a girl coming.

"Hey you! Did you happen to see Mrs Deren downstairs?" asked one of the Sanem employees.

"Um, no. She's not there." replied the girl confidently. "There's only Sanem and Ayhan downstairs at the moment." she specified.

"Ah, go then, back to work." Cey Cey replied seriously and diligently.

"Thank you." replied Bulut.

"Wait I'll try to call her." he said pulling out the phone from the inside pocket of the suit he was wearing.

He dialed the number and waited.

"*The customer you have called cannot be reached at the moment. Please...*" Bulut hung up.

"No answer?" asked Cey Cey.

"No. It's switched off." Bulut began suspiciously.

"Off? Strange. Mrs Deren never turns her phone off." Cey Cey pointed out to him.

Bulut looked at him, nodding.

"There, at least that's what she did before you got married." Cey Cey then corrected himself embarrassed.

At that moment Burak came out of the bathroom behind the counter.

"Ah, brother? Have you seen Deren?" asked Bulut.

"Um, yeah, she was here, had a drink and then... I don't know, she'll be in her office. Did you look?" he asked.

"She's not there." Bulut replied.

"Ah... she must have gone to the bathroom then." he said, pointing to the door of the women's bathroom at his side.

At that moment Leyla passed by.

"Leyla? Come here." said Cey Cey.

"Tell me Cey Cey." she replied apathetically.

"Can you check if Deren is in the bathroom?" asked Bulut.

"Why?" asked Leyla suddenly more alert and awake.

"We are looking for her." replied Burak.

"Here, if you could take a look... you know with the pregnancy and all, the bladder..." tried to say Bulut.

"Okay..." replied Leyla as she approached the door. She entered. She checked, and went out.

"There's no one inside." she replied.

"Ah, I'm starting to go crazy, I swear!" said Bulut in a panic.

"Why?" asked Leyla.

"She can't be found, she's not answering her phone, no one has seen her..." he replied agitated.

Meanwhile, Can had also come up behind Bulut, intrigued by the assembled group.

He had heard Bulut's words and in no time spoke to the entire creative team, asking them to search every corner of the agency.

Emre also took part.

Meanwhile, Burak took his brother aside.

"Brother, what's going on?" he asked. "Seriously." he said.

"Here, I would have liked to tell you under happier circumstances, both to you and Deren, but... well, i come now from the court." he began.

"Again?" asked Burak.

"Yes, and... Burak? You have been officially entrusted to me and Deren." he said.

"Really?" asked Burak happily." But how is that possible? I mean, the evidence..."

"The 'how', I will explain in another chin. I want to find Deren now, brother." apologized Bulut.

"That's why I rushed to the agency. I wanted to tell you both. But Deren cannot be found! Burak? What if something had happened to her and the child?" he asked with a broken heart at the very idea.

It was at that moment that Burak realized.

"With such good news, Deren could not have disappeared. Not now that they had finally really become a family! The family Deren hoped they would become.

"No! Brother, nothing will happen to her. I promise you. We will find her." he said firmly.

"I'll go ask Sanem." he said, running off. In tragedy he tried to call her. Off he went.

Two floors later, transfixed, Burak burst into the office.

"Have you seen Deren?" he asked breathlessly.

"Deren? Isn't she at home?" asked Sanem,

"No, not today. She came to the office with Bulut, then he had to leave and she stayed with me in the agency. Then I stepped away for a moment and poof! Gone. Not to be found! Do you know where she might be?" he asked agitated.

"One minute! She can't be found?" snapped Sanem, immediately taking the phone in her hand.

"She's not answering. My brother and I have already tried. Bulut is worried and so am I. He is now searching the whole agency with Can." he said.

"Come, let's check here then. I'll go with you." she said getting up.

Ayhan tried to get up to follow them.

"Don't you dare! You stay here!" scolded her Sanem.

"We don't want to lose the second pregnant woman we have in the office too." she said before rushing out.

Nothing, she wasn't at the Sanem's and as they went up to Fikri Harika, they discovered she wasn't even up there.

Sanem began to fidget.

"First Deniz, then Ezgi, now Deren who is nowhere to be found..." she thought.

Bulut called Deren's driver. He was unreachable. Perfect. In the agency only the secretary at the entrance had seen her leave with all the commotion.

Can had Bulut check the cameras. From the videos he had confirmation. Deren had left the agency, but the images showed nothing else from the camera position. They still didn't know what her destination was.

"My God if something had happened to her, I..." Bulut began to say, trying to push back the lump in his throat.

"Don't worry Bulut. Don't worry man, we'll find her." Can comforted him by giving him friendly pats on the back.

"Easy, Can? What if she and the driver had an accident? Huh?" thought Bulut.

"Ah, Bulut, though, don't be catastrophic. Otherwise we won't get out of it." said Leyla.

"Catastrophic? Leyla how can I not be catastrophic, I mean, my 9-month pregnant wife is somewhere who knows where!" he blurted out getting nervous.

"Alright. All right. Calm down." said Burak hugging him.

Sanem walked away for a moment with the phone in her hand. She had to talk to someone.

Se dialled the number and hoped for an answer.

After several rings, when he was about to hang up, a voice broke into tears answered.

"Hello?"

"Ezgi? Ezgi, hi, i'm Sanem." she said.

"Hi Sanem, sorry but I'm not really in the mood to talk right now. Can I call you back later?" she asked without losing her politeness.

"Ezgi, wait! Wait, wait, don't hang up!" Sanem blocked her.

"I will only ask you one question." she said.

"Did you by any chance see Deren this morning?" she asked in a rush.

"Why?" she asked, avoiding confirming or not.

"Please, Ezgi, this is important. Deren has disappeared. She is nowhere to be found. Listen, if you know anything, if you have seen her and know where she might be, please say so. Her husband's in a panic. Her phone is switched off, and we don't know where she is. All we know is that she has left the agency." she said worriedly.

"What?! Has she disappeared?" she asked.

"Ezgi, please..." pleaded Sanem.

"I saw her. Yes, I saw her. We were at the bar at the top of the agency road. Then we turned around, and suddenly she was gone. I don't know where she went from there." he replied in a confused tone.

"We turned around?" asked Sanem attentive to her words. "We turned around, who, Ezgi?" she asked.

"Was there anyone else there with you?" she asked.

"Listen, something doesn't add up, OK? I saw you get into a taxi. You were upset." said Sanem decisively,

"What happened in that bar, Ezgi?!" she repeated nervously urging her to answer. Ezgi was crying.

Meanwhile Can joined her.

Reluctantly Ezgi, taking a breath, answered: "Metin was there with us."

Sanem opened her eyes wide.

"Metin..." she replied.

Can looked at her. By now he too was aware of the whole story.

"What was Metin doing there?" asked Sanem.

"Listen, this is an important matter. I'm not asking out of curiosity. What happened?" she repeated.

Ezgi remained silent, then Sanem felt herself pull up with her nose and take a deep breath.

"Ezgi, tell me something." Sanem said resolutely, wanting to know the answer. "Was Deren as upset as you by that encounter?" she asked.

"Yes..." she replied in a trembling voice.

Can seeing his wife agitated like that, he mimicked a "what's up?"

"Ezgi won't tell me what happened. Fine. I'll try to get there then." Sanem said, taking courage.

"Metin did happen to tell both of you something about you?" asked Sanem.

"Something about your past?" she added.

Ezgi remained silent on the other end of the phone. She was surprised.

"Yes..." she finally replied.

"Something that binds one to the other, isn't it?" asked Sanem.

"Yes, but..." replied Ezgi wanting to add more. Sanem interrupted her.

"All right, Ezgi, I understand. Don't ask me how, but I know everything." she hastened to say.

"That she and I are..." tried to say Ezgi.

"Sisters." concluded the sentence Sanem. "I know."

"How?" she asked with a edge in her voice.

"Now is not the time for explanations, Ezgi. Listen, Deren has disappeared. You are both upset, devastated, I understand, but she is missing, and in her condition, we are all super worried... please, if you know something, say so." returned to the point Sanem.

"I don't know, Sanem. I don't know where she might have gone. But... one minute. The driver! When we left, her driver was gone." she thought lucidly. "When I arrived, he was waiting outside, leaning against the car door. I didn't pay attention at first, but then, I saw Deren nod to him." she remembered.

"All right. All right. Ezgi, thank you very much." she said.

"Sanem, if I can be of any help..." she said.

"All right, Ezgi, thank you. If I know anything I'll let you know." she replied.

She hung up quickly.

"Sanem what's going on?" asked Can.

"Wait Can." said Sanem turning back to Bulut and Burak.

"Bulut?" she called him.

"Tell me Sanem." he replied.

"She was with Ezgi, at the bar here down the street. That's where she went. But then left, without knowing where... with her driver." she said.

Bulut's blood ran cold. He really thought that something bad might have happened to her.

"Maybe she went home." thought Ayhan. "You should go there." she suggested.

"You're right. Yes, I'll go and see at home." replied Bulut. "Come on, Burak let's go." he said.

"No, Bulut, don't you think it's better for Burak to look elsewhere?" pointed out Sanem to him.

"Maybe he and I can talk to the bar across the street to find out more, what do you say?" asked Sanem trying to convince him.

"Alright. OK, yeah, we better split up." he said. "I'll run there." he said running off like lightning.

Sanem then called Burak and her husband to review.

Then looking at the creative department, Can said, clapping his hands: "Come on, come on, everyone get to work! Come on!" he exclaimed.

Then looking at his sister-in-law, "Leyla? You take care of it."

"All right, Can." she said, turning back to the team. "But let us know." she added.

"So where were we?" she told them as she walked briskly on her heels towards the headquarters.

Emre's phone rang.

"Brother, I have a meeting, I have to get back to the office." he said.

"Go Emre. I entrust the company to you." he said.

"OK." he said as he answered, "Hello?"

Only Ayhan and Cey Cey remained at roll call.

"Ayhan warn the Sanem that I'm going away. Stay there still, don't move. And if you see Metin warn me." he said.

"Cey Cey, you the same thing here at Fikri harika. Keep your eyes open and as soon as you see Metin alert. Don't let him escape." he said.

"Sister what's going on?" asked Ayhan as Burak asked: "Metin?"

Sanem spat out.

"Metin told Ezgi and Deren everything. That's why she can't be found, and Ezgi too...she was devastated. I saw her leave the bar when I was on the phone. I dare not imagine how Deren is right now..." she said.

"What?!" They all exclaimed in shock with wide eyes. Burak clenched his fists in nervousness.

"Did he say that?" asked Ayhan.

"Oh, sir..." commented Cey Cey. "Poor Derosh."

"How... one minute! Did Metin really tell Deren and Ezgi that they are sisters?" asked Can surprised but also partly pleased that his friend had decided to tell the truth.

"Yes, in the middle of a bar..." commented Sanem.

"Does that sound like the place to say such a thing?" commented Ayhan.

"Yes, but why right now?" asked Cey Cey.

"I don't know exactly..." replied Sanem doubtfully.

"But I bet you have an idea, don't you?" asked Can.

"Yes, but... I'm not sure." insisted his wife.

"It wasn't enough to play dirty with her until now, was it? There was also a need to tell her in the most insensitive and off-topic way possible, in her state then.... Ah, if I catch him..." said Burak, clenching his fists more and more in anger.

"Can! Burak! Come with me, let's go to the bar. Let's hear what the owners say." said Sanem.

"Take care." she said to Cey Cey and Ayhan as they rushed out.

"Alright, sister, we'll take care of it." she replied.

Ayhan at that point, without a second thought, pulled out her phone and dialled a number.

"Hello? Muzo? Red alert!" she exclaimed.

Meanwhile, on their way out, Sanem called for all the help she could get.

"Hello, Volkan? We have an emergency." said Sanem.

Can turned to look at her.

"Deren has disappeared. Metin spoke to her... Yes, yes... All right, OK. Perfect." she replied, then hung up.

Talking to the owners of the café they found out that Ezgi and Metin had a big fight and Deren, they saw her leave. The owners, who know Can very well, even offered to show him the camera images.

Deren can be seen getting out with difficulty, the driver running to help her and the car driving off.

"My God..." thought Burak. "She didn't run to the hospital, did she?"

Can and Sanem exchanged a glance.

Sanem looked at the footage again, it could well have been that her water broke and Deren had herself taken to the hospital.

"But she would have called, wouldn't she?" Can pointed out.

"Here, if you're in labour, you don't think about your mobile phone, but surely in her case she could have had the driver alerted. So I don't think that's what happened." Sanem thought.

"I mean, she might not have given birth, but maybe she didn't feel well..." thought Can.

"I'll call my brother right away." said Burak. Once they had explained what they had seen, they agreed, Bulut and Burak would check in every hospital in the city if necessary.

As they left to head each to their own destinations, Cey Cey called Sanem.

"Hello? Cey Cey?" she asked. Can and Burak stopped.

"Sanem? Metin just came out of his office. He's in a hurry to leave. I couldn't hold him back." he admitted regretfully.

"Ah, Cey Cey! Ah! It's OK... it's OK, I'll take care of it." she said hanging up.

"What's going on?" asked Can.

"Metin is in the agency but he's about to leave in a hurry according to Cey Cey." said Sanem.

"Excuse me, Can. But I need to have a little word with him." she said as she set off at a brisk pace.

Burak and Can went after her, trying to hold her back.

"But..." tried to say Can.

"And nothing, and no one, can stop me this time!!!" she exclaimed stopping only to point her finger at him.

"I'll go with you too!" exclaimed Burak. I have two little words to say to him too!" he said decisively.

"I won't leave you alone." said Can.

"Then we'll do that." said Sanem agreeing.

A few minutes later Metin reached the underground car park of the Fikri Harika where he parked daily.

"Metin?" a firm voice called him.

Metin looked around, and from behind a column came Sanem.

"Sanem?" he asked.

"What's the rush? What's going on?" she asked.

"I have an urgent meeting." he answered hastily.

"I guess..." she replied.

Metin looked at her.

"Why? Why did you decide to tell them, huh?" she asked.

Metin masked his surprise with a smile.

"You know, Sanem, I should have guessed that with your usual curiosity you wouldn't be able to resist." he said.

"I admit that at times I actually had a hunch about it, but... you did well, I admit it." he said.

"Why today of all days, Metin?" insisted Sanem.

"Because it was right for them to know the truth." he said.

"It was right that they should know the truth... interesting." repeated his words laughing Sanem.

"If it was so right, how come you hid it all this time?" she asked.

"I could ask you the same question, I suppose. I bet you haven't known recently either, is that right?" he asked.

"You are wrong on the contrary. I've known for a few months, not years like you!" Sanem replied curtly.

Metin smiled.

"I don't have to give you any explanation." he said. "Since you seem to know many things, you tell me then." he challenged her.

"Let me see if I can guess..." said Sanem.

"Deniz left you because you were smothering her with your jealousy towards Muzo." she began. "Besides the fact that she was made aware of your secret." she added.

"Ah, but the disappointment of being rejected by Deniz as well wasn't the only one wasn't it?" she asked.

"Before her, how many times did you go to Ezgi hoping to impress her? Huh? Because you are smitten with her, aren't you? Kind of like you always were for Deren, or am I wrong?" poked him Sanem.

"But she also rejected you for the umpteenth time, because she has no feelings for you. And you at that point, furious that all women reject you, made that rash proposal to Deniz, thinking she would never leave you... and instead..." said Sanem.

"You're wrong..." replied Metin through clenched teeth.

"Really? Are you sure?" she asked with a smirk.

"That's not what happened." he replied.

"Ah... so let's hear it... how did it go? I'm really curious." said Sanem crossing her arms ready to hear his version.

"It's true. I love Ezgi, and not since today. For a while now." he admitted.

Sanem nodded, smiling.

"And Deniz?" she asked.

"I love Deniz very much, but..." he interjected.

"But you don't love her." concluded the sentence Sanem for him.

Metin remained silent.

"And yet, you stayed with her, because rather than being alone, better to have a plan B. Isn't that so? After all, that's what you learned from your work, isn't it?" asked Sanem.

"Sanem, listen, I have been alone for many years... and I have experienced unrequited loves all my life. For once a good person has reciprocated me, I..." tried to justify himself Metin.

"You jumped in, hoping that that might become love. But then you found out that Ezgi, that girl Ahmet Erdogan had told you about in confidence, was close to you." Sanem began to assume.

"He asked you to keep an eye on both of them so that they wouldn't meet, but when you found out that the wedding dress he bought from her, you got even closer. Didn't you?" continued Sanem.

"It's at the wedding, isn't it? When you came to pick up Deniz you realized that, didn't you? When you saw Ezgi among the guests. That's actually why you came, isn't it? Not for Deniz. Erdogan had sent you to keep an eye on Ezgi, am I wrong?" she asked.

"You are wrong." he replied firmly through clenched teeth.

"Deniz had called me desperate, she wanted me to go and get her, so I did. Seeing Ezgi there was a coincidence." said Metin.

"So that's why the phone calls with your 'sir' became more and more frequent? Is that so?" she continued.

"Don't worry, sir, they haven't seen each other. Of course, I'll keep my eyes open and all that." Sanem quoted.

"You spied on me?" asked Metin.

"Well, you know Metin, the agency is a very open environment. Every room has eyes and ears, even your favourite place. The archive!" said Sanem.

"You thought that no one would hear you there, because you knew very well that the cameras were not there when Muzo worked there, but then he left, and you took advantage of the opportunity thinking that you would not be filmed or heard, but you are wrong." she replied mockingly.

"Isn't that right, Muzo?" said Sanem loudly, making herself heard.

With his usual unmistakable laugh, Muzo peeped out from behind a pillar behind Metin.

Sanem smiled smugly at him.

Metin turned around and was startled.

Muzo was not alone. Hand in hand, there was Deniz.

"Deniz?" he asked.

"Leaving you was the best choice I could have made!" she exclaimed.

"Maybe I waited even too long. I understand that now. All this time I was blind. Anger and pain for the past had clouded my brain. But now I realize that I was angry at the wrong person. You took advantage of me in my darkest time, now you will understand what it means to mess with a 'sick person' like me." replied Deniz, getting out of character.

"Deniz, I..." tried to counter Metin.

Muzo's characteristic laugh resounded throughout the car park.

"My dear Metin, you thought you were better than everyone, but... apparently you are not. And you will soon pay a high price for it, you can be sure of that." replied Muzo confidently.

"What a pity..." commented Deniz with a disgusted face.

Metin reflected and understood.

"I get it... so you weren't alone in this." he said looking at Sanem.

"Everyone has their own means." she replied.

"Why do you work for Erdogan, Metin? Why are you double-dealing in your best friend's company, huh? Don't you think about

Can? Wasn't what happened in the past enough for you?" recalled Sanem.

"What about Deren? Do you really not care about her?" she blurted out.

"You even went so far as to despise her marriage to Bulut. I heard you." she added.

"I know sir, he is not suitable for her, and so on, you said." she mimicked.

"Why is that a lie?" he replied.

"AH! And that's it!" exclaimed Burak, holding back until that moment. He too was listening covertly.

"It's a lie all right! How dare you, huh? Who do you think you are? You don't know my brother at all!" he blurted out with clenched fists, barely holding back.

Sanem approached him, holding him by the arm. "Burak... calm down." she said.

"See, I'm right. Anger runs in the family apparently." pointed out Metin.

"Metin!" quipped Sanem taking him back.

"Watch your words. Don't you dare." hissed Sanem angrily. "Don't listen to him, Burak. It's what he wants." whispered Sanem to him.

"Or what? What are you going to do? Are you going to beat me up? You, in your situation? Against a lawyer?" he said.

"Not even your brother would save you, believe me. It doesn't suit you." he added, full of himself.

Sanem was shocked by the Metin in front of him.

"One minute... one minute, one minute. Now I understand why you said you wanted to say something, but you couldn't. Can doesn't know is that it?" thought Metin with a smile.

At that point, from a black car parked there from the start, two doors opened from which both Can and Bulut came out.

"It's not good for you, dear Metin." said Bulut. "Because not even your 'sir' would save you, believe me." he replied.

"But really? You have that much faith in yourself?" replied Metin.

"I have confidence in law and justice, without position or social rank." replied Bulut.

"You and your sir's days are numbered, you can be sure of that. Justice will take its course." he said.

Metin remained silent.

"What about Metin..." Can took the floor, flanking his wife.

"You thought my wife was hiding something from me, but you were wrong." he said holding her close.

"And apparently there is one more thing I was wrong about." he admitted.

"Your sincerity." he said.

"I trusted you again. And even though you didn't directly wrong me this time, my wife and I don't want partners in the business plotting behind each other's backs. Our agency is based on trust. And every employee must come to work knowing that they are safe. And I have to protect my employees. So I absolutely cannot condone what you did to Deren. And for that... you are fired!" he said.

"I thought so." Metin replied. "But... as you know, work is not a problem at all. On the contrary. I have an offer always open waiting for me in London." he said.

"Good for you." replied Can quietly.

"Evidently you have forgotten what friendship means." had the cheek to reply Metin.

"Evidently you have forgotten that friendship is one thing, and work is another." Can replied quietly.

"And evidently you have also forgotten what it means to be a real lawyer." Bulut added.

"Ah, and you would be one? Wouldn't you?" laughed Metin.

"Don't make me laugh." he added.

"We will see who is a real lawyer. And soon we will also see how you can handle anger." said Bulut.

"You can go Metin." said Can.

Metin looked at them all one last time, without rancor, he already knew he was leaving. Indeed he got into his car and drove to the airport. The destination was obvious.

Once the car disappeared from their sight, it was Muzo who spoke.

"We are going." he said.

"All right. Have a good trip." Sanem greeted them.

"We'll keep in touch." said Bulut.

Muzo greeted everyone with the military salute.

At that moment Sanem's mobile phone rang.

"Mrs Sanem?" asked a deep voice on the other end.

"Volkan, you are on speakerphone, go ahead. Have you found Deren?" she asked.

"Mrs. Sanem, I followed Ezgi and I think I found her,." he replied. "Parked in front of grandmother's building is Mrs Deren's car, I recognize it." he said.

"Let's go!" exclaimed Bulut to Burak.

"One minute. The driver was waiting outside, he just rushed inside. Something's wrong." said Volkan doing the minute-by-minute commentary.

"My God... what's going on?" asked Sanem.

"I think you'd better come as soon as possible." he added.

"We'll be right there." said Burak rushing off with his brother to the car he had gotten out of earlier with Can.

"All right, Volkan, listen. You keep an eye on things until you see Bulut arrive, OK? After that you get to the airport. PHASE 2 begins. At the airport you will find Muzo and Deniz. They will explain the situation to you." Can said.

"Alright, Mr Can, as you wish." he said.

"Thank you very much Volkan." greeted him Sanem, then hung up.

"What shall we do?" she asked in pain as he looked at Can.

"Are you OK?" she then added concerned seeing her expression.

"I'm fine, love." he replied.

"You're sorry." sentenced Sanem.

"I'm sorry but it's only fair." replied Can.

38. VALLEY OF TEARS

While all this was going on, however, someone, having hurriedly left that damn bar, had rushed to the workshop to ask her mother for an explanation, showing the evidence provided by Metin, in particular a photo, in her face.

It was Ezgi.

There was an ugly argument, perhaps one of the worst mother-daughter arguments ever. Ezgi accused the mother of not telling her anything. Because she knew. She had always known.

After shouting and screaming in front of the whole workshop, venting and distraught, she went out. She walked in the open air along the coast, savoring the salty smell of the sea. She found a vacant bench and sat down.

She stood there staring at the peaceful sea of the harbor for a while as tears marked furrows on her face, and thoughts whirled through her head.

Then suddenly her phone rang insistently. She didn't feel like answering it, so she let it ring for a long time until she gave up. She looked at the screen. "Sanem Divit" was calling.

She sighed. As much as she didn't feel like it, she answered. She felt sorry for her.

She cleared her throat and answered: "Hello?"

When Sanem told her in a few minutes update her that Deren was completely lost, she was heartbroken. She felt her heart hammering wildly.

"What?!" she answered, jumping to her feet.

Once the call was over she had to sit down again for a moment to process it all.

Deren... Her sister... was missing. She realized.

Then she got up and started walking aimlessly. Until, after finding herself in the centre of Istanbul, surrounded by luxury shops, she thought of a place.

Without a second thought, she catapulted herself to the side of the road to ask the first passing taxi driver for a lift. She got it in seconds, and for that she was grateful to be in the centre.

Direction? Deren's grandmother's house...And it was at that moment that she realized that that was also her grandmother. Grandmother Pembe.

Also someone else in the meantime, once she arrived at her destination she chased away the driver, who insisted on calling someone to calm her down. But Deren, quite distraught and shaken, wanted no one and as she screamed at the man with the phone to his ear, ready to call her husband, in a fit of rage she took it from his hand and threw it into the garden. The phone broke.

The driver, however, a man loyal to his 'lady', having known her for years, and sorry to see her in that state in her condition, decided to stay there anyway at the car, in case of need, perhaps once she had let off steam she would change her mind, he thought.

He saw her enter, clinging tightly to the railing of the few steps outside to reach the front door. Then she disappeared inside, closing the heavy wooden door behind her.

He waited.

In the meantime, Deren staggering, crying her eyes out, entered the house and without a second thought, reached her small teenage bedroom. That same small room where she had found her grandmother's wedding dress.

Slowly, feeling her legs give way, not withstanding too much pain, thanks also to the pregnancy hormones, what she felt was twice as much as she would normally be able to bear. So she let herself slide down to sit on the large, round, soft carpet laid out at the foot of the bed, opposite the wardrobe. She laid her back on it and remained there for a while, giving free rein to her tears, while from her bag she took out the envelope given to her by Metin. With quick gestures she emptied the contents in front of her and began to look deeply. There was the birth certificate, an account of Ezgi's whole life, and how their destinies were connected. She thought that surely he had a similar file on her.

Then photos. And those hurt the most. For not only had she discovered she had a sister, but also that her father had made a life for himself without her mother. Maybe he had cheated on her? She didn't know. But at that moment, an excruciating rage rose up inside her. An anger held back all those years against a man who was a complete stranger to her. Her father.

Not only had he deprived her of one family, but not content had he created another without even warning her of the existence of a sister. From there the questions began? What about her mother? What had happened to her? Where is she now? She asked herself. Has she also rebuilt her life?

Then she thought about her grandmother.

"What about Grandma? Did she know about all this? Or had she hidden it from me too?"

Her breathing became laboured as anger mounted inside her. She was enraged, shattered, ravaged by a stabbing pain in her chest.

Suddenly she felt hot, and began fanning herself with the contents of the envelope, then suddenly felt as if she were wet as the heat grew more intense. She thought she was sweating like never before, thanks also to the hairy carpet she was sitting on. She tried to change position, but in an instant found herself completely soaked.

"Is the carpet flooding?" she asked herself.

Outside it had started to rain with thunder and lightning. The weather perfectly represented her mood at the time. Perhaps there was water seeping in?

She looked around, and noticed that there was only one spot where the mysterious water was coming from. It was from her.

"Oh, no!" she exclaimed, touching her dress.

"Oh, no, no, no! Tell me it's not true!" she exclaimed in a panic. Her hands were shaking.

"Nooooo! You can't be born right now!" she managed to say before a contraction set in. It seemed to her that the baby was as angry as she was at that moment.

"Ahhhh!" she squirmed.

She began to scream. But no one answered, or appeared. Then she remembered. She had sent the driver away and was in the part of the house furthest from the entrance, a part of the large building that faced the back, overlooking the large garden.

"Noooooo!" she shouted as another contraction set in. "You can't be born here. You cannot be born here. You have to be born in the hospital. Not here, I said." she ranted to herself.

"What do I do now?" she told herself.

The only one was to get up.

She tried, but her legs were weak, partly because she had been fasting for she did not even know how many hours, and the weight did not help. She couldn't do it.

"Ahhhh!" she screamed again.

She tried to take the phone out of her bag, but realized it was dead. Perfect.

Meanwhile Ezgi arrived at the house. She exchanged a few words with the driver and once understood the situation, she approached the front door and taking a hairpin out of her hair, she inserted it in the lock and started to turn it until it opened.

At that point she catapulted upstairs while the driver remained on guard.

"Buluuuut!" she screamed at the top of her lungs. After all, everyone had always teased her about the powerful and determined voice she had when she screamed. She was capable of breaking glass, so said Can. It was time to use it.

Ezgi arrived.

"Deren? Deren?" she started calling her all over the house to see what room she was in.

"Helpppp!" she shouted during another contraction.

At that point Ezgi already in the hallway threw open the door to the small bedroom and found her.

"Deren? Deren!" she exclaimed when she saw her on the floor.

"Ezgi? Ezgi, please call Bulut. My water broke. The baby is coming." she said desperately, catching her breath. She was pale and her forehead beaded with sweat.

Ezgi noticed the puddle on the ground and realized.

"Ahhhhh!" she screamed again at the top of her lungs.

At that point outside, the driver snapped, hearing the screams from the open doorway. He recognized the voice and dashed inside in a second.

In the meantime, Volkan, having just finished his phone call with Sanem, noticing that something was wrong, as he waited for Bulut to arrive, got out of his car, placed it in an unnoticed spot across the street, and casually, as if he were a neighbor, returned to his property, hearing the commotion and approached.

The driver hurried out and grabbed a duffel bag from the boot of the car.

He heard shouting again.

Then Volkan asked to the man: " Is something wrong? Can I help you?" he asked the man who was trying to open the door, which was closed again by the wind.

He was wearing a cap and wrap-around sunglasses, so as not to be recognized.

"Ah, thank goodness. Oh, yes thank you. Unfortunately there is a problem. My lady is locked in, she's in her ninth month of pregnancy, and I just heard her screaming. I don't have a phone. Can you please call an ambulance?" she asked in a panic.

"Sure. Right away. I'll run and get the phone from the car." said Volkan.

It was a tactic to check the road, hoping to see Bulut arrive.

Meanwhile he called the ambulance, and as he gave directions he recognized Bulut. So he got into the car and observed the scene.

MEANWHILE INSIDE...

"Deren? Deren, look at me. Breathe." said Ezgi, kneeling in front of her.

"Calm down. Look into my eyes, follow my breathing." She told her.

Meanwhile Bulut and Burak got out of the car, found the driver and asked for an explanation. A few minutes later from the window of his darkened car, Volkan saw Bulut turn his head towards the second-floor window when he heard shouting. He took the duffel bag from the driver's hand and together with Burak flung open the door with a shove, running upstairs.

"Deren!" he shouted through the house.

"Ahhhhh! Bulut!" she called to him.

Bulut followed her voice that led him to her.

When at the bedroom door, he saw her on the floor, screaming in pain, he immediately rushed to her, while Ezgi stepped aside.

"Love? Love!" he said, looking at her.

"Bulut? My water broke." she said as another contraction made her scream.

"Our daughter is coming!" she said gritting her teeth.

Bulut immediately squeezed her hand, shook her hair in front of her face, and trying to reassure her, saying: "I know love, I know. The driver said so." he said, stroking her.

"The ambulance is coming," Burak said, hearing sirens in the distance. He looked out of the bedroom window.

"I want an epidural!" shouted Deren writhing in pain. Bulut tried to calm her down, but Deren seemed to be under the influence of caffeine from how agitated she was. So Ezgi approached her and said firmly: "Deren, listen, breathe slowly. OK? Look into Bulut's eyes, and breathe slowly together." she said looking at her husband.

"Ah... she will be born here. I can feel it. I need to push." said Deren.

"What!" exclaimed Burak.

"What do we do now?" asked Bulut in a panic.

"Do something!!!" shouted Deren.

Bulut looked out of the bedroom window to see if he could hear the ambulance.

"We have to take her to the hospital." proposed Burak.

"Ahhhhhhhhh!" shouted Deren again.

"We can't move her right now." said Ezgi.

"Deren, I'm sorry but someone has to do it." she said.

Deren understood. She nodded exhausted.

"Bulut, you shake your wife's hand."

"You? Burak?" she said, looking at him. "Bring any towel or sheet you can find." Ezgi said.

Burak, looked at Deren's cot and without a second thought took the sheet directly. "Here." he said, handing it over with agitation.

Ezgi, placed it as a sheet over Deren's raised knees, and looked. She opened her eyes wide.

"I see the head!" she said, smiling.

"What?!" exclaimed the two brothers.

"Ahhhhhh!" cried Deren again, clinging with all her might to Bulut's arm.

Burak, meanwhile, had turned pale.

Ezgi glanced at him and said: "Burak, you shake her other hand."

"If we all do our duty, we will deliver this baby." she said decisively, rolling up the sleeves of her shirt.

"What!? Are you kidding?" said Bulut.

"We have no other choice." she replied inflexibly.

"Deren breathe, remember what they told you in the birthing class." she reminded her.

Bulut having been with her understood how to help her.

"When the contraction comes, push." she told her.

"It's coming!" cried Deren, gritting her teeth.

"Go, go, go." said Ezgi.

Deren caught her breath.

"Do you want to change position?" asked Ezgi.

Deren shook her head. "Just..." he said indicating to lift her legs towards her.

"OK, hear that, guys? Up. Hold her legs firmly so that she can push better." she said.

The two inexperienced brothers obeyed.

Ezgi really seemed to know how to do it. She looked like a nurse.

Burak looked at her admiringly. After all, she was not so much older than him.

He was 18, she was 25...

"That's it, good! That's it. Deren is coming. You're almost there." she encouraged her.

"Come on love, up you go!" Bulut encouraged her.

"A good push, Deren!" said Ezgi.

"Ahhhhhhhhhhh!" cried Deren.

"The last one, come on, you're there!" she encouraged her.

"The last one and you can hug your baby, come on! Push as hard as you can!" she told her, looking her straight in the eyes.

"Ah, enough... I can't take it anymore..." she blurted out exhausted.

"Deren, love..." said Bulut worriedly with fear in his eyes.

"It was at that point that Burak, seeing her without strength, leaned close and whispered in her ear:

"Think of the person you hate the most right now and push!"

Meanwhile in the background could be heard the sirens of the approaching ambulance.

Deren filled her lungs and pushed determinedly with all the strength she had.

"Ahhhhhhhhhhhh!" she screamed.

That scream was followed by a moment of silence, in which Ezgi, smiling said: "There she is! She is born!"

It was answered by the cry of the little one, who, like her mother, had a loud voice.

Deren slumped her head to the cupboard behind her, exhausted, while Ezgi wiped the little one with the sheet.

Burak, without being told anything, took the other sheet on the bed.

Ezgi wrapped it and brought it close to Deren's chest, who was already crying.

"Here is this beautiful baby!" she said, laying it on her chest.

Deren held her close, losing herself in that sweet little face.

She stroked her little cheek with her index finger. "Hello..." she said in a broken voice.

"Hello little brat. You were the one who kicked me all those times, huh?" she said, smiling touched.

Then she looked at Bulut who first looked at her and then at her little girl. Her eyes were shining with emotion. Bulut caressed the small fist resting on her chest.

"Hello, my little one." he said

"She is beautiful." said Deren, stroking her little nose.

"What name were you thinking of giving her?" asked Ezgi.

Deren and Bulut looked at each other and sure of what had been their first choice until then, they had no doubts.

Turning simultaneously towards Ezgi, they answered: Aysegul.

That name had a special meaning for Deren. "Ayse (life) and Gul (rose) in honour of her grandmother."

"Aysegul Cehver." said Burak. "It sounds good. I like it."

Suddenly that little family picture was interrupted by the arrival of the doctors, led by the driver to the room.

They got Ezgi and Burak out and secured mother and baby girl so they could be transported to the hospital.

It was Bulut who cut the umbilical cord.

Meanwhile the whole agency was waiting for news.

Everyone was apprehensive and unloaded the excitement in their own way. Some were throwing paper airplanes, some were walking back and forth, some were having coffee in honor of Deren, some were sitting and looking at the ceiling. They were all gathered in the small lounge in the center of the headquarters when suddenly the phone rang.

"Hello?" answered Sanem immediately. "Bulut? You're on speakerphone. So you found her?"

"She was born!" he said.

"Whattt?" exclaimed Sanem in astonishment.

"How was she born? Who? Deren gave birth?" she asked in confusion.

Yeeeeehhh!" exclaimed the whole office meanwhile celebrating by throwing papers in the air. They were happy that this period of pregnancy was over.

"Yes, it's complicated to explain. There will be a way later, but Deren and I wanted to warn you. I am with her right now." Bulut said.

"Ah! All right, all right. But everything is OK? I mean they are both fine right?" asked Sanem.

"Everything is fine, they are both fine. They are healthy and strong." he said happily.

"Oh, God, what can I say... I'm a moment shocked right now, but congratulations, my dear Bulut, you've officially become a daddy!" said Sanem on speakerphone showing Can her trembling hands.

All the rest of the crew wished in the background.

"I'm so happy for you. Really." she added.

"Congratulations Bulut." added Can to the conversation.

"Thank you! Ah, Can? By the way, the little one got her voice from mommy!" he said laughing.

"Man, I told you so! It couldn't be any other way. Now you're screwed. Doubly screwed!" he said, "But I'm happy for you." he added.

"Thanks."

"We'll leave you now, we'll have a chance to meet and get to know the little one. We will talk later, now enjoy your family." said Can.

"Alright. Thank you all."

"Give the little one a kiss from me." said Sanem.

"Sure, I will. See you soon." said Bulut hanging up.

"So... since Muzo is not here, I'll say it this time!" said Sanem all gassed up.

"Music!!!" she exclaimed.

And so the whole office celebrated.

All's well, that ends well.

39. SISTERS

Meanwhile, in the hospital room, Bulut returned to his wife.

"Did you warn them?" she asked.

"Yes, they jumped for joy. They were all surprised by the news, especially Can and Sanem saying hello to you. They can't wait to hug you back and meet the little one." he reported.

"They jumped for joy? Really?" she asked shyly as a child.

"Yes, the whole team was jubilant." he said.

Deren smiled serenely.

Bulut looked around and then asked: "Where is our daughter?" seeing the empty cot next to her.

"They took her for check-ups."s he said. "She will be back shortly."

Bulut approached his wife and kissed her on the forehead.

"I haven't told you yet how proud I am of you." Bulut admitted.

Deren looked at him.

"I already knew you were a strong woman, but I admit you surprised me." he said.

"To find out something like that was a shock." Deren confessed.

"I want to say.... How my family fell apart and ... secrets..." said Deren with his eyes ready to shed more tears.

"To all this there is only one culprit." she said seriously and firmly looking at her husband.

"And that is Ahmet Erdogan." she concluded.

"He has not only ruined my life and my family, but also Ezgi's." she said.

Bulut squeezed her hand in comfort.

"He is not the only culprit in this affair." he added.

"Metin also has his faults." he said.

"See, I didn't get it. Still, at least he told the truth." said Deren.

Bulut looked at her. He opened his mouth and then closed it again.

Deren noticing his expression frowned and asked: "Why that face? What were you going to say Bulut?" she asked.

"Here... Metin wasn't at all as sincere as you think.... But let's not think about it now. We will talk at home calmly. Don't think about such things now. Try to be calm." he said stroking her forehead, moving her hair.

"Bulut?" she asked.

"Tell me." he replied serenely.

"Is Ezgi here?" she asked.

"Yes... she is outside. Burak is with her." he said.

"Can you let her in, please? I need to talk to her." she said.

Bulut stared at her.

"You're not really going to relax, are you?" he replied, already knowing the answer.

"In order to relax I need to talk to her." she replied. "Please." added.

"Alright." He said.

"I'll call her. I'll be outside. Is there anything you wish to eat? Shall I bring you something?" he asked her.

"I'm craving sushi!" she exclaimed brightening up.

"OK." he replied.

"From my favorite restaurant, mind you." she added.

"OK, i will do." replied Bulut as he approached the door.

"And..." added Deren.

"Yes?" asked Bulut turning back to her with his hand on the handle.

"A cup of my coffee! I need it urgently!" she said.

Bulut smiled. "I didn't doubt it." he replied.

"All right. See you soon." he said.

"Thank you." she replied shyly, softening like a child.

Bulut smiled sweetly at her. He was happy for the birth of his daughter, of course, but seeing Deren in that condition, exhausted, happy, but also sad, her face pale and her eyes circled with tiredness, made him suffer. After one last look, he went out. Outside the room, sitting side by side on the chairs that ran the length of the ward corridor, he saw Burak and Ezgi. They were talking, both looking at the ceiling with their arms crossed and their heads resting on the wall behind them. Bulut approached. Ezgi, was the first to straighten up upon his arrival.

"How is she? Is she all right?" she asked worriedly.

"She is fine. She's hungry." he replied, smiling.

"Let's go get her something then, brother." said Burak.

"Don't worry, I'll go. The driver is waiting outside." Bulut said.

"I'll retrieve my car and give him the rest of the day off." he said. "Poor man." he commented, thinking about what he went through.

"You stay here." he said. "In case she needs anything." he added.

"All right, sure, brother. Whatever. I'll take care of it." he said seriously and diligently.

"Perfect." replied Bulut. "Are you guys hungry?" he then asked. "Deren is in the mood for sushi... and coffee." he said.

Ezgi laughed as he saw Bulut roll his eyes.

Burak smiled too, but his gaze was on Ezgi.

"For me, a nice sandwich with chips." he said in reply.

"OK. You Ezgi?" he asked looking at her.

"Me? Nothing, thanks. I don't have much appetite. My stomach is tight." she admitted, touching her chest.

"There, with everything you've seen... I mean that's normal." Burak said.

She looked at him. And with her gaze down she admitted in a whisper: "It's not that."

Bulut heard the whisper then took the opportunity to tell her: "Ezgi, Deren wants to see you."

Ezgi raised her head towards him standing in front of her.

"Now?" she asked taken aback.

Bulut nodded with a gentle smile.

Flustered, she stood up, picked up her handbag with which she was tangling her hands in her haste to put it on her shoulder, took a deep breath and walked to the door. With her hand on the handle she took another deep breath with her eyes closed and opened it decisively, disappearing inside.

"Come on, I'll see you in a bit." Bulut said to his brother as he walked away.

"Brother?" called Burak to him.

"Tell me?" he replied, stopping, turned to look at him.

"Did you break the news to Deren?" asked Burak pointing with his index finger at himself.

"Not yet." he admitted.

"Ah..." he replied, lowering his gaze sadly.

Bulut approached to comfort him with a pat on the shoulder.

"Everything has its time, brother. Deren right now is going through everything. Childbirth, the discovery of a sister, the past..." he said.

"She still has to process it all. That's why I haven't told her yet. I wanted to, believe me, but... she's not quiet now. And she wants to talk to Ezgi... you understand, don't you?" asked Bulut looking at him.

"I understand, but she would be happy about it, I'm sure." commented Burak.

"Of course she would be happy about it, little brother, how could she not be? But she has to resolve some personal issues first, come to terms with the past, and then she will be free to rejoice fully in the news." said Bulut.

"I understand." he replied.

"Remember that you are like a brother and a son to her, don't forget that. And whatever they say in there, that will not change." she reassured him.

"Yes, but at the end of the day, she is the real sister. Not me." he said sadly.

"Do you think that will make a difference to Deren? I remind you, that she cut ties with her family, with her own blood... if it was important to her, would she have done that?"

"No, that is true. You are right brother." replied Burak realizing.

"So don't get any ideas while I'm gone. Cheer up." he said. "You've become an uncle." he reminded him with a smile.

"Yeah, that's right." he said brightening up with a happy smile.

"Come on, I'm off. See you later." greeted him Bulut.

"Remember my sandwitch." he said behind his back.

"Don't worry." replied Bulut walking away.

Meanwhile, in the room, Ezgi, once had closed the door behind her, slowly approached the bed.

Deren looked at her seriously.

"Hello..." Ezgi greeted her intimidated.

"How are you?" she asked as Deren looked at her.

"That's a very difficult question to answer right now." she admitted.

"Well, if you mean the birth, of course I'm fine now," she specified.

"But if you ask in general, I can't answer that. I don't know exactly how I feel." she continued.

Ezgi nodded, lowering her gaze to her own hands. She felt the same way.

Deren looked at her.

"I understand. Deren, I..." she said suddenly, raising her head to look at her.

"Ezgi..." she interrupted her.

"I thank you." said Deren.

"Why?" she asked blinking in surprise.

"Because if it wasn't for you, I probably wouldn't have made it. If my daughter was born healthy and strong, I owe it to your cold blood and promptness. So on behalf of myself and my daughter, I thank you." she said.

"I... I... I didn't do anything. I mean, anyone would have done it in my place." replied Ezgi embarrassed and surprised. She didn't think the conversation would take this turn.

"I don't think so. Only someone who cares about us, and... unfortunately I don't know many, would have done what you did." said Deren slowly as she tried to keep her tears under control.

"A family person... a sister... an aunt... of heart and blood." said Deren.

"If you want it, of course..." she added.

"Like... what?!" replied Ezgi confused.

Deren started laughing through tears along with Ezgi.

"Maybe I didn't explain myself well, actually." she said, touching her forehead.

"What I mean is... that you were a sister of the heart to me even before, and now... you are a sister of the blood as well. I always felt a strange connection between us, from day one." admitted Deren.

"A connection I had never had before like this with a 'stranger.'" she said mimicking the inverted commas.

Ezgi on hearing those words began to sob. She brought a hand to her mouth to restrain herself.

"So if you want, from now on you are part of my little family." Deren repeated.

"I do... of course I do." Ezgi replied tearfully.

"I thought you didn't want to see me anymore, or resent me..." she blurted out through her tears.

"Be mad at you? And why?" asked Deren grabbing her hand. "You had nothing to do with it. You are as innocent as I am. If there is a person to blame, we know very well who it is." she said.

"And I'm sorry that man ruined you and your mother's life too." Deren tried to apologize.

"Let it go. The past stays in the past. Let's look on the bright side of this, we found each other. Sooner or later. Now at least we know of each other's existence." said Ezgi.

"That's true. And even though he has divided us all our lives, we can be stronger than him. Together." said Deren, returning Ezgi's handshake.

"I thank fate for bringing us together." Ezgi replied.

"No, it is my grandmother... or rather, our grandmother who brought us together, of that I am more than certain." said Deren looking at the sky outside the window.

"Our..." repeated Ezgi uncertainly, like a child learning to pronounce a new word.

"I still struggle to realize." she admitted.

"Why do you think it's grandmother?" she then asked. "Did she know?"

"No, I really don't think she knew. But since her disappearance I have always felt her close. And I think she from up there, where she may have found out, somehow brought us together." thought Deren.

Ezgi nodded silently. She did not know what to say.

"I mean, think about it, our bond was created because of a dress, her dress. My grandmother had bought that dress in your atelier. Maybe she met your grandmother, I don't know..." reconnected Deren.

"Are you saying that my grandmother might have met your grandmother?" asked Ezgi.

"How do you know?" she then asked.

"I did some research after the wedding, and here in the house I found the certificate that the dress was bought and sold. In fact, to be exact, I didn't find it at all, but Bulut did." she admitted.

"I can't believe it." Ezgi replied surprised.

"Yeah... Grandma Pembe was the thread... think about it, you came there... to her house... and helped me give birth." Deren mused.

"See, I believe certain signs." she concluded.

"Well, said like that actually makes sense." Ezgi commented.

"Wait a minute, now that I think about it, how come you came there?" thought Deren again.

"Well, when I heard everyone was looking for you, I thought I'd do my little bit, and I was reminded of that place, I know how important it is to you, and I don't know... something inside me said you'd be there." replied Ezgi truthfully.

"And you were right." Deren replied.

"Why right there Deren?" her sister then asked.

"When I left the cafè, I didn't want to see anyone, I didn't even tolerate my driver, but in my state... I had to." she said.

"At that moment I just wanted to run away. I was confused. My head was hurting. And I didn't want Bulut to worry. That house had always been my hiding place. And so, I knew I could think there in silence." she explained.

"But in your state, Deren... when I heard you were gone, I got so worried that..." said Ezgi, stopping the sentence in mid-sentence.

"I was afraid that it was my fault. If something had happened to you, I wouldn't have forgiven myself." she said between sobs.

"Ezgi... don't be like that. Don't cry. Come here." said Deren, spreading her arms wide in a completely natural gesture.

She, the woman who a few years ago could neither laugh nor hug. The old Deren, Deren Keskin, no longer existed. She had died with her past. In its place, together with her daughter, a new Deren had been born, a stronger, more sensitive, caring Deren that perhaps even she struggled to recognize. Yet there she was, Deren Chever. Wife, mother and sister. She was complete. Despite the evil and unforgiving past, despite the pain that had made her who she was.

She was now the woman she had always wanted to be. The best part of herself.

The two sisters hugged each other tightly.

"I'm so sorry..." said Ezgi.

"I didn't think Metin was working for him.... I didn't know anything, Deren, I swear!" she said.

"I know. I understood that you were unaware of it too." replied Deren.

"Really?" she asked, blinking her tear-filled eyes that spilled onto her face.

"Yes." replied Deren smiling.

"Enough crying though." she said, stroking her back.

Meanwhile Bulut slowly walked back into the room with Deren's lunch. As soon as he saw the scene, however, without being heard he went back outside.

"Don't worry. Those who hurt us will get what they deserve, you can be sure of that." she replied, reassuring her in a motherly tone.

Ezgi, pulled away from her and looked into her eyes. "What do you mean? What do you want to do?" she asked.

"I want to help you. I am ready to do anything." said Ezgi, catching her breath as she wiped her eyes with her hands. By now the make-up was gone.

Deren handed her a packet of tissues.

"Thank you." she said, taking it.

"There will be a time to talk about this, but first, I will need your version. I need to know how Metin approached you and other things." she said.

At that moment, before Ezgi could answer, there was a faint knock on the door.

"But not now." concluded Deren.

"Ah, here we are at Mama's." the nurse said to the little one as she led her back into the room, followed by Bulut and Burak.

Ezgi, tried to move away, but it was Deren, who blocked her by grabbing her hand.

"You must not turn away... remember my words? You are part of the family." she said.

The nurse placed the little one on Mama's chest, as she emitted little squeals.

"Here's mummy." repeated the nurse as she laid her on her.

"Congratulations again, Mrs. Cehver." she said, quickly leaving the room. Her pager was beeping.

"Thank you very much." replied Deren distractedly.

"Hello, my little one..." she said looking at those dark eyes looking at her.

"Oh..." let Ezgi slip out, bringing her hands to her mouth in sweetness.

Bulut and Burak walked over to the right side of the bed, while Ezgi stayed on the left side.

"Are you OK?" asked Burak, seeing Ezgi's distraught face.

Ezgi answered with an affirmative nod of her head.

Bulut looked at Deren and then at Ezgi frowning in confusion.

"All very well, isn't it?" said Deren.

"Me and Ezgi..." she began, then paused.

"I meant, my sister and I were talking." Deren corrected herself boldly. She convinced herself to say it out loud to make it more real.

"You made yourselves clear, then?" asked Bulut.

"Yes..." replied Ezgi.

"Whether you accept it or not, know that Ezgi is part of my family." said Deren taking on her usual firm and somewhat haughty tone to mask her emotions.

"I gathered that from your embrace a moment ago. And why should I be against it, my dear? I am more than happy for both of you." Bulut said.

"Who are we to judge after all?" Burak replied, looking at his brother.

"Well said brother." replied Bulut.

"If Deren is happy, so are we." he added. "We have nothing against you Ezgi, if that is what you are afraid of. On the contrary, we are grateful for everything you have done for her and consequently for us as well." continued Bulut.

"Welcome to the family." concluded Burak, taking a step forward as did his brother.

"See?" said Deren.

"Well, I... I don't know what to say, really." said Ezgi tearfully again.

"Thank you." she said simply.

In the meantime, the little one made herself heard with a few small cries.

"See? She agrees too." said Burak laughing.

"But the family doesn't end here." said Bulut trying to get to the point.

"What do you mean? You didn't get a dog, did you?" asked Deren worriedly.

"Dog? No! What dog?" replied Bulut.

"Ah... I see, you meant the agency then. It's true the agency is also part of our family you are right." she said.

"No... my dear, not even that. If you let me finish..." said Bulut.

"Then what are you referring to?" she asked blinking.

"That's it..." intervened Burak.

"He's referring to me." he said bringing a hand to his chest. "I have officially been entrusted to you." he communicated.

"What?! Really?" exclaimed Deren in her squeaky voice, forgetting that she had the little one in her arms. "But how...?" she asked.

"It's a long story. There will be a way to tell it. The important thing is the result." replied Burak happily.

"Quiet... shhh, you wake her up!" reminded Bulut, stroking the little one's head.

Deren quieted down, and lowering her gaze to her, s he noticed that the expression on her little face was pouty.

"She's going to cry." Bulut said.

"No...no, no, no." said Deren rocking her to her chest slowly.

"No, my little one, will not cry." he said.

"Burak come here! Let me give you a hug right now!" exclaimed Deren.

"Bulut, you take you daughter for a moment." she said pointing to the baby.

"But... I... I don't know how to take her." he said awkwardly.

"Ah! You know, you know... you have to get used to it, my dear. Up, fold your arms as if you were cradling pillows, like you used to rehearse at home." she reminded him.

Bulut took her gently.

"I am afraid of hurting her, she is so small." he said.

"Bulut, aren't you a forester? Then imagine that she is one of the delicate seedlings you look after for Sanem. You must be gentle and make her grow healthy and strong." tried to speak his own language Deren.

"Are you comparing our daughter to a plant?" asked Bulut looking at her quizzically.

"Of course not, my dear fool, it was only an example, I was trying to speak your language!" exclaimed Deren resolutely as in the old days. She was in a very good mood, all that good news had helped.

Bulut took her in her arms like a little bundle, while Deren and Burak hugged each other tightly.

428

"Are you happy Burak?" whispered Deren in her ear.

"So much." he replied.

"Me too... Ah, my heart is exploding of joy, if I were drinking caffeine I'd say I'm about to have a fit, but... by the way! My dear husband, what about my coffee? And my sushi?" she asked, loosening herself from the embrace, and assuming a head position, with her hands on her hips, despite lying in bed.

"It's here." replied Burak pointing to the bags poking out from the table behind her back.

"Ah..." she said looking at him seriously. His eyes narrowed to two slits. "I thought you'd forgotten." she confessed.

"Possibly?" replied Bulut.

The little one at that point began to wriggle.

"She's going to cry." panicked Bulut, stretching the little one towards Deren.

"And sure, if you hold her like that, of course. My poor baby." she said, bringing her back to her chest.

Burak laughed in the corner.

"Come, come, you laughing in the corner. Come here." called Deren to him.

"Time for official introductions." she added.

"You see this handsome boy here..." said Deren speaking to the little girl. "This is your uncle Burak." she said.

Burak came closer and looked at her.

"She is really beautiful, Deren. She looks like you." he said.

"You think so? The black hair is daddy's, though." he said.

"True." replied Bulut.

Burak brought a finger closer, and the little girl with one of her small hands grasped it tightly.

"She got the strength from mummy, though, for sure!" said Burak winking at her.

"Someone here wants to play arm wrestling." said Burak in a sweet tone.

"Ah! Ah, you defeated me, all right. You won. OK." he said playing with the little girl's fist.

Deren cast an emotional glance at her husband. Then she looked at Ezgi, who watched them smiling in the corner.

It was Bulut, who stepped aside. "Come Ezgi, come closer." he said.

Ezgi was hesitant. She was moving with leaden feet.

"Come Ezgi, come. Meet your niece." Deren said. This is Aunty Ezgi." she said to the little one.

Ezgi, stood beside her, and saw the little girl up close.

"Oh, she is so sweet!" she said, staring at her lovingly. With one finger she stroked her small cheek. The little one hinted a small smile as she grimaced.

"Oh, look, she smiled. She likes you." Deren said.

"She's really a sweetheart." commented Ezgi.

"What did you say her name was?" Ezgi asked again.

"Aysegul." replied Deren in a tone completely in love.

"Aysegul..." reflected Ezgi, observing her. "It suits her." she admitted after a brief silence.

"In honour of Grandmother Pembe." recalled Deren again.

"Ayse stands for life and gul stands for rose." she said as he contemplated her. "And she is the rose of my life." said Deren. "In fact, of our life." she corrected herself as she looked at her husband.

"That's very appropriate." commented Ezgi.

"Very nice, isn't it?" confirmed Burak.

"I'm sure Grandma Pembe would have loved it." said Bulut.

"I think so too." confirmed Deren.

"Welcome to the world, Aysegul Cehver." greeted her aunt.

40. THE CEHVER PLAN

Once back home, Bulut, Deren, Burak and Ezgi got together to talk.

It turned out from Ezgi's version that Metin had approached her, not as he wanted to imply, for a long time, but in truth for a relatively short time. He introduced himself to her in the shop after Deren.'s wedding, saying that they both had a mutual acquaintance, that he would soon be attending a wedding abroad and that he was looking for a complete man's suit for this. From there, believing that this acquaintance was Deren, Ezgi was very friendly with him, so much so that a friendship was born. Metin never revealed that he was engaged, and the more time they spent together, the more he began to feel something. Something that Ezgi repeated several times that she did not reciprocate. But she did not want to lose his friendship, because deep down she believed it was Deren who had sent him to her as a client, and she was sorry.

Therefore, they saw each other from time to time and talked, but Ezgi had never suspected that both of their fathers were behind it. Although, she could get there.

Metin, a lawyer, indeed one of Istanbul's most distinguished lawyers, suddenly taking an interest in a wedding dressmaker. Absurd to even think about it. But not at that moment.

He had always been nice, friendly and helpful, but now he realized it was only to keep an eye and get information from her. At the thought, Ezgi cursed herself for her naivety.

At that point, Bulut told her about the plan he had hatched with Sanem.

Deren was now aware of Sanem and other members of the agency's involvement. And although displaced, once she talked to her, she could not help but understand her plight and condition. She did not blame her for anything, in fact she understood her. Because after all, she too had been caught in a lie in the past and knew what it felt like.

In fact, she was really grateful to her for always keeping an eye on the situation around her.

Muzo and Deniz were in London to gather information together with Volkan about Metin and Ahmet Erdogan. It was Deren who had initiated it.

While she had focused all her anger on her father, her only target in that plan, Bulut on the other hand was focused on Metin.

This time it would prove, once and for all, which of the two was really a lawyer with a capital A. All this time, the words of superiority, the cutely snobbish tone with which he had always apostrophized him, making him feel inferior had always stuck in Bulut's mind. He hated those kinds of people.

The whole agency was on hand, they all kept their eyes open.

But in all this situation, there was also good news.

Can asked Bulut to take over Metin's role as the agency's lawyer. It was a great leap forward in his career as a lawyer. Can and Sanem gave Bulut complete freedom to manage. Sanem even proposed to find a trusted colleague, an intern who could help him, and who would be hired at the Sanem, under his guidance, while he was busy with the great Fikri Harika.

It took a few months to get concrete proof, but eventually, thanks to the help of Muzo and Deniz, moved by their unfinished business with Metin for the way he had behaved, and thanks, of course, to

Volkan, Bulut collected a whole folder of evidence, analyzing each document carefully during sleepless nights looking after little Aysegul while Deren rested exhausted.

The day he had been waiting for came. One morning he woke up and after saying goodbye to his wife and daughter went to deliver all the evidence he had in his hand.

Shortly afterwards, with the abundance of material collected, her father's prestigious studio was closed by the police. In the same silent and devious way that he, Ahmet Erdogan, had acted towards his daughter, he saw his great empire crumble before him. An empire of lies and deceit. Not even his team of valiant lawyers was able to protect him, including Metin, who found himself out of a job again. For the judge, the evidence was absolutely overwhelming. And from that long sentence, the two sisters, more united than ever, were repaid materially and morally for all the evil inflicted on them.

Ahmet Erdogan was repaid in the same coin. He was unfit and in prison.

Deren thus showed her father what it meant to turn against her. She was no longer the child to be subdued, or the rebellious girl to be brought down a peg or two. She was a powerful, strong, determined, ambitious woman, capable of protecting, tooth and nail and with such professionalism, what she had created with sweat and tears over all those years. With this victory, she had fought for herself, her sister and her grandmother. But above all, she proved that no one is invincible or untouchable. And who errs, pays.

She was fortunate to have a lawyer with a capital A at her side.

She believed in justice, she had always believed in it, but seeing her husband's passion and dedication for his work, she felt that feeling even more deeply.

Part of the money Deren got from winning the case, she decided to use it for the renovation of her grandmother's house, to which they had agreed with Bulut to move.

Deren had thought of everything. And inside the large mansion, she had already made arrangements for the creation of a room dedicated to her sister, who would always be welcome.

On Burak's side, however, things went like this.

Bulut and Burak's mother, who had remained in the house with the man throughout the court's analysis of the evidence, had taken testimony, recording her companion's voice in which she admitted what he had always done to her and her youngest son.

She had remained in that house for that purpose only. It was not true that she did not want to cooperate, she had sacrificed herself, holding out "in that prison" long enough for him to extract the truth. Exhausted, and trembling, having succeeded, she joined her eldest son at home, rang the doorbell and handed over the envelope in silence. But before she could leave, shattered, her strength failed her and she collapsed before his eyes.

All this happened on the morning of Aysegul's birth, while Deren and Burak were at the agency.

Bulut rescued the mother and, without wasting any more time, immediately ran to deliver the evidence he had in his hand.

And at that point, the judge's final decision was not long in coming.

Once transported to hospital in a state of confusion, Bulut's mother was hospitalized. She later agreed to be treated at a specialized clinic. A long journey of inner rebirth awaited her. She would deal with all the past traumas. It would not be easy, but now that she was free, she could do it. Her soul was at peace, she could finally put the pieces of herself back together.

And Ezgi in all this? What will she have done with the money she got from the lawsuit?

Ezgi, despite the large sum of money that allowed her to completely change her life if she wanted to, decided to invest some of it in her and her mother's business, to repay her for all the sacrifices she had made in raising her alone. For herself, she only took away a small but great whim. She bought a small flat all to herself halfway between her mother and her sister.

41. DISTURBING DISCOVERIES

After the big event, the birth of Aysegul, which had taken the whole agency by surprise, the company was now back to its normal routine.

Burak got a promotion and, after his months of probation, they decided to incorporate him into the creative department as an intern.

His working hours were reduced to make room for the newly started university.

With Deren on maternity leave, and Burak partially absent, as well as the absence of Muzo and Deniz still travelling the world after their misadventure in London, an unreal silence resounded throughout Fikri Harika.

"Look, look..." commented Can to his wife. "It almost looks like a serious workplace." he said, observing from the window of their office their employees all caught up in low head work.

"I've never seen the agency like this since I've known it... I'm almost scared, Can." Sanem admitted.

"I wouldn't say, look, we still get our daily dose of chaos." he replied as he approached the window from behind his wife. He meant Cey Cey, who, like every day, arrived at a time when he would tidy up the employees in the creative department with his usual 'soft and gentle' tone of voice.

Sanem checked her watch. "Precise as a Swiss watch." she commented.

Then she observed her sister, in her office next door.

"Can, we need to sort things out between my sister and your brother. I can't see them like this anymore." she said displeased.

"There she goes again." Can commented. "I was almost in pain that you weren't asking." he admitted.

"Come on, don't joke. What can I do about it? I'm sorry!" she exclaimed.

"Me too." admitted Can.

"No news on the horizon?" asked Sanem now aware of the whole story.

"None." he admitted. "But I talked to the social worker." he informed her.

"What? Why?" asked Sanem.

"Because I wanted to find out if she had any more knowledge about the father." he replied.

"And what's even stranger is that the results aren't in yet, you know? Again. Something doesn't add up." said Can.

"Like Emre hasn't got the results of the DNA test yet?" asked Sanem surprised.

"Yeah..." he commented.

"Strange indeed." she commented suspiciously.

At that moment Can's phone rang.

"Volkan?" he answered. Sanem stared at him.

"Is there any news?" he asked.

"There is, but before I bring you up to speed I need someone's contact details." he said.

"OK. Go ahead and close." replied Can.

"I need a hacker to be able to access confidential information. I wanted to inform you and get approval from you to continue."

"Of course you have it. Go ahead." said Can.

"But what kind of information?" he asked.

"From the family home's paper archive I was able to find out things, but to get confirmation you need access to a digital archive in a person's name." Volkan explained.

"I can't do names at the moment." he added.

"I understand." replied Can.

"Can? Give him Hilmi's contact. He worked with Aylin. He could be a good help, once he realizes he can take revenge against those who put him in that situation in the past." recalled Sanem.

"I'll talk to him if necessary." she added.

"No, no, no. No way! You will not talk to anyone. I'll take care of it. And Volkan will do the rest, please don't get into trouble." he pleaded with her.

"We'll do it together." Sanem replied firmly, looking into his eyes.

Can huffed, but agreed.

"Alright, what should I do with you and your stubbornness, huh? Did you tell me?" he asked.

"That's also why you love me." replied his wife.

"All right, Volkan, then you reach out to the agency. We will contact him in the meantime." he said.

"All right." replied the investigator in his deep voice.

He hung up.

As Sanem had imagined, when Hilmi, called to the office at Fikri Harika, found out what he was supposed to help with, he did not flinch, on the contrary. He showed real curiosity about it.

He immediately set to work with Volkan at his side.

Sanem warned him beforehand. Hilmi was unpredictable, so if he saw anything wrong, he absolutely had to let her know.

Can and Sanem returned to their office. They said nothing to their brothers.

"Can?" asked Sanem once they closed the door behind them.

"Tell me, love." he replied.

"Do you think we'll be able to find out anything by the end of the day?" asked Sanem.

"Well, I don't know, but I hope so." he replied.

That very evening, after non-stop hours of blockades and impossible access, Hilmi, when everyone in the agency had left, succeeded.

In the office, as always, only Can and Sanem, Emre, and Volkan with Hilmi remained.

Called by Volkan, the two rushed into the meeting room.

In front of them, printed out, lay a sea of documents... evidence, as the investigator had called it.

The first document Volkan handed Can was the result of the DNA test.

Can had seized the opportunity by asking the hacker to find out the result.

Can looked at him. Emre is not Hatay's father. He said with a smile.

"Really?" exclaimed Sanem, peering at the papers.

"Here, this result is purely confidential, but it is necessary for Mr. Emre to urge the printed document from the hospital, of course." Volkan specified.

"Of course, of course. But it's true, isn't it?" asked Can as confirmation.

"It is true. I think the hospital hasn't sent the hard copy yet, or there might have been a delay with the mail." said Hilmi.

"Or maybe someone prevented the result from being sent to the receiver." thought Sanem.

"Ah, I have to tell my brother right away." said Can.

"Mr Can... Wait, please, before you tell your brother I think it is only fair that you know the complete truth." stopped him Volkan.

"But if Emre is not the father, then who is?" asked Sanem absorbed as Volkan spoke. She asked the question aloud without even realizing it. A second later she blinked and focused on them.

All three men in front of her were looking at her.

Volkan nodded, and without a word, took a printed document, placed beside him, and handed it to the Divits.

Can took it, Sanem approached him to read it together.

"What?!" exclaimed Sanem bringing a hand to her mouth.

"I can't believe it!" she exclaimed.

Can continued reading the whole document in silence.

"Is this a joke?!" commented Sanem.

"That's it... it doesn't surprise me at all. On the contrary. It confirms suspicions I had from the beginning." admitted Can calmly.

"What do you mean? How could you have known that he was the father, eh, Can?" asked his astonished wife.

The document in question had been hidden in a secret archive. Aylin's network continued even from inside the prison. Someone had concealed the real DNA test, requested by Aylin herself.

Surely she had done it with the hope that Emre would turn out to be the father, but as this was not the case, she preferred to conceal the evidence. From two parents in prison... he wasn't going to get anything.

"Enzo Fabbri, Can! We're talking about Enzo Fabbri!" ranted Sanem.

"Aylin and Enzo Fabbri... a more evil couple could not exist." he exclaimed with his hands in his hair.

"Yes, but Can... that poor child... I, I can't believe it, really." she tried to articulate a meaningful sentence.

"How could anyone do such a thing?" wondered Sanem with his hands in her hair.

"Given the characters, we couldn't expect better. I mean, we both know that Aylin doesn't care about anything other than herself, and I can understand that a child was just a burden to her." thought Can.

"Yes, but Fabbri..." said Sanem.

"I don't think Fabbri knows." Can quickly replied. "Otherwise, it doesn't explain why Aylin wanted an abortion from the start."

"Yes, but she didn't." Sanem pointed out to him.

"Exactly..." said Volkan handing her another document. It was a clipping from a newspaper article.

"ENZO FABBRI AT LARGE AGAIN." said the headline.

"Look at the date." said Volkan. "It matches." He added.

"There... we've explained that too." said Can satisfied with a round of applause.

"Poor Hatay... I mean, I can't believe it. How can you abandon a child to himself like that, huh?" he asked.

"There, Hatay deserves to know he has a free father." said Sanem.

"Sanem... don't even think about it. We will not contact Fabbri! Let it not cross your mind! I don't want to see that bastard's face at all!" her husband closed the conversation immediately.

"He must never set foot on Turkish soil again." he said as serious as death.

"Yes, but that poor child..." said Sanem, "he's been living in a foster home all his life... it's not fair."

"What will happen to him? Will he spend his whole life there while we continue ours as if nothing happened, huh? How can I look that little innocent in the face again knowing the truth, huh?" blurted Sanem.

"I'll contact the social worker right away. She said she wanted to be informed if we found out anything about his parents. She's been taking care of him since the beginning, she'll know what's best to do." said Can.

"She will know what is best to do according to the law, Can, but that doesn't mean it will be best for him. She after all has to do her job you see?" said Sanem.

"And what should we do then Sanem?" he retorted.

"Hilmi, you can go, thank you." Can hastily dismissed him. "Take care, and if a single word gets out about this matter or you will end up back in the company of your former boss. Do I make myself clear?" said Can nervously.

Hilmi nodded, and disappeared as quickly as he had arrived.

"Um... sorry, but I have an idea." said Volkan.

Can and Sanem cheered.

They looked at him.

"Can you go ahead and contact the social worker. But if you want, I could do something. I could trace Mr Fabbri's address and anonymously send an envelope with all the documents about Hatay and some pictures." he proposed.

"Like Aylin sent it." Can thought.

"Good idea." he thought.

"At that point we'll see what happens. You are in contact with the social worker, and if he shows up, surely he will have to talk to her. She will notify you." he said.

Can and Sanem looked at each other and nodded.

"Yes, good idea, Volkan. Thank you." said Sanem.

"Then I'll proceed." he said.

"I'll make a copy for my brother too." said Can.

"We have to go to them right away." said Sanem.

Volkan collected the documents, the envelope and once they said goodbye, he went out.

"Volkan thank you very much, again, as always." Sanem greeted him.

"I'll let you know as soon as I've posted." he said.

"Alright." replied Can.

Left alone, Can and Sanem gathered their things and were the last to leave the agency.

They reached Emre and Leyla's house and there gathered in the living room and explained to them everything they had discovered, but above all, that Emre was not Hatay's father.

"I can't believe it! Enzo Fabbri?" asked Leyla in amazement.

"There... it must have happened before I was arrested, when I was collaborating with him against our agency. That's it, I was also inside that group at the time, because of their blackmail, but... only when I got out... after the incident, I thought there might be something between them, but I never knew for sure." explained Emre.

"Oh, by the way, it looks like Fabbri is out of prison." Sanem informed them. At the mere mention of his name, Can clenched his fists tightly.

"What?!" they both exclaimed.

"Yeah... but don't worry, he'll get a little surprise soon. I'm really curious to know what he'll do. Will he act like a bastard or a man by taking his responsibility?" thought Can.

"Poor child..." commented Leyla.

"What parents he got..." she said with a sigh.

"Yeah..." commented Emre.

"And..." said Sanem. "Leyla what are you doing? Don't you hug your husband? My dear brother-in-law, is innocent! What are you waiting for?" she urged her.

Meanwhile, as the two embraced, Ilker appeared.

"Uncles!!!" he exclaimed, running towards them.

"Ah, here's my handsome nephew!" said Can, taking him in his arms.

"And you? Weren't you sleeping?" said Leyla in a lecture tone.

"Ah, leave him alone..." said Emre.

"He missed his uncle!" exclaimed Can.

"And his aunt, don't you, little one?" said Sanem mussing up that blond hair like a chick.

Meanwhile, Emre and Leyla looked at each other lovingly.

How much 'apology and guilt' was in those eyes...?

Sanem noticed them proposed: "How about Ilker coming over tonight? Huh? That way he can spend some time in nature with his little cousins... and you'll have the night off." she said, raising and lowering her eyebrows mischievously.

"Yessss!" exclaimed Ilker excitedly.

"Sister, won't that be a bother? Four children..." she said.

"But what disturbance..." said Sanem.

Can with Ilker in his arms, hugged his wife, finishing the sentence. "We are used to chaos. We don't like silence, don't we, my love?" he said.

"Exactly." confirmed Sanem.

"Whereas you, it seems, are in urgent need of it." she added.

"Sister, don't be cheeky now..." replied Leyla.

"Ah, how long you make it.... Because what did I say wrong?" she wondered.

"There, actually..." said Emre agreeing with his sister-in-law.

"See? Even my brother-in-law agrees." she said handing him a friendly fistful which Emre returned with a big smile.

"Alright, I'll pack a bag then." said Leyla disappearing into the corridor.

"Come on, let's go." said Can heading to the small room with Ilker.

"Just a minute! But today is Friday!" realized Sanem.

"Yes, sister, why?" asked Leyla stopping.

"Then take the weekend off, we'll keep Ilker." she proposed.

"But..." tried to retort Leyla.

"But nothing but... sister." said Sanem decisively.

Leyla raised her hands and eyes to the sky.

"Alright, whatever." she replied.

"And take advantage no? Once in a blue moon!" said Sanem.

Leyla prepared everything. Ilker meanwhile chose his favorite toys to take with him, they all said goodbye and set off for the estate.

On Sunday evening when Ilker returned to his parents, the two sisters caught up. Everything was back to normal. Sanem breathed a sigh of relief. At last everyone around her was well. And now she could be fine too, she thought, but the week that followed, between the children's perfume launch and finally getting approval from the lab for that secret project of hers, Sanem began to feel as if overwhelmed by all those perfumes. So she did not run towards the intense smell of coffee that characterized Fikri Harika.

And it was while observing the usual daily grind that an idea came to her.

"Why not make a children's area in the office?" she asked herself.

Why hadn't she thought of that before, she wondered. Then she thought of her children, born and raised in the middle of nature, and understood why. But now... Now that other co-workers and employees were expecting or had already had children in the meantime, why not do it? She said to herself.

She thought of Deren, whom she had visited a few days earlier and who was looking forward to getting back to work, then she looked at Ayhan, who was standing in front of her, at the end of her pregnancy

Then she thought about Ilker and later her children, the agency was slowly filling up with new lives, and securing an area would make life easy for anyone. She ran to tell Can.

42. LOVE HAS NO CRITERIA

A few weeks later, Muzo and Deniz returned. The reason? Deniz had been contacted to start a treatment course with a child with a difficult past. That child was Hatay.

One day, the social worker contacted Can and Sanem saying that the alleged real father had come forward.

The two, knowing Fabbri, had warned her, so she was joined by other professionals, all ready to follow the little one in this knowledge.

Nobody knew, however, that Deniz had applied after her break-up with Metin to follow child cases. To this application Deniz had never received an answer until then.

No one knew this. Not even Can and Sanem. They were surprised when they arrived at the agency with the social worker to gather information about Fabbri in a professional capacity. They were amazed, but they were certain of one thing. Hatay was in very good hands.

Meanwhile, Muzo's big day arrived. In fact, his return with Deniz was also due to this.

Once again, the book presentation was held in the great hall of the opera house.

American publishers attended the preview, knowing that Sanem Aydin would introduce this new writer to the world.

The hall was packed. Every single member of the agency and Sanem was present. Osman and Adile also attended.

In the two long front rows, there were Deniz, Cey Cey, Ayhan, Osman and Adile, Deren, Bulut, Burak and Ezgi, Sanem, Can, the children, Leyla, Emre, Ilker, Mevkibe, Nihat, Melihat, Aziz and Mihriban. In short, no one was missing. Behind them, it was easy to recognize some familiar faces from the neighborhood that had seen Muzo born and raised.

They were proud of him. Because after all, he had always been a son of the neighborhood.

They were all dressed up. Once they were seated, with the lights pointed at the lectern in the centre of the stage, Sanem made her entrance, applauded by all.

Her eyes turned to her children and her husband, who were applauding her.

She took a deep breath and brought the microphone close to her mouth and began to speak.

"Good evening everyone. I am Sanem Aydin, and welcome to this special evening." she said.

"The one I am about to introduce is not only an up-and-coming writer, but also a great friend. We have known each other since we were kids, and I can now say that I know him like the back of my hand. He is someone who has really put a lot of effort and dedication into this first work of his. A work that came out of a dark moment. A work in which I admit I saw myself again the first time I read it. That is why, from the first reading, I wanted to support it, because this story deserves to see the light. And that is why I ask you to welcome Muzaffer Kaya with a big round of applause."

"Thank you, thank you." repeated Muzo as he took the stage in his smocking.

Sanem, on the other hand, walked away applauding, leaving the centre of the stage to him, wrapped in a long, black pantsuit.

Muzo cleared his throat.

"Good evening, thank you for coming. And thanks to Sanem for her words. Um..." he said in embarrassment.

"I'll be honest with you, I'm a neighborhood boy, and as such I'll speak very bluntly and simply, because that's how I am." he was careful to point out.

"I wrote this book during a solo trip. It was just me and my pen, the only friend I had by my side at the time. I went through a very dark moment in my life, where... I didn't know what to do, I didn't know who I was... I was lost." he tried to explain.

"So I listened to my friend Sanem's advice and wrote. I wrote whatever was on my mind. You must know that I have always written. It was always easy for me to fill pages with words, though then... whether they made sense was another thing. But still... I wrote for myself." he said, lowering his head. He was in awe.

"I knew I could count on a friend ready to read whatever nonsense I wrote without prejudice or judgement." he said pausing.

"And so I sent it to her. I sent hundreds of pages. At first they were personal thoughts, moods, reflections... but then the writing that seemed to make no sense suddenly took the form of something." he said.

"I didn't know what it was at the time... and maybe I still don't." he admitted, laughing.

"But with a fixed thought, I started writing from sentences... or should I call them criteria. And I analysed them." said, casting a fleeting glance towards Deniz. The book was still secret from her.

"Without realizing it by analyzing those criteria, I also analyzed myself, as I had never done before." he confessed truthfully.

"Once I finished my analysis, as always I sent those hundreds of pages to Sanem, but this time with a title." he continued.

Sanem from her seat nodded.

"Only you know the title, no one else in this room knows anything. It is not just any title. It holds a meaning that is very personal to me. Sanem understood it immediately." he said.

"My dear friend, in those twisted lines saw something, and that is how our collaboration was born. She saw a potential that I did not see, because at that moment I was only writing for myself. But she went much further, she thought that those words could be of help to others. That they could give hope to others who were in the same condition." he pointed out.

"And so this journey began. And I would not have come this far without her support." Muzo said.

"So thank you very much, Sanem Aydin, I will be forever grateful to you." he concluded in front of everyone.

"And now... before I reveal the title, I just want to add one thing." he said.

"This book is dedicated to a special person present in this room. A person who accepts me as I am, unbalanced, awkward, childish, heavy, at times even obnoxious." he said, smiling.

"This person, who, when she reads the title, will understand that I am referring to her, I want her to know that while I was writing, my thoughts went to her." he confessed excitedly.

Deniz listened to him in silence.

"So you are curious?" asked Muzo.

A chorus from the hall answered: "Yes!" Leading this chorus was the clear and powerful voice of Cey Cey.

"It is with great emotion that I present to you: 'Love has no criteria.'" he said as the cover of the book was projected at full height on the cloth behind him.

Long applause followed by the surprise of some members of the agency filled the room.

Cey Cey was the first to understand, and Ayhan with him. He was followed by Deren and Bulut, and Can and Sanem.

The rest applauded but in a more composed manner, not understanding. Among them was Deniz.

Who kept looking at the stage without understanding, despite having her colleagues' eyes on her.

"Why are you all looking at me now? Is there something wrong with me?" she asked looking at the dress she was wearing.

"What? Deniz? Don't you understand?" asked Ayhan.

"What am I to understand?" she asked blinking naively.

"She didn't understand... again." said Sanem.

"What?!" she asked.

"Ah, weren't you the one who had a list of 127 criteria that a man had to meet?" recalled Cey Cey to her.

"I mean, I remember that..." he added.

"Really? You have a list of 127 criteria?" asked Ayhan surprised as she looked at her husband.

"Yeah... she had it.... several years ago." confirmed Cey Cey.

"Ah..." commented Deniz brightening up slowly. "I get it... you say Muzo..." began the sentence Deniz.

"Ehh! Muzo titled the book for you, Deniz! It's you he dedicated it to! Good morning! You were always in his thoughts, don't you understand? He never forgot you!" exclaimed Sanem blusteringly.

"My love, calm down." said Can.

"Ugh... never once did she understand at first..." she commented in a whisper.

Can who heard, looked at her and holding back his laughter, replied with tight lips: "Shame."

"Calm down cupid, calm down, come here, let me give you a hug." said Can welcoming her into his arms.

"You're a little nervous today, aren't you?" he pointed out as he pulled her close, stroking her hair.

"She's the one making me nervous." she said pouting.

Meanwhile, Muzo still on stage looked in the direction of Deniz, who had brought his hands to her mouth, showing that she understood. Her eyes were glazed over.

"Deniz?" he called, making her name resound throughout the hall.

"Could you join me here?" he asked at the edge of the stage, his hand reaching out for her to join him.

"Ah! Go! Go!" exclaimed Deren.

"Me? Why?" began Deniz embarrassed. "I'm ashamed..." she added.

"Come on, don't let the poor guy down! Look, he even dedicated the book to you! Come on daughter, join him, you don't want to leave him there like that in front of the whole room, do you?" said Mihriban leaning towards her from the back row.

At that point everyone urged her to join him. So finally she got up and slowly, wrapped in a long carrot-colored dress like her hair, she reached him.

Muzo offered his hand to help her up the steps.

"Did you really dedicate it to me?" asked Deniz in a whisper so as not to be heard over the microphone, tears in her eyes.

She would never have expected such a thing from him.

"Yes... and now... if you please..." he said looking at the audience.

"Dear audience, before we move on to questions I have to do something." he said.

"Sorry if this is going to be unprofessional, but I must seize the moment." he said and then knelt noisily in front of her. The very thud of his knee could be heard echoing across the stage.

"Ouch..." commented Cey Cey instinctively.

"Hey, am I wrong or did he leave the knee there?" commented Can.

Bulut, a few seats away from him, laughed: "No, no, you're not mistaken, I think he really crashed through the stage."

Burak laughed, while Deren and Sanem exchanged a glance of understanding as they rolled their eyes. "Still... you two... you're really incredible." commented Sanem.

Sanem and Deren, like everyone else open-mouthed at what he was lighting up, attracted by the restrained laughter of the two, glared at them. Then Deren intervened. "Rude! Even in a moment like this... you always manage to be kids... I wonder at you." she scolded them like a mother. Since she had really become one, she had really become everyone's mum.

"Deniz (sea)... my dear, you have twisted and changed my life just like the sea, in an instant... so please, will you become my wife?" he asked in front of all the flashes and the audience in the hall who started clapping.

Deniz was stunned. She had not expected this at all.

While in the audience all the girls were crying, Sanem, Deren, Mihriban, Mevkibe, and even Nihat, handing each other handkerchiefs in chains, suddenly Ayhan's tears took over in a hormonal sob.

Cey Cey looked at her with wide eyes, blinking them in surprise.

"Ayhan? What's going on? Are you possessed?" he asked.

"Ah... but what possessed... I'm just happy for them." she said in an unintelligible tone. Only Cey Cey in those months had learned to understand that language.

Nihat looked at him nodding, he too had had to do the same with Mevkibe.

The whole room turned to look at them.

It was a pity that Cey Cey had already proven in the past that he was not a good interpreter at all.

While on stage everyone waited for Deniz's answer, Ayhan mumbled something again between desperate tears.

"Sister, all right?" asked Osman beside her.

Meanwhile Deniz answered yes, and a roar of applause accompanied the moment.

Suddenly, however, Ayhan shouted, still muttering something unintelligible.

"What, are you thirsty?" asked Cey Cey seeing Ayhan pointing to the small bottle he was carrying.

"And drink. You got excited, I understand." said Cey Cey.

But Ayhan instead of taking it to her mouth poured it on the ground.

"Ayhan? Are you crazy? What are you doing?" he asked.

"Sister what's happening to you?" asked Osman.

Adile next door found her feet wet, looked at Ayhan and realized.

She sprang to her feet. "Ayhan? Ayhan? Did your water break? Is that what you are saying?" she asked.

"What?!" exclaimed Sanem and Deren.

"Did your water break?" Osman asked Adile.

"Ah... all right, if the waters broke it means we'll fix them. What can it be!" exclaimed Cey Cey overthinking.

"What do you want it to be? Cey Cey don't you understand? The children are coming!" exclaimed Osman.

"And if they arrive we'll welcome them." he replied quietly.

A second later he realized.

He shouted. "Ahhhh!!! They're coming?" he exclaimed.

Three seconds later he was already losing consciousness as he fell backwards, but Bulut picked him up and immediately put him back on his feet. Can good-naturedly slapped him on the face and woke him up. But he was still half-dead with his eyes half-closed. Then Sanem intervened and took her water bottle and poured it on him.

"Ahhh! What's happening? They're coming! They're coming!" he came to his senses as agitated as ever.

"I'll go and get the car." said Osman.

Muzo and Deniz also worried rushed to help. Sanem took charge of the situation and with the help of Aziz and Mihriban brought attention back to the stage. The presentation had to continue.

He left the situation in Deren's hands while she ran after her best friend. Can with her. The children stayed with their grandparents.

The moment had arrived.

In the car Sanem was as agitated as if was her to give birth.

"Calm down, Sanem. Calm down." repeated her husband.

"I can't Can. I swear, look! I'm feeling bad for her. My car hurts." she said.

"Do you want me to stop?" he asked.

"No, no, don't stop for anything in the world. Just follow Osman. I'll get over it." she said with a disgusted face.

Can stroked the back of her hand with his free one.

They all arrived at the hospital, Ayhan was immediately checked, while the others waited in the ward.

Hours passed, Cey Cey was let into the room with her. Screams could be heard from the corridor. Suddenly, however, the sound of a dull thud echoed. Shortly afterwards two nurses brought out Cey Cey's 'corpse'.

As soon as Sanem saw him, commented: "I wondered when that would happen... he can't resist the sight of a droplet of blood, let alone this..."

Osman at that point asked to go inside, to be near his sister.

Can and Sanem stretched Cey Cey out, recomposing him on the chairs in the corridor.

At one point, however, his phone rang. Sanem pulled it out of his pocket.

"It's Grandma!" she exclaimed intimidated, showing the screen to Can and Adile along with her.

"I'm not answering it." she said.

"Shall I answer it?" asked Can.

"No, if you don't mind I'll answer it. She doesn't know me." said Adile taking the phone from Sanem.

She had heard too much about his grandmother's phone calls, and she had even heard one once. It was disturbing.

"On the one hand, though, I would have liked to have answered just to find out his homeland" Can admitted in a whisper to his wife.

Adile looked at him, then answered.

"Hello? This is Cey Cey's phone, how can I help you?" Adile asked cutely.

The grandmother not knowing that female voice remained interjected for a moment, then spoke.

"Who is this? You are not Ayhan. Who are you?" she asked in her harsh and direct tone that contradicted her.

"Hello, you are Cey Cey's grandmother, aren't you? I am the wife of Osman, Ayhan's brother." she said kindly.

"Ah!" exclaimed the grandmother softening instantly.

"You are Adile, aren't you?" the grandmother asked confirmingly.

"Yes, I am, ma'am. Hello." replied Adile.

"Ah, Ayhan has told me a lot about you." she said.

Can and Sanem exchanged a fleeting glance. "Ayhan had talked to Cey Cey's grandmother? I didn't know that." admitted Sanem.

"You're such a pretty girl, you know... I always watch you on TV." she said.

"Ah, Cey Cey's grandmother is also a fan of Adile..." commented Can.

"Where is my grandson?" she asked.

"Why is that fool fainted? I see everything." said Granny.

"If she sees everything she should also know why, shouldn't she?" continued Can commenting in a whisper.

"Shh... let's hear what she says." replied Sanem silencing him.

"Alright." he replied.

"Here, ma'am I don't want to scare you, but your great-grandchildrens are coming. Ayhan's water broke and we are in the hospital, we are waiting.

"Ah, fool of a grandson! And how am I to see my great-grandchildren now? He is my eyes and ears." she said.

"Wake him up! Slap him, if necessary! I must see! I cannot miss the birth of my grandchildren!" she exclaimed.

Adile motioned to Can and Sanem to wake Cey Cey, while she tried to reason with the grandmother.

"Look ma'am, my friends here are trying to wake up Cey Cey, but as I'm sure you know, it's going to be difficult considering his blood phobia, so... I'll propose something." said Adile promptly.

"What daughter? My nephew broke his promise!" she exclaimed.

"Madam, I will keep it for him, don't worry. He has done his part after all, hasn't he? She had asked for grandchildren, right? And Cey Cey gave her grandchildren. But now since he is in no condition, I will have her assist." Adile replied firmly.

Cey Cey meanwhile showed no signs of recovery, he was exactly tone sur tone with the wall behind him. White.

"I will go into the delivery room and film everything for her. It will be a memory for everyone, for Cey Cey and for her. Stay on the line." she proposed.

"Excuse me." said Adile quickly, stopping a nurse who had just come out of Ayhan's room.

Can and Sanem looked at her in silence.

Both had given up on waking Cey Cey.

Adile explained the situation. Can and Sanem saw the nurse nodding so, doing OK with her fingers, she waved them off before disappearing inside.

"What do we do?" asked Can then still standing.

"We wait, it seems obvious." replied Sanem.

"No, I meant with him..." he said pointing to the comrade who had fallen in battle.

"Also... the answer is always the same." replied Sanem.

In the meantime, two nurses passed by at full speed, and seeing Cey Cey in that state they thought he was dead, and almost took him away to the morgue.

He was in a real bad state, poor Cey Cey.

Meanwhile, night was falling outside, and Can returned with two hot coffees from the cafè and two sandwiches.

"Just a minute!" thought Sanem.

"What about the bag? Ayhan doesn't have the birthing bag with her!" she exclaimed sharply.

"Um... That's right." noted Can. "We came away in a hurry."

"He needs to wake up! Cey Cey!" Sanem exclaimed, "At least let him carry the bag! That can do it!" she exclaimed, slapping him good and proper.

Suddenly, out of nowhere, like all the other times, Zu Zu appeared, holding a birthing bag.

"Zu zu?" asked Sanem as soon as she saw her.

Can turned around. It was the first time he had seen her.

The eternal child with the usual long, thick braids, approached and placing the duffle bag on a chair next to Sanem whispered something in Cey Cey's ear, who suddenly opened her eyes and sat up straight like a mummy awakened from eternal sleep.

"What's going on?" he asked in a calm voice, as if in trans.

"Cey Cey, wake up! Your babies are being born." said Sanem.

Cey Cey looked at her. "Ahhh!" he exclaimed, immediately plugging his mouth.

At the same moment, inside Ayhan was screaming.

"This is it, Cey Cey! This is it!" exclaimed Can patting his back assertively.

"Mh... thank you, Mr. Can." he said in a whisper, his breath catching.

"Zu zu?" asked Sanem getting more and more curious about that little girl.

"But... how did you get Ayhan's birthing bag?" she asked recognizing him.

She and Ayhan had packed it together.

Cey Cey looked at her. "Sanem, does this seem like the time?" he asked in a daze but as mentally lucid as a freshly glazed bowling ball.

"Ugh, I'm just curious!" she exclaimed.

"Zu zu, can do anything. She is from the village." replied Cey Cey proudly.

Can and Sanem looked at him narrowing their eyes, and approaching him, in chorus asked: "And where exactly is your village, Cey Cey?"

"Ah! This is not the time now!" he exclaimed, cutting off the conversation.

"I cannot say." he added.

"Why can't you say?" they asked again.

"Because the village chief doesn't want to." replied Zu zu.

"The village chief? And who would that be?" asked Sanem.

"My grandmother." replied Cey Cey.

Sanem opened her mouth wide.

"Your grandmother is the village chief?" asked surprised.

"That's right." he confirmed.

In the meantime, Ayhan's screams became more and more intense.

Cey Cey snapped. "What do I do? Ayhan is alone!" he exclaimed.

"She is not." replied Can. "Your grandmother is with her, along with Adile and Oaman." he added.

"What do you mean? My grandmother is here? Did my grandmother show up?" he asked taken aback.

"No, she called, and she should still be on the phone. Adile is bringing her in live. She even said she will make a video for her and you." explained Sanem briefly.

"What? A video?" he asked staggeringly.

"No! No, no, no, no! Don't even think about it!" exclaimed Sanem as Can held him upright.

"Listen to me! Ayhan is the one inside experiencing one of the greatest pains a woman can suffer. So you now, stay here awake and alert and pray for her. At least you can do that, can't you?" Sanem scolded him firmly with a fiery gaze.

"I do, all right." replied Cey Cey frightened in a husky voice.

"You're scary though." he said.

"Fine." replied Sanem proudly.

After yet another scream all of a sudden Cey Cey closed his eyes and grabbed Zu Zu's hands. She saw him move his lips. "Was he really praying? Maybe they had their own village magic ritual?" wondered Sanem.

She closed her eyes and turned her palms to the sky as well.

After a beastly scream, in the silence of the ward, a first cry was heard. Followed shortly after by another.

At that point Adile immediately walked out, leaving Osman to take the pictures.

"Cey Cey! Cey Cey! Come on in! What are you waiting for!?" urged Sanem as soon as he saw her. She had sprung to her feet.

"Congratulations, Cey Cey, you've become a daddy!" exclaimed Adile.

Agitated Cey Cey ran into the room.

"In three seconds we're sure to hear another thud!" exclaimed Can.

"Come on, Can!" exclaimed Sanem.

"What? It's true..." he replied.

At that point as they laughed relieved, Sanem turned around, but Zu zu as she had arrived, was gone.

"I really don't understand!" exclaimed Sanem, slamming her heel on the ground. "How can she arrive and leave like that in thin air? She looks like a ghost!" she exclaimed.

"Who are you referring to?" asked Adile.

"To Zu Zu. You saw her too, didn't you? She was here Can, I didn't make her up." she told her husband.

"Yes, she was here, but she's obviously gone." he replied quietly with a shrug.

"Forget it, love, don't stare at your head. When it comes to Cey Cey, nothing makes sense. You know that." replied Can.

"Anyway... Ayhan, how is she? The kids?" asked Sanem focusing on her best friend.

"They are fine. Ayhan is exhausted. It all happened naturally, thankfully. They are two little angels." said Adile.

"Ah, how beautiful!" commented Sanem.

Can stood there while his wife talked to Adile and alerted the agency.

"And Grandma? Was she happy to attend?" asked Sanem.

"Oh, yes, I even heard her get emotional. Can you believe it?" she exclaimed.

"Really?" replied Sanem.

"Yeah. Just think, she was so happy and grateful that before she hung up, she told me a secret." she said.

"What secret?" asked Sanem curiously.

"Just a minute. I'll write it down before I forget. Wait." she said, opening the phone's notes.

Three seconds later she turned the screen towards her.

Sanem brought her hands to her mouth.

"I can't believe it!" she exclaimed, reading.

"Is that what I think it is?" asked Sanem almost more moved by that, than by the birth of the little ones.

"Caaan!" she quickly called to him.

Can hung up and joined her.

"What's going on?" he asked beside her.

"Read here." she said pointing to the screen with her mouth still wide open in surprise.

"Come on... it's not going to be..." he said.

"The address of the village?" asked Adile rhetorically proud. "I think so. If not, where can I send the CDs with the videos and photos I promised?" she replied, winking at them.

"I can't believe it Adile! But you are a genius!" exclaimed Sanem.

"One minute... one minute... who can tell if that's really it? It could be fake." thought Can.

"Well, it could, but... we can ask Ayhan." thought Adile.

"Right." replied Sanem.

"Or to Muzo. He knows too." she added.

"Or desperate times, we have Volkan." concluded Can jokingly.

"He's become one of the family by now." said Sanem laughing.

"Just a minute! Really! Why didn't we have Volkan investigate this?" she asked thinking back seriously.

"Sanem, I think you got a little out of hand now on the investigator thing...it's not like we can investigate every person we don't know something about?" replied Can.

"Yes, yes... you say that, to be correct, but in fact, underneath it all, I know you would have wanted to do it too, my dear Can Divit." Sanem said, pointing her finger at him in a knowing manner.

A few days after the birth of the two babies, it was learnt that Cey Cey's grandmother, that very night... the night of the birth, had flown into the sky. This explained Zu Zu's immediate disappearance.

Cey Cey had tried to contact her the following days without success. At first he thought it was a joke, that she had been upset about fainting without being able to see the birth of his children, but when Zu Zu reappeared a few days later, the two of them stared at each other in silence, with just a blink of their eyes they understood and silent tears began to fall down the faces of both of them as if they had always been connected by an invisible thread. *A thread that only those from the village could understand*, so said Cey Cey.

Now that her homeland had lost its sage, Cey Cey no longer had any reason to keep the secret, and of her own free will one day confirmed her grandmother's address.

That address was her last goodbye.

Grandma knew. Grandma had always known that she would REALLY not have long to live.

On the day of the funeral, Cey Cey, accompanied by his family, reached the village. His last farewell as the coffin was about to be buried will forever remain bitter sweet.

"Grandma... you always threatened me that you would die if I didn't marry and give you a grandchild, and now look! I'm married, you have two grandchildren and you're gone... what kind of joke is this, is it? That wasn't the deal!" he said, trying to play it down, as he stroked the smooth surface of the coffin. His free hand was clasped in that of his wife Ayhan while Adile and Osman's hands were resting on his shoulders as a sign of closeness and comfort.

Then turning serious he said in a whisper. "Thank you for everything."

Yes, because after all his grandmother had been a mother to him, having been orphaned.

But in that simple 'thank you' was contained much more than he could have imagined.

After all, it was thanks to her that Cey Cey had entered Fikri Harika, spurring him on to try. It was thanks to her that he had met love, and it was always thanks to her that that love had won him back.

The grandmother had seen his future, and although from a distance, had done everything in her power to make everything written in destiny, come true.

She had gone away in peace, serene that she had achieved everything her grandson deserved.

Happiness.

43. STORIES OF A

NOT TOO DISTANT FUTURE

SANEM

There is a phrase I hear very often:

For every bad thing, there is always a good thing.

Here, never before have I heard the meaning of those words.

How much has happened in the last while, huh?

Secrets, intrigues, quarrels, reckoning with the past, goodbyes, but now, as I sit here, at sunset, on the green lawn beside the jetty, I realize that each one has been followed by a beautiful episode, ready to erase what has hurt us most. The present and the future always erase the past.

Take Deren for example: in spite of the past, she now lives her fairy-tale love, happy and content with her little Aysegul, her husband and her brother-in-law in her grandmother's big palace, just like a princess.

Ezgi, too, despite her past disappointment, now seems to have found serenity with her sister, her niece and a certain feeling with Burak.

After Emre's scare over Hatay's alleged paternity, however, the marriage with my sister is going well. In fact, Ilker will soon have a baby sister on the way.

Cey Cey and Ayhan, after their grandmother's beating, are slowly finding serenity by focusing their attentions entirely on the twins, both of whom have decided to honor their parents or whoever their parents were.

Therefore the female was named Nuri in honour of Cey Cey's grandmother, which was the nickname everyone called her in the village. While the male was named Bata in honor of Ayhan's father, it was the nickname she used to call him when she was little.

Well, considering Cey Cey's initial options which included: Can, "Su samuru" given his boundless love for otters, or coffee, espresso, and cay (thè)... I would say the final choice is the most apropriate one.

Muzo and Deniz are getting married soon, and in the meantime she is continuing to follow little Hatay with great interest.

Well? And what about us? Now you will find out.

AT SUNSET...

Can, and the children were at the top of the pier, feeding the ducks that live around there. They had also brought their fishing rod with them, which Can had just placed there.

Sanem watched them sitting on a picnic blanket on the green grass near there. Suddenly she saw Can reaching out to her.

"Take care! Watch out the movement of the water! If you see anything, call out." said Can.

"Alright, Dad!" they exclaimed.

Can sat down next to his wife, beginning with: "I'm so hungry!"

He opened the basket they had prepared together.

"Are you hungry, my love?" he asked.

"Um... not really. My stomach is a bit upset." said Sanem giving him a pointed look as he continued to rummage through the basket.

"Are you alright?" he asked, still with his gaze searching for something specific inside.

"Here, I'm a bit tired lately..." admitted Sanem.

"Eh, I've noticed..." he commented distracted.

"But where did they go?" he asked more to himself than to her.

"What?" asked Sanem.

"The cutlery. didn't I take it out earlier?" thought Can again.

"Ah, yes, wait..." said Sanem pulling out from behind his back, a rolled up napkin.

"You know, with the wind I preferred to cover them." she lied.

"Ah, you did well." said Can.

"And... you were saying?" he asked as he opened the container with some fresh fruit.

"Well, I was saying that…" said Sanem watching as Can unrolled the napkin.

At that point, Can was in for quite a surprise.

His gaze went from the positive pregnancy test in front of him to his wife's face.

"Are you... this time?" he asked.

"Am I what?" she replied wanting to hear the conclusion of the sentence.

"Are you pregnant?" he asked surprised.

"Oh, yes, it looks like the Divit family will be six soon." she said nonchalantly.

"Really?" he asked.

Sanem hunched as a smile lit her up from ear to ear.

"Oh, my love!" exclaimed Can squeezing her vigorously, disappearing into those strong arms for a moment.

"Can, that's how you squeeze me though. In fact, you squeeze us." she pointed out breathlessly.

"Oh, sorry, I didn't mean to, i mean..." said Can all flustered as he tried to put the words together.

At that point he looked at her, took her face in his hands, caressed it observing every tiny detail and covered her with kisses.

"Are you happy?" she asked.

"Am I happy? I'm over the moon!" he exclaimed. "I could scream for joy!" he said.

Then he leaned over the still invisible tummy and placed a kiss on it.

"Are you OK? Are you nauseous? Is that why you have no appetite? Are you tired? Shall we go home? Do you need a rest?" he immediately started peppering her with questions.

"Look, don't play games this time, huh!" he continued to say seriously.

"Can? Can? Shhh... calm down." said Sanem stroking his cheek.

"I am fine. True, I'm nauseous and a bit tired, but I'm fine." she reassured him.

"When did you find out?" asked Can.

"This morning." replied his wife. "Well, actually I've been feeling something different for a few weeks already, but it was only this morning that I tested positive." she admitted.

"We have to go to the hospital." said Can. "We have to do a check-up."

"And we will...we will, but not today and not now." Sanem replied.

"Tomorrow." he quickly said.

"Alright. We'll go tomorrow. And... think, Dr. Levant even won the bet." said Sanem. "He'll be happy to hear that." she added.

Can meanwhile on his feet, moving, unable to stand still.

"Do we tell the children?" he asked, watching them as Ates and Deniz bickered as usual, with Yildiz acting as referee.

"Not today." replied Sanem as he stood up. Can immediately offered him her hand, which she accepted.

"Today is just for us." understood Can.

"Exactly." she replied.

"Ah... look at them!" she exclaimed as she observed them. "Aren't they too sweet?" she asked.

Can positioned himself behind her, gently hugging her belly.

Sanem leaned her head back on his shoulder.

"They sure are. And soon they will be even more so." he said, stroking her belly. He kissed her cheek.

"Let's hope it's a boy." said Sanem.

"Ah, you say? There, I'm used to my women of the house by now. So I gladly accept being in disadvantage." he said looking at Deniz.

"There, that's what I'm hoping for Deniz, not you!" she exclaimed feigning a mock snobbish tone.

"Ah... thank you." he replied.

Sanem laughed. "I'm joking, of course."

"Well, let's say if I imagine him, I dream him male." Sanem said.

"But it's too early to tell." she added.

"That's it, my beautiful and very sweet, and very intelligent Mrs Divit, the important thing is to never stop dreaming." he said as Sanem with her eyes closed and a sly smile, with her head resting on his chest twirled her hand in the air towards herself with every compliment he whispered.

"Dad?" called Ates from the dock in her usual schoolmarm position, hands on her hips.

That romantic moment faded. Can at distance replied as happy as a child. "Tell me Ates."

"Shall we have a diving competition before dinner?" she asked and then looked at him with her big soft eyes, her hands clasped in prayer.

"Go!" whispered Sanem to him.

"Eh, but if my daughter tells me so, how can I say no?" he replied.

"OK, but the first dive is mine!" he warned her.

"Alright!" she exclaimed.

"I love you to death Sanem Divit!" he said waving her off with a passionate kiss before running off towards the dock and diving in with a liberating scream. "Yuuuuhuu!!!"

The children instantly followed him one after the other.

Sanem watched them laughing.

There really was nothing more beautiful than her family. As they swam carefree illuminated by a breathtaking sunset, she caressed the tiny being growing inside her, thinking that this was not the end of the story, but just the beginning of another wonderful chapter of their lives.

THE END

Made in the USA
Middletown, DE
03 November 2023

41879961R00286